The Old American

Other Novels by Ernest Hebert

Hardscrabble Books — Fiction of New England

Rowland E. Robinson (David Budbill, ed.), *Danvis Tales: Selected Stories*

Roxana Robinson, *Summer Light*

Rebecca Rule, *The Best Revenge: Short Stories*

R. D. Skillings, *Where the Time Goes*

Lynn Stegner, *Pipers at the Gates of Dawn: A Triptych*

Theodore Weesner, *Novemberfest*

W. D. Wetherell, *The Wisest Man in America*

Edith Wharton (Barbara A. White, ed.), *Wharton's New England: Seven Stories and* Ethan Frome

Thomas Williams, *The Hair of Harold Roux*

The Old American

A Novel by

Ernest Hebert

Dartmouth College

University Press of New England

Hanover & London

Dartmouth College

Published by University Press of New England, Hanover, NH 03755

© 2000 by Ernest Hebert

All rights reserved

Printed in the United States of America

5   4

Library of Congress Cataloging-in-Publication Data

Hebert, Ernest, 1941–

The old American : a novel / by Ernest Hebert

p.   cm.

— (Hardscrabble books)

ISBN 1–58465–073–7 (alk. paper)

1. New England—History—Colonial period, ca. 1600–1775—Fiction.
2. Blake, Nathan, 1712–1811—Fiction. 3. Indian captivities—Fiction.
I. Title. II. Series.

PS3555.B425 O44 2000

813'.6—dc21   00–008467

This book is dedicated to the old Americans in my life, my father, Elphege Hebert, and my father-in-law, Leo Lavoie.

So many people read parts of the nine drafts of this novel that I don't dare list them for fear of leaving somebody out. My thanks to all, but especially to Nicola Smith and Tom Powers, who were the first to see the promise in an early draft. I also want to thank the librarians at the Baker Library at Dartmouth College and The Historical Society of Cheshire County in Keene.

Contents

The Old American

Grief

APRIL 1746

The old American wears a red turban with white feathers sticking out of the last turn at the peak, a strategy designed to conceal a bald head. His habitual pose and features resemble that famous profile to the north that both English and native refer to as the Great Stone Face. Many years ago he named himself Caucus-Meteor, for he'd lost his childhood name. He uses no war paint, but his ear lobes are split and stretched an inch long and from each hangs a French coin. Except for the turban and highly decorated fringed moccasins reaching almost to the knee, he's dressed like a French soldier with brown pants and a blue waistcoat, which hides burn scars on his arms. He carries no musket, sword, or hatchet. A short knife with a bone handle dangles from a neck cord, but it's more a tool than a weapon, for the old American has no use for the excitement of bloodletting; he's too feeble to fight well, and the French hired him as an interpreter, not as a warrior, so he's not expected to engage in combat; even so, for the purposes of continuing instruction

I

in those matters that concern a king, he always immerses himself in battle.

Because Caucus-Meteor knew he couldn't keep up with the troop, he had left the camp an hour early under moonlight to time his arrival with the outbreak of hostilities. He likes to wander among the carnage, the exercise making him feel like a living ghost, which he reckons is another of those emotions unique to a king. And, too, there's something else in him, a wish; as his old mirror, adversary, and sometimes intimate, Bleached Bones, was fond of saying: "Call sudden death the best of luck." In an attempt to see into his future, Caucus-Meteor tries the conjuring trick of the ancients. But it doesn't work. He's too hale for release from the responsibilities of mortality.

He's surprised that he's arrived before the fighters. Something must have delayed them. He knows that this village is one of the newer settlements on the borderlands of New Hampshire, but he does not know its name and he wishes he did. To destroy a place without bothering to learn its name strikes him as disrespectful. It will be dawn soon, and he should stay in the woods until his comrades launch their attack, but he'll walk boldly into the town, for he enjoys the shiver along the spine when one is close to one's enemies without their knowledge.

He sees perhaps half a hundred homesteads, log huts, and timber-frame houses under construction. Most of these structures are strung along a muddy path. Beyond is a stockade with wooden pickets and turrets for sharpshooters at the four corners. But Caucus-Meteor has little interest in military matters. He's drawn to a light, a warm glow from a single pane of glass in a log cabin. He peers through the wavy distortion. The sources of light are a whale oil lamp and a blaze in a stone fireplace. Caucus-Meteor sees a man sitting on the edge of the bed putting on leather shoes held together with gut laces, a woman poking the fire with an iron. A two-year-old lies in a cradle only a few feet from the old American. He could break the pane and snatch the child, but he only watches its blue eyes suddenly widening, blinking, mouth opening, crying out, fists doubled. Caucus-Meteor guesses that it's a girl. The mother comes to tend to her offspring. Caucus-Meteor makes no attempt to conceal himself. Since his wife died, he never lets practical matters, such as possible threats to his life, stand in the way of satisfying his curiosity, and for the moment he's engaged by this English family behind the glass. The mother sweeps up the child, carries her to the hearth, and sits her down on a low stool.

The woman spoons white bacon fat in a pot and hangs it from one of the irons over the hearth. Through the cracks around the glass, the old American catches the aroma.

The husband has finished putting on his shoes, and now takes notice of his wife at her cooking pot. The two begin to talk. Caucus-Meteor presses his ear against the glass. He enjoys listening to English. It's an unmusical language, weak in ability to convey feeling but full of expressions for things and actions. He catches only a few words through the glass, but he surmises from the woman's tone and the pained expression on her face that she brims with sorrow.

"You peer so deeply, Elizabeth, even into the bottom of a pot," the man says.

"I have half a notion that God made the world and all the creatures in it merely for the pleasure of His viewing." The woman's eyes are wild, disturbed.

"Merely?"

"It's a mere world. Or perhaps only meager. But does God ..." She halts in the middle of her thought, in order to hold the man immobile, keep him from breathing for a moment. It's the way of some women even in their lovemaking, thinks Caucus-Meteor, admiring the woman's trick. Finally she speaks. "But does God 'smell' his works as well? And touch? What of God and touch?"

The conversation goes on, and Caucus-Meteor begins to understand that there's a strain between these two that they're both pretending is not there.

The woman reaches into a plain ceramic pot for a handful of dried corn. She scatters the kernels into the sizzling bacon fat, and places the lid on the pot. Then she pours cow's milk into wooden noggins.

Caucus-Meteor realizes now how much like the woman he feels: tired, hungry, and full of despair.

Inside, the man notices what Caucus-Meteor has already seen, a tightness in the sinews of his wife's face. The man makes as if to speak, then falls silent, as if he understands her sorrow but has no means to deal with it. Caucus-Meteor bends his ear to the window.

The woman says, "If a cook could slow time to watch corn burst open, she might feel a little closer to heaven, do you think?"

"Aye," says the man, puzzled and disconcerted by his wife's strange question.

A few tears make her eyes glisten. She wipes them away angrily, and makes herself smile falsely. The man mumbles to himself. These people are like us, Caucus-Meteor thinks; it is only their learning that is disgusting. The man on the other side of the wavy glass is perhaps thirty or thirty-five years old, or maybe forty. It's hard to tell the age of white people; even those that live long lives often show time-wear early on. The man's movements, nimble and fluid, are unlike most Englishmen's. His face, sharp as rocks split by frost, seems to be a frame to display a long pointed nose and eyes the dark brooding gray of ledge. The hair, tangled and the same fusty brown as last autumn's fallen leaves under Caucus-Meteor's feet, is offensive to the old American. Don't these Englishmen know how to use a comb? The man wears a trade shirt, dark gray trousers, and white stockings under the laced boots. Lying on the bed is a buff-colored waistcoat and a tricornered hat. Caucus-Meteor concludes that an Englishman with no belly fat, no wig, and no buckle shoes cannot be very important in his world. Still, even an ordinary man has value as a captive, either for trade or enslavement. Not that the old American wants a slave. Slaves are trouble; he himself was once a slave and he was trouble for his owner. Still, it would be nice to have a captive for others to admire.

The woman is pale as if with fright; her hair is the color of corn silk and eyes like a winter sky on a clear day. She's small and doesn't look very strong, though it's obvious she can bear children. He guesses from her face, fighting itself, that she would make a stubborn captive, especially if her children were killed before her eyes, as they were likely to be, for they are too young to endure the march to Canada as captives. Only their scalps have value.

Caucus-Meteor notices a musket leaning against the inside wall by the door. He knows this kind of gun well. It's almost as ancient as he is, a 1680 New England trade fowler, the kind of weapon his own father carried in his great war. This farmer probably inherited it from someone in his family, and probably has fired it but half a dozen times in his life, if that.

When the corn finishes popping, the woman takes the pot from the hearth, empties the contents in wooden bowls. Another child appears as if by magic, scrambling down the ladder from her loft bed, and takes her place on a bench and drinks from her noggin on a slab-pine table. Caucus-Meteor estimates her age at four.

An Englishman, a Frenchman, or even a Mohawk, might regard the cabin as crude, for it has only one room of unpeeled softwood poles laid on the ground with no foundation, a dirt floor, logs chinked with mosses—a temporary affair until a proper frame house can be built. But for Caucus-Meteor even the cabin is too refined, for he has always lived the nomadic life and structures built to last more than two seasons strike him as unnecessary and subtly corrupting of the spirit; also, prone to insect infestation.

The man shows little emotion, but Caucus-Meteor can read his eyes, for the old American has witnessed this kind of trouble in families before: the man cannot bear the sorrow in the woman, and cannot tell the woman that he cannot bear it. The man turns away from his food, grabs his coat, and starts for the door.

"What's the matter?" the woman says.

"Naught. I'm going to the barn. Breakfast can wait." He hesitates at the door, looks at the musket, and frowns.

"Nathan?" calls the woman, a touch of harshness in her voice.

The man responds sharply. "A man cannot chop wood and carry a musket, nor can he hoe the ground, pitch hay, scythe grass, plane a board, or even haul a bucket up from a well . . . carrying a musket." His outburst stops abruptly, and he is instantly contrite. "I am sorry, Elizabeth. I did not mean to lose my temper." She gives him a bare nod, and he goes outside. The weapon remains inside, the woman's eyes wild and fearful.

The man needs only to look in the shadows twelve feet away, and he will see the profile of the great stone face in the old American, but he continues on, for he is more in his thoughts than in his environs.

He pauses at the barn, turns his eyes toward his town, gazes at it for the longest time with an expression that is a queer confluence of pity and confusion, or perhaps, thinks the old American, I am only mirroring myself, as I am wont to do when I require company to fend off morbidity. Caucus-Meteor wonders now what was here before the arrival of these invaders—a meadow, swamp maples, and strange gods that have long withdrawn. Caucus-Meteor is aware that the English divide land into measured lots, but the sight—fenced boundaries, cabins and frame houses under construction, and barns, and pigsties, everything lined up in squares—sends surges of revulsion through him. He wants to tell the Englishman, who like himself is still looking out, puzzled, over the town, that Christian hell must be like his village, row upon row of square-made structures. In this near-dawn light all is shapes and shadows, though in the distance Caucus-Meteor can make out the log fort and under construction a kind of church, which the English call a meeting house. It's a good idea to mix religion with statecraft, for the errors of one can be blamed on the other. Before Caucus-Meteor can meditate further on this notion, before the Englishman breaks off his attentive gaze, they're both distracted by the pop of a musket. Then another. The attack has begun.

The woman is already out the door with both children in her arms when she meets the man. In the dawn's first light and in their silence and fear-frozen expressions, they resemble something like statues Caucus-Meteor saw in Europe. The man takes the children from the woman. She hikes her skirt, and the family runs for the fort. Caucus-Meteor is glad they got away.

The old American listens for the sounds of war. In times gone by, Americans believed that devils could be frightened by loud noises, so warriors whooped and hollered in battle. These days Americans have largely discarded these beliefs, but they still whoop and holler. The old American pulls back his mind so that the gunshots, yells of alarm and terror, war whoops, threats, curse words grow dim. He thinks only of his hunger and fatigue. The door to the cabin is ajar, and Caucus-Meteor enters. He takes note of a sagging mattress of straw and feathers, a spinning wheel, tools on wooden hooks. He picks up one of the whimsy-doodle toys that the English father carved for his children, inspects it, and puts it down gently. Englishmen beat their children, and yet they make toys for them. How can such brutality and kindness be reconciled? He walks over to the stone fireplace hearth, tosses on some fatwood kindling, and a couple of hard-wood sticks.

Familiar images from a thousand brooding moments float through his mind: a house of poles, birch bark, tied grass-bunch for insulation, a tiny fire in the middle on the earthen floor. The wigwam fades, replaced by a stick castle complete with moat, stained-glass windows, mannequins in armor with feathers sticking out of the helmets, a king's throne of lashed-together sticks upon which sits a younger version of the old American himself; people of all races appear in adoration at the foot of the king of America.

The vision fades, and Caucus-Meteor turns his attention to the food on the pine table. He sits on the bench, a disagreeable and unfamiliar position. Caucus-Meteor thinks in various languages, favoring none, no more than the wind favors a particular leaf that falls from a tree. Now, in an Englishman's cabin, he thinks in English: How can people sit like this? He picks up a bowl of popped corn and the child's deserted noggin of milk, brings them by the fire, and puts them on the floor. He drops to both knees, sits on his heels, and starts eating popped corn, one kernel at a time. He used to lecture his children and later his grandchildren, "No two popped corn kernels are exactly alike, nor is the circumstance of eating them. So, to obtain the full benefit, don't stuff your mouth." The old American takes a long drink of the creamy milk. It satisfies, though later it will probably upset his stomach.

After he's finished eating, he walks to the bed, tears open the mattress with his knife. Feathers and straw spill out. He unstops the cork from the Englishman's ceramic rum jug. The stink fills the old American with anger and loathing. He pours rum on the straw and feathers and the log walls. He grabs the fireplace poker and pulls the fire out of the hearth onto the earthen floor. Flames catch the rum-soaked straw and flare up into a wave of orange and black.

He's about to leave when he glances through the windowpane. The cabin owner, the man named Nathan, has returned to his home. Caucus-Meteor watches him pause at the barn and go in. The pine siding and split-cedar roofing are eggshell brown, softly iridescent. No sag in the roof, no rot in the boards at ground level. It strikes Caucus-Meteor now that the Englishman built the dwelling place of his animals to last beyond his own years. Moments later two oxen lumber out, then a cow, a pair of sheep, chickens, pigs, geese. Apparently, the man left the safety of the fort to free his animals from the barn. An odd but endearing vanity, thinks Caucus-Meteor.

The smoke from the burning cabin now obscures the old American's vision. He grabs the musket and goes out the door. A score of raiders, mainly Iroquois, run toward the front of the barn. These men may be his brothers in battle, but they are also his competitors, for under the rules of engagement established between the French and their native allies, captives belong to those who capture. Caucus-Meteor goes around the rear of the barn. Coming out a back door is the man Nathan. He's holding a lamb in his arms. The man Nathan sees him, drops the lamb, and the animal scampers off.

Caucus-Meteor cocks the musket, and muses that he hasn't fired one of these things in years.

Seconds later warriors pour out of the back door of the barn, while others appear from around the sides. The Englishman is now surrounded. He extends both hands palms upward, turns a half circle to show he is unarmed. The man's demeanor, apparent mild amusement and the kind of radiance found only in saints and the insane, elicits admiration in Caucus-Meteor.

"You've come too early. I've not had a chance to eat," the man Nathan says. Caucus-Meteor understands the technique: in the face of disaster, act casually defiant.

Caucus-Meteor translates the man's words first in Iroquois, then in Algonkian, and finally in French. The warriors laugh at the captive's joke. Then Caucus-Meteor utters his own response in the three languages. More laughter. Finally, the old American speaks in English, "It must be a poor Englishman who cannot go to Canada without his breakfast."

The man Nathan appears shocked that his captor has responded to him in his own language.

Caucus-Meteor ties the man's arms to a stake shoved crossways against his back. The captive's brazen front falls away as he watches white smoke pouring from his barn. "Can you smell your hay burn?" Caucus-Meteor says. "Your cabin, Nathan—that is your name, is it not?"

"Nathan, Nathan Blake," the man says in a whisper.

"Nathan, your cabin, it burns with the sound of a winter wind, does it not?" taunts Caucus-Meteor.

The captive's body shivers along the spine where the strain of the stake is. He is no longer able to pretend contempt for self-concern. Other than the experience of false cold, he'll be an empty vessel of feeling for a while, thinks Caucus-Meteor. Which is what a master desires from his slave in the early stages of captivity.

Minutes later the attack is over. The raiders leave as swiftly as they arrived. They cross a meandering stream on a single-log footbridge, felled precisely to drop on the further shore, one side hewed flat. Caucus-Meteor finds the cleverness behind the idea as well as the skill used in carrying it out suspicious and oddly disheartening. It's strange but interesting to be old, he thinks. The troop moves swiftly west in single file and in silence. The old American strains on three counts, to keep up with the younger men, to pretend he is not close to exhaustion, and to keep an eye on his prisoner.

An hour away from the battle site, the troop slows briefly. Caucus-Meteor blindfolds his prisoner, ties a rope around his neck, and half drags him as he starts for the head of the column, winding his way through the men. Some are the sons of the northern Algonkian tribes whose territory is now inhabited by the English—Penacooks and Squakheags and Abenaki—who have banded together in the French missionary towns, but most are Christian Mohawks from Kahnawake across the river from Montreal. Only Caucus-Meteor represents the mixed-tribes' village of Conissadawaga.

At the front of the column he's met by the commander, Ensign Pierre Raimbault St. Blein. The ensign is very young, with flowing locks of dark brown hair, blue and silver eyes. He has a pretty face, little nose, almost like a girl's, and like a girl sometimes he pouts; nonetheless he is already a veteran of many campaigns and his men respect him, for he never shows fear. Before a battle he trims his thin mustache and hair patch under his lower lip and parades before his men. "I defy the Englishman to take this scalp," he'll say, pulling on his hair. "Come, my savage brothers, let us fight together." Then he'll laugh, a laugh that inspires confidence.

With the ensign is Furrowed Brow, a middle-aged Mohawk with a deeply lined face, features permanently fixed in gravity so extreme he inspires in Caucus-Meteor the opposite emotion of giddiness. Furrowed Brow is holding a tether to which is tied a big white man whose wrists are crossed behind him, his mouth gagged, his eyes covered.

"Now I know why you were late to the battlefield," Caucus-Meteor says in Iroquois.

"We surprised this fellow and three others in their camp while they slept," Furrowed Brow says, and he makes a motion with his hand to his temple, which tells Caucus-Meteor that the other men were tomahawked.

"Is he a soldier?" Caucus-Meteor addresses his question in French to St. Blein.

"From his papers, an English naval officer," says St. Blein.

"I did not know the English could bring the sea so far into the mountains," says Caucus-Meteor.

St. Blein laughs; Caucus-Meteor laughs; Furrowed Brow's permanent frown deepens. The old American is aware that he and the French officer share a sense of humor that unsettles others, especially humorless men like Furrowed Brow.

"More likely the Englishman lost his ocean," says St. Blein. "We will discover why when we interrogate him and your own prisoner at our camp by the great river."

In the tongue of the destroyed tribe that gave him life, Caucus-Meteor speaks the name of that river—Kehteihtukqut—and feels a pang, a longing, for his parents.

The old interpreter and the young commander start talking in the friendly dueling way of French intimates until they are interrupted by Furrowed Brow. "The two of you speak too fast and too cunningly in a language where I am slow and seek certainty."

"Our apologies," says the ensign in French.

"You have a worthy captive—you're a credit to your kind," says Caucus-Meteor in Iroquois. The old American is annoyed that the Mohawk has a more important captive than he does.

Furrowed Brow is not sure whether he's being insulted, teased, or complimented. In frustration, he tugs on the tether of his captive.

Minutes later, the march resumes. The men walk until late in the afternoon, when they reach the river.

Caucus-Meteor takes the blindfold off his captive. Nathan is coming out of the shock of capture, and Caucus-Meteor decides to address him to see how he behaves.

"Can you swim?" he says, knowing that the water, icy cold from snow melt, would kill a man before he could cross.

"If a savage can ford this stream, an Englishman can," he says.

Does the Englishman really think that we are going to plunge into the waters? wonders Caucus-Meteor. Is he confused, stupid, or merely inexperienced in the ways of native humor? He attempted some humor himself back when he was captured. But that was only nervousness and bluster in the face of personal disaster. Perhaps he will be funnier and wiser when he is nervous again. When the local Abenaki fellows arrive with the canoes, the old American searches the captive's face for a reaction. But the Englishman conceals all emotion. He is cleverer than Caucus-Meteor had thought. Already his captive is probably thinking about escape, perhaps even laying a plan. I admire him very much, thinks the old American.

The brown water of the river is high, moving with the treachery of malicious whispers. Two canoe men ferry the raiders to the other side. It's flat above the river banks, good soil. The troop makes camp in the woods just off the flats in the cover of the forest. From this vantage point, they can see the open areas along the river where distressed cornstalks from the last growing season stand like weary sentries. The corn was planted by the wandering and secretive Abenaki. The old man gives Nathan some pemmican. Later St. Blein arrives, talking to Caucus-Meteor in French. Then the old American says to Nathan in English, "Come. Follow." And then a dangerous idea sends a shiver of excitement through him. He pulls the blindfold off. "If you should happen to escape," Caucus-Meteor says, "I wouldn't want you to get lost going home."

Another French commander might be appalled at the action of the native, but St. Blein is only amused; Caucus-Meteor thinks: the pleasure of amusing one's superiors is a remnant of my slave days.

He leads Nathan to a huge sugar maple tree with rot oozing from its crotches, the bark twisted and colorful. "You are a farmer, are you not? And a woodsman?" Caucus-Meteor strikes a formal tone.

"Aye," says Nathan.

"What will happen if I hit this tree with that fallen branch?" asks Caucus-Meteor.

St. Blein looks on, a sardonic smile on his pretty face. Nathan is confused. Perhaps he suspects he's being made sport of. But he answers the question. "Likely, it will ring hollow," Nathan says.

"And why is that?"

"Because the maple dies from the inside. In old age, the core is likely to be rotted out. Eventually, the weight of the tree will bring it down for the weakness of its empty chamber."

"Let us test it." The old man unties Nathan from the stake at his back, and points to the fallen branch. Nathan's arms are so stiff he can barely pick up the branch, but finally he gathers the strength to swing it against the maple.

"It makes drum music," says Caucus-Meteor. "You know your trees—is there a god in the tree?"

The Englishman ponders the question, apparently trying to devise a cunning answer. Finally, he says, "The Lord God is everywhere, so in the tree, too, I imagine."

"Surely, you must be right, for I can see that you are a man un-used to falsehood. Know this as your god knows it: I am Caucus-Meteor, and by force of arms I am your master. Now repeat for me your name, and your position within your community."

"I am Nathan Blake, one of sixty proprietors of the town of Upper Ashuelot that you burned."

"Your town by birthright? Or perhaps by the grace of your god?"

"By English law. I was born and bred in Wrentham, Massachusetts."

"What a coincidence. I was born in the same area, Mount Hope."

"The home of the rebellion during King Philip's War," Nathan says.

"That is correct. I was a boy during the war. Do the local English folks still talk about Metacomet, the leader they called King Philip?"

"They still tell how the head of King Philip was placed on a stake outside Plymouth town and how the preacher, Cotton Mather, ripped off the jaw to silence the king forever."

"What do they say happened to the head?"

"They say after twenty years the devil came and got the head and brought it down to hell."

"If it be so, King Philip has a place to call home, which is more than can be said for his people."

Unsure how to respond, the Englishman bows.

"Your captive is somewhat naive, but he is no fool," says St. Blein in French.

Caucus-Meteor now shifts his accented English to sound like the fine-wigged nobles from old England: "Nathan Blake, this man is Ensign St. Blein. He and I will ask you some questions. Let them not ring hollow like the tree, lest you topple from the weakness of your own answers. Understand, Englishman?"

"Aye," says Nathan.

Caucus-Meteor makes Nathan drop to his knees and ties his

hands behind him. "Now you can properly pray to your god," says Caucus-Meteor. He builds a small fire only a few feet from Nathan's loins, shoves a stick in the ground behind Nathan, and leans the stick against his spine so that he has to strain to keep from toppling into the fire. Caucus-Meteor kneels opposite his captive, the fire between them. St. Blein sits on a log a few feet away, hands folded, face assuming the meditative aspect of an interested observer.

"I wish to begin by asking my captive a series of benign questions," says Caucus-Meteor in French to St. Blein.

"Seems like a waste of time. Fear is the only emotion necessary to instill," says St. Blein.

"Information obtained through fear is unreliable and debases the inquisitor."

"Then why the fire?" asks St. Blein.

"For warmth." What Caucus-Meteor doesn't say is that he believes that the process of inquiry debases both parties on any account, for it subverts the ancient religious rites surrounding the torture of captives, but he keeps this point to himself.

The old American stirs the fire with a stick, and says to Nathan, "I note that a glass window graced your cabin."

"I have no cabin—you burned it."

St. Blein, who understands English and speaks a little of it, interrupts, and says impatiently in English. "You have no cabin, but you have your life. You will please us with your cooperation."

"I brought that glass all the way from Boston. It replaced oiled parchment," Nathan says.

"Why?" says Caucus-Meteor.

"Why, for light. My wife and I met at a New Light meeting, and she is sorely afraid of the dark."

"I watched you through your glass, Nathan Blake. It told me that your wife was full of sorrows. Is that the real reason you left the fort: to escape a difficult family situation?"

"Whatever my motives, I had no wish to be captured by a savage."

"And yet you did risk life and limb."

Nathan starts to speak and then goes silent, his eyes distant and his jaw tight with a private pain.

"You are thinking about your wife—her sorrow," says Caucus-Meteor.

Nathan says nothing, avoids the eyes of his interrogator.

"I doubt it was sorrow; the man's wife was probably afraid of an attack. Why dwell on this unimportant matter?" says St. Blein in French.

"Because it interests me, good ensign," Caucus-Meteor says, then he asks Nathan in English if his wife's distress was provoked by fear of an impending attack.

"Nay. My wife was grieving the loss of our son, our eldest child, who died of the distemper in the fall of the last year."

"And you?"

"Myself?"

"He doesn't understand," Caucus-Meteor says to St. Blein in French.

"But I do understand. Can we proceed with the interrogation? I want to know where the Massachusetts militia is. Our safety may depend on his answers."

"I doubt it, Ensign. He's my captive, and I'll handle him in my own way." Caucus-Meteor switches to English. "I am curious, Nathan Blake. Why does an Englishman abandon his family and risk his life to free animals from a barn, since he must know that most will be slaughtered anyway?"

Nathan Blake remains silent.

"What does an Englishman do for comfort when his wife is sorely lost in sorrows and he himself grieves the loss of his son, and yet cannot speak of it?"

Caucus-Meteor grabs a stick from the fire, and holds the burning end inches away from Nathan's eyes. He brings it closer and closer until perspiration pours from Nathan's brow. His mouth gapes open. He's a man suppressing a scream, not from pain, for the heat has not touched his flesh, but from fear. And now he does cry out—a terrible gasp—and from neither pain nor fear, but from bearing witness to the uncanny, for the burn end does touch flesh, though not Nathan's. Caucus-Meteor suddenly pulled the stick away, and burned his own arm. Nathan's cry is followed by a soft moan from Caucus-Meteor, and a softer curse from the French commander.

"Your idea of mirth astonishes me," says Ensign St. Blein.

"Surprise always gains over repetition," says Caucus-Meteor to the Frenchman, as if he knew exactly what he was doing. In fact, he burned himself out of an impulse that he realizes now was ignited by his own grief. The pain will alleviate his weariness, he knows. He turns his attention to Nathan. "Speak now, Nathan Blake—speak."

"You wish me to speak of my comfort?" Nathan says in a whisper. His voice is under control, but sweat runs down his forehead into his eyes, and his flesh trembles.

Caucus-Meteor answers in Nathan's own accent, "Aye, of your comfort."

"For comfort I pray."

"I asked what you think. Prayer is not thinking. Every man thinks of something to give him comfort. I wish to know what you think. When you came out of your cabin, upset by your wife, you paused before going into your barn. You had a look on your face of a man searching for . . . something; I cannot say what it was, but it was not comfort. What were you thinking?"

Nathan says nothing.

"Speak or I will burn you."

St. Blein says in French, "You burn yourself, now you threaten to burn a captive over trivialities?"

"My curiosity is not trivial, Ensign," Caucus-Meteor answers in French, and then addresses Nathan in his language. "Speak—speak."

"I was thinking about my oxen, Reliant and Intrepid, their warm breath, their mild nature, their unconcern over such matters as mortality, territory, and pride."

"By the look on your face, you were thinking something else."

Nathan blushes, like a boy caught in a lie. He hates falsehood, especially in himself, thinks Caucus-Meteor.

"I was thinking of my oxen; then my thoughts turned to . . . a far place," Nathan says, and his tone is so serious, so dark that even St. Blein cannot find amusement in the utterance.

"Where is this 'far place'?" asks Caucus-Meteor.

"West of here, I cannot say exactly. Only that it is far, and I think of it often."

"So it is a place of your thinking, and not of the world."

"Of my thinking it is, but also of the world, for I believe that if I think it so, it must be, else my desire means nothing."

"Such thinking surely goes contrary to your prayers."

Nathan now cries out as if burned, though the old American has not touched him. For the first time since his capture, Nathan Blake appears on the verge of breaking down. "I have no answers on these questions of desires and prayer."

Caucus-Meteor turns to St. Blein, and says in French the opposite of what he believes. "This man is a simple farmer."

"That may be, though I fail to see the relevance. Let us turn now to questions regarding military matters."

"We will do better when we question the naval officer."

"I think you are protecting your captive, Caucus-Meteor," says St. Blein, but there is no venom in his accusation, no justifiable outrage, not even exasperation. The ensign is a good soldier —why is he so accommodating? Caucus-Meteor concludes that his commander has something besides warring on his mind these days. What can it be?

After more questioning, it becomes obvious to soldier and savage that Nathan Blake is a farmer with no information of any immediate use to the force. Caucus-Meteor is pleased with his captive, for he remains an interesting puzzle.

"Watch my prisoner, please. I wish to tend to my burn," says Caucus-Meteor to St. Blein, and then goes into the woods. He has no interest in medicating his wound, for it is not serious.

What he really wants to do is feel cool air on his bare head, but in private so others do not see his bald pate. Out of sight of the other men, he removes his turban.

Around nightfall, another raiding party from the south joins up with St. Blein's men. They have a third captive. Through questioning of Nathan, Caucus-Meteor learns the new prisoner is Samuel Allen, a youth of eighteen, and a nephew of Nathan's friend John Hawks. Nathan is also acquainted with the naval officer. The big man is known to Nathan only as Captain Warren. "He marked my pines," Nathan says with some bitterness. Caucus-Meteor doesn't understand what Nathan means, but he decides to let the mystery sit for a while.

That night the men make fires for feasting and fellowship. Someone has looted rum during the raids, and the men sing and drink and dance and celebrate their victory. Caucus-Meteor releases Nathan's hands, but hobbles him with ropes tied around his ankles. He can walk well enough to pick up dead branches from the woods and hemlock boughs for bedding, but he can't run away. Caucus-Meteor follows him around, pointing the musket at him, saying nothing.

After the beds are made, Caucus-Meteor orders Nathan to lie on some boughs on his back, and ties his wrists and ankles to maple saplings at the base. "There," he says, "I've arranged you like Jesus on his cross so that you can comfort yourself with the idea of martyrdom."

Caucus-Meteor and St. Blein interrogate the other prisoners. Each is tied to a tree. One of Furrowed Brow's cousins brings some fire from the main fire, and lays it at the feet of the captives. The interrogators rate Samuel Allen as a frightened youth; he has wild red hair and a kind of hysterical curiosity in his eyes. Captain Warren remains more interesting to Caucus-Meteor and St. Blein. Warren is big, powerfully built; he raises his head at the sight of the interrogators.

"Captain Warren," asks St. Blein in French, "what is a naval officer doing so many miles away from a navigable water body?"

Warren blinks with the terrors of confusion.

Caucus-Meteor translates the question into English. "You understand English, Englishman? You are, perhaps, a pirate?"

"I am an officer in His Majesty's navy, and thus a valued personage," Warren says. "I will remain silent."

St. Blein ambles off, turns his back on the proceedings, folds his arms. Caucus-Meteor picks up a burning stick and touches it just for a moment to the ear of Warren. He screams, first in pain, then in fear. The old American feels the hurt of his own wound. "Captain Warren, how long do you think you could stand this burning stick under your armpit before you answered the question in some fashion?"

Warren speaks all in a breath, "I am not a commissioned officer in the navy. Captain is an honorary title."

"Which you have bestowed upon yourself," Caucus-Meteor says.

"That's correct."

"And you are not a son of Old England but of New England."

Captain Warren nods in the affirmative.

St. Blein returns, takes the stick from Caucus-Meteor, and tosses it into the fire. Caucus-Meteor says to Warren, "Now please answer the good ensign's question. What is a navy man doing so far from the sea?"

"I am a timber surveyor hired by His Majesty's navy to scout pine trees to be used as ship masts."

"Did you mark trees belonging to a proprietor of a border town east of here, a man named Nathan Blake?" asks Caucus-Meteor.

"I do not recollect all the names."

"Thank you, Captain Warren," says Caucus-Meteor. "With your cooperation, I will personally see to it that no harm comes to you."

"You have a generous heart," says St. Blein sarcastically.

Caucus-Meteor smiles a little, and then both men laugh. The laugh does more to terrorize Captain Warren than the questioning, for he begins to perspire heavily and his bowels loosen.

"Take him down to the river and clean him," says St. Blein to the guards.

Upon return, Warren answers all of St. Blein's questions. He tells everything he knows about numbers of troops, location of barracks, kinds of weapons, and plans for future campaigns. The most important information the raiders learn is that no Colonial force is near enough to offer pursuit.

In concluding his inquiry, Caucus-Meteor asks, "By what device does the English heart remain so hard?"

"By the device of cannon and musket," says Warren.

"He doesn't know what you mean," says St. Blein in Algonkian.

"I know. He has little capacity for understanding, this man. I just wanted to see what he said."

"I will tell you that there is more than musket and cannon," says St. Blein in French. "There is the device of dividing the tribes by the wedge of their ancient animosities; there is the device of the promises of convenience."

"Which is followed by the breaking of such promises," says Caucus-Meteor. "And the spreading of disease, and the rum, and the terror, and the killing of women and children while avoiding warriors. These were the devices that the English employed to destroy my parents and their people. But all these devices we Americans have used to undo one another." Caucus-Meteor switches to English and addresses Captain Warren. "The most important device of the English and, yes, the French, is your Christian god, who allows all things convenient in his name. With such a god, even a savage such as I could be king."

Caucus-Meteor notes the expression on Warren's face, which tells him that though he speaks in the captive's tongue, his words are lost on him.

"Fall on your knees, then, old man," says St. Blein in French. It's the dark humor between the Frenchman and the American, and their laugh makes the captive tremble, for he understands less and less.

Afterward, St. Blein talks to Furrowed Brow. "The Mohawks now have two captives. What do you plan to do with them?"

"The fellow who captured young Allen owed me a debt, so they are both mine now; I am reserving judgment until after we see how they perform in the gauntlet."

"I think the governor-general would pay a good price for Captain Warren, for we could exchange him for more than one of our own," says St. Blein.

"I do not know if I want to sell him. He looks strong; he might make an acceptable Mohawk for adoption," says Furrowed Brow.

With that speculation, Furrowed Brow loses the respect of Caucus-Meteor, for the old interpreter is convinced that, despite his superior physique, Captain Warren is mediocre as a man.

Later, St. Blein visits Caucus-Meteor at his campsite, and sits with him by the old man's personal fire. They converse in French. Nearby, Nathan sits, bound with his own bootlaces. Caucus-Meteor likes to tie the captive in different positions, to keep his blood circulating and to keep himself entertained.

"You know, Caucus-Meteor," St. Blein says, "in man-to-man combat I'd wager on an American any day over a Frenchman or an Englishman, but as soldiers you're impossible. You don't follow orders. You'd rather groom yourselves than keep your equipment in order. You desert nation for self."

"I have seen the ensign groom his mustache and patch." Caucus-Meteor touches himself under his lower lip.

"True, but I groom myself *and* keep my equipment in order, and I plan, and I fight for Canada. But the savage puts his person ahead of state, church, even family."

"Count your blessings, St. Blein," Caucus-Meteor says. "If the American could be ruled from on high like the Frenchman, we'd kick your ass out of Canada."

"Yes, I've thought of that, old king. But if the American and the French-Canadian could truly be brothers in the heart"—he thumps his chest with his fist—"instead of just allies of opportunity, we could take this continent for our own, make it one country, free ourselves from all European influence."

"You mean French and Americans without France?"

"That's correct, my friend; that is my vision."

"A very ambitious idea that could get you stretched on that Old France torture machine in Montreal," Caucus-Meteor says.

"Yes, the rack—it frightens me not. I used to keep my ideas to myself, but now I don't care any more because I'm likely to be killed anyway, either in combat or through betrayal. So I've resolved to speak with an honest voice."

"Are you disturbed by thoughts of death?" Caucus-Meteor asks, and now he is thinking of his own death. Surely, it must lurk close by. He remembers the words of his captive, "a far place . . . west of here."

"On the contrary, thoughts of death relax me," the French ensign speaks with the confidence of a young man unable to contemplate his own mortality. "Dead, I won't have to carry on my father's despicable business. Dead, I won't have to wrestle with my confessor, who questions my ideals. The only fear I have remaining is death not by violence, but by disease or starvation or exposure alone in English territory."

"With no priest to give you absolution."

"You are being sarcastic again, Caucus-Meteor. It's the reason I befriend you."

"How would you feel about being shot and scalped by an English bounty hunter?"

"It pleases my vanity to imagine a lock of my hair hanging in a Boston government office."

After that there's a long silence until St. Blein says, "You seem a little frail for the rigors of war, old interpreter, and a little too philosophical for the enterprise."

"You thought I came out of retirement because I like war so much."

"I'm afraid I didn't think anything. We needed an interpreter, and when Adiwando wasn't available we were happy that his mentor and father-in-law agreed to accompany us. Nor did I think my interpreter, during the inquiry of a prisoner, would burn himself."

"I had private reasons for involving myself in this campaign. I thought going to war would take my mind off my grief. The throat distemper took thirty members of my village, including my son-in-law, two of my grandchildren, and my dear wife, Keeps-the-Flame. All that remains of my immediate family are my two daughters, my youngest, Caterina, and Adiwando's widow, Black Dirt. It was the grief of my daughters that drove me away. I couldn't bear their suffering."

"War with nature is far more terrible than war with man, Caucus-Meteor. I knew Adiwando had died; I didn't know about the others. You have other reasons?"

"Who can say why a man does what he does when the man himself is not so sure?" Caucus-Meteor is thinking about his captive and his decision to leave the stockade. "I will say that my village has use for the interpreter's salary."

"Conissadawaga is poor? I thought your village did well in the moccasin trade."

"We do, but because we're cold to the priests who come to take our souls, the church will not protect us from . . ." Caucus-Meteor cuts himself off. "Do you know what I'm saying, good ensign?"

"François Bigot!" He emphasizes the name in his musical language, bee-goh!

"Correct. I am required to pay the intendant a tribute every spring. You see, twenty years ago I negotiated with some Montagnais for property where our summer village now rests and for hunting rights in the hills beyond the lake. We didn't bother with French legal documents. Naturally, from the intendant's point of view, the legal documents are everything."

"The vultures from Old France are stealing Canada blind," St. Blein's normal blasé demeanor falls away. He's full of passion and belief. "They steal from the peasants, they steal from the soldiers, they steal from the king, and they steal from the savages."

"We should be flattered they treat us as equal to the king."

St. Blein smiles a crooked grin, as if remembering that it is more productive to pretend indifference. "It's getting late, Caucus-Meteor. I'm going to bed. You should go to bed, too, old king." St. Blein rises to leave.

"Not me. I'm going to sit here all night, and eat this fire."

Caucus-Meteor watches the Frenchman vanish into the darkness, then he huddles very close to his fire, lets the smoke sting his eyes, the heat burnish his skin. With the help of his fire and the nagging hurt of his self-inflicted burn, Caucus-Meteor finds powers to pluck out of memory a vivid picture of his late wife. She was in her sixties when she died, a woman with big shoulders, big bust, very dark skin. He says something in Algonkian to the fire. The fire responds in Iroquois. Suddenly, Keeps-the-Flame, young and beautiful and naked, appears in the flames. Caucus-Meteor, with a full head of hair in braids, drapes her body with wampum belts, bits of white and lavender seashells held together with thread—the old currency.

The old American dreams but he does not sleep; he sits with a blanket over his shoulders by a small fire, and rests by concentrating his attention on the fire, watching the flames and smoke, listening to the crackles and hisses, inviting dreams. Sometimes he closes his eyes, and is able move on to other places, other times, but he's never unaware of the world in which he resides, so when the captive awakens in the middle of the night, cramped, cold, aching from the thongs cutting into his wrists, Caucus-Meteor hears his labored breath, his moans, and finally his cry of startled anguish as he comes out of a nightmare.

Caucus-Meteor puts three sticks on his dying fire, picks up the musket, then walks a few feet in the darkness to the prisoner.

"Good evening, Nathan Blake," he says. It's a test. If Nathan complains about his obvious discomfort, Caucus-Meteor will walk away and let him suffer from cramps, but Nathan only returns the greeting. The captive has passed a test. Caucus-Meteor frees Nathan from his bonds so he can stretch his limbs.

When a man dreams, he is righting himself, believes Caucus-Meteor, and a righting man is dangerous. Nathan Blake will pray to his god, and he will plan for escape. At this point, Caucus-Meteor is uncertain how violent and capable this farmer can be. He's feeling his burn when the dangerous idea he had earlier returns: if my captive kills me my worries will be greatly reduced.

Next morning on the trail, while pretending to be more exhausted than he really is (though he is exhausted enough), Caucus-Meteor watches his prisoner very carefully, and determines that his analysis was correct. The prisoner is planning an escape. The technique is simple enough: twisting his tied wrists until he can slip out in the slime of his own blood. Old tricks, born of desperation, are always a little sad as well as annoying.

The troop begins a long ascent through the mountains, following an ancient trail that winds with a river that tumbles over rocks, runs fast through pebbles, and never seems to meander. The rocks are different here from the ones in Nathan's land. They're lighter in color, more brittle, the slates more layered. The water in the stream is different, too, not tea-colored, but clear with just a taint of green. Further up, the hardwoods give way to fir with groves of white birch and yellow birch.

As Nathan Blake walks he continually turns his wrists against the ropes. Surely, thinks his captor, he believes that toil, blood, and belief will free him, for that is the way of his religion. All during this long march, Nathan Blake must be imagining himself killing his enemy, fleeing through the woods—to his family, to his own kind, to his ruined home, or perhaps not; perhaps it is that far place west of here in his secret heart where his hope resides.

That night in the mountains it is cold, and Caucus-Meteor is so tired and weak that he doubts whether he can go on. After the captive has gathered firewood and boughs for bedding, Caucus-Meteor stakes him down, sits by the fire, and stares into it.

Next day the pace slows somewhat because the troop is beginning to feel safe from pursuit. Even so, Caucus-Meteor has to push himself hard to keep up. As the pain of his burn wound subsides, the limits of his stamina close in, for pain gives a man energy. He hopes the weather holds. These mountains, like mountains anywhere, play tricks. He entreats the god in the mountains for a continuation of kindly weather. Caucus-Meteor distrusts all gods, but who else but gods can one pray to?

The old American notes that his captive's wrists bleed, but he still cannot pull his hands free. Another day or two, and he'll be so far away from English territory that even if he can escape he'll have no place to go. He must be excited in his desperation. "I envy you, Nathan Blake," Caucus-Meteor says, but he speaks in Algonkian, so that the captive understands only the sound of his name.

The following dawn the troop leaves the stream behind, goes through a notch, and then begins a downward trek, picking up another path along another stream. Caucus-Meteor thanks the mountain god for deliverance.

Soon they arrive at the big lake the French call Champlain, a blue ribbon in the mountains, appreciated for its beauty by white and red people alike: it's a thought that cheers Caucus-Meteor. The troop retrieves their birch-bark canoes. The crafts were filled with stones and sunk in the lake for concealment. The men are in a good mood. They believe themselves safe from English muskets. From here to Quebec there will be no more long marches; they'll move swiftly in their crafts with only a few short portages.

"Do you know where you are?" Caucus-Meteor asks Nathan.

"I've heard tell of this lake," says Nathan. "They say a monster lives in its depths."

"The monster does not live in the depths, but across the waters in the long houses of the pagan Iroquois. Perhaps some day, Nathan Blake, you will visit the English and Dutch town of Albany, or perhaps the native town of . . ." and he speaks the local name in his native tongue. "You will have to learn our language. Speak now the name as I have uttered it."

"Synecdoche," Nathan says.

"Good start," says Caucus-Meteor.

Caucus-Meteor checks the wind. It's blowing from the southwest, and that means easy going. He realizes now that he has enough strength to make it back to Conissadawaga, an observation that sends a charge of despondency through him, for once he has returned to his village he will no longer allow himself the luxury of contemplating suicide; he will feel the weight of the responsibilities of his throne, the gnawing hound of want chewing the bone of his ambition.

For the old American canoeing is not as exhausting as walking; canoeing is just stiff joints, aching back, cramps in thighs, pain in the elbow, bee buzzing in the buttocks, and sloshing bladder. For Nathan, it's the first time since he's been captured that his hands and legs are untied for long periods of time. The raiders chant, an activity that helps with the rhythm of the paddling. Nathan is quiet; it's a while before Caucus-Meteor realizes that his captive is passing the time in silent prayer.

In the same canoe with Caucus-Meteor and Nathan are two brothers from the town of Odanak on the St. Lawrence River, and this is their canoe. They keep to themselves, laughing and joking and singing. Caucus-Meteor tells Nathan that they're Squakheag réfugiés.

"Their families once lived in the river valley where your farm is, Nathan Blake."

"In 1736 when I built the first log cabin, no one challenged my claim to the property," Nathan says.

"Most of the Squakheag proprietors were driven out by the pagan Mohawks, the same people who are now the English allies. Just as you have never stepped foot in Old England, these brothers had never stepped foot on their ancestral lands until the day they burned your town, and that is why they are jovial."

The canoes ride low, but move fast, since each person paddles.

Only the old American cheats at paddling. As the hours slip by, Caucus-Meteor finds himself thinking about matters long interred in memory. It's this captive, his enslavement to me, that has disturbed my mind, he thinks.

As a slave in boyhood, Caucus-Meteor had moments when he no longer wanted to be an American, but he didn't want to be a Frenchman or a Dutchman either, and certainly not an Englishman or an African. He thought maybe he wanted to be a Spaniard. At night, he would lie still in darkness, trying to remain awake to think, for only the moments before drifting off to sleep were his own. He would imagine himself in armor, face painted gold and silver, ears decorated with brass crucifixes, a ring in his nose, as the pope might wear. In those days he thought the pope was a Spaniard. He enjoyed picturing himself in full armor. He didn't know whether in the interest of accuracy he should picture the shiny metal armor he heard tell Champlain wore, or the stick armor of American warriors before the age of firearms, or the strange cloth armor he saw in his dreams. He settled on a compromise, stick armor painted shiny. How did a Spaniard behave? With that question, he had realized he had no understanding of such matters. The whole idea fell apart in his head. He was no Spaniard. He was not an anything or an anybody. Goaded on by that notion, he'd started planning an escape from slavery. He wonders now whether his own slave is having similar thoughts.

Later that night the company reaches Missisquoi at the northern end of Lake Champlain. A few Abenaki leave the troop, for this village is their home. Under the stars and moonlight one can see a couple of log huts and maybe a dozen stick-frame structures covered with layers of birch bark, pine needles, and grass tufts between the layers for insulation. St. Blein visits with Father Etienne Laverjat, the priest who operates the mission. Caucus-Meteor muses that the gatherings of Frenchmen, though admirable for their intimacy, leave out natives.

The company camps under some pines in a cove sheltered

from the wind on the eastern shore of the lake. Caucus-Meteor sets up his camp out of sight from the others. The warriors sit around a fire, chewing their pemmican; Caucus-Meteor can hear them talking of war, women, weapons, wagering, and weather. The mild south wind pushing the canoes has turned them into giddy optimists. Caucus-Meteor wants nothing to do with people in such a mood, so he's content to guard his prisoner.

Caucus-Meteor sits on a log, raps it with a middle finger. It's not hollow, no good for drumming. The sounds of laughter and easy talk come to him worse than taunts. He's thinking about his wife, his grandchildren, his mother, his father, scores of fallen comrades—all the dead ones. Why have I lived so long? he wonders. He decides to walk down to the shore, where the sound of the waves will drown out the sounds of happiness. "Come, let's have a drink of water," he says in English to Nathan. He hobbles the captive's feet with thongs. As he ties Nathan's wrists to the stake across his back, the old abrasions open and he feels Nathan's blood on his hands. He pulls up his sleeves and rubs the blood against his burn. Is this the omen he's been looking for? It doesn't feel like an omen. Even so, Caucus-Meteor leaves some slack below the knots. "Now you can escape," he says to Nathan in Algonkian. He picks up the musket, holds it for a moment, leans it against a tree.

They walk on ledge, down through ground made soft by pine-needle cover, to the rocky shore. Gentle waves slosh through stones. Caucus-Meteor is certain now that he does not want to return to Canada to face the burden of his responsibilities as a king. St. Blein will travel to Conissadawaga and report that he was killed by a prisoner. He'll trust St. Blein to turn over his salary to his eldest daughter, Black Dirt.

From Nathan's squirming movements followed by no movement at all, Caucus-Meter determines that his captive has freed his hands. Caucus-Meteor drops to his knees to drink. He can hear the captive shuffle behind him. He's picking up a rock, thinks Caucus-Meteor; he will bring it down on my head. The lake water is cold and very tasty. Caucus-Meteor enjoys a surge of intense feeling very similar to the feeling of gambler's excitement. He'd like to turn and deliver a long oratory on the nature of choosing the time and instrument of one's death, but this is not the place for oratory. It's the place for submission to those unknown gods who rule by whim and mystery. Something like the lights that fill the northern skies in the winter dance in his head, and the image of the Spaniard is back, huge and metallic in his armor.

Caucus-Meteor senses the decisive moment. Nathan Blake throws a rock ten feet over his head. With the sound of the splash, Caucus-Meteor leaps to his feet, and pulls his knife.

The captive lurches forward, trips on his hobble and falls to his knees. Just as moments earlier, Caucus-Meteor awaited death, so now does Nathan Blake.

Caucus-Meteor says politely, "Do you wish to drink?"

"Aye," says Nathan.

After Nathan drinks, Caucus-Meteor marches Nathan back to camp, and ties him down.

"You could have killed me, but did not," says the old American.

Nathan says nothing, gazes off into a place his own.

"I am your master. You must answer my question," says Caucus-Meteor.

"I have not heard a question," says Nathan, and the insolence in his voice tells Caucus-Meteor that his prisoner, through his refusal to kill, has found powers within himself that he did not know he possessed.

"You know the question. Why did you spare my life?"

Nathan Blake remains silent. For the first time, Caucus-Meteor feels anger toward his captive. Perhaps he is a Christian devil, or maybe a trickster from olden times returned in a new guise. Perhaps he should kill Nathan Blake, or sell him to the Iroquois, or burn him, as in olden times, as a rite to assuage his own pain. But Caucus-Meteor has lived too long to be mastered by anger or fear or even hope.

"It's just you, me, and the Great Now, Nathan Blake," Caucus-

Meteor says, and suddenly he's thinking about himself from a
time long ago. He switches to the tongue of his parents, so that
Nathan can feel the emotion within him without the disguise of
word-meaning. He speaks in the manner of his father, addressing the multitudes before the king's seat in Mount Hope. "I wish
I was a young man again so I could go on a vision quest, as we
natives used to do before the French and English arrived. It used
to be that young fellows would go off into the forest to seek
dreams to understand their lives and place in the world. These
days they get drunk, and think they're having visions. They go to
war, not to avenge a wrong or to make just an indignity or to assuage the grief of their mothers, but so that French merchants in
Paris can have fur hats to sell."

Caucus-Meteor does not finish his thoughts with speech, for
they would embarrass him, even if he did speak them in a language only he comprehends. Still, the thoughts bring him a
mellow feeling, for wistfulness has given way to that wonderful
feeling of ambition. He silently mouths the words of the dog-
gnawed bone: "One day I will be king of all North America; I
will lead one tribe, one people with castles to rival those in Europe, with corn ten feet tall and canoes with so many paddlers
their singing can be heard in the countries across the oceans. I
will throw out money as a medium of exchange and bring back
the wampum belts, which combined money and diplomacy with
adornment. What else besides money, diplomacy, and adornment is of worth in the public domain? A condition of permanent and excited peace will ensue." The old American tries to
cast his mind out into the void like a net to embrace his vision,
but all he catches is a headache.

Next day, on the water, the troop glimpses the Lake Champlain sea monster. Actually, it's a sturgeon. Quite a fish, but disappointing as a monster.

The troop paddles off the lake onto the Richelieu river. From
here on in, it's downstream into the heart of Quebec. The Americans' good mood continues as they paddle for home.

"What is to become of me, Caucus-Meteor?" asks Nathan. "Are you my master forever, or truly do I belong to the French?"

Since Nathan spared Caucus-Meteor's life, a change has come over both men. Nathan is more forward, unafraid; he has gained something, while Caucus-Meteor has lost something. What can it be? And then the answer comes to him. Now that he's back in Canada, the old American once again is in bondage to the idea of life and the difficulties involved in continuing life.

"I captured you," Caucus-Meteor says. "You are mine, a fair prisoner in war. I may, as I am sure is your wish, sell you to the French, which means you would probably be exchanged for a French prisoner held by the English. Or I may keep you as my personal slave, for I am an old man with an old man's needs."

Nathan seems somewhat relieved. Perhaps he believes that it's unlikely he will be harmed, for if an Englishman understands anything it's that a damaged slave is not of much use.

"Are your people papists?" Nathan asks. "I hear tell that many of the Canada savages have been converted by the Jesuits."

Caucus-Meteor thinks: what a wonderful opportunity for speech-making. The old orator begins to speak, and as he does he's no longer addressing his captive. He's talking to the familiar throngs inhabiting his imagination, though now his words are in English.

"I will tell you about my people," he says. "My village, just north of Quebec City, is called Conissadawaga. In every language, some words mean more than one thing. Conissadawaga means two things. It means, roughly put in English, makers of shoes. Our women make the best moccasins in North America, and our men trade them. But it also means People-in-Exile, for a people with shoes too good are tempted to wander far from home. Our citizens are from tribes taken by the English in New England in the days when the Colonials called us Americans and before they began to call themselves Americans. We are, therefore, the first American tribe. We are the children of war and disease and gods who have abandoned us. A few of us worship Jesus, a few the old American gods, some no god at all. Most live in great confusion. When I was in Europe where I was a slave trained in languages, I heard of a king in China, who was known as Confusion. The Chinese would have sayings, as in: Confusion say, 'English fellow going to Canada to have breakfast with the People-in-Exile.'"

"You turn a man's mind to mush, master. I know nothing of these things," Nathan says.

"Corn mush for the belly of the savage, and prayer to purge the bowels."

"Does my master worship Jesus?"

"I argue with all the gods, except the god of rum and brandy, whom I despise with constancy since he has no redeeming virtues. You, Nathan Blake, must make do with your one God. You will need your English Jesus when we arrive in Montreal." Caucus-Meteor waits for Nathan to ask why, but Nathan remains silent. His restraint pleases Caucus-Meteor. He says, "In Montreal, you will be tested in the gauntlet."

"If my blood is spilled, I'll make a poor slave," he says.

"That's true, but the gauntlet is a venerate tradition among the tribes, and there's nothing I can do to protect you. I will give you a bit of advice, though. Don't think about blood; think about behavior."

The Gauntlet

That night Caucus-Meteor drifts off into one of his waking
dreams. He sees a forest filled with people and trees he
can't identify. In the background is a rushing noise. A figure
representing himself dangles from the claws of a crow. Below is
another figure with folded arms and colorless eyes. The crowd is
boisterous though not violent, merely excited in a way Caucus-
Meteor cannot determine.

The crow does not injure him; indeed, the crow's claws embrace rather than grasp. The man with the folded arms and the
colorless eyes is obviously an adversary, though he makes no
threatening gestures. In the dream Caucus-Meteor hails the
man, who says nothing but unfolds his arms, producing two
small stones from the air and placing them on a large flat rock.
The Caucus-Meteor figure, still dangling from the crow, places
one stone on the rock. The mob cheers, and half a dozen runners
appear. Caucus-Meteor tries to enter more deeply into the dream
to study the runners, but he cannot. Usually he has the power to
alter his dreams as he wishes, but not this one. The sound of the
cheering crowd rises, then subsides, and now Caucus-Meteor
can hear the mysterious rushing noise again. The men have
stopped running. The crow releases the Caucus-Meteor figure,
who picks up the stones. The man with the folded arms walks

away. The figure representing himself in the dream mingles with the crowd. The figure seeks out one of the runners to congratulate him on his performance, but the runner has disappeared. The crow scratches marks on the ground that Caucus-Meteor understands as advice telling him that finding the runner is of great importance. Then Caucus-Meteor sees the runner in the shadows. Before he can recognize the man, the old gods return and disrupt the dream.

The feeling of fulfillment that accompanied the dream suggests that it's important he learn what the dream means. Why? Why do I think this? he asks himself. Once he's asked himself the question, the answer is readily apparent. The purpose of the dream is to set him on a course to conclude his stay in this realm. The dream is the beginning of the middle of the great and last adventure of his life. The end of the beginning was his capture of Nathan Blake. A major task that lies ahead of him will be to determine how Nathan Blake fits into his dream.

Next day it's more of the same—paddle paddle paddle, sing sing sing. It's night when the raiders arrive at a village across the great St. Lawrence River from Montreal. Caucus-Meteor lectures Nathan, "Tomorrow you will run the gauntlet. Until that event is finished, you belong less to me than to the spectacle to come. You will be isolated until that time." He locks Nathan in a gloomy storage shed full of hides, stinking of animal blood, musk, and oil, but he's not bound.

Caucus-Meteor is the guest of Furrowed Brow, the captor of Captain Warren and the owner of young Allen. Furrowed Brow occasionally teases Caucus-Meteor by calling him king. Caucus-Meteor pretends to be amused, for he is the guest. The men talk and smoke outside by a fire, and soon the old chief is exhausted, not only from the journey, but from the strain of holding his tongue, for he finds his Iroquois host overbearing and full of himself. Or perhaps I am merely envious, thinks Caucus-Meteor, for Furrowed Brow has *two* captives, one of them a military officer.

The villagers build up the fire; drums and rattles play. This place is the home of most of the fighters who destroyed the English frontier town, and they're celebrating their victory.

The next morning Caucus-Meteor brings his slave some breakfast, the corn and grain mush that the Iroquois are so fond of, and then takes him outside. Nathan blinks into blasts of hard light. He sees clusters of log huts on the bank by the river, a few more elaborate than his own burned-out log cabin, some more primitive.

"Is this Quebec?" Nathan asks.

"You are not in Quebec. You are in the Christian Mohawk village of Kahnawake. You and the other two Englishmen will be taken across the river into Montreal, where you will run the gauntlet. If you survive, you will go on with me to my village of Conissadawaga, which is just north of the place where you thought you are now, Quebec—one hundred sixty English miles more canoeing."

"I stand corrected," Nathan says. "You are the sachem of this town of . . ." Nathan tries and fails to pronounce Conissadawaga.

"I am king of Conissadawaga."

"Aye," says Nathan, and bows slightly.

I like his subtle insult to my pride, thinks Caucus-Meteor.

Captain Warren and young Allen appear with their guards. In the next few minutes, scores of men, women, and children empty from the cabins and surround the captives.

"Remember what I told you about the gauntlet—behavior," Caucus-Meteor says. "I can do nothing for you until after that test."

The captives are pushed and shoved, moved on down to the shoreline. Caucus-Meteor takes note of the town: log cabins with plank roofs, iron stoves for heat, a few cows and horses, many chickens. He watches a girl lead a couple of dogs pulling a cart on wheels. She's headed for work in the fields that surround the village. Maybe eight hundred to a thousand Mohawks live here. There's even a public building, a long log cabin with a cross on top. The place is more advanced than his own village, and even the English border town they burned. The Iroquois, whether Pagan, Protestant, or Catholic, know how to organize themselves. Caucus-Meteor feels a mixture of envy, resentment, contempt, and admiration.

Half the village's canoes will cross the St. Lawrence to Montreal. The atmosphere is festive, for a gauntlet day is a holiday. The people laugh, exchange witticisms, place bets, pack food and brandy into canoes. Many of the men adorn themselves extravagantly. Furrowed Brow himself is bare-legged and bare-chested in chilly weather to show off white-dot body makeup. Another man halves himself with blue and yellow paint. An old man, a survivor of tortures by a rival tribe, accentuates his burn scars with subtle red and gray makeup. The women wear colorful beads, but no paint. Everyone is carrying an instrument for inflicting harm—a stick, a spear, a hatchet, a whip, a club, a bundle of thorns.

Caucus-Meteor studies the faces of the captives. Nathan's lips move; his slave has detached himself from the situation through prayer and perhaps the consolations of memory. Young Sam Allen walks as if the bones in his legs have been removed. Captain Warren, broken by his interrogation, seems like a man with an unworkable but soothing plan, he's so calm. Ensign St. Blein likewise seems preoccupied with his own thoughts. Once in the canoe, Caucus-Meteor suddenly hears the background rush of the Lachine Rapids, which prevent oceangoing crafts from penetrating any deeper into the continent. Where has he heard that sound before? Why is it taking on importance in his mind?

Montreal is a bustling trade center of three or four thousand people, a town surrounded by wooden palisades; the gauntleteers march their prisoners through a gate manned by soldiers in blue and brown. Inside are paved streets, impressive houses made of wood and stone, along with stone churches, and a huge open market. Furs coming in from the western and northern tribes keep this place humming. Hung in open stalls for viewing by buyers are pelts of beaver, wild cat, lynx, martin, mink, deer, bear, moose, wolf, skunk, and seal; the feathers from scores of different kinds of birds; and porcupine quills arranged by size and sold with dyes for coloring same. With the money they make from animals they hunt and trap, the tribal emissaries shop for kettles and other kitchen ware, beads, brandy, guns, powder, lead, cloth, brandy, brandy, hardware (such as door hinges), knives, scissors, axes, and brandy. The bargaining is conducted in different languages, accompanied by politic hand signals and facial expressions. The raiders display their prisoners to curious onlookers. The word has circulated. Today is going to be a gauntlet day.

The French merchants wear trimmed beards, bright baggy pants, shirts in colors that don't match the pants, and floppy caps. They tip those ridiculous hats to everyone who approaches them. Their outfits are also influenced by fashions from the tribes, including feathers, beaded belts, and earrings. French matrons at the markets wear neat jackets buttoned prim and proper at the throat, but dark blue skirts that reach only to a dimple between thigh and knee to accentuate shapely calves. Women from the tribes wear colorful tops but skirts identical to ones worn by the Frenchwomen. The facial makeup of the tribal women is spare, and their hair is long and straight. The men cut their hair according to their own whim. They spends hours with body and facial paint. Some have tattoos of wild animals and designs whose meaning is known only to them. They wear earrings, nose rings, neck beads, bright sashes, beaded belts, and feathers sticking out of every body nook, hook, crook, and crack. Adornments feature crucifixes, pendants, holy medals, coins, bones, beads, and hair tufts from reluctant donors.

Others in the marketplace include priests and nuns wearing black. Caucus-Meteor recognizes the old Ursuline Nun, Esther

Wheelwright, captured in a raid in New England in 1703 and converted by the French to their side. Others include seamen in woolens, a few escaped black slaves from the southern English plantations; even the enemies of Canada, the English and the Dutch, are represented, for a few traders from Albany have won the right to peddle their goods in the French market through the tried and true persuasion of bribery. The priests and nuns, grave but confident in bearing, and the seaman, curious and severe, seem to be comfortable in plain dress. The rest of these folks, myself included, thinks Caucus-Meteor, if you judge us by our outward appearance, are struggling to find ourselves through display and decoration.

A handful of voyageurs stand out from the rest. One can tell these small, bearded Frenchman from the merchants, seamen, farmers, and tradesmen by their deep tans, leathery skins, buckskin apparel, and knotty muscles. One of them comes over to Caucus-Meteor. The two men exchange greetings, and the voyageur joins Caucus-Meteor in the processional walk with the prisoners. They converse easily, partly in French, partly in Algonkian.

"I haven't seen you for a couple years, Row-bear, where have you been?" Caucus-Meteor asks.

"Out west, up north, all over. You look good, old king," says the voyageur.

"You lie."

The voyageur laughs. "How are your people? How's Black Dirt and that interpreter you persuaded her to marry?" The voyageur is Robert de Repentigny, a trapper, trader, curious explorer of western lands, and an old friend of Caucus-Meteor and his family. Like most voyageurs, he's short, wiry, and very strong, perfectly sized to paddle a canoe for hours.

"She is a widow, Robert. And I am a widower. Black Dirt's two daughters were also taken by the sickness."

"I am sorry. I heard about the plagues. I didn't realize they had harmed your village."

Caucus-Meteor shrugs. "Are you going to join the gauntlet?"

"The novelty has worn off for me."

"The rite of the gauntlet is more profundity than novelty."

"I am sorry if I offended you."

"No offense." The two men shake hands, and de Repentigny leaves.

In the background, music plays. Like the garb of the folk, the music is all mixed, the sounds not exactly comfortable in each other's company, thinks the old American. He can hear the drums, rattles, and cedar lutes that move him so; Catholic hymns sung by French nuns in Latin, a language nobody understands but the clerics and the lawyers, but which sounds impressive; even some kind of a fiddle screeching, maybe Scottish, that Caucus-Meteor heard as a boy in New England and that now suggests to him another hidden reason he came out of retirement: somewhere in the back of his mind was the dim hope that the raiders would continue south to that place his parents had called home.

The captives are paraded through the market. Nathan and Sam, hands bound in front, half walk, half stumble; Captain Warren appears to be growing more detached, devoid of emotion. This one may already be dead, thinks Caucus-Meteor, a man at the gates of his own personal Hades. They reach an expanse of pasture grass, muddy and drab with patches of old snow, waiting for the green of May, the field extending almost to a little mountain, the "mont" of Montreal. A few soldiers practice marching and gunnery, but most of the field is used for athletic contests — foot races, wrestling matches, lacrosse games. On the edges are crude stick booths where men can buy liquor or food, and adornments, including tattoos. Some day, in my old age, he thinks, I will tattoo my skin until I cannot recognize myself. Perhaps in that action I will find release from ambition. His attention is drawn to the gambling arbors where men shoot dice, play other games of chance, and wager on the athletes. Drunks of varying races, tribes, nations, and persuasions slither through the crowd.

A few stray Frenchmen, and some tipsy sailors, join the gauntlet. More and more people line up, until eventually several hundred have formed a twisting human labyrinth—how like the canals of a wolf's ear, thinks the old American. Hundreds of others hang back to observe. Everybody knows that whatever happens here will be remembered and talked about for years to come. By now the contestants must realize that no amount of human strength, speed, nimbleness, and determination can get a man through these lines. The captives have been told that the gauntlet is a test. But it's a test not only of the individuals passing through the hellish corridor, but of itself, thinks Caucus-Meteor. The gauntlet is a register of shifting human moods. Each captive is to be taunted, provoked, driven to behave beyond the cunning of the self that faces the world. The resulting behavior, revealing the inner man, will turn the mood of the gauntlet, which will change its behavior toward the captive, which will change the mood of the runner, who will change his behavior, and so forth to an unpredictable conclusion. There is no correct or incorrect technique for running the gauntlet, because each member of the line is a mystery with his or her own personal chronicles and dispositions.

But general principles of conduct do exist for the gauntlet. It's considered graceless as well as impractical to strike a killing or disabling blow. The purpose of the spectacle is not to maim or even to punish, but to determine the character of the contestant, so that he can be dealt with accordingly. The captive of good character, brave but respectful, can be brought into the tribe as a slave or even as a full-fledged citizen. The captive of bad character, cowardly or defiant or obtuse, can be killed or, in these times, sold to another tribe or to the French. If Caucus-Meteor understands one thing about the gauntlet, it's in an old saying among the Algonkian-speaking nations: you never know. The reason for the success of the gauntlet as an institution is the charm of its uncertainty. The old American, like most on the field, enjoys the suspense and anticipation of the crowd. Many a clever talker can produce convincing oratory about what will happen, but nobody knows for sure the outcome, and there are always surprises.

Caucus-Meteor takes his place in the middle of the twisting corridor of the gauntlet. Others in the line carry all manner of mayhem—sticks, switches, spears, hatchets, whips, chains, knives, stones, handfuls of sand to throw in the eyes, but Caucus-Meteor is unarmed, except for the knife on his neck cord. He doesn't plan to administer any more than a casual and light touch to any of the runners of the gauntlet. Even though he has as good reason as any to inflict harm on Englishmen, there is no malice in Caucus-Meteor, not a trace left of his youthful rage. His wife, Keeps-the-Flame, taught him to put hatred and vengeance behind, for her tribe was an enemy of his father's people. Their union was an act not only of love, but of reconciliation. Caucus-Meteor is not in the line to seek satisfaction for injury, but to seek guidance in the revelations sure to unfold in the ceremony of the gauntlet. His thoughts spin away from logic: he imagines that he finds some secret in the behavior of the gauntlet runners. From this secret, he'll make a speech about the secret heart of humanity. Great speeches do not a French or an English king make, but an American king must stand or fall on his oratory.

The first runner is Samuel Allen. The more frightened he becomes the younger he seems. He can barely balance on his feet while his bonds are cut, and he is stripped of his clothes and shoes until he is naked. Surely, the gauntlet must look to him like the gut of an endless serpent, fangs running through its intestines; he can't even see the end of the tail for the twists and turns, the raised sticks, the grinning jaws. He will understand nothing of what is said, but perhaps he'll hear the echo of a familiar mocking tone in the voices. His father, his uncles, his elders, his brothers and sisters—they all had their fun with Sam, as Caucus-Meteor learned from his interrogation. Lazy boy, clumsy boy, dreamer, tripper (as one who trips over his own feet)—he'd heard a thousand taunts, and he'd laughed loudest with those who mocked him, while inside (in the secret heart that the old

American believes will be revealed in the gauntlet) he wept bitter tears. His own people tormented him because they sensed he hated farm life, the dreary labor, the confinement. They could not know the yearning within him, because, as Caucus-Meteor determined, Sam Allen himself was unsure of its nature. Family, church, and town robbed him of . . . what? He could not tell his interrogator. Now perhaps what frightens him more than anything is the shadow cast by the mystery of his ignorance. Young Allen, you fear that you will go to your grave without an explanation for your woes, without a chance to reach out for a life you can call your own, or to experience complementary joys with a like-minded soul. Your despair deepens until you wish only for oblivion.

And then something happens to give him hope, or so Caucus-Meteor reads in his eyes. One of his tormentors takes pity on him, or anyway that's the way it seems to Sam. A fellow about his own age with a painted face says something to him. Sam doesn't understand the words, but the tone tells him he's being reassured. Actually, the fellow had been drinking, and he was being sarcastic, posturing for his friends. But in that small moment of benevolent misunderstanding, Sam's fear and despair leave. Sam, this is not a finish but a start. Hope connects head to heart to feet. He takes a deep breath, and dashes into the yawn of the serpent.

Seconds later an extended foot sends him flying. He jumps up, starts running helter-skelter, and then it's whap (pain), whap (pain), whap (no pain). Soon he's not feeling anything; he's just a function of the rite. He falls, somebody grabs his hand and pulls him to his feet, aims him deeper into the gauntlet gullet, and gives him a boot in the behind. He lurches from one side to the other, taking blows. Whap, whap, whap—down again. Pulled to his feet, pushed back out onto the field. Whap, whap, whap—down. Up. Run. Five times he falls. About two-thirds of the way, a kick knocks him through the line; he falls, rises, cannot keep his feet, collapses without a hand being laid on him. Caucus-Meteor waits for the rain of blows that will take the life of this young man, for he has not completed his journey, a violation of the tenets of the gauntlet. Instead someone grabs his hand and pulls him to a standing position. A moan, laughter from the crowd, and he's allowed to collapse in a clump of new spring grass.

Furrowed Brow and a couple of kinswomen, one about fifty, the other perhaps sixteen or seventeen, come over to Sam. Furrowed Brow, the master, stands with arms folded across his chest while the older woman feels Sam up from stem to stern. As she works, she recites the results of her findings for the enlightenment of the young woman, who appears passionately engaged with the medical facts if not with the patient. No broken bones, no open arteries or veins, no signs of internal bleeding or brain injury. Many cuts and bruises. Vision unimpaired. A knock on the head will leave him with a slightly disfigured ear, but the drum that plays the world's music does not appear to be ruptured. The younger woman gives Sam a wooden noggin. "Water," she says in her own language. Sam hesitates, drinks. Caucus-Meteor can predict the outcome. Some ethereal substance outside Sam's experience until this moment surges within him until he's filled with the wonder of it. A minute passes before he knows what he's feeling: happy just to be alive and, in a way he doesn't understand yet, appreciated. Caucus-Meteor is glad, blessed by the young man's emotion; the old American knows that if he feels it, so do the other members of the gauntlet.

The next runner, stripped to the buff, is Captain Warren. Caucus-Meteor guesses that the gentle southerly breeze sashaying around his privates is as close to intimate touch as he's ever allowed. The tormentors, admiring the deep chest, thick neck, powerful arms and legs, generous male dangle, are thinking that this fellow might be of some consequence as a man. That body hair, though, thick and matted, is repulsive to them. Only Caucus-Meteor is not sizing up Captain Warren. Caucus-Meteor's eyes are on his own slave, Nathan Blake, who has also been stripped naked. Caucus-Meteor has seen legs like these before, on the Pure Men runners of the northern tribes. The women of his village make moccasins for such runners, who compete in races at summer trade fairs.

Captain Warren starts his run, and Caucus-Meteor remembers something the captain told him during his interrogation. "People admire my body, it is my currency; do not harm it, and I will tell you what you wish." He holds his head high, runs steadily, does not seem to feel stings inflicted by his tormentors. A woman with a licentious eye touches him on the shoulder, as if giving a blessing. Captain Warren bows. Others in the gauntlet follow the example of the woman. Captain Warren runs slowly down the line, and no one strikes him with any force. Given his character, he feels by now a little more than human, thinks Caucus-Meteor. Cheers from the crowd behind the gauntlet urge him on. Surely, he believes his performance is winning over the heathens.

The gauntlet roughed up the young fellow, but allowed him to bow out before he actually finished, a definite strain on tradition. Now the gauntlet was giving the second runner free proceed. It will not allow a third captive through so easily. Caucus-Meteor calculates that his own slave is in for trouble.

At the halfway point in the line, a Mohawk warrior stops Captain Warren, gives him a bear hug, and shakes his hand. Everyone laughs, even Captain Warren. He resumes his run at a slow jog, bowing with each light touch as he goes through. He's looking down the end of the line, noting pleased looks on people's faces, thinking perhaps that he will be given a savage woman tonight to bed with, when Caucus-Meteor steps in front of him. Captain Warren recognizes the interrogator who burned him. He catches the old American's eyes now, full of intensity. He's watching the eyes, so that though he discerns the motion, it doesn't register that the interrogator is reaching for the knife he carries from a cord around his neck. He doesn't see Caucus-Meteor turn the blade toward himself. The butt end of the knife catches Captain Warren in the mouth as he runs by.

Caucus-Meteor knows what it's like to be surprisingly struck so: the impact in the skull, an explosion detonated behind the eye sockets, the sound of one's own throat crying out, crystals of maple sugar sparkling in the vision, until one can taste sweetness on the tongue. Captain Warren drops to one knee, brings his hand to his wound, feels the lacerated lip, the slick blood, the jagged mess in his mouth. A tooth falls into his cupped hand. Captain Warren takes a moment to gather his powers. Is he praying, wonders Caucus-Meteor? And then he remembers the captive's behavior under interrogation. Probably the captain is not praying; probably he is meditating on the justification of his anger. Meanwhile, the gauntlet folks, men and women both, watch the big Englishman huffing and puffing on one knee. All sense that this is the decisive moment in his run. Caucus-Meteor thrills inside. This, he thinks, this feeling is the difference between his own kind and the animals and even the gods. It's the reason the gods envy us; it's the feeling inside the apprehension of mortality.

Captain Warren shoves forward and at the same instant grabs the knife from Caucus-Meteor. The cord snaps off the back of the old American's neck, the turban flies away revealing the bald head, and the captive raises the knife into stabbing position. Caucus-Meteor thinks: Well, finally, I'm going to die, which will simplify everything. Captain Warren never completes his follow through. In a few seconds, the weapon is wrenched from his hand, and then blows begin. What's done to him appears to be just a beating, but in fact the mayhem is refined and systematic.

The tormentors crack kneecaps, dislocate hips, shoulders, and wrists, chop off thumbs. After they finish, two women stop the bleeding, tend to the more serious wounds, and examine the work closely to make sure the damage has been done properly. Captain Warren will soon realize with horror he's not going to be martyred. The tormentors have conspired to keep him alive, but permanently deny him use of his magnificent body.

Caucus-Meteor is not seriously injured, but he feels something of the trauma of the captives, queasiness in the stomach, a slightly deranged view of his world, as if hidden fingers were pressing on his eyeballs from the inside. He returns the turban to his head. Someone inquires as to his health. It's a moment before he recognizes St. Blein.

"Where is my prisoner?" Caucus-Meteor asks.

"He is about to begin his run."

"Counsel him well. I must rest." Caucus-Meteor watches his commander approach the naked captive.

St. Blein says in heavily accented English. "Now it is your turn, Nathan Blake. I suggest you show a little humility. And may God have mercy on your soul." Nathan responds in heavily accented French. "Mercy bohcoo."

Caucus-Meteor is outside the lines getting over the dizzy spell brought on during his encounter with Captain Warren. The gauntlet reassembles, the participants sullen and watchful. Who can guess their mood when they're not sure themselves? The old American is thinking that the tormentors are waiting for the gauntlet spirit to manifest itself when he hears a voice in the crowd calling to him in French.

"A man your age testing a bully in the gauntlet—you should know better."

Caucus-Meteor is looking at a wizard as bald and almost as old as himself, and gaudily attired with beaded headband, and like himself with split ears, red sash, but unlike himself, reeking of liquor and tobacco, bone through his nose, and heavily armed with two knives, a hatchet, and a hand musket in a shoulder sling. Caucus-Meteor remembers his dream.

"Bleached Bones!" says Caucus-Meteor. "I'm surprised that none of those people you cheated has killed you yet."

"It's because I say my prayers and think pure thoughts."

"Between the two of us, pure thoughts gather the attention of the gods for their rarity."

"What was impure between us for you was pure for me. This fellow about to run—he's yours, no?"

"I captured him myself back in New England."

"He has legs for running. Do you think he can make them go fast enough to get through this mob?"

Caucus-Meteor is mulling over his dream. The adversary was Bleached Bones. The runner must be Nathan Blake, and the stones must be a wager. The tormentors in the gauntlet are the crowd in the dream. But who or what was the crow with the delicate claws?

"I think you are mocking me, Bleached Bones."

"If I mock you, old king with his turban for a crown, it won't be with such subtlety. I was testing your confidence in your slave."

"He has my confidence," Caucus-Meteor says, but what he's thinking is that his confidence is in his dream.

Bleached Bones smiles, tweaks the bone in his nose. Caucus-Meteor remembers the day they pierced each other's nostrils many years ago, but Caucus-Meteor removed the bone through his own nose because it was a bother. Bleached Bones says something in Iroquois, in English, in Dutch. It's a joke. Caucus-Meteor and Bleached Bones were once interpreters in the employ of the French. Playing with languages was their shared art. In spite of his better judgment, Caucus-Meteor, as he has done in the past, succumbs to the wiles of Bleached Bones and bets his entire interpreter's salary that Nathan Blake will make it through the gauntlet. Bleached Bones, who knows how much Caucus-Meteor despises alcohol, offers him a drink from a noggin he carries in his belt pack. Caucus-Meteor takes a tiny swallow to be polite.

"You make a good living as a gambler?" Caucus-Meteor asks.

"Excellent, but I don't do it for the money. I like the travel, the excitement, the desperate characters you meet."

"You're not afraid to lose?"

"The feeling—it's better when you lose." The conversation is interrupted by a stirring in the crowd. "I think your man is preparing to make his run."

Caucus-Meteor watches. Nathan is about to begin his test.

But Caucus-Meteor is thinking about his bet. Even if he's not killed, Nathan Blake might be too injured to be of any use as a slave. Caucus-Meteor will be forced to sell Nathan to the French for a prisoner exchange. It's doubtful he will bring a very good price if he's broken up the way the last fellow was. Caucus-Meteor will have to return to Conissadawaga without any gifts for his people. It's likely he will lose favor among them, and that his rival in the community, the great hunter, Haggis, will be crowned king. So, then, Caucus-Meteor thinks, if I lose this bet I stand to lose everything I value. I will be a free man. Bleached Bones is right: it's better when you lose. Still, Caucus-Meteor does not think he will lose. The dream was too powerful.

From the tense muscles in Nathan's legs, Caucus-Meteor can see that Nathan's impulse is to break into a run. The old American is thinking about his slave, when, out of nowhere, the conjuring trick that he has been trying to perform all his life is suddenly before him, but it comes unsummoned, in spite of himself. It comes like the dream. Nathan, you are naked and the gauntlet winds a long way. Caucus-Meteor sees his slave's lips move. You are praying again. You stand before your tormentors, smelling their sweat and bear grease and cheap French brandy and your own anxiety. Someone shoves you forward. Instead of heading for empty space between the rows, you walk toward one edge of the gauntlet. What are you doing, Nathan Blake? Nathan Blake doesn't know himself what he is doing. Prayer is guiding him. Or something else. Maybe the devil who resides in the far place. He wants you to join him there, Nathan—go with him. He wants you to run, Nathan—run. Run from your life.

A stick cracks you between the shoulder blades, like the lash of a whip but cutting deeper. You wince—run, Nathan, run. But no, you walk to the other side, offering yourself for abuse. Stones strike your face and chest. You take another step forward, but keep your head up. The old Mohawk with the burn-scarred face grins at you, a man driven insane by torturers in a time gone by. Another stick slashes you across your back, and you cry out involuntarily, as you did the day I burned myself instead of you. I feel that wound now, a tender place like a sorrow or a remembered hope. Do you know, Nathan Blake, that black slaves who are especially disrespectful are sometimes whipped to death by their English masters? A couple of laughing fellows shove you to the other side of the gauntlet. A woman raises a switch to strike you. You see the blow coming, but you don't try to avoid it, only to suppress your need to cry out in pain. The switch smacks you in the face.

You smile at the woman. Are you insane, Nathan Blake? Someone strikes you in the temple, and now you stand in a rain of colored lights. A second later something falls at your feet. You blink, your head clears, and you bend to pick up the walking stick belonging to the mad old man with the burn scars. The stick is decorated with a swatch of your skin and blood. You return the stick, bow, and say, "Your cane, sir." The Mohawk accepts his implement with a handshake and a thank-you.

The people in the gauntlet find this exchange between a captive and one of their elderly touchingly amusing. They don't laugh ha-ha, or hee-hee, or har-har, more like ho-hoh-hohh. Nathan, can you taste blood running down the back of your throat? You step forward, see the lights again, but they're dimming, changing in color with fading music that may be coming from angels. What does your Protestant Jesus think about angels? Tell me, for I am uninformed on this matter. You hardly feel the next blow. Then another. In your determination to keep your head up and look into the eyes of your abusers, you continue the strategy you started with—don't run the gauntlet, walk it.

The conjuring fades until Caucus-Meteor wonders whether it was within him at all, for now he is merely thinking, thinking the word *pure* in the language of his father. For a while Caucus-Meteor is resigned to losing his bet with Bleached Bones. Nathan Blake staggers, is knocked about. Any minute he'll lose his temper like the previous runner or he'll just crumple from meekness. Then Caucus-Meteor notices something that gives him cause for optimism, an improvement in demeanor—head held high but without French haughtiness or English arrogance or American defiance, without the rancor of nation versus nation, a man. Exemplary behavior. Now the captive adopts the unusual tactic of walking the gauntlet, as if to say, "We are here together." In olden days, when defiance was so admired, Nathan Blake's behavior might not have saved him, but these days the folks on the line see in him an emblem of the Christianity they've embraced. Caucus-Meteor chuckles to himself, thinks these people must be unnerved. He wishes he could predict the outcome. Will they crown this man with thorns or laurel?

He's surprised when Bleached Bones settles the wager between them.

"But he's not through the gauntlet yet," says Caucus-Meteor.

"I've seen enough—he will walk to the end of it without harm. These Iroquois might be Christian by baptism and inclination, but they're pagan by ancestry and habit. The old gods rise up in them from time to time. They secretly suspect that your slave is a sorcerer. They may be right. You watch out, Caucus-Meteor, else your man visit upon you a plague you cannot now imagine."

Caucus-Meteor stares into the eyes of his once and future adversary and companion. He sees a happy glint.

"You've lost your bet, and you are still a man. I admire you, Bleached Bones."

"I am a man falling off a cliff contemplating the rush of air in his throat while the ground flies up to impale him. It is not so bad to feel what you can before you die." Bleached Bones tweaks the bone in his nose, turns his back, walks away.

Nathan Blake, you kept your head up, you talked respectfully, but respect is not how you'll be known in the stories told; you'll be known as the man who walked the gauntlet. Nathan Blake, you will be the last to appreciate your accomplishment.

Nathan has minor cuts, bruises, and bumps. His most serious injury is a bloody nose. Caucus-Meteor throws Nathan's head back, puts pressure on his forehead and neck, and the bleeding stops. The old American conducts a brief examination, pronounces his patient fit, gives him a blanket. "Remain quiet, Nathan Blake, until your stomach tells you it is all right to stand," Caucus-Meteor says. "Then you may dress and resume normal activities."

Nathan throws the blanket over his shoulders, sits on a log, shivers. He's banged up, weary, a little nauseous, but calm.

"We will stay the night here in Kahnawake with my cousin, Omer Laurent," Caucus-Meteor says. "Omer and his wife live by the European custom of ambition, hard work, chicanery, prayer, and luck. Tomorrow we will start for Conissadawaga."

The Squakheag brothers decide to paddle home to Odanak under the stars. They don't bother to tell their commanding officer. By French law, they're deserters, but as a practical matter the military service is over and the mercenaries will return to their villages whether their commander wishes them to or not. Meanwhile, in Kahnawake, a big celebration rages all night. Caucus-Meteor and his slave, Nathan Blake, watch from the darkness just outside the fire glow. Sam Allen stands naked beside a huge pot of water bubbling over irons straddling a fire. Most of the village has turned out for this event. The Mohawk men and, worse, the women, make fun of Sam's scrawny body.

"They going to kill him?" says Nathan, his jaw tight, his eyes feigning slight interest. He's more upset about this than he was about his own safety.

"Watch, Nathan Blake—you will discover something you never encountered in New England."

The younger woman standing beside young Allen pinches her nose; the older woman and the rest of the Mohawks laugh.

"What deviltry is this?" says Nathan.

"No deviltry; you look too deeply. All they're saying is the obvious. The boy stinks."

The two women wash Sam Allen from head to foot. He winces where they touch his cuts and bruises. Finally, he stands clean and shivering, and they give him a blanket to dry and warm himself. Then Furrowed Brow dips his right index and middle fingers in a bowl of red paint. He marks first the right side and then the left of Sam's face. The women bring Sam a Frenchman's baggy trousers, trade shirt decorated with bead and quill work, moccasins, red sash for the waist, blanket with an arm hole, headband to keep hair in place.

"Those clothes belonged to his 'brother' in the family, killed in the wars against your people, Nathan Blake," says Caucus-Meteor.

Furrowed Brow thumps himself in the chest with his fist and speaks a word in Iroquois. Caucus-Meteor translates for Nathan's benefit—"Father." Sam repeats the word. The mood of the onlookers changes from jovial to solemn. The older woman points to herself, and utters a word—"Mother." The young woman takes her turn—"Sister." Sam asks a question in English, and the Mohawks look away from him. "From here on in, he's not to speak any English," says Caucus-Meteor. "Your young kinsman is not sure what he is to these people yet—a brother, a son, a slave—but he knows that he has become something more than a captive."

Caucus-Meteor looks in Nathan's eyes to see if the lesson he has just completed has had an effect, but Nathan does not betray himself with word or facial expression. The gauntlet has made Nathan more confident. He'll be known as the man who walked the gauntlet. Such a man, rash but not violent, can pose great danger, thinks the old American. I admire him very much.

The Great River

Caucus-Meteor gently declines Furrowed Brow's hospitality, and he and Nathan walk along the shore of the river to a sheltered cove, where, tethered to a tree, is a huge log raft on which is built a wigwam. "Stay here for a moment," the old American says to Nathan. It's a test. Caucus-Meteor is wondering if walking the gauntlet gave Nathan ideas about walking away to freedom. He goes inside the wigwam to converse with his subjects, comes out in a few minutes; Nathan is still waiting. "We'll spend the night here where I can smell the river," says the old American. For the first time since the journey north began, he doesn't bind his slave for the night. While Nathan sleeps, Caucus-Meteor sits in front of a small fire in sleepless rest. At about the time that Sam Allen is going to bed after a night of revelry, Caucus-Meteor and Nathan are rising to get an early start.

They're met in the raft wigwam by Omer and Hungry Heart Laurent. Omer is hard-muscled, with almond eyes and sallow skin. Hungry Heart is light-skinned, heavy-bodied, with iridescent green eyes and skinny legs. They're mixed blood. Omer is mainly Montagnais, the Algonkian inhabitants of the St. Lawrence valley when Samuel Champlain arrived in 1608. Not that the Montagnais can claim the region as their ancestral home.

They replaced a tribe of Iroquois-tongued people laid low by war and epidemics following the arrival of Jacques Cartier in the century before Champlain. That's how it goes in these lands, thinks Caucus-Meteor, festivals of destruction, duplicity, and disease. Hungry Heart was a niece of Caucus-Meteor's late wife, Keeps-the-Flame. When she's had one too many brandies, Hungry Heart claims that she's a descendant of Champlain himself through a dalliance with one of his so-called native "daughters," that Champlain is the source of her green eyes, but no one believes her.

"Where do they go when the river freezes in the winter?" Nathan asks Caucus-Meteor.

"They live in the winter village of Conissadawaga, in the hills."

"Winter village — different villages for different seasons," Nathan nods his head, as one gaining understanding. "You truly are a nomadic people."

"Aye," says Caucus-Meteor, gently mocking Nathan's speech. "We are like the ancients, like all the American tribes. The rule of the nomad makes this land what it is."

Caucus-Meteor remembers when the Laurents were dispossessed children given succor by the dispossessed people of Conissadawaga. Their business is river transport. Omer will tell you that some day millions of people will live in Canada, and the only practical way they'll have of travel will be by birch-bark canoe. He envisions a day when he and his heirs will control the river. At the moment the Laurents own and operate six canoes. Hungry Heart, who can cipher and read some French, takes care of the accounts and the bribes to French officials to steer business their way. Omer works the waters. Business is good. All the Laurent boats are in service except for Omer's personal craft. Accordingly, Omer himself will bring Caucus-Meteor and his slave 160 miles downstream to Conissadawaga.

After some food, the men are ready to depart when a French officer arrives with his gear. He explains that he is a soldier en route to Quebec, where he will report to the governor-general and visit his family. He's heard that Omer could transport him to Quebec quickly. It's St. Blein.

Caucus-Meteor smiles. He can see that Hungry Heart is about to show why she and Omer are equal partners in their enterprise. Because Caucus-Meteor is a relation and leader of her village, she could charge him only for expenses. Now with the appearance of a stranger, she has a chance to turn a profit. She can tell by his clothes and bearing that St. Blein is an aristocrat with coins in his purse. She shakes her head sadly, explaining that his presence will overload the canoe. It's probably best that he wait for another canoe, or go across the river to Montreal and charter a French bateau. St. Blein could bow, thank her for the advice, then pretend to leave, and she'd practically beg him to accept a seat on the canoe. But Caucus-Meteor and perhaps even Hungry Heart know that St. Blein counts himself too good for such tricks; sons of gentlemen do not lower themselves to the level of American women. He is honest with her. He tells her that a French bateau will take an extra day or more to reach Quebec. He wants to go home as soon as possible. Well, all right, says Hungry Heart, but because of the inconvenience he'll have to pay extra. Omer looks away. He hates this part of the business. Caucus-Meteor catches St. Blein's eye. The ensign smiles, and pays the fare. Caucus-Meteor is first amused and then deflated by this little drama. What Hungry Heart has gained in coins, she has lost in nobility.

The party shoves off in the hour before dawn. From his position kneeling in the rear, Omer steers his craft toward the center where the water moves fastest. Later he'll follow a line where the tide runs. Coming back upriver to home port, he'll work the eddies near the shoreline, where currents turn upon themselves and push upstream.

"If you all paddle mightily we can make St. Francis by nightfall," Omer says.

"If the weather holds," says St. Blein.

"The big 'if' of the river," says Omer.

Caucus-Meteor notes that Omer said "St. Francis," the French name for Odanak. Omer is trying to worm into the good graces of St. Blein. Perhaps such shameful behavior is necessary during these times, thinks the old American, which leads him to his own shame. As usual he will cheat at paddling, pretending to pull the paddle through the water, but actually letting the boat motion push it.

Nathan paddles hard and steadily. He finally reveals something on his bruised face—appreciation, approval—at the sight of meadows and cleared fields in the river valley. Caucus-Meteor tries to see what his slave sees, but in the end sees only through his own tired eyes. He says to his slave, "Sometimes the river makes its own music, singing in its incomprehensible language."

"You confound me, master, with the very words of my own language," Nathan says.

"I am a mystery even to myself, as most men are; my only grace is my reverence to these mysteries. I saw you looking at the land with something of majesty in your eyes."

"I thought I would see more wild lands."

"You had a misshapen idea of Canada."

"Aye. I expected howls out of the sky. Instead, the wind brings in sounds from the land—clack of tree branches, birds, cows, and, pigs, damn, comical pigs, rooting among stumps, yes, and the sweet lowing of oxen."

"You like oxen."

"The oxen of an English farmer are his hoofed brothers—loyal, uncomplaining, productive in their enterprise."

Caucus-Meteor understands that he and his people have been subtly insulted, for they have neither oxen nor the notion of enterprise. Already Nathan Blake is rebelling in the manner of a slave: in lieu of freedom, attempting to wear away the happiness of his master. "Perhaps," says Caucus-Meteor, lapsing into oratorical tones, "it is servants such as those that we think we love, rather than those we regard as our enemies, who do us the greatest harm."

The party arrives in St. Francis slightly ahead of the optimistic schedule set by Omer Laurent. He's elated, projects a sense of accomplishment after a day's work well done, behavior that depresses his king. St. Francis, called Odanak by the residents, is a réfugié village of various Algonkian-speaking tribes about the same size as Kahnawake, with clusters of square log cabins and some wigwams. As he pulls the canoe up on shore, Omer remarks in French on the improvement in recent years in heating of wigwams with the introduction of iron stoves and flues to vent the smoke.

"I don't see it as progress," Caucus-Meteor says in Algonkian. "Without an open fire, a wigwam loses sway for the spirits that help keep a man content." He suppresses the urge to launch into a long speech. This is not the time and place for oratory.

St. Blein visits the families of his Squakheag fighters to inform them that they'll be coming home soon, only to discover that they've already arrived. When Omer learns that the two brothers who transported Caucus-Meteor and Nathan on Lake Champlain pulled in six hours ago, the corners of his smile drop.

"I shouldn't have let you talk me into going to bed last night," he says to Caucus-Meteor. "We could have steered by the moon, beat them by two or three hours."

"Don't feel bad, Omer," teases Caucus-Meteor. "They're too happy to be home to boast that they beat a river man." Which of course is not true.

The travelers spend the night in a lean-to shelter made by the canoe and a moose hide tarp. They could have lodged in the brothers' cabin, or with Omer's cousin. But Omer insists they avoid friends and relatives, because they'd be duty-bound to exchange gifts, dance, visit, drink, chat, and otherwise waste time. Omer wants his paddlers strong, awake, and alert before the dawn. He's given himself over to work, schedules, and whimsies for a life in the future very much like a Frenchman's, and he has no patience with those of his own kind who think like those of his own kind. Caucus-Meteor admires him very much.

Surely, home is on the minds of all here this night, thinks Caucus-Meteor while the others sleep. Nathan Blake had a home, but we wrenched him from it. St. Blein is returning to Quebec to visit his parents, but it's not home; the Canada he envisions as home doesn't exist yet. Omer's homesick for a life of wealth, power, and prestige that's not only out of his reach and talents but would not make him happy if he achieved it. Omer's happiness is in the strain, privation, weather, scenery, and danger of the river; he doesn't recognize that he's home in his canoe.

All his life Caucus-Meteor has dreamed of being a king, like his father, the famous King Philip. The English may have been sarcastic when they dubbed Metacomet a king, but his father came close to making them eat their words, uniting the New England tribes to fight a war he almost won before the English hunted him down, killed him, put his head on a stake as a reminder of English ferocity and American futility, and sold his wife and son into slavery. Caucus-Meteor often imagines himself heir to a throne of sticks and beads, though in his day-to-day dealings with the world he regards himself as next to nothing. He escaped from slavery, made himself into an American, married a woman who was half black slave and half Iroquois, raised a family, gathered réfugiés that no tribe in Canada wanted, and with his wife established a village. Ask Caucus-Meteor where home is and he'll tell you, "My kingdom is Conissadawaga." But in his heart home was never a place or even an idea. Home was the comfort of a woman's arms, first his mother's, so fleeting her touch before she was taken from him, and later the arms of his wife, Keeps-the-Flame. With the loss of his women, home is a remove. The old American is thinking that he'll find a home only in the reuniting ceremony following death. Where, when, how this ceremony should take place is another burden Caucus-Meteor carries, which is why he hopes for a sudden death. Nathan Blake, Omer, Hungry Heart, St. Blein, all of us are homesick for a place we cannot reach, thinks the old American.

Omer breaks camp before dawn.

"No fire?" says Caucus-Meteor, whose ancient joints request time to loosen.

Captain Omer picks up a paddle, holds it like a staff, and repeats. "No fire—river. I smell one more good day with a south wind."

Starting a day without a fire—Caucus-Meteor is appalled. But he won't say anything. Out here on the river, Omer is the authority.

"Everybody do your toilet, and let's dig the water," Omer says in French.

St. Blein winces at Omer's slaughtered French, and Caucus-Meteor translates to English for Nathan's benefit, then puts three fingers on Nathan's lips, and repeats Omer's order in Algonkian, as if he could pass on his own gift for articulation through his fingertips.

"Speak now the words as I have given them to you," says Caucus-Meteor.

Nathan attempts to voice the words in Algonkian. Caucus-Meteor, Omer, even St. Blein break ribs with hilarity at his pronunciation. Nathan smiles bashfully.

"What's that smell?" he asks in English as they're about to board the canoe.

"Iron foundry," says St. Blein in halting English.

Caucus-Meteor points to a whaleback hill and says in English and Algonkian, "That mountain, put there by gods who left the earth before Jesus was born, is full of iron."

Nathan repeats the phrases in Algonkian, and this time the laughter is more subdued. Nathan appears to wonder at this new development, so Caucus-Meteor lectures him.

"I am your master, Nathan Blake—never forget that," he says in English. "I expect you to refashion your thoughts, feelings, expressions, dreams, yea, your very prayers into the Algonkian language. Once you have mastered that language, we will work on Iroquois and then perhaps French."

"Yes, master," says Nathan, his eyes looking off in the west to that far place that so intrigues him.

"And after you have mastered those languages, we will learn Latin together and become priests." Caucus-Meteor is joking in French now for the benefit of St. Blein, who laughs uproariously.

The old American switches to Algonkian, and addresses Omer or perhaps the river, for Omer is not listening. "The day will come when Nathan Blake will forget he is an Englishman with an English wife, children, parents, brothers, sisters, friends, peers. His dream to build a homestead will vanish in the intoxicating light of new experiences. He will forget his god, or, more likely, his god will forget him. What worries me, Omer, is that there is something else in the man, a yearning that he does not understand, and because the slave does not understand, I fear it cannot be governed by a master."

Paddle paddle paddle, dig that paddle north, downstream. Must be a bit disorienting to Nathan Blake. Where he comes from the rivers flow south, and they're not nearly so immense. The dawn is misty, not too colorful, a slow descending radiance that suddenly evaporates until the canoe is in blazing sunshine. This will be more like a summer than a spring day. Omer serves a breakfast of bread and dog meat to be eaten in the canoe as they keep moving, but the portions are generous and Nathan is given an equal share with the others. He appears pleased by the canoe master's evenhandedness. Caucus-Meteor knows that Omer is thinking he has to feed the slave if he's going to keep him paddling hard.

All along the river are rolling fields and pastures, the earth being prepared for planting. Nathan watches a pair of oxen pulling a plow, frowns, mumbles something under his breath. Apparently, the teamster is not measuring up to the Englishman's standards. The canoers pass well-manured fields, barns with thatched roofs, farmhouses of timber or stone or logs; fences of poles and split poles; windmills to pump river water for irrigation; and hewed poles squared into Calvary crosses erected at crossroads and on promontories, some standing twenty feet tall.

Omer steers the canoe toward the shore, where a rip of tide gives the craft more push. Then, a miracle. The wind carries the sound of a woman's voice singing, a farmwife working the fields with her husband. The delicacy of the voice carried by the delicacy of the breeze sends a tremor through Caucus-Meteor. He notices that the other men are also affected. They cannot see her face, obscured by the glare of the morning sun, but they do see her shape bent over a hoe, dress loose, long hair. They listen to her sing. The old American can pick out the words *coeur* and *amour*. It's all any of them can do to restrain themselves from jumping overboard and swimming toward the wail of that voice. The wind shifts, and now the only sounds are the hush of the current, the beating of their hearts, the strain of their labors. Caucus-Meteor is thinking of his dead wife when he notices that his slave is silently choking back tears, a man lost to home and unsure perhaps of his wife's love.

The next item of interest is men working fish traps. "Some kind of basket contraption . . . what is its purpose if not to catch schooled fish?" Nathan asks, his feelings under control now.

Caucus-Meteor repeats his question in Algonkian. Nathan mouths his English words in the Algonkian language. Caucus-Meteor answers in Algonkian, then translates into English. "The ocean tide hundreds of miles away brings eels to the baskets." Nathan nods with the satisfaction of received knowledge.

"I would like you to practice saying the name of the place where I am taking you." Caucus-Meteor pronounces the name of the village—Conissadawaga, makers of shoes, People-in-Exile. "Twist thy tongue, Englishman."

Nathan tries three times to pronounce the name, and eventually succeeds. "Very good, Nathan Blake," says Caucus-Meteor.

"Are the people of Conissadawaga like the people of Kahnawake?" Nathan asks.

"The people of Kahnawake are Catholic Mohawks who still

maintain some ties with their Protestant and pagan brothers and sisters in the Iroquois confederacy," he says. "My wife was Iroquois, but I have already told you about my people, who do not even speak the same language as the people of Kahnawake and who in olden times fought the Iroquois." Caucus-Meteor speaks first in English, then Algonkian.

"How did your people come together?" Nathan asks.

"Why, through sorcery," Caucus-Meteor says in English only.

Omer addresses Nathan in his peculiar French, "Your master, Caucus-Meteor, gathered these people as one picks fruit fallen from the tree." He turns to Caucus-Meteor and says in Algonkian. "Can I tell him?"

"You might as well, for he will learn eventually."

Omer says in French to Nathan, "Your master, Caucus-Meteor, is the son of a great king."

But Omer's French is too much for Nathan, who blinks in confusion. Caucus-Meteor laughs, says in English, "Omer was bragging on my behalf. He was telling you that I am the son of King Philip."

"Yes, I know the story," Nathan says, "but I did not know that the king had a family."

"My father was killed, his people defeated and scattered; my mother and I were sold into slavery in the islands in the southern sea, but on separate plantations," Caucus-Meteor says. "I never saw my mother again, nor heard word about her. During one of those brief periods of peace between England and France, my slave master brought me to Europe to train as an interpreter. I saw both London and Paris. In those days, my master dressed me in robes, feathers, and war paint. He'd show me off as a creature part Roman centurion and part New World warrior. I loved the admiration. I still do."

Caucus-Meteor doesn't say that the son of King Philip was never allowed to learn to read or write, so that despite his demonstrated intelligence and gift for languages he could still be regarded as an ignorant savage.

"Listen, Englishman, while your master teaches you to be a proper slave," St. Blein says to Nathan in broken English.

"I have no experience in the enterprise of slavery," says Nathan in the kind of haughty tone that's not fit for a slave, but Caucus-Meteor lets the insolence go.

"I would think it would come naturally, given the disposition of your people," says St. Blein.

"Nathan Blake, can you smile falsely?" asks Caucus-Meteor.

"How long can a man live within himself if he smiles falsely?" Nathan asks.

"Longer than if he displeases his master with offensive honesty," says St. Blein.

Nathan frowns, grins, grimaces. He's confused now, thinks Caucus-Meteor.

"In your own way, you are very funny, Nathan Blake," says Caucus-Meteor. "Make note that a man, like a child, can learn all he has to know by pretending."

"Yes, master," says Nathan, but his face says no.

"Perhaps you are thinking of what you can lose in addition to what you have already lost," Caucus-Meteor says. "You are worried that you will lose the struggle to determine truth from falsehood, which is always the problem even if a man is not a slave. Surprisingly, for a slave, the distinctions are easier to grasp, because pain teaches the difference."

"You are a slave no more," Nathan says. "Did your master grant your freedom?"

"My master treasured freedom for himself. I ran away. The first time I was caught after a week of wandering. My master's feelings were hurt that his slave should betray him so. He whipped me almost to death. But he did not defeat me. I survived by devising a secret plan." Caucus-Meteor translates his English into Algonkian. The exercise gives him pleasure.

Omer Laurent is interested now; he breaks in, speaking in Algonkian, "This plan, if I had a piece of it, would it help my canoe transport?"

"Some victories are better savored in private, so I will not reveal my plan. Whether an understanding of my cached heart would help your business I cannot say." He switches now to English, "Slave, you'll need a plan of your own to survive the rigors of your captivity, so pay attention."

Nathan laughs a little. "My father's favorite expression was 'pay attention.'"

Caucus-Meteor is thinking that even after he'd escaped and carried out his plan, it still took many years to remove the slave inside the core of himself so that he could be a true, free American. But if he can say one thing about his life, it is that eventually he did succeed. Today he stands like an old maple tree that rings hollow, his core of hatred rotted out, empty, a living drum that makes music from the blows of life, in danger of toppling from the weight of his accumulated knowledge.

Caucus-Meteor catches St. Blein's eye.

"You've been unusually quiet, my commander," Caucus-Meteor says.

"I worry more when I am not at war. Perhaps it is time that I spoke my mind. Omer," he says, "you pay a bribe to the intendant's man in Montreal?"

"Why do you ask, do you work for him?"

"No, I work for Canada. I despise the intendant," St. Blein says.

Omer doesn't like this kind of frank talk. It could get him in trouble, and he attempts to change the subject. "There used to be a sand bar there"—he points with his paddle—"gone today. The river never lets you rest, because your knowledge of it is never entirely true."

"And so it is with a leader of a nation, for a people are like a river. My ensign," Caucus-Meteor addresses St. Blein in the familiar *tu*, "you didn't talk so wildly when we were fighting Englishmen and burning their barns."

"I was too busy making war to express my political beliefs."

"You seemed to enjoy the business of war." Caucus-Meteor is teasing, but the young French officer remains serious.

"I like to make war, because there's no room for conscience or consideration. Everything is as simple as life and death. Now, however, I am not at war"—he stops in midsentence to laugh without mirth, then adds—"except with my beloved enemy—moi."

"You are thinking about your destiny, then; this is common and admirable among young men," says Caucus-Meteor. His mind suddenly and unaccountably a conjuring apparatus, Caucus-Meteor notes that Omer Laurent is no longer listening. He can tell we are testing one another, that the true subject matter is palace intrigue; Omer Laurent is interested in our talk only in so far as it affects his enterprise. And anyway since we are talking rapidly in formal French, he has lost the meaning. Caucus-Meteor's mind turns away from conjuring to the world of time and event-present; St. Blein is about to speak.

"I do think of myself as one destined," says St. Blein, "but I think first of my country, and I am not talking about Old France."

"You are wasting your nobility, Ensign," Caucus-Meteor says. "Nothing can be done for New France as long as Old France rules Quebec."

"Perhaps you are right," says St. Blein. "The logical conclusion, well, I dread to speak it."

"But you must."

"Yes, I must. Something more than talk must be the instrument to halt the demise of Canada. One has to act." St. Blein launches into a long speech, criticizing corruption in the government offices. But the speech ends in frustration and a grimace.

"What you need," says Caucus-Meteor, "is what is known in the English language as a motto. I think what you are trying to say is: Canada for Canadians."

"Yes, that's it—Canada for Canadians!" St. Blein speaks the phrase as if he had invented it.

Omer Laurent doesn't like the tone of the conversation. Grand ideas, grand emotions, especially coming from privileged young

Frenchmen, usually mean some unforeseen difficulty for his own kind.

St. Blein enjoys the feeling of one who senses that his long felt ideas have come to the surface and now can be expressed. "The people of North America—French, native, English, Dutch, Scots, even the freed African—have more in common with one another than they do with those of Europe," he says. "We quarrel amongst ourselves because of interference from Europe."

Caucus-Meteor smiles. St. Blein conveniently set aside his knowledge that the tribes were at war with each other long before the arrival of the trading ships from across the sea. He imagines love and peace, if only the governments of France and England were driven off the continent.

"Good thinking," says Caucus-Meteor in a tone of gentle mockery.

Omer's canoe party arrives in Quebec City in midafternoon. Nathan gazes at the stone fortifications surrounding the city. He appears impressed.

"Is it the massive walls that move you so?" asks Caucus-Meteor.

"More the order in the design and the cunning behind the labor," Nathan says.

Caucus-Meteor suddenly feels very inferior to his slave. It's not what these Englishmen say, he thinks, it's how they say it, with self-assurance.

Omer counts thirteen oceangoing vessels in the harbor and many smaller French skiffs and canoes. "The sun tells me we're an hour later than I'd hoped," he says, looking critically at Caucus-Meteor.

"Don't feel too embittered against your king for not paddling hard—he is an old man," Caucus-Meteor teases. He puts a hand on the shoulder of his kinsman.

Omer forces a laugh. He brings the canoe to a dock, and tells

Caucus-Meteor that he and Hungry Heart will join the tribe when ice clogs the river.

"And you will bring me part of your profits for tribute to be paid to the intendant, correct?" Caucus-Meteor smiles without showing teeth. Omer winces, but nods in compliance to his king's request. Caucus-Meteor knows that Omer's resentful because he's paying double taxes, tribute to the intendant's man to operate his business in Montreal and tribute to Caucus-Meteor to fulfill his obligation as citizen of the village of Conissadawaga. Maybe if I provoke him enough, he'll drown me one day, thinks the old king, watching Omer depart. Omer will loiter around the docks until someone is ready to pay him for transport, maybe a red-capped voyageur heading north to Tadousic, where the furs come down the Saguenay from the Hudson Bay region, or some traders going south to Montreal or west on the Ottawa.

Caucus-Meteor turns his attention to Nathan, who appears to be studying the city. He likes things, thinks Caucus-Meteor, he likes buildings, he likes man-made structures; people leave him disturbed.

Quebec is divided into two sections. Here in the lower section is a marketplace with shops selling leather goods, candles, clothing; alongside the mercantile establishments are churches, convents, taverns, and inns. Strolling streets paved with stones laid like brick are priests, nuns, merchants in colorful garb, seamen, and Americans.

"These houses are considerably more elaborate in style than even the houses of your own cultured town, Boston," says Caucus-Meteor.

"Too fussy," Nathan says. "Though I admire the stone work of the streets and houses, I prefer timber-framed dwellings with clapboard siding painted white, plain, square corners."

"My own preferences run to sticks," says Caucus-Meteor. "I don't like to see wood mutilated with saws and irons."

Nathan responds with a polite nod. The idea that boards are

inferior to branches is not only alien to him, it's seditious. Caucus-Meteor is pleased that he's dumbfounded his slave.

"We soon will enter one of those buildings you admire, for we
are going to the intendant's palace to see the intendant's man."

Nathan nods wisely, the way people do when they don't understand. Caucus-Meteor doubts whether he knows what an
"intendant" is.

Caucus-Meteor bribes the intendant, whose "man" keeps
priests, soldiers, fur traders, ambitious Americans, and earnest
public officials from taking over Conissadawaga. Without public succor from the intendant, the village of castoffs would dis-
appear, for unlike the Hurons in nearby Wendake or the Mohawks of Kahnawake, or the various Algonkian peoples from
Odanak, its inhabitants don't have the power of numbers, the
blessing of the Roman church, or the influence of arms needed
for survival in Canada.

Caucus-Meteor senses that St. Blein has strange matters on
his mind. He wonders what they are. After Omer leaves them,
Caucus-Meteor says in his most aristocratic French, "Ensign, I
believe your family lives near the intendant's palace. I am going
in that direction, so perhaps we can walk together."

St. Blein gestures wildly as he answers, "Better yet, let's ride
by carriage—I'll pay."

"Excellent," says Caucus-Meteor, though he's a little suspicious. When a Canadian offers to pay an American, it means the
Canadian wants a service.

St. Blein hails a horse-drawn carriage. The driver has a salt-
and-pepper beard and smokes a long-stemmed ceramic pipe.
The men look where they step, which is the common-sense rule
in streets dominated by horse traffic.

Off they go in the carriage, the ancient American interpreter,
the rebellious French officer, the stalwart English captive. For a
few minutes, no one speaks; they listen to the pleasant sounds of
horse hoofs on stone-paved streets.

"How do you think the latest war between the French in Europe and the English in Europe will go?" St. Blein asks casually, though by the stiffness of the question, the insertion of the word "latest," and the repetition of the word "Europe," Caucus-Meteor can tell the ensign is entering into something more than small talk.

"I cannot say," says Caucus-Meteor.

"Our fate in Canada is being determined by men who have never and will never set foot on our soil," St. Blein says. Caucus-Meteor thinks, more anti-France talk. He decides to taunt the ensign a little to see how he behaves.

"Fate . . . determined by men?" Caucus-Meteor says with false incredulity. "I thought the believers of your faith hold the finger of the one true God to be in every pudding."

"And so it is . . . said, but let us not discount free will, for as long as any man's will is free, by God's grace, luck, and fortitude, he will be free to err." St. Blein chuckles without mirth.

Caucus-Meteor thinks that this young man is far more humorless in peace than in war, on his home ground than on foreign lands. "Why don't you file your complaints with the governor-general—he's your commander, isn't he?" Caucus-Meteor says.

"I have complained, but Galissoniere is a naval officer, an interim governor, an old man. He wants only to return to the sea. He will not involve himself in civilian affairs, because he knows Bigot has important friends in Old France as well as here in Canada among the merchants."

An awkward silence ensues. Caucus-Meteor hates sitting like this, ass off the ground—downright unnatural, hurts the back. If there were more room, he'd kneel on the floor and sit on his heels.

St. Blein breaks the silence, erupting into a long harangue about corruption in Canada. It's the same speech he gave in the canoe, but then it just seemed like traveler's talk, easy and of no consequence. Now, something else, something as yet unspoken, is at stake. The missing idea titillates the old king's curiosity.

St. Blein ends his speech with a flourish. "Canada for Canadians, my friend."

"Fine words," says Caucus-Meteor.

"Yes, I believe so. No more tribute, no more drain of our capital to Old France. Canadian, native, réfugié—all will be the same people. Remember this well, my savage friend: Canada for Canadians." St. Blein has already forgotten that it was Caucus-Meteor who gave him his motto.

Suddenly, Caucus-Meteor understands what the ensign has not yet said. "You've made a decision. You're really going to knock a hole in the French canoes."

"It's done. From here on in I will work for a free Canada. Caucus-Meteor, I need your help."

"Much as I respect you, Ensign, I doubt there is much wisdom in your ideas. I cannot ask my people to join a rebellion."

"It's too early for a call to arms. I ask only that you discuss the matter with other chiefs this summer during the trade fairs, gauge the sentiment, perhaps plant the seed of the idea."

"I don't think I wish to be associated with this matter."

St. Blein looks away, gazes out the window, listens perhaps to the wheels on the paving stones. Finally, he says magnanimously, "Of course. I am sure that Caucus-Meteor is doing what is right for his people."

The carriage travels to a second lower town on the banks of the St. Charles river, close to where it flows into the mighty St. Lawrence. "Here, driver—stop here," calls the ensign. They've arrived at the intendant's palace, a two-story stone building covered with tin and larger than even the governor's palace.

"I will now go on to my father's house," says the ensign.

"Quite a house it is, I understand," says Caucus-Meteor, to be polite.

"Yes, with a mother who prays with the nuns, three younger sisters who change dresses four and five times a day, and a father slickened by the oils of corruption." Ensign St. Blein shakes the old American's hand, and Caucus-Meteor and Nathan step out of the carriage.

The guard at the palace back door recognizes Caucus-Meteor,

nods to him, goes inside, comes back a few minutes later, and ushers Caucus-Meteor and Nathan into an office with book-cases, cat-claw chairs, a red velvet–upholstered couch, a map of the vast emptiness of North America on the wall, and an ornate and polished desk, brought over from Old France. Behind the desk sits a pocked-faced, slit-eyed man in his fifties wearing a long powdered wig, with slender, manicured fingers and nails painted pink, a green coat with white lace frills at the throat and sleeves, a strong flowery aroma emanating from the perfumed pores of his skin.

Caucus-Meteor is taken aback. It's not the intendant's man, it's the intendant himself, François Bigot. He's warm and friendly with Caucus-Meteor, asks about his adventures on the war-path, jokes with him, compliments him on the good behavior of his slave, takes his money with a casual "merci." He gives Caucus-Meteor a fat nugget of tobacco he claims is from Virginia. Caucus-Meteor knows he's being flattered for a purpose, but at the same time he thinks he must be somebody special for the intendant to give him a gift. He's visited with the passing thought that he might yet be not just chief of a small village of American réfugiés, but a true king. He's talking in French, but his feelings come through in English, the language of his slavery, in two little words with an exclamation point at the end—"a king!"

"Fine-looking slave," Bigot says, with a dismissive glance at Nathan. "Are you going to sell him to us or use him for your own?" The disposition of prisoners of war is the domain of the governor-general, so Bigot has no interest in Nathan Blake. Caucus-Meteor wonders whether the intendant is making small talk or whether he's pursuing another idea.

"The fate of the captive has yet to be determined. I must meet with my council to discuss his situation." In truth, Caucus-Meteor doesn't have a council.

Bigot reaches into a desk drawer and withdraws some papers. Now Caucus-Meteor begins to see the world through the yellow glow of nervous exhaustion. He knows that when papers appear, Americans are going to lose in the transaction.

"Do you know what these are?" Bigot asks with a sly smile.

"Of course, they are the royal parchments," Caucus-Meteor says.

"It is the legal title to the lot where your summer village is presently located."

"I see," says Caucus-Meteor, picking up the papers and looking at them with a studious expression. He used to imagine that if he could touch paper, smell the ink, gaze at the marks with deep concentration, the writing would come to life; now the real thing in his hand mocks his imagination. Back during the raid, Caucus-Meteor was often tired, but he was never afraid. Now he is more weary than ever—and afraid. He struggles to maintain a calm exterior. "I bought the land from some Montagnais when Conissadawaga was established by myself and my late wife."

"I think liberties were taken, old prelate. The deed states that the property was sold by the Montagnais to a Frenchman, who defaulted on loans to the government. The land you purchased was not for the seller to sell. The land that you claim for your village belongs to the crown, and therefore is my burden and responsibility to administer."

Caucus-Meteor understands now what's going to happen, and he tries to head it off. "We are a poor village of réfugiés from a dozen different tribes driven to Canada by your enemy to the south. It would be expensive and burdensome for the French government to relocate us."

"We understand the great difficulty and sensitivity of the situation," Bigot says sympathetically. "Relocation is not even a consideration, nor is dispersion. But let us be honest. Conissadawaga is not so poor. We hear that your moccasins are highly prized."

"How much in tribute do you want?" Caucus-Meteor asks.

"France needs currency for its war effort not just here, but in Europe," says Bigot, and then he writes a figure on a separate parchment, and announces its meaning. "The tribute will be due one year from the day you plant your corn, understand?"

Caucus-Meteor nods.

"I am sure your village can raise its share, and the king will be grateful for your contribution. Now, please excuse me, I have other appointments."

On the way out, Caucus-Meteor says to Nathan first in Algonkian and then in English. "We are going to the stables now."

On one side of the palace is a storehouse, on the other a prison. In the rear of the palace is a large garden, and then the stable. Caucus-Meteor and Nathan are alone briefly as they walk from the palace to the stables. "I know what you are thinking, Nathan Blake," says Caucus-Meteor. "You could overpower me, steal a canoe, and make your way south."

Nathan Blake cracks a crooked smile, which tells Caucus-Meteor that his attempts to read his slave's mind have only partly succeeded. The man is harboring a secret, he thinks.

"A master who reads thoughts has little need for a slave," Nathan bows.

His words halt the old American. His English captive is full of both pride and humility, ignorance and knowledge, caution and daring. Bleached Bones is right, he thinks. If I don't kill him or sell him, he will do harm to my village in ways I cannot fathom. But he won't kill Nathan Blake, at least not soon, for the captive, this man who spared his life, has found his way into the dreams that will guide him into the next realm.

The two men enter the royal barn, where they find a man in his thirties mucking out stalls. He's dressed like a Frenchman, though with beaded belt and moccasins. On his homely dark face he carries an expression of perpetual patience, like a porcupine up a tree waiting out wolves. From thongs around his neck hang a knife and a Christian cross. "This is Norman Feathers, my kinsman, a man who remembers everything that has been said and judges none of it," Caucus-Meteor says in English to Nathan. "He's a villager of Conissadawaga, but works for the

French. He'll transport us in his canoe. It's about ten English miles north just off the big river."

On the canoe ride to Conissadawaga, Caucus-Meteor and Norman Feathers converse, switching back and forth between Algonkian and French. Norman doesn't have much prestige in Conissadawaga, because thus far he has refused to marry, but he's a self-contained man, very sincere, very honest, and Caucus-Meteor ranks him as trustworthy if not particularly interesting.

Caucus-Meteor shapes a plan to deal with the intendant. He says to Norman in Algonkian, "Go to the home of my commander, St. Blein. Ask to see him in private. Tell him that Caucus-Meteor has changed his mind, and will comply with his request. Tell him to contact me after I've returned from the summer trade fairs."

"I will do it," says Norman.

"Norman, you are still a follower of Jesus?"

"I confess my sins, take communion when I am near a church. I am sorry, Caucus-Meteor. I know you were against my conversion, but my faith in Jesus is strong."

"I am not angry with you, Norman. Long ago I had a falling out with a priest, but probably it's time to give Jesus another chance." Caucus-Meteor switches to French, tells Norman about his run-in with the intendant. "Do you think if the village allowed the priests to establish a mission in Conissadawaga that the church could protect us against the intendant?"

"I don't know about the church, but Jesus can do anything."

"It's worth a try. Go to your priest and tell him that Caucus-Meteor would like him to say mass in the American village of Conissadawaga."

Conissadawaga

They're less than a mile from their destination when Caucus-Meteor stops talking, stops paddling. He's gathering his little remaining strength for his entry into his village. He cannot show how weak he is. He kneels in the canoe, head on arms spread over paddle straddling the thwarts, body resting, but mind at work. He's trying to think of a way to assuage his daughters' grief; he's scheming to retain his authority as a leader; he's brooding over potential trouble with the intendant, trouble with St. Blein, trouble with soldiers, with the Iroquois, with ghosts, with weather, with mysterious forces that no man can understand, anticipate, or control in any way. Twice he might have been killed by the hand of the people who killed his father, and twice he was spared through no action of his own. Why won't the gods let him die? It's that damned dream—he has to fulfill its portents. His worries are all too much, and he soothes his mind by imagining himself sitting on a stick throne, the king of North America.

Two boys appear on the bluff above the river. Norman spots them, hollers a greeting. Caucus-Meteor sits up, waves, calls out the names of the boys. "The older boy is Sebec, whose father was killed in the wars. The younger, well, I cannot speak his name in English, nor can the meaning of the name be translated into

English," he says to Nathan, "but it's something like way of freedom, with the words running together in one excited breath."

"Free way?" says Nathan.

"Freeway—yes, that will do."

Norman Feathers says something in French, and Caucus-Meteor translates first in Algonkian, so that Nathan can repeat the words, and then in English, so that he can understand them —"Freeway will spread the word that the king of Conissadawaga is home from the wars." Caucus-Meteor is not tired any more.

The canoe passed some hills a few miles back with cliffs reaching right into the water, but here the land is more gentle. The river is wide, broad, and benign. The land on the bluff is flat to gently rolling. Beyond the plain are wooded hills which block the north wind. The men paddle into a slow-moving branch of the big river that twists and turns for maybe half a mile through dense swamp maples and willows growing off the banks. They're the kind of trees one might expect to find two hundred miles south. It was the trees as well as the good soil that caught the old American's attention years ago when he'd bargained for this plot.

The men can hear a waterfall ahead, and suddenly after a bend in the river they're paddling hard upstream through riffles, and coming into view are the falls themselves, a fifteen-foot cascade over a black granite outcropping, dropping into a frothing pool that grows quiet by the time it reaches a rocky shore where a single crude stone-faced wigwam stands. Villagers run down a path from the bluff to the shoreline—men, women, children, all laughing, waving, carrying on, welcoming home their leader, who gestures with the paddle over his head as a king might with his scepter.

As he steps from the canoe into the shallow water, Caucus-Meteor is greeted by a frail girl maybe fifteen years old; even she is not certain of her age. Her face is pretty but disfigured by smallpox scars. "Caterina, my little pumpkin," Caucus-Meteor says in French to his adopted daughter, then switches to Algonkian, the words spoken with resonance so that the gathered can hear. "I've been gone too long, but now I am home; now I know that a contented people makes a king happy."

Caterina comments in Iroquois on the state of the occasion of the king's return, and then ends in French, "Father, you don't look well."

"I am just tired, dear daughter," says Caucus-Meteor.

Out of the crowd emerges a tall woman in her early thirties, very dark, almost like an African, dressed in a blue robe with bright designs above the hem, a black mourning ribbon in her black braided hair, bead necklaces around her neck, moccasins embroidered with dyed red, blue, and white porcupine quills. She's the only villager not laughing or joking or hopping around in exuberance. Caucus-Meteor feels the weight of his responsibilities as a father. He remembers the day when his daughter was six years old and digging in the earth with her tiny hands, and he gave her a name to carry into womanhood. He doesn't embrace her, but stands before her, and calls out that name. "My daughter, Black Dirt." He doesn't say what he's thinking, but he knows that she is thinking the same thing: they are the only two remaining of the same blood. She leaves, and starts back up the path to return to her mourning.

As soon as Black Dirt is out of sight, the good humor of the crowd returns. Caucus-Meteor puts Nathan on display, as one might any piece of property worth boasting about. The captive stands proudly with his head up, his legs wide apart, hands at his side, fists slightly clenched. The villagers like his bearing, though his beard stubble, matted hair, and dirty face give them pause. Caucus-Meteor's people are of mixed race. Though most have dark brown or black hair, some have lighter brown, red, and a couple even have drab blond-colored hair. Eye colors vary from black to blue, from brown to green. Most have never seen an Englishman, and now the sight of one is alternately exciting and revolting.

"He has good legs," says Wytopitlock, one of the single women in the village; she's thin as a reed, with big ears and a clipped nose, from an enraged husband suspecting infidelity. The villagers sometimes joke that Wytopitlock was a widow before her husband died.

"It seems to me that these men from European loins, whether French or English, are all too hairy, and with long noses you wonder how they get a clear view to see," says Parmachnenee, another single woman, stocky, full-busted, about thirty. She belongs to a small clan, current whereabouts unknown.

The crowd of perhaps fifty people or so moves up the narrow path onto the bluff. Hanging in the background is Haggis, Caucus-Meteor's rival for leadership in the tribe. Caucus-Meteor notes that Haggis's son, Wolf Eyes, is not with his father.

Caucus-Meteor watches his captive for any telling gesture or reaction that might signal future success either as a slave or member of the tribe. Nathan seems preoccupied by an old stone foundation of a French farmhouse that was never built. Then he gazes out toward the fields behind the foundation, then at the cluster of huts on the east shore of the lake. There his gaze stops, not bothering with the majestic view of the hills beyond or the clouds above the hills or the heavens above the clouds. These Englishmen, thinks Caucus-Meteor, pretend to be enchanted by the Maker of the Universe, but their eyes do not dwell upon His works but upon things made by man.

The old American pushes thoughts of his slave out of his mind and takes in his town in a long visual embrace. It comforts him that he sees no log cabins, barns, or permanent structures of any kind. The dwellings consist of poles covered with bark in a roughly conical shape and woven mats for doors, wigwams of the type used before the arrival of Europeans. Caucus-Meteor dreams of wigwams as big as European castles. The only animals his people keep are dogs for pulling loads. On stick racks hang hundreds of fish, mainly salmon. He sees drying racks for skins, one stretching a moose hide. A tri-stand holds a recently killed porcupine. The quills will be dyed and used to decorate moccasins.

"Understand, Nathan Blake, we are not like the French or the English, nor like the Mohawks or the mixed peoples of Odanak, stationary nations all—we are a tribe of nomads." In fact, Caucus-Meteor is talking to himself, for his slave is out of earshot. It's a nice spring day, so everybody gathers by the communal fire. Some of the women are tending to cooking pots. A couple of men shake rattles and beat drums. A few villagers start dancing. Somebody passes around a jug of brandy, which eventually reaches Nathan. It always amazes Caucus-Meteor how brandy suddenly appears, seemingly out of the air. His people know how he feels about strong drink, so they do not talk of drink in his presence, nor reach for drink in his presence; drink just appears when he is not attentive to them. So, too, it must be in the struggle between the Christian Satan and the Christian Jesus. Satan does his business when Jesus is not paying attention. Nathan accepts the brandy with an Algonkian thank-you phrase that Caucus-Meteor taught him on the canoe ride, and drinks.

Caucus-Meteor scans the area looking for Black Dirt, but she's nowhere to be seen. People talk to the slave. He says a few words he knows in Algonkian, and everybody laughs at his pronunciation. He blushes, but he is not frightened; he must sense that for the moment there's no malice or instability within the villagers. The mood is festive. Mica, a little tipsy, wiggles her rear end at him, and speaks a word. Nathan understands her meaning, and repeats the expression as best he can—dance! They want him to teach them an English dance. The slave is light on his feet, and though the music isn't right for the steps, he dances.

During the festivities, Caucus-Meteor tells the story of how he captured Nathan Blake, how one Englishman made it through the gauntlet and how another did not, how Nathan tricked the gauntlet by walking it, how Caucus-Meteor made twice his interpreter's salary on a wager with the famous Bleached Bones. He omits the disturbing scene by the lake when Nathan Blake spared his life. The more he talks the more dangerously pleasant his mood becomes until the old familiar feeling of largess comes over him. This is the feeling that the king of Conissadawaga lives for. Caucus-Meteor starts giving away his money until everybody in the village has some of his coins. He gives away the tobacco that the intendant gave him. He gives away the medallion around his neck to the boy Freeway. And by malicious design, he gives Nathan's musket to Wolf Eyes, the sullen son of Haggis. He gives away all his valuables but his turban, for he is terribly ashamed of his bald head. Stripped of his possessions, he takes the hand of his adopted daughter, Caterina, and walks over to the wigwam that he shared with Keeps-the-Flame, his wife. Together father and daughter sing a brief lament, and then Caucus-Meteor gives away his iron stove. Caterina does not protest. There's a longing within her. She herself is not even sure what she longs for, but it has nothing to do with material goods.

The old American delivers a speech in which he recounts the history of the village. The villagers have heard it all before, and when the children begin to fidget, Caucus-Meteor knows it is time to stop talking. After that Kineo and Nubanusit approach Nathan Blake. They sniff him. Kineo pinches his nose. Haggis comes forward along with other prominent men in the village — Seboomook, Seekonk, and Kokadjo. Caucus-Meteor breaks a stick and tosses it into the communal fire. The villagers grow quiet; they sense a moment of struggle between the great king and the great hunter, the two most powerful men in the village, and they want to see how it turns out.

Haggis steps into an imaginary circle near the fire and addresses the townsfolk. "The captive must be tested, and better clean than no — for our own sake, if not for his, since an Englishman does not have the capacity to take offense from himself no matter how much offense he gives." A few people laugh at his not very funny joke.

Haggis is dressed in buckskins, like the natives of the previous century. His hair is very long, very black, though his skin is almost fair in complexion. By contrast, his son, Wolf Eyes, is very dark, with startling blue-green eyes, with a shaven head, except for a tuft down the middle. Haggis says something that Caucus-Meteor doesn't catch, then Kineo and Nubanusit grab Nathan, and are about to haul him away. Caucus-Meteor stops them with the raising of his right hand.

Haggis laughs, steps out of the circle, walks away. The crisis has passed.

"Come," Caucus-Meteor says softly to Nathan, and Nathan follows him to the wigwam with Caterina. Nathan and the king sit on skins on the ground. Caterina goes off to an edge of the wigwam, and stitches moccasins. Even though she's only ten feet from the men, her body is turned away from them, her attention on her work. It's the method the villagers use to attain privacy within the confined spaces of the wigwam.

Caucus-Meteor surprises Nathan. "Nathan Blake," he says, "I forbid you to drink spirits in my presence."

"Caucus-Meteor objects to strong drink?" Nathan is confused.

"Caucus-Meteor despises strong drink."

"But his subjects drink."

"The men and women in this village are free to do as they please."

"How does the king rule if the will of his subjects is equal in authority to his own?" asks Nathan.

"The king rules by oratory and by example." Caucus-Meteor stops, laughs a little. "Actually, I don't rule. No one rules a Conissadawaga citizen but himself, and even then the subject often disobeys his own commands."

"But you rule me. You just now ordered me not to drink in your presence," Nathan says, and Caucus-Meteor looks at him with a wry smile. Suddenly, Nathan Blake remembers what he is to these people. Nathan says, "I forgot that I am a slave. I am not used to being a slave."

"And before you were a slave, what were you? An Englishman

absent from his native land? One who kneels before a king he has never laid eyes on?"

"I have knelt before no king."

"But you swear allegiance to one, through a belief unexamined; you refuse to busy yourself with matters you cannot tend to with your hands. With trials to come, now might be a good time to consider all matters previously unexamined."

"There's enough today for me to examine," Nathan says. "You, an old man who went off to wars, return home with your booty and give it all away, and still you claim to be their king. Those men, your villagers, they gave me, a slave, their liquor."

"Sharing comes naturally to us. It doesn't necessarily mean I am less of a king, and you are less of a slave."

"Why did they hold their noses and take hold of me?"

"Isn't it obvious?"

"They liken me to a skunk."

"They want you to wash, Nathan Blake," Caucus-Meteor says.

"In New England we believe that bathing is dangerous to health," Nathan says.

"Perhaps you are right, for if I know one thing about the people of New England it is that right is their inheritance, but wash you must. The people require it before you are tested."

"If Caucus-Meteor wishes, I will do it," Nathan says.

"It no longer matters what Caucus-Meteor wishes, for Caucus-Meteor is no longer Nathan Blake's master."

Nathan blinks. "Am I free?"

"I have bequeathed you to my village."

"You mock me, master."

"Since our fateful meeting and union, I have indeed mocked you, for you are easy sport. Forgive me; one should not mock one's inferiors. But in this case, I am not mocking you. You were my last gift, Nathan Blake. I am retiring to my wigwam to eat my fire to give me the energy to go on the trade missions with the other men. The ones who took hold of you were going to wash you; I was afraid that in their enthusiasm they might offend your lungs with too much water. I asked them to turn you over to me until such time as you are to be tested. You will stay in my wigwam with Caterina and myself. When the tests begin, I will surrender you to my people, and they will determine your fate."

"Who is my master?" Nathan asks, and from his anxious tone it's clear that uncertainty disturbs him.

"I did not give you to any particular person. You belong to the people of Conissadawaga. I want them to think as a village, and you are an instrument for that purpose. But I will tell you that the most influential of the men, after myself, is Haggis. Haggis wears no French or English clothes. He is even more of an opponent of change than I am."

"A very impressive looking man."

"Come, let us wash," says Caucus-Meteor with gentle command.

The old American is thinking about his rival. It's the kind of thinking that brings him great pleasure, so he accompanies his thoughts with visualization. Haggis showed up at the village ten years ago with three wives—sisters, Katahdin, Mica, and Millinocket. Keeps-the-Flame advised Caucus-Meteor to turn them away, but he could not deny succor to desperate people. No one knows for sure where Haggis came from, not even he, for he has only the dimmest memories of a mother and father, and they themselves were réfugiés who went from tribe to tribe. Haggis was named as a cruel joke by a Scottish trapper who enslaved his parents briefly. He wields his name as a reminder of betrayal and humiliation. He is committed to the nomadic life of the northern Algonkian. Caucus-Meteor respects him because he is a moderate drinker and a great hunter, the best in the village. Like him, his wives are mixed blood, but they're known to have kin among the northern Cree. Katahdin is at least ten years older than Haggis. She has a very powerful personality, and rules the other two wives. Haggis has since taken a fourth wife, Chocura, a widow from the Penacook tribe. Haggis also has an adopted son, Wolf Eyes, a young man who offends his stepfather. Caucus-

Meteor gave Wolf Eyes Nathan Blake's musket, knowing it would cause mischief between father and son. Haggis's wives are his strength in the village, but they are also his weakness. Haggis has a very powerful enemy, the Catholic Church. The priests say he and his wives are going to hell. Caucus-Meteor wonders if hell is a proper place for Haggis.

"Do you believe in hell, Nathan Blake?" Caucus-Meteor asks.

"I do, yes. And I fear it."

"I think if one is uneasy in crowds, hell would be a good place to avoid."

"I think I am there now."

"And yet you are not so filled with fear."

"You can do with me what you will, take from me what you will, but my fear I reserve for my God."

Surely Nathan Blake understands that his life is at stake, but there's little anxiety within him. Caucus-Meteor is uncertain why. His refusal to kill and his performance in the gauntlet gave him powers. But there's something else in the man, something that was in him before the gauntlet. Then a possible answer dawns upon Caucus-Meteor. Nathan Blake is pious. He has put his faith in his god, and this action has released him from fear. But that is not enough. Something in him outside of his piety adds to his courage.

"You will be tested," Caucus-Meteor says. "After that you might be adopted into the village, kept as a slave, sold to the French, or killed. What is your preference?"

"I wish to be sold to the French. I believe I stand a better chance in a French prison waiting to be redeemed than in this village."

"You are right. And your wish will probably come to pass, though I suggest you heed an old Algonkian saying: you never know."

"How will I be judged in these tests?"

"That is impossible to say. Your behavior will determine much, though in the end it may mean nothing. I suggest you do the best you can. If you deliberately do poorly because you think it might help send you to a Quebec prison, the people will divine your insincerity; they might think you are a sorcerer, and kill you. Like most people confused about religion, they are superstitious, though in their heart they want to be fair. From what I know of you, Nathan Blake, I do not believe you are capable of insincerity, which is a turn of mind that presents different problems."

"I do not understand what you mean, Caucus-Meteor."

"That is the point I am trying to make."

Caucus-Meteor rummages through a moose skin, and comes up with some clothes. "They belonged to a Frenchman who unsuccessfully attempted to settle this land."

"The fellow who laid the stones for the house foundation."

"Yes, alas he died of disease before any house was built. You can wear his clothes while yours are drying. Come, let's go wash you."

Caterina looks up from her work, and speaks. Caucus-Meteor answers, then says to Nathan. "I told her to speak in Algonkian. My daughter is Seneca by birth, and prefers her native Iroquois language, but I think it best that you are exposed to only one language, the one of this village, very much like the speech that was spoken in your own lands of New England before there was a New England."

"What did she say to you?"

"She said she will speak as she wishes, and to mind my own business. She also said she will prepare a meal for us, and then she said, 'Father, you must eat to regain your strength.'" Caucus-Meteor smiles. "You see how it is with a man? Even if he's a king, first his mother rules him, then his wife, and finally his daughters. It's only with his enemies that he can have his own way."

"Your other daughter, the one I saw down by the water—"

"Black Dirt."

"Yes. She doesn't live with you?"

"Keeps-the-Flame and I had four children of our own, and one adopted child, Caterina. One died at birth, two died from disease. Black Dirt is the survivor. She has her own wigwam, once filled with a family, now empty. Adiwando, her husband, a boy of nine, and a girl of three were killed by the same throat distemper that killed the children of your English village, as you related to me during your interrogation. She will remain alone in her wigwam until her mourning period is over next year."

Nathan and Caucus-Meteor walk down by the waterfall. Nathan appears to be full of apprehension. It's his most worrisome moment thus far in his captivity. For him, a bath is worse than the gauntlet—it's such wonders in the human mind, the ability to make good seem bad and bad seem good, that keep old men attentive, thinks Caucus-Meteor.

The stone-face wigwam at the base of the falls is a room designed for cleansing the body. Water is poured on hot rocks. The moist heat opens the pores of the skin. Nathan and Caucus-Meteor undress. Caucus-Meteor marches naked except for his turban into the wigwam. Caucus-Meteor doesn't mind exposing his wrinkled body, his shriveled sex organs, but the bald head—never! Over an hour they sweat out the grime. The bath ends under the waterfall, where he must expose the bald head. Perhaps this humiliation is more cleansing that the bath. "Instead of the waters feeling frigid, they are cool," says Nathan in amazement.

"The secrets of heat are easily available through thought if one only reflects with persistence and an open mind," says Caucus-Meteor.

"An open mind like an open pit is subject to whatever a passerby may whimsically discard," says Nathan.

"Good point," says Caucus-Meteor.

They dress, the captive in the Frenchman's baggy pants, trade shirt, but his own coat. Caucus-Meteor offers to give Nathan a pair of moccasins.

"My boots are wet and cracked, but they are comfortable," Nathan says.

"And you don't trust American shoes."

Nathan bows slightly. Caucus-Meteor thinks: I like this fellow's sense of humor, if that's what it is. The old king addresses the crowd. "Clean is an odd feeling for Nathan Blake, itchy and wanting in aroma, but bearable perhaps." The crowd laughs.

It's dusk when Caucus-Meteor, Nathan, and the villagers start back. They've almost reached the village when Caucus-Meteor eyes Black Dirt silhouetted against the red sky, body arched, planting corn.

"My daughter," says Caucus-Meteor.

"In the fields all this time, working—alone," Nathan says.

"And you thought her name might refer to her complexion, darker than the other Americans. Now you realize Black Dirt refers to her love of the soil. Like you, Nathan Blake, she's a farmer."

She doesn't even notice us, thinks her father. She's lost in private thoughts. Her grief is so painful that she can barely stand her feelings. Or perhaps—and this strikes him hard—perhaps it is he she cannot stand. He will test her.

It used to be that Caucus-Meteor, his wife, and Caterina would join Black Dirt and her family for meals. They would eat outside over an open fire, except during the most inhospitable weather, in which case they would crowd together in one of the family wigwams. The old American remembers the laughter and mischief of his grandchildren, the portentous if honest speeches of his son-in-law, the biting quips of his wife, the Catholic choir chants Caterina had learned. Meals were always a good time. The reduced family still sits around the kettle boiling on the fire, but the feeling is not the same. Meals are a reminder of what has been lost, the good noises of clan. Today even Caterina, who has sung all her life, is silent.

The father and his eldest daughter exchange pleasantries. Caucus-Meteor wants to tell Black Dirt that she wears her mourning ribbon with great dignity, but something else in her demeanor, a tightness, tells him that she's concealing something from him. Instead of complimenting her, he decides to provoke her; perhaps in anger she will reveal herself. He gestures in the direction of his slave, and says, "I brought you back a husband."

"Please, father," she says.

"Do you feel that my coarse wit degrades your condition as a grieving widow: is that the source of your aloofness?"

"Your wit is yours alone for judgment, father, and I do not mean to be aloof."

"Black Dirt, something has changed in you since I went off to the wars; something more than your sorrows makes you cold to me."

"All the time you were gone, a storm has raged in me."

"It's your grief—it's normal."

"It's my grief and something else. It's this village. Good, king and good father, something is wrong here."

"Wrong? What?"

She does not answer.

"Conissadawaga is a good place, inhabited by good people," he says.

"It's not the place—it's how we live that troubles me."

"We live the life that brings joy, the life of the nomad. How we live makes us what we are—Americans, at ease in familiar or strange lands. Only the nomad has such freedom." When again Black Dirt does not respond, Caucus-Meteor, nervous and sorrowful, comforts himself by falling into repetition and oratory. "We live as we've always lived. The men do men's work—trading, hunting, warring; the women do women's work—house building, craft making, and farming. Together we care for the children. As king I lend pomp to the proceedings."

"I am sorry if I upset you, father."

Caucus-Meteor did not know he was upset until his daughter pointed it out. Now he realizes she is right—he is upset, and something *is wrong* in Conissadawaga. Perhaps it is him—his interest in morbidity. "What is it—what is wrong?" he asks.

"I don't know, father."

That night in Caucus-Meteor's wigwam, Caterina makes

hardly a sound as she sleeps; only the rise and fall of her chest signals that she's alive. He calculates that she, like her sister, is in the midst of changes. Nathan sleeps restlessly while Caucus-Meteor sits by his fire, so close as to be baked by it; all through the night the old American hardly moves a muscle except to put a stick on his tiny fire. Caucus-Meteor has given away everything that he owns. He has nothing, so that now he truly feels like a king. In some future time, after St. Blein and the rebels have taken over the government and installed him on the throne of Canada, he will acquire huge amounts of coins, gifts, trade goods, property, loot from the English colonies—and give it all away. His dream of a worthy reign as king is to begin each day rich and end it a pauper.

By morning the wigwam has become stuffy and smoky. Caucus-Meteor believes that a depletion in air for breath is good for his health. He goes outside at dawn with Caterina, who leaves him without a word and walks into the woods. Her mysterious behavior has always worried him. Caucus-Meteor removes the embers from the fire inside the wigwam and builds a small fire outside. Nathan comes out of the wigwam to do his morning toilet.

Later, Caterina returns and prepares a meal. She gives Nathan the same share she gives Caucus-Meteor, a pancake of dried corn and a piece of smoked salmon. She says to Nathan in Iroquois, "Your breakfast, good slave." Caucus-Meteor translates her words first in English, then in Algonkian. Nathan bows, thanks Caterina in English for the food. Caucus-Meteor translates his thanks in Algonkian, and insists Nathan repeat the words.

Black Dirt has already been working in the fields, and presently, carrying a hoe, she returns with Katahdin. Caucus-Meteor has always been attracted to Haggis's primary wife. He likes Katahdin's big shoulders, wide back, thick neck, and spindly legs. The women are looking over the slave, not sure what to make of this fellow yet.

"He seems haughty and docile at the same time," says Black Dirt.

"He's measuring us, as we are measuring him," says Katahdin. "We will see how he behaves over time."

"We've never had a slave before, so I'm not sure what to expect," says Black Dirt.

"I've had some experience in these matters, and I'll tell you that captives change over time," says Katahdin. "Some fall into despair, and lose their usefulness; some plan revenge, and must be killed; some transform themselves from the inside. It's such as these who become good slaves. Or even passable husbands. Our village needs husbands."

"For today our need is for a laborer in the fields," says Black Dirt. She turns to Caucus-Meteor. "Father?"

The old American nods. "Tell him yourself in Algonkian. He must learn our language."

"Today you will work with the women in the fields," Black Dirt says.

Nathan blinks, retains a stoic expression, which impresses his master. "He still doesn't understand," Black Dirt says to her father.

"I believe your manner offends him. In his world women do not talk to men in officious tones." Caucus-Meteor turns toward Nathan, and says first in Algonkian and then in English, "Our village has no horse, no ox; you, slave, are the beast of burden."

Nathan bows, and Black Dirt hands him the hoe, points to the ground, and watches while he marches out with the women. The slave is subservient enough, though he keeps his head up, his shoulders squared; his eyes are observant, his mouth shut. I admire him very much, thinks the old American.

Soon Nathan Blake will learn that only women and slaves work in the fields. The sole crop men raise is tobacco. Presently, the men are busy socializing, making gun flints and casting bullets for their flintlocks, and patching and building canoes. Small ash logs are split, shaved, steamed, and bent to make the frame; the birch bark is sewn and sealed with spruce gum. The men are preparing to embark on trade missions, selling the village's prime product, moccasins, which are made by the women mainly in the winter. The men will divide up into trade groups, taking their wares to Quebec, Montreal, Tadousic, Odanak, Wendake, Beaucancour, Silery, Sault St. Marie; a few even venture to Albany in English territory. Caucus-Meteor eats his fire to gain the strength for the trade fair missions.

That night a cold rain falls. At the end of the day's work, in the dark of the wigwam by the tiny fire, Caucus-Meteor tells Nathan about trade.

"Some will trade well, and others will be disgraced," he says. "Some will lose the coins and goods they trade to gambling and drink. One or two will come back as followers of Jesus, which is what happened to Norman Feathers. Two or three will not come back—the deserters and the dead. The successful ones will exchange our magnificent moccasins for French coins, iron stoves, stove piping, pots, pans, fabric, beads, needles, dyes, axes, knives, tobacco, liquor—far too much liquor—rope, weapons, farm tools, and even some wampum, which is still used for adornment, though no longer as currency or for diplomacy. The traders are also expected to bring back news regarding relatives, friends, enemies; the gossip of the trail enriches the lives of the men while the trail itself meets the demands of the women for household goods and news. You English call trade items goods because they are good for women, no?"

"We English believe you enslave your women with burdensome labors, such as field work," Nathan says.

"Because they do the work that men choose to do in New England? That is not slavery, Nathan Blake. Excuse me now while I eat my fire." The old American turns his head from Nathan and stares into his fire.

Caucus-Meteor left off his trade list matters he does not think Nathan Blake is ready to deal with—personal adornment items, such as combs, clam shells for pulling out facial and body hair, and various kinds of paint, earrings, medallions, bracelets. American men spend much time primping themselves. Every man owns a mirror, and he spends part of his day plucking out hairs, applying paint, arranging feathers. Most wear European fibers with some buckskins, the clothes garnished with medallions, bracelets, necklaces, ear and nose rings. Each individual wishes to put himself forward in a unique way. It's not an idea that an English frontier farmer will understand, except in the most general way, and he wouldn't have much sympathy for it, and it would only confuse him. Also Caucus-Meteor doesn't tell Nathan that he's worried he won't have the strength to go on a trade mission this year. If he has to remain behind, he will lose prestige in the village. His people will look elsewhere for a king.

A week goes by. Nathan is picking up a few words of Algonkian. Caucus-Meteor speaks less and less English to him. He still hasn't been "tested"; in fact, the men hardly pay him any mind, though he is the butt of a joke that he finally grasps— "The slave works very well as a woman." Until this moment, he has showed little emotion, but now that he understands how the men regard him, his feelings rise to the surface and spill out; he blushes with shame and resentment. For him, farming is noble and manly, thinks Caucus-Meteor. "Nathan Blake, do you despise us for what you believe are our peculiar ideas, do you pity us, or do you question yourself?" Nathan is too wrought up with humiliation to do anything but mutter. Caucus-Meteor says, "I will answer for you. Perhaps it is better, Nathan Blake, if you withhold judgment. For the time being your task will be to observe, to pray, to await your god's will."

"Yes, master," Nathan bows.

Each morning the women meet to discuss the day's work. Nathan can't understand their words, but surely their demeanor tells him that they talk as farmers talk anywhere—of weather, crops, land; and no complaints, please.

At night around the fire, the old American attempts to give his slave some learning regarding his predicament.

"The leaders of the women are Katahdin and Black Dirt. Katahdin is imperious without being queenly. She argues with everybody except her husband, Haggis, whom she seems to adore, though who can say what really goes on between a man and a woman. Though Katahdin is quick to anger, she is also quick to forgive, to laugh, and to praise. Her strengths are energy and fearlessness. She bullies the other women into doing her bidding, and they are more or less grateful."

"Such a woman might be made more humble by being dunked or fitted with a scold's bridle," says Nathan.

The old American is amused. "The women look to Black Dirt for a different kind of leadership," he says. "She never offers advice unless it's asked for and does little to influence the group, but she's the hardest working woman in the fields and she knows more about farming than anybody else. When there is a problem to be solved, the women, even Katahdin, come to her."

"You have more women than men in your village."

"Our men keep getting killed off in wars and accidents. Married women with children have great influence and authority in the village; women with children but no husbands have some influence; women without children almost no influence." After a week, Nathan is able to pronounce the names of the head women. Besides Black Dirt and Katahdin are Leyanne, Ossipee, Azicochoa, and Contoocook.

"Here is a test for you, Nathan Blake," says Caucus-Meteor in the whimsical tone he uses when he wants to abuse the slave with confounding ideas. "You have been here a while. Tell us now what is our most valued product?"

"Why, the three sisters—corn, beans, squash."

"No."

"Peas."

"No."

"The moccasins the women make."

"No."

"Trade."

"Trade is not a product."

"I do not know the answer, master," says Nathan.

A week later, Nathan Blake says to Caucus-Meteor. "I know the answer to the valued product question. It is the same as in our nation—children."

"But how can you value children, if you strike them?"

"The child, out of its nature, is unruly, and thus must be ruled through a good whipping now and then, and certainly a scolding once a day. The will of the child is the char from Adam and Eve's original sin, and thus must be burnished until it glows into exemplary behavior."

"In our village the child might be pulled from danger, and certainly must suffer the common hardships of the community, but the child is never struck or chastised, for we believe that the will must be kept intact. It is the will—or, as you would call it, the sin—that is the valued product within the individual. Does whipping and scolding create behavior more exemplary among your own children than what you have witnessed among ours?"

"Nay, your children are as exemplary as ours, that I admit; though your adults seem dominated by a child's will."

The conversation leads Caucus-Meteor into worries about his youngest child, Caterina. She is fifteen, and has had several suitors, but has rejected them all. Since his return from the wars, she's distant, sullen. She goes off in the morning and sometimes at night away from the village to be alone. He'd like to think that she is having an affair with a married man, but something tells him the matter is more serious than that.

Nathan remarks to Caucus-Meteor that the women ignore him, which surprises him; he'd heard that native women are licentious even with captives.

"Some are licentious, and some are not. Our women, like our men, do as they please—it's the American way of life," says Caucus-Meteor.

"I suppose I am repellent to them because I am an Englishman and white and hairy."

"You are repellent to them because you are a slave."

In fact, thinks Caucus-Meteor, Nathan is beginning to think

like a slave. He keeps his true feelings to himself. He snaps to when he's called. He reacts to every minor emergency with passivity, for authority outside his own self rules all. Perhaps he feels like a boy again growing up on the farm—frustrated, yearning for something not quite known, but also free from civic worries. I would envy his position, thinks Caucus-Meteor, if I hadn't been a slave myself.

One morning Haggis and half a dozen men approach Caucus-Meteor. "We feel it is time for the captive to be tested," Haggis says.

"Good idea," says the old king.

The men walk as a delegation into the fields where Nathan is working. The women ignore them, pretending to be uninterested in the proceedings.

"Are you ready to be tested, Nathan Blake?" asks Haggis.

Nathan looks to Caucus-Meteor for a translation, but the old American says nothing and shows nothing on his face. Haggis repeats his question. Nathan doesn't know exactly what's going on, but he drops the hoe.

Haggis puts his right hand over Nathan's chest to check the captive's heartbeat.

"Is he frightened?" asks Caucus-Meteor.

"Hard to tell. His heart is beating strongly, but not like a man in panic. I think he is excited."

"A good sign," says Passaconway.

Black Dirt approaches the men. Haggis appears pleased. An idea formulates in Caucus-Meteor's mind. Haggis is obviously attracted to Black Dirt. When she's finished her mourning period, she'll be expected to take another husband, and provide children for the village. Haggis might be more easily controlled if he married Black Dirt. Caucus-Meteor watches her carefully. She says nothing to the men. She does, however, reveal her purpose in coming forward, walking to the place where the captive was working, picking up his hoe, and striding off with the valued implement.

Haggis speaks to Wolf Eyes, plainly dressed in French clothing, wearing only a single streak of red paint from the tip of his forehead winding down across his nose, lips, chin, throat. "Will you allow us to use the musket that Caucus-Meteor gave you for the test?" Haggis asks.

Wolf Eyes stiffens. The old American guesses that the son is thinking of some new way to defy his father, and the father is thinking, I doubt he can do it: if he declines to offer the weapon, he will be reduced in the view of the men; if he agrees, he bends to my will. But as always Wolf Eyes finds a way to insult his father by responding, "Oui," using the French language for agreement instead of Algonkian. Caucus-Meteor is pleased. He knew if he gave the musket to Wolf Eyes, he would cause some mischief.

A target is set up about fifty yards away, an old wasp nest on a rock.

The captive spreads out the powder, ball, a ramrod in front of him, and then loads the weapon. He proceeds with care and deliberation, but not with speed. Caucus-Meteor thinks if this is his way of performing a chore, then this is a careful man. But likely it's something else, fear or incompetence with weapons.

"This was your musket, was it not? You have experience in using it?" Haggis says, but the captive speaks very little Algonkian and Haggis does not know how to formulate words in English, so there is no answer to the questions. Nathan might not understand the particulars, but it's clear that he understands that he's being tested and that he's not to look to Caucus-Meteor for help.

Nathan brings the musket to his shoulder, aims, wobbles a little. With that wobble, Caucus-Meteor knows that Haggis has learned everything he needs to about the captive's skills as a hunter.

"He has one shot," says Caucus-Meteor. "Perhaps he will waste it on one of us. Who shall it be?"

The other men laugh. Risk, suspense, danger, and uncertainty are part of the amusement of the test.

"If he wishes to kill his tormentor, he has not far to look," says Haggis.

"The victim never kills his tormentor, but his benefactor. It is one of those rules the gods made long ago to confound us all," says Caucus-Meteor.

Nathan fires off a shot in the general direction of the wasp nest. What was clear to Caucus-Meteor with the wobble is now clear to all: Nathan Blake is no marksman. Minutes later the captive will find himself back in the fields working with the women.

That night by the fire Caucus-Meteor explains to Nathan why he'd been called to demonstrate his abilities with the musket.

"Haggis believes that the problem with Americans nowadays is that guns have made them lazy," Caucus-Meteor says. "The fine art of bow and arrow construction has been lost. Young boys no longer practice archery for hours on end. Americans think guns will do everything for them. Guns need maintenance, lead, powder, and, to be effective, marksmanship. With a war on—and there is always a war on—it's difficult to buy ammunition, so we haven't had much practice with our muskets. Result: Americans who can't shoot straight. Haggis and I are in agreement on this matter. The test was to determine whether you might be a second line shooter for the fall hunt."

"I am no hunter."

"Probably Haggis figured that out right away. I think he was really testing Wolf Eyes, to see how he reacted when you, a slave and an Englishman, fired the gun that I won from you in war and gave him in kingly largess."

"Haggis is a cunning man."

"That is true, but it is also true that the second most cunning man in a group lives in a state of constant frustration."

"What is the next test?"

"That will be up to the whim of the village men, but I suspect it will be foot racing."

A small, secretive smile plays on the captive's face. Before Caucus-Meteor can question it, Caterina breaks into the conversation. She spends so much time facing away from the men, so silent that often she seems not even to be breathing, that the sound of her voice is disturbing, something in the tone desperate. "I'm going to the woods to pray," she says.

"It's very late, and there is no moon," says her father.

"I must pray alone."

"Do not return with the god," Caucus-Meteor says.

"I will do what the god demands," she says.

Caucus-Meteor doesn't mind a god in the wigwam if the god minds his own business. It's a god's courtship of his daughter that troubles him. She has adored many gods over the last two years, and every one has led her into difficulties of one kind or another.

Nathan retires to his bed of sticks and mats, but the old king remains by his fire. He's quiet for a few minutes, then begins chanting, partly a traditional chant he learned from his mother and partly some Latin. He doesn't have the faith and he doesn't understand the priests' secret language, but he's always enjoyed the Latin choirs, so he puts a few words he's heard together and calls it a song—Espiritus sanctus in dayo, da-hey-ohhh, specularum, odorum, hic, hike, hok, da-hey-ohhh. He's in the center of the wigwam by his tiny fire, a position he assumes twenty hours a day. He sings in a voice low but audible. He stops abruptly—jolted by a surprise feeling of conjuring; perhaps the god has come to him. "What do you want from me?" he asks. The answer to his question: Go to your loved one. He rises up, leaves the wigwam, and goes in search of Caterina. But it's very dark. Not only is there no moon, the stars are blotted out by clouds. He thinks he hears Caterina moan in the woods, but maybe it's an animal. Eventually, he gives up his search and returns to the village.

He sees light through the cracks of Black Dirt's wigwam. "Are you asleep?" he says at the mat door. He knows the answer, but he's giving her a chance to feign sleep in case she doesn't want to talk to him.

"Come in, father," Black Dirt says.

"It's almost like day in there," he says.

"I like candle light—the shadows it makes are sisters to my sorrows," she says.

Black Dirt has turned her home into a storage shed of moccasins. Perhaps supple moose and deer skin made soft by smoking bring her a small comfort. She'd rather be with the products of her people than with the people. Grief is drawing her away from the very notion of touch.

"When I was in New England marching off to war, I remembered you singing a lament," he says, and he repeats it for her in song:

> Let me hold my babies one more time;
> let me braid my husband's hair one more time;
> let me seek my mother's counsel one more time.

He sings the lament two more times, each rendition sadder and slower than the one before.

Father and daughter embrace. "The gods are cruel," Black Dirt says. "They say to me: Those times are gone by."

"Time is like a milkweed pod, bursting open, flying in the wind, starting anew in neighboring soil." Caucus-Meteor is repeating an old Algonkian saying; he's not sure if he believes it or even exactly what it means, but it seems like the right thing to say.

"Don't let your grief keep you away from the people," he says. "They need you, Black Dirt. Without ambition or conscious effort you've replaced your mother as head woman in this village." She shakes her head in denial. "You took charge of the moccasin enterprise, and now you're making all the important decisions regarding planting the fields."

"I would rather count moccasins, stack them, even smell them than oversee the performance of my sisters. Let Katahdin do that."

"Where's the profit in the smelling, the counting, and the stacking of moccasins? The smell of moose? I do not understand, daughter."

"It's not the smell of moose I'm thinking of, it's the smell of money. Why do I think this? What does money mean? I ask myself these questions."

"In the old days," says her father, "wampum was the medium of exchange between tribes. The polished shells had to be worked and shaped into belts before being brought into circulation as currency. Wampum held powers of ceremony, beauty, and even speech, for the design of a wampum belt conveyed a message. But for all its power, money is only money. Money even more than war and liquor and white settlement is wearing away the American way of life that Keeps-the-Flame and I taught you to value above all."

"I feel no threat—I feel a pull . . . toward the money . . . in violation of your teachings, father." She looks up. "Dear mother, forgive me." She looks now at her father. "This too is my lament. Father, do you understand now—do you?"

Caucus-Meteor begins to tremble. Grief is changing not only his daughter's heart; it's changing her head. Or perhaps (and this thought pierces him) she was already changed before the distemper epidemic, and death and grief are making her see that change. He remembers a transforming moment in her life. She was a child, sick with fever, and he and her mother had thought she would die. His wife woke him at dawn. Their child was gone. They found her among the corn. She was eating, not the corn, but the dirt. Keeps-the-Flame had said, "Dirt is her medicine—it will restore her." And it did. Later, Black Dirt bore her children "in this dirt," as she said. For a long time, Caucus-Meteor had wondered why she had said, "this" dirt. Now the solution to the mystery comes to him. His daughter is not, has never been, in her heart a nomad. As the father eats fire, the daughter eats dirt, this dirt, on this land, in this place. He thinks: despite her love for me, she will betray me. He wants to shout to the gods: Why couldn't you let Nathan Blake stone me dead!

But in a calm voice, he says, "Come, my daughter, be a child again for a few minutes."

Black Dirt puts her head on her father's lap, as she did as a little girl. He strokes her hair and chants in his pretend Latin until she grows sleepy and lies down on her mat. He covers her with a blanket, kisses her on the forehead, and returns to his wigwam.

Back eating his fire, Caucus-Meteor is passing the night when his other daughter, Caterina, appears from out of the darkness, gives him a bare nod, and starts for her bed.

"It's late, and no one is up to give me company," Caucus-Meteor says.

Caterina hesitates, then sits on her heels across the fire from her father. They sit for a long time, saying nothing. Finally, Caucus-Meteor speaks.

"Did you see a god in the woods?"

"I did not see a god because I am unworthy," she says.

"You were in the woods a long time."

"I did penance."

He doesn't understand what she means, but he feels a profound disturbance from the tone of her voice. He attempts the conjuring trick—fails. "Tell me what you desire, dear daughter," he says.

"When the priest comes to village, I wish to make a confession."

"I am not a priest; I am your father, though not your natural father, so perhaps you may use me as a priest and confess your sins."

"I was the first in our village with the smallpox. I was scarred but I did not die."

"The priests you wish to confess to brought smallpox to our village. It's the reason I drove them away."

"I also survived the throat distemper that killed so many of our family last winter. I think there is a devil within me, father."

"It's not a sin to be sick, Caterina."

"I believe I have sinned, so surely I have sinned. Give me forgiveness."

"I cannot forgive what is not a sin. Caterina, you must believe me when I tell you that you have not sinned, and that you are worthy of the company of any god or man. Come now, I will give you my blessing, which is something that all the gods sanction for fathers and kings."

Caterina rises up on her knees, and Caucus-Meteor whispers some pretend Latin into the air, tells her he loves her, and, as he did his other daughter, sends her off to bed.

The next day he notices that Caterina has changed her blouse. He inspects the soiled garment and finds drops of dried blood on the back. She'd told him that she had done penance, but had not confessed. Now he understands what she meant. Caterina went into the woods to flog herself. He looks at the burn scars on his arms. Most strangers think he's survived tortures from enemies. Caterina knows that when he's upset he burns himself.

The next day, in the early afternoon, Haggis and other village men fetch Nathan from the fields again. Nathan Blake is to be tested in a race. Caucus-Meteor's mood lightens. It will be good for the king to get away from family problems and mingle with his subjects.

The Conissadawaga Americans are known for the quality of the moccasins they make, so foot racing is important to them and everyone turns out for the contest. The women leave their work in the fields, and the children stage races of their own. Everyone knows the fastest runners in the village—Haggis and Wolf Eyes—so the suspense is in how the English slave will do. The racers will run through the village, down to the lake, and back again, a distance of perhaps half a mile. Caucus-Meteor feels the old urge to bet, but he has nothing to bet with, and anyway it's not a good idea for a king to gamble with commoners.

Then again, we are all common enough, he thinks. He wonders: If I were betting, would I bet on Nathan Blake? The man looks like a runner, and by his demeanor now it's plain that he's competed in races before and that he has confidence. But something about Nathan, a shadow of the stupidity and arrogance that he saw in Captain Warren, suggests to Caucus-Meteor that Nathan is a poor bet.

Passaconway, who is even older than Caucus-Meteor and who was a great runner in his day, starts the race by dropping a feather. When the feather hits the ground, the runners burst forward. Nathan, not used to this starting method, is the last to move his feet, but within fifty yards he's caught up with the leaders. He looks relaxed and strong, thinks the old American. As sure as I am a king, he will win this race. Nathan accelerates; the power of his body surges into the soles of his feet. A second later the worn leather laces on his right boot burst. Suddenly, he's running in a sloppy shoe. Nathan finishes the race last.

He holds up his shoe as an excuse. The village men taunt Nathan Blake. Their words mean nothing to him, thinks Caucus-Meteor, but surely he can read their faces: no complaints, no excuses, eat your defeat, Englishman; surely he can see the women laughing. If Nathan Blake could answer in our language, he'd taunt us right back, challenge us to another race with new shoes, thinks Caucus-Meteor. But he's trapped in his own language, defeated by pride and bad luck, as when he left the safety of the stockade to let his animals out of the barn for reasons mysterious even to himself. Perhaps this young man with imperfections compatible with his own was sent to serve him in ways as yet unforeseen. Caucus-Meteor squeezes his eyes shut, and presses on his eyeballs in an attempt to see into the future, but only the blindness he experiences strikes him with any vigor.

The village men gather in a circle to discuss today's events. They look to their king for leadership. "I gave Nathan Blake to the village, so let the village determine his fate based on his performance. I will give no speeches on this matter."

"No doubt Nathan Blake can run," says Haggis. "But that is not important. What is important is the omen of the burst shoe."

"I think before he brings his bad luck to this village, we should kill him," says Kineo.

"If we do that, we will have insulted our king, who gave him to us as a gift; thus, we will have insulted ourselves," says Passaconway.

"I will not take insult from someone so small in status as Kineo, or any of you for that matter. Do what you wish with your slave." Caucus-Meteor knows that the magnanimous gesture more than the threat is a weapon of control.

"What has this slave done to deserve death?" says Seboomook.

"It's not what he has done, it's what he will do," says Kokadjo.

"Omens are not to be taken lightly," says Kineo, and makes the throat-cut sign.

"Sometimes when one does not know where the quarry is, it's best to stand and wait until it comes around again, for all creatures move in great circles," says Passaconway, mouthing an old Algonkian saying.

"Wait and do nothing, I think not," says Seekonk.

Argument rages until Haggis speaks, and all listen. Caucus-Meteor admires Haggis's strategy. He's learned through experience that it's best to let others talk out the mad ideas, and reveal one's own position only when the group is fraught with uncertainty. Everyone knows now that though there will continue to be discussion, debate, argument, bluff, humor—for the men love opportunity for oratory—in the end Haggis's opinion will prevail.

Haggis concludes his speech by saying, "Let the slave return to the fields where he can work like a woman."

That night in the wigwam, Caucus-Meteor says to Nathan, "You took your defeat hard."

"I was more disappointed at losing that race than at watching my cabin go up in flames," Nathan says. "I have never lost a footrace in my life. Why don't you people just kill me and get it over with?"

"You are very comical," Caucus-Meteor says softly.

Nathan gives the old man a savage look, and Caucus-Meteor bursts into laughter. Then Nathan laughs.

"Why am I laughing? What is happening to me?" Nathan says.

"Joy in the face of disaster—what else can a man brag about to the gods? Nathan Blake, it's probably to your benefit that you lost your race. The village men have decided that you would not make a good American man. Haggis has suggested that the village sell you to the French. It appears you'll be in a Quebec prison before the men leave for the trade season."

Nathan takes a moment to let this news sink in, but he can't seem to get excited.

"I think you do not like to lose," says Caucus-Meteor.

"I think I do not trust anything that is said by a savage," he says.

"You talk boldly for a slave."

"Forgive me, master."

"I'm no good at forgiveness, because I cannot see sin where the sinner sees sin. You think we are not honorable men?" Caucus-Meteor feigns outrage.

"I think you are a people ruled by whim."

"So I am to be the king of whim. Thank you for unburdening me."

Norman Feathers brings word to Quebec and in a few days returns with two priests and soldiers from the office of the governor-general. The village is buzzing. It's the first time in years priests have come to Conissadawaga. Caucus-Meteor greets the clerics—Father Esubee Goulet, smooth-shaven face, bald head, pink skin, and Father Sanibel "Spike" Morrissette, youthful, bearded.

"Let us welcome the visitors," Caucus-Meteor says. "We will talk to the soldiers about selling them our slave, and the priests will talk to us about Jesus. But first let us have something to eat."

The villagers always react the same way when visitors come. They bring out the drums and rattles, stoke their pipes with tobacco and bark, load the cooking pots, and pass around jugs of brandy.

Father Spike, as he is known, mingles with the villagers, talking with them in French, asking them to teach him words in their Algonkian dialects. He blesses them with the tiniest hands Caucus-Meteor has ever seen on a man. Only Black Dirt and Nathan Blake remain in the fields, Black Dirt because she thinks it unseemly to carouse during one's mourning period, Nathan because he is a slave. Meanwhile, Caucus-Meteor meets with Father Goulet in his wigwam. They talk in French.

"It has been a while since we have broken bread together," says Father Goulet.

"If I remember correctly it was ten years ago. You baptized the Iroquois orphan my wife and I adopted."

"Yes, and I named her—Caterina Aratta, after my Italian grandmother. I thought in those days yours would be a mission village. But later you banished us."

"You brought smallpox to the village."

"You cannot blame Jesus for the mischief of the devil."

"No doubt what you say in this instance is true, if everything else you say is also true. Truth aside, I see now you were right all along," says Caucus-Meteor with just a trace of sarcasm in his smile.

"So?"

"So, let us say that I am repentant."

"Now that you are close to death, you are having a change of heart? A little fear, perhaps?" Though Father Goulet talks with a lisp, he doesn't come across as weak or without courage.

"You are very wise, a good priest, I imagine. I am wondering about the power of your church."

"It is very powerful because it is sanctified by Christ."

"I would like to test this power."

Caucus-Meteor then launches into a long, rambling speech

about French law, the governor-general, the intendant, and finally tribute. "My villagers bring in more French scrip per person than any of the mission villages, and yet we remain poor. We live the nomadic life because it pleases us. I would like my village to have parchment title to this land; I would like to stop paying the intendant tribute."

"If this village becomes a true mission, that is possible."

"By a true mission, you mean everyone in the village has to be baptized."

"I mean that everyone has to be instructed. Children may be baptized, but adults must be instructed. They must elect to receive Jesus before they can be baptized."

Caucus-Meteor pauses for a moment to think. He's going against his experience and feelings by inviting the church men into his village. He wants to say that Jesus is too demanding a god, but of course one cannot argue religion with a cleric, for there is no possibility of an exchange of beliefs. If the priests take over the village, they'll retain him as head man, since he invited them. So he withholds his true feelings. If he sends them away, it's likely that he will lose his position as king to Haggis in the coming months. Finally, Caucus-Meteor says, "Let us test it. Also, you can do me a personal favor."

"If it is within my powers, good king."

"Hear the confession of my youngest daughter, Caterina. She is weighted down by guilt. Perhaps, as you clerics say, Jesus can bear some of the weight of her cross."

"We will test it both ways, with the intendant when we return to Quebec and here with your daughter."

Elsewhere, the villagers and soldiers haggle over the worth of the slave. Eventually, the villagers agree to accept the soldiers' offer for the slave. The soldiers will wait until the priests finish their work. For three days, the priests circulate among the villagers. They preach the word of Jesus. Norman Feathers, the only practicing Catholic among the group, acts as the interpreter with the few Americans who don't speak French. Most of the villagers are cautious. They're waiting to see what their king, Caucus-Meteor, will do. If he submits to instruction and baptism, most of the villagers will go along. The exceptions are Haggis, his wives, and their followers, who make up nearly one third of the villagers. They stay away from the priests.

The Conissadawaga villagers talk mainly in various dialects of Algonkian, but a few speak Iroquois, and once in a while there are outbursts of French and even a few words in English or Dutch. It amuses Caucus-Meteor to imagine that even the village dogs bark in dialects. All these languages come out in verbal melee with the priests, whose presence has caused the villagers to examine themselves. Haggis and his wives are upset, because the priests tell them their union is not sanctioned by Jesus. Mica, Haggis's second wife, claims that angels (beasts half woman, half eagle) will swoop down and take her away from her children and clan. Haggis suspects the priests want to incarcerate him in a church. Wolf Eyes has no interests in the priests, but he has been hanging around the soldiers, showing them the musket that Caucus-Meteor gave him. Most of the villagers are charmed by the priests and their mysterious Latin incantations. The mood at the moment is to vote to become a mission village. Haggis and his band will have to go along or strike out on their own. Caucus-Meteor believes he has seized control of the village. Is it the feeling of control and achievement that makes one side of his face numb?

That night the Americans bring their private discussions into the public arena by the outdoor fire. The soldiers and priests watch and listen. "The evening gathering has turned into a town meeting," says Nathan to Caucus-Meteor. In place of a moderator, there is the imaginary circle by the fire. When a citizen has something to say, he or she steps into the circle and makes a speech, often a very long speech. When the citizen is finished, he or she steps out of the circle and somebody else steps in. The villagers of

Conissadawaga, like the villagers of Upper Ashuelot in New Hampshire, enjoy hearing themselves talk. They agree on a price for the captive, but take no action on the conversion question.

Caucus-Meteor knows that this is the time to make a speech. If he converts to Catholicism, his villagers will allow the priests to build a mission. He'll have some leverage he can use against the intendant; the powers of his rival Haggis will be greatly reduced. But the old American had a dizzy spell earlier in the day, and yesterday for an hour, the side of his face felt numb. Maybe Keeps-the-Flame, who was violently opposed to French missionaries and their religion, was chastising him from the beyond. He thinks it best to hold his tongue, and wait for an omen.

Father Goulet has the last word in this night of oratory. "We will leave in the morning with the soldiers for Quebec. We will be back in a week with payment for the English captive and with soldiers to transport him to Quebec for prisoner exchange. We will say mass, and listen to the will of the people."

Caucus-Meteor understands that Father Goulet is giving him a week to accept a mission.

Later, the old king watches his daughter go off with Father Goulet, who has agreed to hear her confession. When they return, his daughter appears radiant, blessed, while the priest has a smug expression on his face. Caucus-Meteor feels the pangs of jealousy.

Next morning the village turns out to say goodbye to the departing visitors. All are at the landing by the waterfall when Caterina springs a surprise. She makes a long speech ending with the words, "I wish to marry no man; I will be the bride of Christ." Caterina is leaving with the priests to enter a convent.

Black Dirt's face flares with anger. She says harsh words to her sister, who remains passive but determined. Caucus-Meteor is more than surprised by this development; he's traumatized. He's thinking: this is the same feeling I had when they took my mother away, and when my wife died. Jesus is punishing me for my insincerity.

All day the village is somber. Every loss of a villager is like a death. If Caterina had married and brought children to the village, she might have enjoyed great prestige. Instead, she goes off with the priests. Villagers whisper among themselves that the priests are sorcerers whose goal is to reduce the village to nothing. Only Haggis is secretly glad, thinks Caucus-Meteor. He senses changes in the air, which can only be to his benefit.

Caucus-Meteor keeps his vigil, eating his fire. One would expect that the king would be fraught with worry or anxiety, some strong emotion in reaction to his daughter's leaving. But the disturbances in his mind are nothing like that. The old man is shutting down in the universal way: his face twists, body slumps forward, unseeing eyes stare at the fire only a few feet away.

It's not until the next morning that he registers events that can be filed in memory. He awakens, and thinks, now isn't this grand. I have awakened, which means I must have slept. I must be rested. He reaches down to see if he has a morning erection, which will tell whether indeed he is rested. But before the hand can complete the journey another of his senses has a message for him. His fire is cold and silent, and smells old. He hears a voice now. "What's wrong, master?"

It's his slave, but the voice has brought him round to the state of things. He says, "Go fetch Black Dirt," his words slurred as if he had been drinking too much.

When Nathan returns with Black Dirt, Caucus-Meteor utters two words. "I'm blind."

Her response comes in a voice mushy as spring ice. He can smell and hear and his sense of touch is uncanny, so that he feels odd sensations in his nipples and along his spine, but no pain. This is good news, he thinks. I am experiencing events in a different way. Perhaps I am closer to death, or to truth, or to time—whatever out there is of import. Finally, I've reached the station in life where I can begin truly to conjure. But he soon realizes that he's not conjuring. He is merely falling asleep. Well, all right. He hasn't slept in ten years; perhaps it's time for a long night.

All that day the old man is confused. Mainly, he is silent, but during odd moments, he makes speeches that don't quite make sense, and circle back on themselves. He thinks, my but these speeches are better than the ones I make when I am calculating them. He says: "I am a child lost in the woods. I have entered that terrible hollow tree of the one true self. I'm you. But do not be frightened. That place where thoughts, feelings, and behavior are one has its rewards when one is in the hollow . . ." He can tell from the activity around him that his villagers are unsure what to do or say. He feels no sense of responsibility, no ambition, no call to control situations around him. He thinks: this must be what it's like to be content. I think I will nap.

By the second day the king of Conissadawaga has gotten his wits about him, though he still can't see.

He confesses weakness to his people. "It's bad enough that Father Goulet steals my daughter for Jesus, but this—" Caucus-Meteor points to his sightless eyes, his paralyzed facial muscles —"shows a sense of humor more profound than I ever imagined could come from a priest. I think it is time for me to digest the fires I've been eating all these years, and perhaps instead of the usual stuff some wisdom will come out the other end."

The villagers suspend labors to discuss the crisis. They talk long into the night. Afterward, Black Dirt meets privately with Caucus-Meteor; when she leaves, the old king delivers the news in English to Nathan.

"I am no longer king of the Conissadawaga Americans," he says. "The people have replaced me with Haggis, Passaconway, and Black Dirt, who will serve as chiefs with equal powers until I am healed or dead."

"Women as rulers?" Nathan grimaces.

"Do not the English have queens who rule?"

"By blood, but not by election, and not in New England." Nathan pauses.

Caucus-Meteor knows that like a good slave Nathan is waiting for his master to speak, but he decides to remain silent to see how Nathan behaves.

An hour goes by, until Nathan blurts out the question that has been on his mind. "What of me? Am I to be delivered to the French? Will I leave with the priests when they come next week?"

"The priests will be turned away. Conissadawaga has voted to remain a pagan nation. The people have decided that you, Nathan Blake, are to replace my daughter, Caterina, who was stolen from me by Jesus and the priests."

"I do not understand, Caucus-Meteor."

"Blind I cannot care for myself. You will care for me. What I'm trying to tell you, Nathan Blake, is that my villagers have loaned you to me; you are once again my slave."

Nathan does not respond. Caucus-Meteor cannot even hear him breathe, though he can smell the stink of his disappointment. Finally, Nathan says, "This means I am not going home."

"This means your fate is entwined with mine."

Nathan's anger suddenly flares. "I had a chance to kill you once, but..." Good, thinks Caucus-Meteor, he's going to tell me now why he spared my life; perhaps then I can understand with greater clarity how the gods fashion the instrument of death. But Nathan seems to gag on the words he's about to utter, and in the end he says nothing.

"You can kill me, Nathan Blake," says Caucus-Meteor, "or, if Jesus is not done punishing me, you can watch while I die of this curse or that. Either way, know this, my people have determined that if I die, you die. My fate is your fate."

For a long time the slave says nothing. That night, Caucus-Meteor sleeps for a few hours. When he wakes, his fire is cold and dark. He can hear a whisper. For a moment he thinks that Jesus has come from the beyond to punish him more, but it's only the sound of his slave praying.

"Nathan?" he calls. No answer. "Nathan?"

"Yes, master."

"Get me some fire," says Caucus-Meteor.

"Yes, master."

He hears Nathan shuffle by; he can smell Nathan's disappointment exuding from his armpits. Caucus-Meteor cocks his ears at the open flap of his wigwam while his slave sifts through the ashes of the communal fire of the village until he finds some coals. He returns, carrying the coals on a couple of sticks. Caucus-Meteor opens the flap to the smoke hole on the wigwam and builds a small fire. He's sorry he can't see the fire, but at least he can feel its heat, listen to its peculiar language, and smell the burn. For a long time neither man speaks. Finally, Caucus-Meteor says, "I heard you praying; what did your prayers bring you?"

"You can enslave my body, old king, even my will, but there is a part of me you cannot own," says Nathan.

"I'm delighted," says Caucus-Meteor, "for already, you are thinking like an American. You have made great progress. See that you don't enslave that secret part of yourself. Myself, I have no desire to enslave it. I am merely curious to know it, and perhaps learn from it."

Slave

Weeks go by; it's June. By now the men should have departed on their trade missions, but some contagion in the air prevents any activity. Nobody moves. Like the men, the women too are unsettled, sullen, watchful. The people of Conissadawaga are waiting for the crisis that follows the crisis. Only the old king knows the true nature of the contagion, for he has created it with his illness. With a mix of smugness and sadness, he calculates that his people believe that the new crisis will be his death. Caucus-Meteor is not so sure his demise is imminent. He wasn't quite sick enough for enlightenment. A little sicker and he might have been able to use the powers of delirium to move a little closer to Keeps-the-Flame, his mother, his father, those countless ancestors he'd be pleased to meet in the great circle. He's waiting for a visit from the God of Opportunity, who hides behind the stone face of a moment.

His slave brings him to his toilet, prepares and presents his food and fire, listens to his speeches; such dependence is instructively humiliating. "We share not only our food and lodging," he tells Nathan, "but a common condition, for we are both piteous creatures. You've acquired the habits of an old man, getting through the day with prayer and mind-drift. The difference is I will not get over my old age, but you may one day rise out of your slavery." This speech is the best he can do by way of giving his slave hope.

Every night the Americans meet around a campfire to drink, dance, converse, laugh. But the night before the first trade mission is set to depart, they're somber. Caucus-Meteor hears a buzz among the people. He thinks: if I could see I would see the moment sparkle. "What is it? What's happening out there?" he asks his slave.

"It's Black Dirt—she's going to speak," Nathan says.

"This is news indeed. Bring me outside."

Black Dirt really doesn't like the circle. She's not a speech maker, nor is she impressed by speech makers. But since the people have elected her as a sub-chief, she must realize she has to reveal her feelings. Perhaps she will disown me, thinks the old king. I hope so, because then I really would be free to die.

Caucus-Meteor's sensibilities as an orator are offended when Black Dirt launches too quickly into the substance of her speech. He wants to tell her that it's not earth but air that people breathe.

"I'm haunted by a belief that something is not right with this village," she says, speaking not in oratorical tones, but softly and intimately, as if to a loved one. "My father tells me that my grief is affecting my judgment, and he may be correct. But I must speak, and leave it up to you to decide. I have come to the circle to ask the traders to purchase some stock for the village—a cow, a couple of piglets, chickens, maybe even a horse or an ox to pull a plow."

Everybody knows the meaning behind Black Dirt's request. Right now the tribe is nomadic, in the tradition of the northern Algonkian peoples, hunter-gatherers who abandon the summer farming village for hunting camps in the hills in the fall. Black Dirt wants the tribe to settle permanently in this, the summer village of Conissadawaga.

Passaconway, another of the chiefs established when Caucus-Meteor fell ill, supports Black Dirt, but then he undermines the idea by launching into a disorganized speech about days gone by.

Caucus-Meteor doesn't know whether to be amused or appalled by his friend's oratorical ineptitude.

"The crowd respects the old athlete for his accomplishments in youth, but they'd just as soon he'd quiet down," he whispers to Nathan.

Katahdin steps into the circle. She "honors" her "sister" Black Dirt, but thinks she's gone too far. "The Conissadawaga Americans are not a people defeated in battle, like the Hurons of Wendake, and not a people seduced by mission gods, like the Algonkians of Odanak or the Iroquois of Kahnawake. We are the only true American people remaining on the St. Lawrence river. If we are to remain American, we must think, act, and feel like Americans. Livestock will imprison us on the shores of this lake, where the wind blows cold in the winter. Buying livestock will be the beginning of our downfall."

Caucus-Meteor tells Nathan, "Now, that's more like a speech. It has authority, passion, and exaggeration. And it doesn't hurt that the king agrees with the sentiment."

A couple of men make short, impassioned pleas.

"What are they saying?" asks Nathan, for he values their opinions over those of the women.

"It all amounts to the same thing: soon the women will want us to pull plows like French peasants. They're afraid to think deeply on the matter."

Caucus-Meteor summarizes the debate, in part for Nathan's benefit and in part so that he himself can better calculate the situation. Several women, upset by the dismissive attitude of the men, speak in favor of buying livestock. Sentiment for a permanent village seems to be taking shape. The villagers are tired of living poor; they're envious of the other réfugié towns that have log cabins, meeting houses, churches. Nearly all the men are opposed, but most of the women are in favor, and since women outnumber men, Black Dirt's proposal has a good chance of being adopted. Caucus-Meteor is proud of his daughter's powers, but he opposes her ideas. He's not quite sure what to do.

Norman Feathers steps into the circle. His speech is brief. "We have no barns, no feed. I am the most experienced among you in dealing with large animal husbandry, and I am just now learning the skills of the keepers." Norman goes on to support Black Dirt, but he's unintentionally sounded an alarm. The villagers are thinking that no one knows how to go about the purchase and upkeep of farm animals. It's at this moment of weakness that Haggis steps into the circle.

"What excellent timing he has," Caucus-Meteor says in admiration.

"We are poor not because we are nomads," Haggis says. "We are poor because we pay the intendant tribute. I say we leave Conissadawaga after the fall harvest. We will go north by sled, stay in the Cree village where three of my wives have family. We will live like the Americans of old, free to hunt and fish and trap, free from the confinement imposed by farm life and French law. We will follow the beaver, the caribou, the salmon, the seal, the whale, the bear."

Most of the men cheer and chant in exuberance.

Black Dirt enters the circle and stands beside Haggis. "The nomadic life appeals to the wild in heart. The ones who die in battle. The ones who starve in winter. My dream for the future of Conissadawaga removes the wildness, this I admit, and regret the loss. But we must plan for our children. We must fold the notions of the French, the English, the Dutch into our own behavior, or our children will die in the cold."

"There, Nathan Blake—I don't agree with my daughter, but I do admire her speech very much."

The speeches go on, and a mood of fear and desolation grips the villagers. For the first time they understand how divided they are. It begins to look like the Americans are going to split into two groups and go their separate ways. Out of this confusion a raspy voice shouts in English, "Where is my slave?"

Actually, Caucus-Meteor knows that Nathan is standing right beside him—he can smell him—but he needs a device to attract attention. He's had enough of listening to others; the time has arrived for real oration. He reaches out for his slave's hand.

Nathan leads the old deposed king into the light of the camp-fire. Caucus-Meteor knows the effect he must be having on his villagers. He's seen old men who have survived shocks, and he knows what they look like. With his paralyzed face, his skin greased and blackened by close proximity to his fire, a rank, sour odor emanating from his pores, he must look and smell like a smoked man. But the turban on his head will remind them that he is still their king.

"Listen, my children," he says. "When I was a young slave in training in Paris of Old France, my teacher, who was a gap-toothed and aged priest with a reputation for touching that which a priest is forbidden to touch, read to me a translation of my father's oratory delivered to the English before his fateful war." The old king speaks each phrase clearly and musically. "I memorized those words, and I want you to hear them now."

Caucus-Meteor delivers the speech of King Philip. "'The English who first came to this country were but a handful of people. My father was then sachem; he relieved their distress in the most kind and hospitable manner. He gave them land to plant and build upon . . . they flourished and increased. By various means they got possession of a great part of his territory. But he still remained their friend until he died. My elder brother became sachem . . . He was seized and confined and thereby thrown into illness and died. Soon after I became sachem they disarmed all my people . . . their land was taken. But a small part of the dominion of my ancestors remains.'" Caucus-Meteor changes his tone from formal to intimate. "My father was speaking of the land in New England which was called Mount Hope. My father ended his speech with the words, 'I am determined not to live until I have no country.'"

Caucus-Meteor pauses to let the words find a proper resting place, and then he continues with his own speech. "Sequestered in my wigwam, eating my fire, recovering from an illness brought on, I am sure, by the priests who stole my daughter, I have been praying to my father. I called to his spirit and said, 'Father, I have no country, I have never had a country. I have, however, this small dominion, this village of reprobates. May the old disgraced American gods and may Jesus and his followers bless them. My dominion is on the brink of annihilation. The people have pushed me aside, and elected three sub-chiefs. Passaconway is a noble person, but he cannot lead because he has no will for the enterprise, and I, a blind man, have more vision. My daughter, Black Dirt, is a true leader. She would see us as herdsmen and tillers of the soil. If my people do as she says and buy a goat or two, buy a cow, our children soon will be talking and behaving like Frenchmen, praying to the French Jesus. Every wigwam will have an intendant's man outside. The children will not know their mothers and fathers as Americans, and their mothers and fathers will not know their children as Americans. Haggis is also a true leader and a true American. But he's a well-meaning fool, who would take the people back to the drifting, wandering days of winter starvation.'

"All these things I prayed to my father. I also admitted that I too have been a fool. I invited the priests to come to the village, not knowing they would steal my daughter. I also made a rash pact with a childish nobleman that one day may come back to trouble this tribe. But that is all to come. After admitting my faults, I asked my father: What should I do? Take my people into conflict with the French? Withdraw to the north? Sit and farm? Seek more tribute for the intendant? Kill Haggis? Kidnap my daughter from the priests? Succumb to my fatigue and illness? I called out, 'Help me, father.' I listened in my heart for my father's advice, but he did not respond to my prayer. King Philip stayed dead and quiet. My father was denied speech in the afterworld because Cotton Mather ripped the jaw from his skull before it was raised on a pole in Plymouth town. I have thought about this matter for a long time, for a blind man has the leisure to think—how lucky I was to lose my sight. I have learned in my thinking that if I were purer in heart, I might encourage the gods to let my father speak once again. Surely, my father was pure.

"My father became sachem only after his brother died; my father went to war out of desperation for the future of his people, not for personal honors. I can claim no such noble motives. I have always been sick with ambition. I am less worried about you villagers than I am about my own position among you. I gave you everything I own in return for your admiration and the surrender of your will to my own. I have not taken my demotion well. I believe that even blind, dependent on the slave Nathan Blake, I can lead you better than Passaconway, Haggis, and even my beloved daughter, Black Dirt. My children . . . my children . . ."—Caucus-Meteor's voice drifts off in the foggy ocean of forgetfulness of an old man, then returns to the pier: "my children I would be king not only of Conissadawaga but of Canada, and of the lands south, I would be king of America, and my father would speak my lost boyhood name, if only . . . if only I were pure."

Suddenly the old king is exhausted, a little befuddled, unable to conclude his speech. He bows his head, turns. Nathan takes his hand, and slave and master walk into the darkness toward the wigwam.

After an hour in which he can neither sleep nor concentrate on events in the waking world, Caucus-Meteor comes again to his senses. It's not until the next day, though, that he learns that after he spoke no one said a word. The circle broke up and the people returned to their wigwams.

"What does it mean?" asks Nathan.

"It means that by confessing the secret sin of my ambition, I've regained some authority. The people know that the struggle for the soul of the tribe between Black Dirt and Haggis is over for the time being with neither side emerging as the victor. But the discord everyone sensed but never talked about until this night is now in the open."

In the days that follow, the men set forth in their canoes to trade the village's products. Staying behind are the old men, who fish the lake and streams, the women, who work the fields with the help of their slave, Nathan Blake, and the children, who also are put to work. Their task is to act as human scarecrows, chasing the birds that would feast on the crops.

The short Canadian summer flies by in more ways than one. The biggest excitement occurs around the fourth of July when a flock of passenger pigeons fifteen miles long and a mile wide passes through Conissadawaga. The birds blot the sun and darken the sky. With sticks and nets and muskets and arrows and spears, the villagers slaughter far more birds than they can eat, but they don't make an impression in the flock.

By now Caucus-Meteor can see light and shadow, and the birds are shadow. After they've gone he announces that the light has returned, and in the feasting that follows the pigeon kill, he holds up one of the small sleek pigeons, and makes a short speech. "This little fellow is our national bird. Long after the red people have been wiped out by the white people, long after the white people have been wiped out by the black people, long after the blue people of the northern tropics have wiped out the black people, long after the gods have wiped color from human skin, wiped color from the human heart, this pigeon will remain to honor us all as one nation."

Caucus-Meteor's health improves dramatically during the warm weather. The paralysis in his face disappears. Day by day he sees more light, then objects, and finally motion. When the trade missions come drifting back before harvest time, he can distinguish faces and make his way without having to hold Nathan's hand. However, he is still physically weak, and spends most of his hours by his fire. Even so, his presence in the community is greater than ever. It used to be that he went to his people, offering advice or largess in return for their cooperation.

Now they come to him. By the vote of his subjects, he's no longer king. But in reality, he's retaken the reins of power in the village. The ferocious beast of his ambition gnaws at him. How can he keep his hold on the village when the traders come back?

Upon his return to Conissadawaga, Haggis learns that two of his wives are three months pregnant, great cause for rejoicing. He took his trade mission north to Tadousic and beyond on the Saguenay. He traded moccasins for furs, which he then traded in Quebec for household items demanded by his wives. In the north he met with his Cree relatives, learning more about territory where the hunting and trapping were good and where his people would be accepted. Haggis is clear in his mission: persuade the people of Conissadawaga to move north. When he comes to visit the old king for a talk, Caucus-Meteor guesses that for once they're both thinking along the same lines.

"With winter, a year will have passed since the epidemic that decimated our people," Haggis says, speaking very formally. "Black Dirt's official mourning period will come to an end. In the spring, I would like to marry her, make her pregnant, and through our child unite the tribe."

Caucus-Meteor does some quick thinking. Haggis believes that, with Black Dirt under his control, the village will make him sole chief, perhaps even king. But as a son-in-law, he might find himself more an heir to the throne than the resident of the seat. By continuing their power struggle within a joined clan, there will be less chance that the village will be divided. Caucus-Meteor concludes it's best to keep the villagers together, even if it means that in the end Haggis will have his way and move the people north.

"I will not stand in your way, but neither will I influence my daughter's decision," Caucus-Meteor says.

The men part, both knowing they are gambling on the pre-eminence of their own respective characters.

❦

All during the summer Caucus-Meteor plays host to visiting tribes from all over Canada—traders, relatives, pilgrims, travelers. In casual conversations, Caucus-Meteor brings up the subject of Canada for Canadians, thus fulfilling his obligation to St. Blein. In late September, after the men have returned and the women are hard at work with the harvest, St. Blein, looking dapper and handsome as ever, arrives with several soldiers and the voyageur Robert de Repentigny. The ensign is still fearless and fresh-faced, committed to revolution. Caucus-Meteor thinks: such an idiot, I admire him very much.

De Repentigny pays Black Dirt a visit. The old American watches them walk down to the stone ruins, the tall, stately woman and the short, common man. It was Robert's father who tried to make something out of this land, but it was too much for him and, after he and his wife died of disease brought on by hardship, the local natives took over the land and later sold it to Caucus-Meteor. Robert de Repentigny was Black Dirt's first lover, and the two of them are still friends.

Back at Caucus-Meteor's wigwam, the old chief parleys with the young ensign.

"I don't think Americans wish to involve themselves in a fight between Paris and Canada Frenchmen, because they won't see anything in it for them," says Caucus-Meteor.

"We must teach them, Caucus-Meteor," says St. Blein.

"My vision is weak, but I can see the stars in your eyes."

"We must teach them," St. Blein repeats in a passionate whisper.

"We must teach them? We?"

"All right—me. I will teach them." St. Blein bursts into laughter at his little act of vanity.

He's a charmer, thinks Caucus-Meteor. Maybe he really can change the New World. Maybe charm is the main requirement for leadership. "After your revolution, you will need an American king to unite the tribes."

"I hadn't thought of that."

"I will be the king of Canada and New England, for in your revolution you might as well grab the disputed territory to the south. I wish to rule from Mount Hope Bay, where my ancestors lived for generations."

"You are teasing me again, Caucus-Meteor."

"I'm an old man recovering from a shock. I have nothing else to do but tease a Frenchman with crazy ideas."

St. Blein smiles without mirth. Caucus-Meteor has accomplished his objective. St. Blein is unsure whether Conissadawaga will side with him or not in his war. For the time being, he has more mundane matters to deal with, Caucus-Meteor knows. In his role as a soldier for Canada, St. Blein is recruiting fighters for more raids on the New England border lands. "I would like to recommend one of our young men for your army," says Caucus-Meteor.

When the French canoes leave, they have one extra passenger. Against Haggis's wishes, Wolf Eyes has joined the army. Caucus-Meteor claims a great victory over his rival. All of Haggis's other children are too young to pose a threat to Caucus-Meteor, but Wolf Eyes had come of age. If he and his father had made peace, together they would have enough followers to lead the village.

A week later a half dozen Huron mercenaries from Wendake and another Frenchman in civilian garb come to Caucus-Meteor's wigwam. Caucus-Meteor doesn't require sight to recognize the man; he knows him by the smell of his perfume. It's the intendant's man. The rent has been raised again. The intendant expects tribute next spring, and also the following fall. Caucus-Meteor thinks the intendant has gotten wind that he's a sympathizer with rebellious elements in the Canadian army. Caucus-Meteor has no idea how he's going to raise the funds to pay in spring and fall. Probably he'll have to sell his services to the military again and go to war as an interpreter. Where will he find the energy? Maybe he should succumb to Haggis's dream and go north. Or try to yoke his village to another réfugié tribe; maybe the Hurons would take them in. Or simply stay put, but defy the intendant and see what happens. Caucus-Meteor suffers all these worries alone. He has no one to confide in. Now that his health has improved, he feels only the gnawing hound of his ambition. He acknowledges to himself that he more than deserves the terrible loneliness that goes with a scheming mentality.

The harvest season is an even busier time of year for the women than the spring and the summer. Squashes stored in cool, dry stone cellars will keep into the winter. Corn is dried, then stone-ground by hand. Beans are hung on racks. Green vegetables are devoured throughout the season as they are picked. The women also make time to forage in the forest for berries, and later nuts from beech, hickory, and oak trees, which are of low quality since this is the northern limit of the nut trees, so every tree lives a stressed existence.

The women break down the summer village and prepare to move to winter quarters in a valley that catches the winter sun on the southern flank of the mountain ten miles away, where firewood has been cut and stacked the winter before. The old bark walls are stripped off the frames of the summer wigwams and burned, a necessary procedure to rid the area of bugs. Nathan tells his master that his people live too close to the earth.

The men move the tribe's belongings across the lake by canoe where they build sleds, using the same steam-box, bend-the-ash technique for the land carriers as for the canoes. After the first snow, men and dogs will pull the tribe's cooking gear, tools, weapons, personal effects, stoves, and stove piping to the winter village. Even Haggis will admit that the French brought one useful skill to Canada, a refinement of metal-working to make guns, steel axes, and iron stoves.

The fall hunt in November is Haggis's season to demonstrate his talents and largess. He's not only a skilled marksman with a musket and bow and arrow, he's a master tracker and organizer of hunts. He sends out parties of hunters, telling them where they'll find game, how best to bring down the animals. He's almost always right. Some men whisper that the same sorcery he uses to mesmerize women he also employs to locate game. But Caucus-Meteor understands that Haggis uses no tricks, and makes no contracts with dark forces. He just pays attention. During free time throughout the year while other men primp themselves, drink brandy, or gossip, Haggis goes off in the woods by himself. He's gone sometimes for days. Another man might go into the wilderness to pray or to meditate or to examine himself or his beliefs, or to mull over a problem, or just to enjoy the outdoors and solitude; Haggis goes to educate himself. He studies plants, animals, insects, rocks, birds, soil, scrapings, tracks, broken twigs, droppings, the effects of rot, and so forth. He studies with all his senses. He'll stop abruptly before a clump of disturbed grass, stick his nose in and smell it, touch it to test its texture and moisture content, and finally taste it. He'll think: an owl dropped onto an unsuspecting mouse here last night. Caucus-Meteor thinks: if only I could bring down a deer with oratory.

Haggis's purpose is to locate and dispatch animals that his tribe can use for food, clothing, medicine, and trade. By hunting season, Haggis has done ninety percent of the work of the hunter, for he knows where the animals are, their food sources, their habits, the state of their health, the quality of their vigilance. Just as Caucus-Meteor gave away all his money and belongings, Haggis will give away the game he kills. When he's finished, the tribe's larder will be well stocked with meat, but Haggis himself will have neither a trophy head nor personal food store to call his own. Haggis doesn't know it, thinks Caucus-Meteor, but we are kin both in our vices and our virtues.

Through the summer and fall, the slave lives and breathes and labors by the whims of his master, acting as his companion, launderer, cook, and valet. In Nathan's experience, Caucus-Meteor sees a mirror of his own as a slave. Physically, emotionally, and spiritually Nathan lives a marginal existence. He has enough to eat, though often he has to ask for food. His only entertainment is an occasional handout of brandy dispensed by a generous (drunk) villager. Together he and Caucus-Meteor are the poorest members of the tribe with not even a stove to keep them warm. By the time winter sets in, Nathan has earned the small admiration accorded to a good slave. The villagers like his work habits; they like his strength and health; they like that he's not a complainer. They never think about him. Only I think about him, the old king reflects. I am beginning to love my slave like a son. I must conceal my affection, lest he take advantages. And with that thought an idea grabs hold of him. Perhaps his own master really did love him. And what of it? What if the master does love the slave? Suddenly, the old man feels weak and needy, as he did as a boy slave, desperate for the love of his master. The love within slavery is terrible, terrible, he thinks, for it contains the implements to kill both lovers.

He remembers now that his master was convinced that his slave possessed magical powers, for his facility with languages. Now Caucus-Meteor has grown convinced that his own slave also possesses gifts outside his realm. Sometimes late at night Nathan calls out in his sleep, using English words that Caucus-Meteor is unfamiliar with, words such as chalk lines, gimlet, twybil, and scorp. These words are accompanied by mumbled numbers, and moans of exasperation. Even when he is awake, Nathan's lips move, whispering these strange incantations. His own master used to fear that Caucus-Meteor would kill him out of the spite inherent in his slave condition. Now Caucus-Meteor is thinking that Nathan might overcome his pacifism and kill him. The idea that he might be murdered by his slave turns his mood from gloomy to cheerful. All of his vanities would vanish, and he'd be spared the difficulty of fashioning a reuniting ceremony with the heavenly hosts. But it doesn't happen—Nathan Blake shows no sign of impending violence, just as he himself never thought seriously of killing his master. So what in lieu of rebellion or surrender can the slave do? Caucus-Meteor determines that Nathan Blake has an escape plan, just as he himself did—an escape of mind alone. If I could reach into him for some of that magic, he thinks, if I could join it with the old magic that was within me that perhaps only my master saw, I might yet be the king of North America.

In early November, the tribe moves into winter quarters, a narrow valley in the hills by a brook. The area is chosen because it's near the deer yards; it's protected from north winds; and it's in the middle of a stand of maple trees, which the American women will tap for sugar late in the season. The winter wigwams are designed like the summer wigwams, except they have insulation of bunch-grass and moss between the bark layers. The big fear in the winter is fire. An ember escaping through an iron chimney sticking out of the smoke hole can ignite the bark roofing. Caucus-Meteor and Nathan move into Black Dirt's small winter wigwam. The villagers try to do as much as they can outdoors, even in the winter, but often the weather drives them into their cramped dwelling units, which are warm but dark. More than the cold and the storminess, it's the darkness of winter that rubs nerves raw. Even so the old American feels ennobled by the darkness, and it's all he can do to hide his disapproval of his daughter's use of candles.

A few days before the St. Lawrence river ices over, Omer and Hungry Heart Laurent arrive in the winter village. As promised, Omer gives money to Caucus-Meteor to be used toward the spring tribute for the intendant, then he and Hungry Heart give away their summer earnings to the rest of the tribe. Caucus-Meteor can tell by their impatience and lack of humility that they do not possess true largess. One day as Omer approaches, Caucus-Meteor says to Nathan, "No doubt the Laurents are hoarding much of their money. They live by the snake tails of guilt and exuberance. Watch how Omer's guilt hinders his happiness." Caucus-Meteor tells Omer he loves and admires him. Omer turns ashen. After Omer leaves, Caucus-Meteor says to Nathan, "Only the river will save Omer."

The men set out on the fall hunt. Though it's obvious he has no taste for hunting, Nathan is bitter and resentful to be left behind with women, children, and old men. Caucus-Meteor is amused; his slave might have some magic in him, but he's still a man. Black Dirt stitches moccasins, absorbed in her work. Caucus-Meteor misses his open fire, but he huddles by the stove and rambles. He talks in Algonkian, and by now Nathan can understand as well as converse in the language.

"We hunt in the northern Algonkian tradition," Caucus-Meteor says. "Only one-quarter of our territory is used per year, leaving the other three-quarters to replenish the game. Since the land is hunted only once every four years, the animals forget the hunters. The game will be skinned, cleaned, quartered, and strung up high in trees to keep them out of reach of wolves and bears. Some of the meat will be smoked, and some will be preserved by the gods of cold. After the men return from the hunt, they'll run trap lines, fuss with their weapons and tools, and discuss grave matters relating to war, hunting, fishing, and the training of dogs. Our women will make moccasins. Late in the season after the snows have fallen, settled, melted, frozen into a hard crust, imprisoning weakened deer and moose in their winter yards, the men will go out on the winter hunt, which will be followed by the midwinter festival. Later in the season, the women will tap the maple trees, boil down the sap to sugar. Come spring half the tribe will go north to a stream for the salmon run, while the other half breaks down the winter village and sets up the summer village along the lake."

Black Dirt remains quiet, removed. It's as if her physical being is in the wigwam, but her soul is elsewhere. She's in the last and most intense period of her mourning, though she never complains. Her father attempts through conjuring to absorb her suffering, but he cannot. His own pain—loss of physical powers, loss of influence, loss of loved ones—is good, for it makes him a little bit humble, which is accompanied by a little bit of contentment, but the pain within his daughter is unbearable.

It's because of her pain that he decides he can no longer live with her; accordingly, he devises a new method of suicide.

One day at the evening meal, the king says to Nathan, "I have good news for you. You and I are leaving this place. We have a saying: young men hunt, old men fish. Black Dirt needs privacy in these last days of her public grief. You and I will leave the winter village. We will camp on the ice, and fish in the lake. Periodically, you will bring the catch to the village in the hills. I do not want to be a burden on my people. With your help, I will contribute something to our necessities."

"Father, you will sicken living by the lake where the wind makes it colder than here in the hills," Black Dirt says, and then switches to Iroquois because she knows Nathan cannot understand that language. "Your slave might kill you and try to escape."

"In his own way Nathan is a mighty man, but he doesn't have it in him to kill—it is part of his frustration."

Nathan hears his name used and cocks an ear.

"Father, I cannot let you leave," Black Dirt says.

"You have my pride and my life in your hands. Which do you think is more important to me?"

Black Dirt turns away from him, and moves to the edge of the wigwam for privacy. "We'll leave in the morning," Caucus-Meteor addresses Nathan in Algonkian.

Later that night, for the first time since they've relocated to the winter village, Black Dirt asks to see Nathan alone. Caucus-Meteor accedes to her request and they leave the wigwam and are gone long enough that Caucus-Meteor has to replenish his fire. While he's alone Caucus-Meteor attempts to move his mind outside the wigwam so that he can eavesdrop upon his daughter and slave. But he's too healthy right now for such tricks and his efforts fail.

At dawn when they're preparing to leave, Caucus-Meteor asks Nathan what his daughter said to him.

"She held a knife under my chin," Nathan says. "She said, 'My father believes that you are incapable of murder. I am not.'"

"What did you say to her?"

"I took her hand, the one not holding the knife, and I held it against my heart. She felt it beating, and stalked away."

Nathan and Caucus-Meteor leave the winter wigwam in the protected valley in the hills and return to the lake where the wind blows hard and cold. Nathan and Caucus-Meteor live huddled in a hide shelter by an open fire by the lake. It's a miserable and chilling existence, chipping ice with an iron bar, checking tip-ups, crawling into a cold, smoky hut. Nathan lugs Caucus-Meteor and the first shipment of fish ten miles by sled to the village. They take a meal at Black Dirt's wigwam, then with Black Dirt visit Haggis and his huge family and followers in their long house. Haggis, returned triumphant from the fall hunt, is in a good mood; he takes a few moments to pay his respects to Black Dirt. He tells her that though they are adversaries, he has great admiration for her.

"And I admire a man who can hunt and bring food to the cooking pot," she says, mouthing an old Algonkian saying.

Haggis nods and continues the polite conversation by addressing Caucus-Meteor. "How do you like it by the lake?"

"It is stimulating—I think I would be eternally content if only the winter did not give way to the spring," lies Caucus-Meteor.

"And the slave, how does he like it?" Haggis asks.

Something about Haggis's tone, taunting and superior and insincere, does something to change Nathan's demeanor. Caucus-Meteor watches carefully. He's less interested in the outcome of the drama about to transpire than in its process.

"My master and I cannot go on like this through the winter," Nathan says. "After a storm or two, we will freeze in the cold."

"Like most slaves, he is timid and exaggerates," says Caucus-Meteor.

"He doesn't sound timid to me. He sounds insolent. I think he wants you to beat him, for the English beat their slaves as well as their children. Beat him so he can feel at home."

"Give me an axe," Nathan says softly insistent, looking Haggis in the eye.

"The Englishman speaks our language now, but does he understand what he is saying?" Haggis says with a mocking grin.

"With an axe I can build a proper shelter for Caucus-Meteor and myself," Nathan says.

Haggis turns to Caucus-Meteor. "Do you want an axe?"

"We have no need of an axe. I am perfectly comfortable."

"The old man will freeze to death," Nathan says.

"If we give him an axe, he will kill Caucus-Meteor and escape," says Kineo.

"My people, your concern for me is flattering and touching," says Caucus-Meteor. "I am not worthy of it."

"I could have killed Caucus-Meteor a hundred times over." Nathan says in a low voice that can only be heard by Haggis and Caucus-Meteor.

"But not with an axe," says Haggis. "A man without an axe in hand is less likely to be tempted than one with."

"Let us test it," Caucus-Meteor whispers.

Haggis rises, goes outside, comes back with an axe. "Here, we will see," he says, loud now so everyone can hear.

Nathan picks up the axe, holds it up and down with arm extended. His hand is rock steady, though his lips tremble and something like love crosses his face.

"Too bad he can't embrace a musket with the same ardor," says Haggis to his followers.

Nathan looks over the axe, runs his fingers along the edge. He frowns. Before setting out for the lake, Nathan grinds down the axe and sharpens it. He's watched closely as he works. "By Jove, I'll show these savages what an Englishman can do," he mutters in English so slurred that only Caucus-Meteor understands. The deposed king laughs. Out of the corner of his eye, he catches sight of Black Dirt watching Nathan grind the axe. Her revulsion for the slave has been replaced by dim curiosity.

Later that day, at the lake, Caucus-Meteor stands with blankets wrapped around him and watches while his slave works. Nathan chops down some black spruce trees growing along the shore. He cuts trees only six inches or less in diameter. "If I had my ox to pull logs, I could cut bigger trees, and you'd have a more spacious structure," he says.

"It's better you don't make it too good," Caucus-Meteor says. "A king should not live ostentatiously."

Nathan builds an eight-foot square log house on the ice. He splits the logs with hardwood gluts, notches the ends with the axe, stacks them. Caucus-Meteor helps by chinking between the logs with moss. On the third day, Black Dirt shows up in a sled pulled by half a dozen dogs. She watches for a while, and without a word leaves by sled. She's back the next day with pieces of iron on the sled and some French blankets and skins for floor covering and a door flap. "Can you use this iron to make a stove?" she says.

"Yes. Can you get me a pipe to vent the smoke?"

"I will try."

Next day she's back with iron pipe and some firewood.

While Nathan builds, Caucus-Meteor watches through eyes whose vision improves day by day; Black Dirt gathers the lower dead branches of spruce trees to add to the store of dry firewood. The old lake man soon loses interest in the building activity, and turns his attention to more important matters. Another failed attempt at dying. It's obvious that he's not trying hard enough. He's only playing with death, but what's wrong with that? Death plays with a man, so shouldn't a man play with death? Listen, Death, I have the advantage in this wager. I have nothing to lose but my life, which you have already won anyway. I feel sorry for these loved ones, Black Dirt, my dear daughter, and Nathan, whom I have grown to love like a son. They are trying to keep me alive, Black Dirt out of the duty of love and Nathan for reasons mysterious to me and perhaps more mysterious to him.

Nathan makes the shed roof with poles covered with split logs and birch bark. Bowlegged on snowshoes, Norman Feathers arrives with a piece of glass from Quebec. He's returned from church worship, walked many miles over hill, through frozen swamp, with the glass. "Now you will have some light, and I will pray for you," he says. Norman and Black Dirt leave by dogsled under an ugly, glowering sky. That night a howling blizzard maroons all living creatures in the St. Lawrence valley. Nathan and Caucus-Meteor are warm.

"A stove fire is not a fire a man can eat, but it nourishes nonetheless; I can barely see fire through the cracks in the iron, but the sound is interesting—I will listen," says Caucus-Meteor. Caucus-Meteor has decided that this winter is proving too interesting for him to make any more attempts at suicide.

The old American and his slave spend the winter on the ice. They chip out holes all over the lake and even inside the cabin itself to catch trout, pike, and yellow perch. Fishing is a twenty-four-hour activity, but the work is enjoyable for the Conissadawaga ice fishermen, and they don't have to haul fish to the village. Black Dirt and Norman Feathers spread the word, and once a week a villager or two, usually with a child present, brought along for educational purposes, arrives with a sled and dogs to view the Englishman's log house on the ice and to bring the frozen catch back to the village. And so the season passes. At one time or another every American in the tribe makes the journey to the lake.

The old American reflects on this particular winter experience, time for reflection being the great gift of winter. Never has he been in a position to wield so little power, and never has he been so content. Usually he and Nathan work in silence, and when they aren't working they are also silent, listening to the weather or to their own thoughts. But every once in a while, when they are eating (corn and fish, or beans and fish, or corn and beans, or corn and venison, all of it boiled in a single pot, served in wooden bowls, eaten with spoons carved from birch), and outside a storm rages, making them both feel lonesome and small but also snug and smug (because of all of God's creatures, only they have a fire), they talk. It's not the talk of old, however, for English has given way to Algonkian. Caucus-Meteor notes that Nathan seems to enjoy conversing in the language, musical and direct, in which a notion must be felt as much from the expressiveness of the speaker as the shared understanding of the meaning of words.

"Nathan, what does the English word *sill* mean?" asks Caucus-Meteor, as the men sit around the makeshift stove, propped on sticks in the shanty.

"It is a beam that rests on a foundation upon which the remainder of the house is built. Where in your travels did you find that word, master?"

"Not in my travels, but in yours. In your sleep. Your dreams sound a little to me like your prayers, but the words are different. Times are I think you are a sorcerer, for you speak words such as sill with incantation."

"Nay, I am only a common man."

"Common in the head, yes, but in the hands you are a sorcerer. The barn we burned, the cabin we burned—you built those places less out of need than enjoyment. You built the first log cabin in Upper Ashuelot. You built the barn and back door where you hoped to escape, and where I cornered you. You built whimsy doodles for your children. You built this shanty to save an old man from freezing to death. Nathan, why was your barn bigger and grander than your house?"

The question unaccountably upsets Nathan Blake. A flood of emotion envelopes his face. He says nothing. Caucus-Meteor inspects his eyes. "You are full of shame and magic, Nathan Blake. How can a question regarding a barn fill a man with shame and magic?"

"I wish to speak no further on this matter." And he turns his head away for privacy.

Days later Nathan Blake pours out the story to Caucus-Meteor. "I keep myself from falling into madness by building my wife's imagined house in my thoughts."

"So there's no magic in you," says Caucus-Meteor. "It is only memory and prayer and sheer loneliness. Tell me now what you think."

"I think about sills, placing them on good stone sunk deep into the ground for a structure not to be upset by frost. I think about the pleasures of using a good, sharp chisel. I think about the triumph of a square saw cut all the way through a piece of pine. At the approximate location of the four corners of the basement site, I pound wooden stakes into the ground with a maul made of a maple branch with a burl for the hammer end. Run tight lines from stake to stake. Level the lines."

"The labor of mind brings some satisfaction. You wish now to shout from the tops of the wigwams that unlike the savage who enslaves him Nathan Blake believes in Jesus Christ, and he believes in . . . what is the language for straight boards?"

"Plumb, square, and level," Nathan says in English.

"And, surely, too, you think of heaven."

"Yes, I think of heaven, to soothe me during this hellish experience. The earth may be a rank and wild place, fit only for savages, but in my reckoning, heaven is well laid out with a good stone foundation and squared corners."

Nathan stops talking, exhausted by emotion. "Congratulations, Nathan Blake. You are becoming less of an Englishman and more of an American, for you are expressing yourself through oratory rather than actions. But your tale is unfinished. The other day you spoke to me of shame. Where is the shame?"

"The shame is double. The house was never built. I brought my Elizabeth to a log cabin, but I promised to build her a house. But the barn came first. You see, master, in my heart of hearts I have never wanted that house to be built in New England, or in any known realm at all. I dreamed of a place I called Paradise Lots, a farm town where the only vote was mine."

"And in these paradise lots were women for the having, but no wife to scold, no family to tie you down."

"Aye," says Nathan in English.

"You speak as if your shame is large and unique. But you are like men anywhere, unreliable in the things you say to a woman, and imaginative in the things you truly desire. You are possessed by these thoughts today because of your slave condition. I suggest you reduce the size of your shame to its proper proportion. Let us move on to a related matter that interests your master. Suppose a great ruler, a king of kings, were suddenly to appear in North America. Could you build him a palace?"

"If I had the tools, the stone, the timbers, a foundry to shape iron, beasts of burden to carry the loads."

"This ruler's palace would be of sticks no thicker than a man's wrist, and none straight."

"Why such inferior material?" Nathan asks.

"Because such is the palace that appears in his dreams. It is like the castles he saw in Europe, but instead of stone laid on stone, his castle is a wigwam of bark and sticks that goes on forever. It is a house for Americans."

"I think you know this ruler well."

"He hardly knows himself. But this palace of sticks, could you build it?"

"To build a castle or sticks, a man would need divine guidance."

"When I see you on your knees, Nathan Blake, do you pray to build your own castle to please your demanding wife?"

"Nay, my prayers and my imaginings are a far piece from one another."

"Perhaps that is why the god of echoes does his work. If I had a god as powerful and meddling as yours I would think about him more, and ask him for more favors, for the king of heaven should be heavenly in his largess."

"To use one of your words, Caucus-Meteor, I would think it ostentatious to think about God, and presumptuous to beg favors from him."

"Then why pray?"

"I pray for guidance."

"What you really mean is you don't know what to think about when you do think about god, nor what you should ask for or how. Your prayers, therefore, are worship without purpose. God must think you a comical creation indeed. Perhaps it is this knowledge of what god requires of him — so lacking in a man — that is what a man really prays for when he prays for guidance; I suspect your god sees you as you see him, as one looking through a wavy glass pane. Which reminds me of the first time I saw you with your family at the dawn of the raid."

"The glass pane allows light to come through," Nathan says, and then something of his personal loss comes to his face.

"What's the matter, Nathan? What are you thinking?"

"That like you I've suffered a shock, for my mind's eye is blind to my wife. I can no longer picture her."

"That is no shock," says Caucus-Meteor. "That is merely another condition imposed by your slave status. I will picture her for you, for my shock has brought me sight within." The old king takes one of his slave's hands and holds it the way he held his children's hands when they were very young. "Shut your eyes. Your wife had hair like corn silk. Her skin was pale with a blush on the cheeks, and she had little blue eyes full of fright. I suggest that you practice thinking about her mouth as she cups water from a stream in her hand and brings her lips to it."

Now Nathan kneels before his master, who is still holding his hand. The old king recounts in great detail all he can remember of Nathan's family. Soon Nathan's shoulders and chest begin to heave. He is a man weeping with his body. After the moment of intimacy passes between the two men, Caucus-Meteor releases Nathan's hand, and the slave shifts his body position until the two men are sitting across from one another, conversing in a casual manner as if nothing profound had just occurred.

"Old king, what do you think about when you eat your fire?"

"I think about being reunited with my mother and my wife in the next world."

"And what of your father?"

"I revere the memory of my father, but I confess that I cannot think about him. He's too removed from me. I suppose he is to me as your god is to you, a superior being who does not speak."

"My god is not a man, and yet he does speak."

"Words given to prophets for the purposes of instruction are not speech. They are rumor."

Nathan smiles sardonically. "You remind me, old man, a little of Mark Ferry, the hermit of our town."

"Is the hermit a king?"

"The hermit is never a king."

"But the king is always a hermit."

"I never quite understand you, Caucus-Meteor, but I think I trust you, as savages go."

"You would best be more wary."

"You think of me as one who is gullible, then."

"I think of you as a sometime son."

"Then release me from this bondage, father."

Caucus-Meteor mimics Nathan's sardonic smile, but says nothing.

"The tribe assigned me to care for you, but you are healed," Nathan says; "you can care for yourself. You no longer need a slave."

It's minutes before Caucus-Meteor answers, because he has thought so long and hard on this matter with no definite conclusion. "I would give you your freedom, for you deserve freedom, as all men do. But I cannot. I gave you to the tribe. It would take a vote, and they would never let you go."

"You are lying to me, old king."

"I am half-lying—it's the way of a king. The truth is you are too docile, the perfect slave, like the oxen you speak so fondly of."

"Perhaps, but you lie when you say it would take a vote. Caucus-Meteor could release me, and his people would part the water for my walk to Quebec City."

"I could let you go, but I will not."

After that the fishers in the ice hut are silent for a while until

Caucus-Meteor says, "Now you are thinking that maybe you will kill me."

"Yes, that is exactly what I am thinking."

"But you cannot."

"You told me earlier that I was starting to think like one of your own people, so perhaps another day I will find it in myself to murder like a savage."

"If you decide you can kill, I suggest you do it as an Englishman, for your guilt will be less, and when you die, Jesus will be more likely to let you pass into his realm than if you kill me as a savage."

The exact timing of the midwinter hunt is never the same, though it tends to come late in February. Caucus-Meteor watches the weather, trying to guess the right moment, for he's decided to join the hunt this year with his slave. Haggis picks the day of the hunt based on the conditions of snow. Some years the snow is never right, and the hunt can be difficult and unproductive. This is not one of those years; this year promises to be ideal. A warm spell a week before melted the top layer on the deep snow cover. When a hard cold following creates a crust on top of the snow, Caucus-Meteor announces, "We will return to the winter village with the next visitor with a dog team."

They arrive the following day just as the men are about to leave with their weapons and gear—muskets, clubs, bows and arrows, knives, toboggans, dogs, noggins, pemmican, coats, mittens, blanket rolls. They've been waiting for this day for weeks: when the top layer of snow can hold the weight of men and dogs, but not the sharp-hoofed deer or the heavy moose. Sleds pulled by dogs skim the surface nicely.

All able-bodied men will participate in the hunt except for Omer Laurent. Hungry Heart has had a miscarriage, and she is very ill. He will remain in the village to be by her side.

"From what I can tell by the symptoms," Caucus-Meteor tells

Nathan, "I think she probably induced her womb to abort, a trick they teach in Montreal among certain women who cater to the sailors."

Haggis leads the hunters to a narrow gorge where young hemlocks grow, and the steep rock walls block the wind. "How do the hunters know to come here?" Nathan whispers.

"Haggis has been snowshoeing to this deer yard all winter, observing the herd below, letting them observe him, so they are used to his presence," says Caucus-Meteor.

"What is beyond the gorge?" Nathan asks, and Caucus-Meteor can tell from the dreamy look in Nathan's eyes that he's thinking again of his "far place." The old American decides to tease his slave.

"Why, a great river that flows west."

"Really?"

"Who can say in truth what one will find in the west?" Caucus-Meteor says coyly. "I have not been there myself, but I've heard tell of deep soil and tall grasses." The old slave master decides to say no more. He's titillated his slave just enough to keep his mind occupied with pleasing if false matter, which is the best thing a master can do in his own interest with his slaves.

Haggis divides the men into three groups. At one end of the ravine are the beaters. Caucus-Meteor and Nathan are beaters. They start down the ravine whooping and hollering. Behind them are a second group of beaters with dogs. The beaters and dogs panic the moose, which leave their winter home foundering in deep, crusty snow. At the mouth of the ravine awaits the third group, the shooters, led by Haggis himself. Haggis fires his musket, and the slaughter begins. The few animals that slip past the shooters are run down by the dogs, and clubbed to death by the beaters. Not a single animal escapes. The hunt has been a great success.

The real work comes afterward—skinning, gutting, and hacking up all those enormous animals into manageable units for transport on sleds. It's bloody work, and Nathan is in the middle of it. When it's over, Nathan's clothes are stained with blood; his hands sticky with blood; mouths of many of the Americans drip with blood, for they spoon it like a broth.

"Your slave is better with the butcher knife than the gun," says Haggis, in the teasing manner that men reserve for those they respect. "You think, old king, he'll carve you up one of these cold winter nights?"

"He could have filleted me back on the lake, but he doesn't have the heart for human killing." Caucus-Meteor calls to Nathan, who is cutting away the musk glands on a big buck. "Nathan, tell us what our slave thinks of our hunt."

"It's a messier kind of slaughter than I remember for our cows or pigs, though, I will admit, more . . . more . . ." He lacks a word in Algonkian to express his thoughts and goes silent.

"I think he wanted to say more like the pleasures denied those who enter Christian heaven," says Caucus-Meteor.

"And what does the slave's master think about our hunt, for you have not participated in years?" asks Haggis.

"I wanted Nathan to have a taste of it. As for me, let me put it this way. In Nathan Blake's language, the expression he used for our hunt is 'messier,' a word that sounds like the French title for men, messieurs. It is such slaughter—fine butchery work with languages—that nourishes me more than the meat." He might have added that Nathan's nourishment came from his imaginings of what was west of the gorge.

In March Caucus-Meteor and Nathan accompany the women into the sugar bush to tap the maple trees for their sweet sap. Caucus-Meteor gashes the bark with a knife, fastens onto the wound with his mouth to taste the sap.

"Is a light sweetness a favored food for the old king?" Nathan asks.

"This light sweetness is what he does in place of love," Caucus-Meteor says.

The old American names each tree in the sugar bush after

some characteristic of women. He'll say to Nathan, "Go collect from Sister Silver," and Nathan will know to collect sap from a particular tree with a streak of gray bark. Or he'll say, "Let's put another tap into Aunt Anger," for a tree with wind-twist in its trunk. The women who do the real work in this enterprise tolerate the presence of their sometime king, but they wish he would go elsewhere with his advice.

Caucus-Meteor and Nathan remain on the lake through slush and rotted ice until one night in April when the wind shifts. Caucus-Meteor wakes Nathan. "South wind," he says.

"Yes, I can smell it," Nathan says, pulling on his shoes.

"Do you think we should wait until dawn?"

"I think we've waited too long."

"Waiting until danger arrives is always the most interesting way."

They'd hoped to dismantle the logs and drag them off the lake, but there's no time. They save the metal stove parts, the skins, their baskets of personal belongings, and that's all. They reach shore, and minutes later their winter cabin collapses in the frigid water.

With the end of winter, the tribe separates temporarily. The old men and most of the women move out of the winter village and rebuild the summer wigwams over the frames left from last year. Most of the men and the strongest of the women depart for the salmon river. Some will catch fish with crude nets and spears, while others smoke the fish on drying racks. For the first time, Freeway is allowed to go on the salmon run. He's fourteen, practically a man. In another year or two, he'll make decisions about his life. Right now he's not sure if he wants to be a great trader like his father, Seboomook, a great hunter like Haggis, or a soldier in the pay of the French like Wolf Eyes. The fishers return with a good catch about the time the wigwams are set up. "If there are two things we can count on in America," says Caucus-Meteor, "it's passenger pigeons in summer flights and salmon in spring runs."

No formal vote has been held regarding the leadership of the tribe; even so, Haggis, Passaconway, and Black Dirt know better than to refer to themselves as chiefs. In point of fact Caucus-Meteor is king again. He makes the rounds from family to family to collect tribute to pay the intendant. Last year was easy. He had money from his interpreter's fee, and from winnings over Bleached Bones. This year is difficult. He has to tease, cajole, and persuade to raise the funds. Reluctantly the tribal members give what they have left from last summer's trading season. He gathers just enough to make the payment; now it's not only Caucus-Meteor who has nothing, it's the entire tribe. All except the Laurents and Norman Feathers, who blurts out to his king one day that he has squirreled away savings from his employment in Quebec.

"Surely, you must have confessed this sin to your priest, so why tell me?" says Caucus-Meteor.

"He told me it was not a sin, but I think it was a sin, so I seek your forgiveness," Norman Feathers says.

"I forgive you, Norman," says Caucus-Meteor, and he waves a hand over his subject's head as he has seen the priests do with their penitents. "What else have you confessed to the priest?"

"That I'm a bachelor."

"What did the priest say?"

"Not a sin."

"What else?" asks Caucus-Meteor, pretending great seriousness.

"I confessed that I prefer the company of large animals, especially oxen, to people." Norman Feathers is trembling with the thrill of shame.

"And the priest said?"

"Not a sin."

"Sounds to me like getting into Catholic heaven is easy," says Caucus-Meteor. "I forgive you, as your priest has forgiven you. Next time you pray to Jesus, put a good word in for your king."

One matter troubles Caucus-Meteor. Omer and Hungry Heart are talking about breaking away from the tribe. Maybe after the canoe season they won't come back. Maybe they'll winter next year in Montreal. They're not sure of anything right now. Hungry Heart is still weak following her self-induced abortion. Omer's restless and morose. He tells Caucus-Meteor that the only thing that will make him happy will be more canoes and more French scrip. Caucus-Meteor knows that Omer won't cheer up until he's back on the river.

Norman Feathers brings Caucus-Meteor to the palace to pay tribute. Caucus-Meteor imagines that the intendant himself, like last year, will greet him personally. Caucus-Meteor will make a long, eloquent speech, and the intendant will be so moved he will burst into tears and return the payment to Caucus-Meteor, who will give it back to the villagers. But of course it doesn't happen that way. The intendant's man tells Caucus-Meteor that His Excellency is far too busy to meet with a village headman. He accepts the bribe without a word or a change in expression, then reminds Caucus-Meteor that a fall payment will be due this year. Caucus-Meteor leaves with the knowledge that his people won't tolerate another blow from French authorities without some kind of reaction. Unless Caucus-Meteor can raise some money on his own, come fall Haggis will use the intendant's demands as an excuse to bring the people north. It will be the end of Conissadawaga, as conceived by Caucus-Meteor and Keeps-the-Flame.

His slave has been a captive now for one year. He looks strong and robust, though he has lost some weight over the winter. Caucus-Meteor admires him for his devotion to his god. The old American has it in the back of his mind that his slave, if he keeps praying with the same earnestness that he did over the winter, might eventually reach his English Jesus, who then might take action either in destroying the Conissadawaga village or in empowering it, depending on divine whim. Caucus-Meteor wonders whether he has a better chance of keeping his village whole with Nathan's god than with the intendant. He'll brood over this matter.

Though Black Dirt's official mourning period has ended, she still wears the black mourning ribbon in her hair. Even so, Caucus-Meteor advises Haggis that now is as good a time as any to pay her a courting visit. The great hunter walks out into the fields to talk to the great grower.

Later, he visits Caucus-Meteor and tells him of the encounter with his daughter.

"She said to me, 'This is the only time I can remember that Haggis stepped foot in the women's garden.' She excited me with her challenging manner, for I like a woman with fight in her. It's woman's spite that I cannot bear."

"What did you say to her?"

"I thought this is the time for charm, so I said, 'The Christians say mankind was lost by a woman's curiosity in a garden.' And I smiled at her.

"She said, 'I believe the culprit was a snake, an animal that has a difficult time in our extreme climate.'

"I said, 'You mean the extreme climate of Canada, or the extreme climate of Canada American woman?'

"She said, 'You are here, Haggis. Are you the snake in my garden?'

"I must admit that I was excited now as the snake at the mouse's hole, for I had been bested by a woman, and the feeling is quite pleasant. I said, 'You and I have different hopes and dreams for our people. Even so, I have always thought well of you, Black Dirt.'

"She said, 'And I have thought well of you, Haggis.'

"I said, 'Your mourning period has ended.'

"She said, 'Yes, I will always grieve for the loss of my family, but by thinking of nothing else for a year, I find that now it is easier to think of other things.'

"I said, 'I am glad to hear that.' I spoke very gravely and formally. I said, 'You are still young enough to bear children for our tribe. If you and I were to marry, the strife in our hearts and the strife in the hearts of our people would melt away.'" Haggis pauses.

Caucus-Meteor's heart is pounding with anticipation. He compliments Haggis on his storytelling abilities.

"Thank you," Haggis bows.

"And what did Black Dirt say?"

"She blushed, and said, 'I am flattered, Haggis.'

"I thought: I'd better use good words, for this is a woman on an edge between an idea and a feeling. I said, 'I know that you are very independent-minded and ambitious for a woman, which are further reasons I admire you, Black Dirt. All my wives are independent-minded. I never interfere with their desires. I have one wife who will sleep with me only for the purposes of procreation, and I love her no less than the others. Do not answer now. Think about it for a few days. If you refuse me, I will not hold it against you, but I warn you that I will do all in my power to persuade the tribe to follow me and not you.'"

Caucus-Meteor throws up his hands in disgust. "As usual, the butcher work is messier than the hunt, Monsieur."

"What are you telling me, old king?" Haggis is annoyed now.

"That you can't propose to and threaten a good woman at the same time."

"Well, I think I did well enough. I think she will marry me," says Haggis. "She promised me an answer on the morrow."

"I will speak to her tonight after supper," says Caucus-Meteor. Haggis bows and leaves.

That night, Caucus-Meteor says to his daughter. "What do you think of Haggis?"

"I think he would make a good husband and a middling father," she says.

"Which is all a woman can ask of a man."

"That's true, father."

"You are thinking perhaps that with marriage to Haggis your dream for a purely farming community will vanish."

"That would make you happy, father. If you wish, I will marry Haggis and make you happy."

"It doesn't matter what I wish, nor is my happiness of any

consequence whatever to this village. I command you to follow
your heart, daughter."

The next day, Black Dirt respectfully declines Haggis's offer
for marriage. Haggis's wives spread the word, and Black Dirt loses
prestige in the village. Conissadawaga needs strong, healthy
children. Black Dirt still has another decade or more of child-
bearing. The consensus among the people of Conissadawaga
is that by rejecting the best man in the village, she's turning her
back on her people. Caucus-Meteor worries that, given her
strong personality, Black Dirt will begin now to change deep
within her heart with the possibility that eventually she will
become a sorceress. The Algonkian word for such a woman has
undergone some changes in the last hundred years, he thinks. It
now includes nuances of the English meaning for *witch*. A sorceress is to be respected, feared, and perhaps killed to prevent her
from extending her powers.

The men prepare to leave for the annual trade missions, yet
another excuse for celebrating, and all the villagers are dancing
and chanting in the late evening spring light of Canada when
Nathan Blake steps into the circle and announces that he wishes
to address the tribe, a breach of etiquette by a slave. But the
Americans are curious, wondering what he'll say. Nathan has
many names among the villagers. Most call him Ox-Man for his
manner and attitude toward work. Others put a twist on the
word for ox that translates as Not-Very-Intelligent. A few refer
to him as Ox-Head-Deer-Foot, because though Nathan might
think and behave like an ox, he moves with the nimble feet of
a deer. He's also called a name that means Old-Man's-Dog-
Team, a reference to his services to Caucus-Meteor. None of the
Americans has a name for him that would describe him as an orator, so he catches them off guard with a prepared speech in their
primary language.

Caucus-Meteor is as surprised as any that Nathan is speaking
in the circle. Now that his health has returned, he's come to take
his slave for granted. Now Caucus-Meteor wonders how Nathan

will behave in the circle. He has taught Nathan that it's important not only to express wishes, but to phrase them in the best
language one can put forward. By now Nathan's use of Algonkian is acceptable, and though his accent is still amusing to the
ear of the native speakers, his pronunciation is clear, his words
carefully chosen, and his manner sincere.

"I have been away from my church, my family, and my town
for more than a year," he says. "I have done all you've asked of me
and more; I have never complained. I asked for food only when
I was hungry—and you gave. I thank you. I asked for a coat and
trousers to replace my worn and torn garb—and you gave. I
thank you. You asked much of me, too. I've served Caucus-
Meteor as well and faithfully as I am capable of. I've worked like
a woman in your fields, but I tell you I am as much a man as any
of your men. Unlike my people, you do not attempt to break the
will of your children, but coddle them and encourage them in
subtle ways to develop their own will. If God ever grants me
more children, I will follow the American way in raising them. I
will never break the will of a child or a man or a woman. I know
that what an American values most is personal liberty. Accordingly, you will understand in your hearts that Nathan Blake can
be a slave no more. You must release me, kill me, or change my
status in the tribe. Thank you for listening."

Nathan folds his arms in front of himself, and stares off into
the distance. Caucus-Meteor can shut off debate with a word.
Everyone in the village knows the king has grown fond of his
slave and could adopt him into his family. The king's first impulse is to announce to his people that Nathan Blake is his son,
but something tells him this is not a wise move. He's not sure
why but he has an idea that Nathan Blake must be like a son, but
not a son, for he did not see a son in his dream. Caucus-Meteor
steps into the circle, and Nathan leaves it.

"Not a bad speech—for an Englishman," says Caucus-Meteor. He smiles, and folds his arms the same way Nathan did to
remind his slave where he picked up the gesture. "My health has

returned. I no longer need a slave to tend to my every need. It's unbecoming of a sovereign to keep slaves. My wish is that Nathan Blake live with me as a . . ." He pauses long. Everyone is thinking that the old king is taunting them in the time-honored tradition of the orator, withholding the flourish that creates meaning, but actually Caucus-Meteor, for once in his life, is at a loss for words. Finally, he backs up in his speech and repeats. "My wish is that your slave be granted conditional citizenship; I request that he live with me as a provider of services, providing companionship and perhaps doing a few chores for an old man. You've been kind enough to lend him to me, though in truth he still belongs to you. Therefore, you, the people of Conissadawaga, must decide Nathan Blake's fate."

Following some buzzing and milling about, the men and women separate and hold councils among themselves. An hour later the two groups convene.

Haggis steps into the circle. "The men voted that the slave, Nathan Blake, be adopted into the tribe as a provider of services."

Katahdin comes forward. "The women voted that Nathan Blake should be tested further. We remember that he did not do well on the marksmanship test, nor on the running test. We know that Nathan Blake can work like a woman in the fields, and we know he can serve an old man as any wife or daughter might, but can he perform the duties of an American man?"

"What sort of tests?" Haggis addresses his wife not as a member of his family, but as a citizen of Conissadawaga.

"Manly tests. We want to know: Can he fight? Can he run? Can he do what a man can do?"

The last comment brings titters from the women.

After the people have gone on to other matters, Nathan asks Caucus-Meteor, "If I pass these tests will I be a free man?"

"By the standards you are used to in New England, yes; by the standards of an American already free, no."

Nathan blinks in confusion and frustration. "That phrase you used in your speech, I haven't heard it before."

"Provider of services."

"Yes, what exactly does it mean?"

"There's a word for it in English, but it escapes me at the moment. If you pass the tests, I will continue to be your master, but your status otherwise in the community will be equal to any citizen's."

"I will no longer be a slave—I will be a servant?"

"Yes, your position will improve to servant." He pronounces "servant" with a French flourish. "Thank you for providing the word. Your service is appreciated."

"And the women, what did they mean by manly tests, and laughing afterward . . ." Nathan abruptly stops talking.

Caucus-Meteor smiles. He can see that it has dawned on Nathan that if he passes the tests, a woman will come to his bed.

Pure

*F*irst test—wrestling. The women come in from the fields to watch the matches. Nathan's opponent is Agawam, the son of Seekonk.

While they strip down for fighting, Caucus-Meteor advises his servant. "Agawam is very young, fluid in his movements—you are probably stronger, though. Do you have experience in wrestling?"

"More than you might expect from a farmer. When I was growing up in Massachusetts, young men wrestled for prizes and prestige, just as you do here. I see no torn ears, gouged eyes, dislocated fingers among the Conissadawaga men, so you are not as ferocious as some Englishmen I have fought."

"You—a fighter, I can't believe it."

"My father taught me to fight, but within restraints. He cautioned me about fighting for vengeance, which possesses the will; money, which violates a man's dignity; and about punching with the closed fist, an offense against one's livelihood. He told me more than once—aye, he told me everything more than once—'God protects thy soul, thy wife thy heart, and thyself thy hands. A farmer can do his chores without soul or heart, but not without hands.' So you see, Caucus-Meteor, my upbringing allows me to fight with a savage's fury if not with a savage's heart."

He is confident and obnoxious, thinks Caucus-Meteor. I admire him very much.

The atmosphere for the match is festive. Revelry is at the core of this society, thinks Caucus-Meteor; if we can't agree on anything else, we can agree to make music, sing, dance, be merry, or, in this case, cheer a contest. Agawam circles Nathan. He still thinks of Nathan as a slave, an Englishman who works with women, and as a result is careless in his attack. Nathan tosses him over his hip, and pins him. The match is over in two minutes.

This action elicits loud response from the women. They're urging Nathan on, not because they're against Agawam, but because they're hoping to add one more able-bodied man to the tribe. Caucus-Meteor feels the old urge to wager on the next match, but he holds back. It is impolitic for a king to wager with his subjects, and anyway he owns nothing worth betting, except for his turban, whose loss he would never risk.

The next opponent is a follower of Haggis, Nubanusit, a huge, good-humored rowdy fellow, at the moment drunk. Nubanusit offers Nathan a hand in mockery. "Don't confront this fellow," Caucus-Meteor shouts in English. Perhaps Nathan's success against Agawam has overextended his self-assurance, and he takes the hand. This will be the end of him, thinks Caucus-Meteor. Nubanusit pulls Nathan to his knees and leaps upon him. But the big fellow is drunk, and Nathan is able to squirm free. After that Nathan lets Nubanusit lunge at him, but avoids grappling with him. The two men dodge and feint until finally Nubanusit loses both balance and breath, and Nathan is on him. A minute later, the match is over, Nubanusit lies helpless with Nathan's foot against his throat. Caucus-Meteor was wrong in his judgment. He's grateful for the feeling of humility. If only I were wrong more often, he thinks, I might be reduced in pride and ambition, and would be happier.

By now Nathan has attracted the attention of two women in particular, Wytopitlock and Parmachnenee. They cheer him, stamp their feet, call to him—"Nay-than, Nay-than, Nay-than!"

Nathan appears tired but excited. He bows. Now all the Americans cheer him.

Just when it looks like Nathan is going to be the man of the hour, Haggis steps forward. "I would like to try the champion," he says softly. Caucus-Meteor recognizes an old hunt strategy that Haggis is using against Nathan: wear down your quarry and he will present himself for the kill. Two minutes later he has Nathan across his knee. Could break his back with a whisper. Nathan raises his hand, the surrender sign. Haggis pauses, releases him to rousing chants.

Afterward Nathan tells Caucus-Meteor, "If I wasn't tired, I would have defeated him." Caucus-Meteor concludes otherwise, that from the way both men moved Haggis appeared just a little stronger, a little quicker, and far craftier. Caucus-Meteor smiles. He suspects that Nathan will always believe he could have beaten Haggis.

After the matches, Nathan and the American men drink brandy and boast. They tell stories of contests past, and exchange notions on how to defeat an opponent. Nathan teaches the Americans the New England "trip and twitch" method of separating an opponent from the perpendicular. The back and forth between Nathan and the village men is on an equal basis. Haggis makes an announcement. The next test will be foot racing, tomorrow, same time.

Caucus-Meteor withdraws. He doesn't mind the bragging and foolishness of the men. It's the drinking that disgusts him. And, too, it nettles him that the competition has been a great success for Haggis, who has demonstrated to his people that he is still the best fighter in the tribe.

Nathan doesn't return to the wigwam until very late. He's tired but sober, and a pleased expression on his face tells Caucus-Meteor all he needs to know.

"Whose wigwam did you visit?" he asks.

"Wytopitlock's and Parmachnenee's."

"Your performance in the matches gave you powers to overcome your modesty," Caucus-Meteor says. He's teasing Nathan at the same time that he's probing to determine whether goading will persuade Nathan to reveal his exploits with the women.

Nathan says nothing, and Caucus-Meteor thinks: good, you don't know it, but you have passed another test. Later that night Nathan rises from a troubled sleep, kneels, bows his head, whispers. When he returns to his stick bed, Caucus-Meteor calls to him from his fire. "Excuse me for asking a man about his prayers, but were you thanking your god for this sudden good fortune?"

"I was asking forgiveness for sinning with Wytopitlock and Parmachnenee," Nathan says in a voice far too resonant for a penitent.

"These are not loose women looking only to pleasure themselves, Nathan Blake," says the old American, falling into oratorical tones. "Their seduction of you is serious business. The village has a shortage of children and men. These women are among a particular kind of réfugié—the lost woman, the widow, the deserted woman, the outcast woman, the woman whose baby has died, the woman whose people have been wiped out by one disaster or another. Their serious business is to make babies and replenish their adopted tribe, and thus justify themselves. They would prefer a good American husband to Nathan Blake, but they'll take what they can get. After watching you all this year as a slave, noting how well you worked and without complaint, after hearing your speech, and after watching you wrestle, they've seen enough to convince them that you have the right qualities to give them good babies. Never mind that you belong to another nation, another complexion. They follow the old American adage: it's not the blood, it's the behavior that makes an American."

Next day is race day. The villagers remember that last year Nathan's shoelace burst, slowing him down. At the time, that seemed like a bad omen, a sign that Nathan Blake was not worthy for adoption into the tribe. Now it's an element of uncertainty. Will the Ox-Man become known as the Deer-Man?

That's the big question. In fact, Passaconway, the former great runner for the tribe, predicts that Nathan will do well, though he won't win. He remembers that even hobbled by a bad bootlace Nathan showed ability.

Running has an added importance to the tribe, because its women produce special shoes for trained racers at trade fairs. But nobody locally, not even Haggis, would think of reserving these special shoes for himself.

The competitors will run down to the lake, touch the water, and race back, a round-trip distance of about five hundred strides.

"You look eager," Caucus-Meteor says.

"Back home I was a darned good wrestler, but not the best. My pride is in running."

Caucus-Meteor wonders now what is in Nathan Blake's head and heart. Is he anxious to prove himself? Does he want to humiliate his captors? Has the touch of American women made him confident and hungry for more? Surely, he should worry a little about his shoes. He's wearing a Frenchman's clothes, but he's shod in the leather boots that he was captured in. They're worn down, and though he has new laces, the shoes themselves might just split under the force of racing. Caucus-Meteor translates his own uncertainty as a sign that the gods have a stake in this race. I must be on the lookout for omens, he thinks.

Haggis is among the competitors. Caucus-Meteor can see that vanity is making him go against his instincts as a hunter. He's expected to win, so he has nothing to gain by racing. Haggis, you fool—you never give a quarry this kind of opportunity. You can't imagine Nathan defeating you and the best runners in the village. You can understand an Englishman pinning an American in a wrestling match, but in a footrace that requires explosive power, plus grace—not possible!

Nathan breaks out in front at the drop of the feather from the hand of old Passaconway. After fifty yards, Nathan begins to pull away, Haggis a good ten steps behind. The gathered are thinking that the Englishman will tire. Instead, Nathan lengthens his lead. By the time he reaches the water he's twenty steps ahead. He loses five steps at the lake because he doesn't have the correct technique for touching the water and making the turn, but that doesn't matter. He wins the race by fifty steps. Not only Caucus-Meteor, but everyone who witnessed the race knows that Nathan is the best runner in the village.

The old American cannot conceal his glee at Haggis's defeat. Surely, he is angry for putting himself in a position to be defeated. He's lost some prestige. Haggis, note how the women, even your beloved wives, are looking at Nathan Blake. You'd better kill this Englishman, before he proves to be more than just an annoyance, and emerges as a threat to your position in the community. Ah, but you can do nothing now, for the village needs good men, and if you don't sanction Nathan's entry into the tribe, the women will rebel. Haggis praises Nathan. Good hunter that he is, Haggis will bide his time until he can remove Nathan as a possible threat to his authority, but without injuring himself or the tribe.

After Nathan has accepted the congratulations from the villagers, Caucus-Meteor steps into the circle to make a speech. Everyone quiets down. It isn't the time for speech-making, which makes the king's action that much more effective.

"Listen, my people, while I tell you my dream," he says in grave oratorical tones. And with a few embellishments he relates in a long, drawn-out way his dream back on the war trail last year. "I worried about the running figure, what he meant. I thought he might be the ghost of my fears. I thought he might be a demon who took offense to a man my age going to war. For the money, you understand. It is honorable to go to war to avenge a wrong, but I did it for money to pay the damn intendant his damn tribute. I thought about the running figure when I was blinded, my face paralyzed. I realized the running figure was" — Caucus-Meteor abruptly stops talking, makes a shape like a wave with his hand—"was pure. Pure. Now, following the events today, I understand the meaning of the dream. It was a message from my father's ghost. He was trying to tell me that the runner was a Pure Man, sent to save this village by earning us lots of money. That Pure Man is Nathan Blake."

By now Nathan understands Algonkian, so it's not the diction that confuses him. It's his ignorance of the phrase *pure man*. That night in the wigwam after supper, and after Caucus-Meteor has shooed away Nathan's female admirers, he tells Nathan what a Pure Man is.

"Many years ago, before the coming of the Europeans, as now, trade fairs were held all over North America. With trade came gaming and contests of physical prowess. Specially trained men participated in these events. I'll tell you right now that I would never consider you for these competitions if these were the old days, because you wouldn't stand a chance. But these are not the old days. The best of the young men go to war, men like Wolf Eyes, who fight not for their people or for vengeance or even for glory, but for money or to satisfy a hidden anger. The ones who do compete are poorly trained. In the old days the runners were known as Pure Men. They ate a special diet of deer meat, vegetables, no oily fish or corn mush, no stimulants, no long hours without sleep, no women, and much exercise."

Before Caucus-Meteor can go on, Nathan interrupts, his voice ringing in alarm, "No women?"

The old American is suddenly possessed by a disturbing possibility: it's unlikely that a man can be truly free and truly pure at the same time.

After his illness Caucus-Meteor was able to sleep for short periods, but now that his health is restored, he no longer sleeps. It's as if when he's awake, he's in a dream, and when he's dreaming he's awake. With the arrival of warm weather, there's no need for a stove, and in a state of partial rest, partial excitement, partial wakefulness, partial sleep, he can sit eating an open fire and doze. He's recovered much of his strength, and calculates he has enough life-force left for one more campaign. He's going to race Nathan against the best runners in Canada. His aim is to acquire French scrip by betting on Nathan in order to pay the intendant's tribute in the fall. He'll give whatever is left to Black Dirt. After that, Caucus-Meteor plans to be reunited with his loved ones—the children lost through disease, the wife who made a man and leader of him, the father who was a king, but mainly his mother, who was taken from him and enslaved. He prays to no god in particular that in the afterworld he will be allowed for a short time to be a child again so that he can feel his mother's arms as only a child can.

Even the hard drinkers—Nubanusit, Holyoke, and Pisgah —refrain from imbibing while Nathan is being sworn into the tribe. The children are quiet, and the crows seem to know enough to stop squawking—a good omen, Azicochoa will re-mark later. The old king notes that everyone is on hand for the ceremony except for Black Dirt. She's now well past her official mourning period, but the black ribbon is still in her hair, and she remains in partial seclusion. Black Dirt, the other women come to you for advice in raising crops, but as a leader you have lost powers.

Caucus-Meteor is much moved by the ceremony. Nathan is stripped naked, and his body and face are painted red, yellow, and black. Wytopitlock and Parmachnenee cut his beard and shave his face with a French razor, braid his hair and fit him with a headband to keep the hair looking neat. Wytopitlock gives him a comb as a present. He thanks her, his voice quivering with emotion. Nathan's clothes, the clothes of the slave, are burned. These days most men from the tribes wear more French cloth than animal skin, but Nathan is given the garb of an American of the last century—deerskin loin cloth and breeches, beads and bones around the neck, bracelets of animal claws for his wrists, and feathers in his headband. Seems like everybody in the tribe donates something to his wardrobe. The only apparel he wears that's not native is a white trade shirt. When he's finally dressed, he looks more American than the Americans, except for Haggis. Only Nathan's feet are bare. The shoes are presently under construction, and will have to wait.

Finally, Caucus-Meteor taps Nathan on the shoulder with the flat side of a hatchet and gives him a new name. "From this day forward I will be your godfather. Will you be my godson?"

"Yes, I will." Nathan bows his head.

"As your godfather, I will bestow upon you a name for our tribe. You will be known to us as Nathan Provider-of-Services." Each person in the village walks by him as he remains still. Some give him a hug, others a handshake, or just a light tap on the shoulder. After the ceremony drums play, the brandy flows; the people sing and dance in celebration. Nathan Provider-of-Services is officially a citizen of Conissadawaga. He spends the night in the wigwam of the two single women, Wytopitlock and Parmachnenee.

Caucus-Meteor visits the wigwam of his daughter. She's stitching the racing moccasins for Nathan Provider-of-Services.

"I'm worried about you, daughter. You must learn again to celebrate the joys of life," he says.

"I tell you, father, that I feel my grief less, and reflect upon it more. The anguish of lost loved ones will always be with me, but the numbness and anger are gone. Sorrow has made me stronger."

"You are now able to feel the emotion that supports the pain. Do you remember what your mother used to say on this matter?"

"'An empty vessel will be filled with the first rain if only the lid be lifted.'"

Caucus-Meteor points to the shoes she is stitching. "What do you think of Nathan Provider-of-Services? You think he will be a good citizen of our village?"

"I cannot say. I know he has survived the ordeal of captivity through prayer to Jesus. I wonder if Jesus might in some small way alleviate the suffering of an American woman. But in truth I don't think about Nathan Provider-of-Services. I think about my sister, Caterina, in a convent somewhere, and I regret my anger at our parting. I would like to make amends. Perhaps Caterina could teach me to pray in the Christian manner."

The next day Nathan sits on a log. Standing beside him is Caucus-Meteor. Kneeling at his feet, shoes in hand, is Black Dirt. The old American watches his daughter slip clean French stockings on the bare feet of his godson. She tucks the tops under his leather leggings. The moccasins slide snugly over the stockings. Since some people have different-sized feet, she'd measured each of his feet before cutting the smoked moose hide and shaping the shoes. Nathan's feet are the same length, slightly longer than average, wider at the arch. Caucus-Meteor wonders if she likes touching Nathan's feet as much as Nathan appears to like the touch of her hands. He wonders if she has become one of these women who has shut off feelings for men.

"How do they fit?" asks Caucus-Meteor.

"Perfect," says Nathan softly.

"Your voice lacks enthusiasm."

"The shoes are plain, no bead work or dyed porcupine quills to give them distinction."

Now that Nathan is an American man, he's acting like one, vain about his appearance, thinks Caucus-Meteor. American women often joke about how long it takes their men to get ready in the morning.

"I would have put in some color and design, but father said no," says Black Dirt.

"I don't want the gamblers on the trade fair circuit to inspect you too closely," says Caucus-Meteor.

The king plans to take Nathan all through Canada for the summer. Because Caucus-Meteor himself owns nothing, he has to borrow a canoe from Omer Laurent. Omer wants to charge him a fee, but Caucus-Meteor shames him into donating it for tribal services. Holding up under the wear and tear of travel is Caucus-Meteor's main worry. It nags at him, too, that his mission, even if successful, might mean nothing in the end. If he raises ten times the tribute money, his village will still be at risk because of his ignorance of French law and French writing. A man might do all that is expected of him, but the gods will still laugh for their own reasons.

Caucus-Meteor gives Nathan three weeks of training, which includes running every day at various distances, wood chopping for strengthening the arms and chest, and listening to oratory regarding methods of running—gaining a fast start, racing on different surfaces, elbowing fellow runners who try to pass, stepping on the heel of a competitor.

Nathan ignores Caucus-Meteor's caution about frolicking with women, often slinking off with Wytopitlock and Parmachnenee. The old American watches a pattern develop. In the wigwam with himself Nathan is attentive, humble, and he prays. With the women he is licentious, conceited, and he boasts.

One day he sees his godson chatting with his two women, and he sneaks up on them and eavesdrops on the conversation.

"Most of Caucus-Meteor's talk of racing is cow patties," Nathan tells the women. "I have done enough racing to understand that while the old king might have gambled on races in his day and thus closely observed runners, he was never a pure trainer of pure men."

"But you are his Pure Man," says Wytopitlock.

"Like all men, I am a sinner; no man is pure."

Caucus-Meteor slinks off, humiliation putting him at peace for the moment.

Nathan's not too happy with Caucus-Meteor's special diet for him—deer meat and summer greens. No corn soup, nuts, beans, smoked fish, maple sugared bread—foods Nathan has grown to enjoy. Nathan cheats on the diet. For the entire summer, Caucus-Meteor will talk as if Nathan remains on the Pure Man diet, as if discussion of same provided the necessary nourishment, but Nathan will eat what he likes. One aspect of Caucus-Meteor's training methods that Nathan takes to is what the old king calls concentration of the mind. He teaches Nathan how to prepare himself mentally before each race. "The Pure Man must clean the head as well as the bowels before competition," he says.

"Concentration of the mind is not too different from trusting in God through silent prayer," he says.

"Then you have the skill to do it."

All told, Nathan goes along with Caucus-Meteor's training routines, and the trainer is pleased.

Three weeks pass, another. Caucus-Meteor still doesn't think Nathan is prepared. The able-bodied American men have departed on trade missions. Another young fellow, Sebec, the fatherless boy, the grandson of the great Passaconway, has joined the army. Unlike Wolf Eyes, he promises to return with his salary. The corn is two feet high before Caucus-Meteor announces that Nathan is ready for competition. Before they leave, Caucus-Meteor takes up a wagering collection—every last penny he can squeeze out of his people. Men, women, children, and dogs come down to the waterfront to bid the travelers farewell. Wytopitlock and Parmachnenee weep, not so much because they're going to miss Nathan Provider-of-Services, but because both have had their monthly flow. Neither will bear the child of Nathan Provider-of-Services.

Black Dirt is the last to say goodbye.

One chore Caucus-Meteor won't be burdened with will be gathering information for St. Blein's rebellion. Caucus-Meteor did his part last summer, so he owes his former commander nothing. Caucus-Meteor heard from Norman Feathers that the intendant suspects St. Blein is part of an anti-France group. What's saving the ensign is that he's a good soldier, a pet of Galissoniere, the governor-general, and, more important, that his father is a rich merchant with influence in the French government. Caucus-Meteor suspects the intendant will try to rid himself of St. Blein, but cunningly, so that the ensign's father won't know upon whom to take revenge. When Caucus-Meteor examines his own life, he sees many errors. One of those was his involvement with St. Blein and his dangerous ideas. He knows that St. Blein's rebellion is a story with an ending yet unknown. He hopes that his people are not the ultimate victims of their king's mistake.

On the bluff, watching the old chief and the new American, is the boy Freeway. Something in his pose tells Caucus-Meteor that the boy is thinking about running away to sea, to hunt whales, to set eyes on distant lands, or some such boy-thinking that he himself never quite experienced because of his slave status.

Nathan's first competition is in nearby Wendake, the Catholic Huron town only a few miles west of Quebec City. The Huron were once a proud people farming on lake plains but they were annihilated in wars with the Iroquois confederacy. Many of the réfugiés ended up in Wendake. Caucus-Meteor often mocked the Huron, saying they'd become more French than American; now it pains him to observe that the Huron have their lives in better order than his own people. They're tall, good-looking, healthy, Christianized, even pious in their behavior; they raise livestock, work and fight for the French, wear French clothes, live in two-room houses with permanent foundations very similar to the French peasants who pay to farm lands owned by signeural royalty, men such as St. Blein's father.

The race will be held in a pasture. Caucus-Meteor notes that Nathan's concentration breaks; it's important to bring him back to the matter at hand.

"What are you thinking, Nathan? Your mind seems suddenly occupied."

"I can smell a barnyard in the distance, I see horses, a cow. The grass shows patches of brown from drought. Need rain."

"Wistful is wasteful—that's a Massachusetts expression?"

"I think not. I think it is a Caucus-Meteor expression."

Caucus-Meteor makes the purge sign.

"Aye." Nathan's expression goes blank. Soon his concentration returns.

In part of the field, badly made wooden stalls have been

erected. Local men act as brokers, buying furs from the northern tribes, which they in turn will sell on the docks in Quebec. Caucus-Meteor studies the crowd—traders, merchants, gamblers, and spectators from Wendake. Near the stalls are the pole gambling arbors. First, the runners are announced, and they parade in front of the crowd so people can size them up. Then there's a period of frantic buzzing and bartering as people wager on the runners. Every bet and every bettor is a little different. They're all looking for victims, while pretending to be victims. Caucus-Meteor enjoys the atmosphere; he thinks that gambling etiquette is a most refined form of insincerity, more sublime even than diplomacy. The contestants run in place, do stretching exercises, and pretend that nothing else matters but the minutes at hand.

Most of the runners are local fellows. Caucus-Meteor estimates that only two are Pure Men. One, from the look of him, is mixed-blood, African and Cherokee, an escaped slave from the southern colonies who likely was adopted by one of the smaller réfugié tribes. The fellow is a little too big in the upper body to be a threat in a race requiring more than three great breaths, and this course is almost half an English mile, many breaths. The other Pure Man is a slender full-blood, presently wearing a triangle-peaked birch-bark cap; he's probably a Micmac. Caucus-Meteor guesses these two fellows will have godfathers in the crowd. For the time being he should avoid the gamblers who follow the trade fairs, bet against the local runners only and with local gamblers until he's more confident in his own runner, for he's still not sure how Nathan will do under the pressure of serious competition. Having thought out the right thing to do, Caucus-Meteor does the wrong thing. He bets every penny he's raised on his man. If Nathan Provider-of-Services loses, Caucus-Meteor will be broken forever as king of Conissadawaga. He will be free from the burden of the responsibilities of kingship. He secretly hopes for failure.

In discussions earlier, Caucus-Meteor and Nathan determine that Nathan doesn't have enough experience racing in Canada to size up the competition, so he'll race against the course. He walks the grounds with the other competitors. "The distance is a little long for your talents," says Caucus-Meteor. "You'll have to pace yourself."

"That may be, but I can't let anyone get too far ahead. The first couple hundred yards suit me just fine, packed down grass in front of the crowd."

The athletes will circle a pole stuck in the ground where some hogs have been rooting and the earth is wet, soft, and mushy, a place where one could easily fall. Caucus-Meteor and Nathan form a design for the race based on this obstacle. Nathan will attempt to be the first runner to reach the disturbed earth. By the time the fifth or sixth runner has passed the pole, the ground will be treacherous; the first few runners will have the best footing. After circling the pole, Nathan will coast a ways, perhaps letting a few runners take the lead, and then he will put on a burst of speed at the end.

In the crowd, Caucus-Meteor bumps into an old ally and adversary. They stare at each other for a long moment. Caucus-Meteor notices that the man looks more bent, flesh softer, skin more sallow with new blemishes. He's about to remark on the change, but Bleached Bones speaks first.

"You look like bear scat, Caucus-Meteor."

Caucus-Meteor points to the sky at some turkey vultures. "Soon they'll be feeding on us both."

"I pity the poor bird that seeks nourishment from my meat," Bleached Bones tweaks the bone in his nose, and maybe smiles. It's hard to tell by looking at his eyes or even, if it was possible, searching his mind what's inside the man. He's one who keeps the same facial expression and control no matter how he feels. "I thought I recognized that English racer you brought in, the gauntlet walker in Montreal. Looks like you made an American out of him."

"I'm not so sure about that. I will tell you, though, that he can run," says Caucus-Meteor.

"I find it amusing that a man who made a reputation walking the gauntlet should now attempt to distinguish himself as a runner."

"It's such surprises that keep old men like you and me interested."

"True," says Bleached Bones, "for we've seen too much repetition. I've already bet on your man against the local fellows. I like the footwear and the long upper thighs. Do you think he'll beat the Micmac?"

"Is the Micmac your runner?"

"Bleached Bones is godfather to no Pure Man. Bleached Bones is godfather only to his own suspicions—and a well-placed bribe. I say the Micmac beats your man by two body lengths."

Caucus-Meteor figures that Bleached Bones has seen the Micmac before. He must be a superior runner. This test will be a good one for Nathan, but Caucus-Meteor reminds himself that the race should not be a test of his own exuberance. If he's to help his people he must refrain from exuberance, such as betting against gamblers like Bleached Bones.

"I bested you once before, but only because the gods of luck were generous that day," says Caucus-Meteor. "I have too much respect for you to test them again. Besides I have no more money; I've bet it all with the local gamblers."

"I respect you, too, Caucus-Meteor, and that is why I will accept your slave in place of French coins."

The king considers this proposition for a long moment before he speaks. "He is not mine to wager with. He is a citizen of my village; he is my slave no more, but an honorable servant."

"The old servant ploy—I know it well. You can fool your captive slave and your dull-witted subjects, but you can't fool me. For a king, all men are either pretenders to his throne or slaves to his will. And as a king's will earns him authority, I will accept a modest account from a modest sovereign—your turban."

"You have always coveted my turban."

"It has little worth. I will bet these"—he spills coins from his bag—"Spanish silver, worth more than French scrip."

It's not so mad a wager, Caucus-Meteor knows. Bleached Bones wants to fleece him of his dignity.

Caucus-Meteor considers Bleached Bones's challenge. If Nathan fails to defeat the Micmac, Caucus-Meteor will have to leave the tribe not only broken, but in disgrace with his bald head revealed for all to see. A wave of emotion rolls through him, and with it a clearer understanding of why he frequently goes against his fine judgment. No thrills exist in fine judgment. The feeling he is experiencing now, anticipation of total failure and humiliation, is too good to resist. Finally, he says to Bleached Bones. "I accept the wager. You mesmerize me, old sorcerer."

"You mesmerize yourself. It's because you have a heart, while I am all liver." He takes Caucus-Meteor's hand and places it on his side to feel the swollen organ. It pulsates under the old American's touch, and Bleached Bones moans in pain. "Good," he says. "Good."

Minutes before the race, Caucus-Meteor takes Nathan into the trees where they cannot be seen.

Nathan kneels, and the old king stands over him like a cleric and speaks in a soft voice. "Remember my teachings."

Nathan nods, glances away, hides a half grin.

Caucus-Meteor thinks: he half believes me. The other half, the secret half he holds dear, mocks me, despises me. He is becoming very much like me. I love him like a son. Surely, he will betray me. "Pray to your god, godson," Caucus-Meteor says.

Nathan prays aloud in English. With the "amen," Caucus-Meteor says, "Good prayer. Now empty mind of trivialities."

Nathan shuts his eyes.

"Now empty mind of desires."

It's working, thinks Caucus-Meteor. For the purposes of the race, Nathan has set aside the issue of his divided loyalties and resides in a hollow that is neither American earth nor Christian heaven.

"Now gather your powers for the task that awaits you."

"Thank you, godfather," Nathan says, and stands. He appears ready to run—strong, clear-headed, pure.

Just before race time, Caucus-Meteor learns from an acquaintance that the Micmac is undefeated on the race circuit.

A mixed-blood Huron man with a sparse goatee and a beret comes forward with a musket in hand.

"That is Mr. Poisson," says Caucus-Meteor, pronouncing the name in French. "He is a Wendake chief. Mr. Poisson will fire the musket, and at the sound you will run."

"Good for Mr. Poison," Nathan says in English, summoning the arrogance that a man needs to defeat another in an athletic contest. "I am glad to be off at a shot instead of the drop of a damn feather." And Nathan takes his position in the middle of the pack of about twenty runners, most of them mere boys. Caucus-Meteor can see that Nathan has already made a mistake. The best line to the turn-around pole is the inside very close to the crowd. The runner who has taken that position is the Micmac. Presently, he removes his birch-bark hat and hands it to a young woman.

Nathan bursts into the lead, but only for a fraction of a second, for the big African-Cherokee runner is soon side by side with him. Within fifty steps Nathan pulls ahead; at a hundred steps the Micmac catches up. The two are ten steps ahead of the African-Cherokee and fifteen steps ahead of everybody else. Nathan beats the Micmac to the turn-around pole. He goes against the strategy by lengthening his lead. Though he fades a bit at the end, he's so far ahead that he wins easily.

Caucus-Meteor whoops, hollers, does a little dance as Nathan crosses the finish line. Victory is sweet. He chuckles, walks among the crowd to collect his winnings.

Bleached Bones pays his debt to Caucus-Meteor.

An old Algonkian saying pops into Caucus-Meteor's head, and he practically sings it to his adversary. "This is more fun than dancing barefoot on burning snakes."

Caucus-Meteor knows that his reaction is too openly gleeful, a violation of gamblers' etiquette. He thinks: my joy crawls into the cracks of Bleached Bones's mind like vermin. But he's been so long without a feeling like this that he can't help himself.

"This is the second time you've defeated me," Bleached Bones says softly. "Somewhere during this racing season I am going to break your royal balls."

Wendake is the first of a series of successes for Nathan Provider-of-Services. He will lose two races early on until Caucus-Meteor realizes he can't compete with the best runners in distances over half an English mile. After that Caucus-Meteor enters him only in short races. From that point Nathan is undefeated in trade fairs at St. Francis, Kahnawake, Silery, and many smaller villages along the St. Lawrence. The runner and his godfather march triumphantly through Montreal, where Nathan races on the same field where he once walked the gauntlet. They head west on the Ottawa river all the way to Sault Ste. Marie.

"Your reputation is spreading," says Caucus-Meteor.

"We have a saying in New England: spreading like wildfire."

"Nathan Blake's reputation spreads like wildfire, while the summer drought deepens and wildfires spread like reputations," says Caucus-Meteor.

Everyone is eager to compete against the Pure Man from Conissadawaga. Caucus-Meteor gathers in more French scrip than he thought possible, and his strength is holding up. He's thinking maybe he'll not die soon after all. Maybe he'll last another year or two, or five, or ten. Maybe he'll be around for St. Blein's rebellion, and the Canadians will make him king. He'll rule from Mount Hope in New England. Maybe he will live forever, a punishment imposed by the French Jesus for his insincerity.

As the short Canadian summer wears to an end, something goes on in his runner's mind that excites Caucus-Meteor's curiosity. The mind divides, not just in two but in threes and fours.

A small part of Nathan Provider-of-Services remains the Ox, a slave. When Caucus-Meteor makes decisions and gives him orders, he responds with the loose compliance of a slave: no responsibilities, a dim faith he'll be taken care of, buried resentment, a slightly unsettling feeling that he's missing out on more than the obvious, that there's something out there for the free man that the slave cannot even imagine.

Another part of Nathan is the Englishman, working like a fiend from his Christian hell for reasons uncertain. Surely he has moments when everything he remembers about his past seems like a story, something somebody told him, not his own experiences. The vagueness that came over him during the shock of his capture has returned. "I can think about my wife in words, but I cannot picture her except in that moment you related to me in our ice shanty, as seen through the windowpane. My dead son is more complete in my thoughts than my living daughters, who exist only in the memory of the carved toys I made for them. You see, old man, how you've reduced me."

"But Nathan you love objects. I've heard your dreams and your waking mutterings. I've heard you speak in your dreams of the smell of freshly cut pine going through a saw mill. You've spoken of the thuck of your mallet striking a birch peg in an oak beam."

"Aye, but she, my wife, she is neither in my dreams, nor in my thoughts except as an idea. And this place I build in my mind, it is not located on my proprietorship lot, it is . . . it is . . ." He cannot go on.

"It is the paradise lot in that far distant place you speak of in your dreams."

"Aye, it troubles me so."

"For the anguish?"

"For the gratification. It is almost carnal in its extreme."

"You told me once in great confusion about a far place in your mind. I think you know better now its locale, for your captivity has allowed you to picture it."

"It's a river that flows west into a warm sea, a place called India where Indians reside, a numerous and fair people. West is where I build my wife's house, but you see what troubles me about this vision—she is not there, nor are my children, or any of my loved ones from New England."

"You are right to be troubled. You must count yourself lucky to suffer so. It will earn you a place in Christian heaven," says Caucus-Meteor.

The old American notes that at the same time that Nathan Blake the Englishman is losing an old self, Nathan Provider-of-Services the American is exploring a new self. Every time he wins a race, people tell him how splendid he is. For a man who's passed the last year as a slave, praise and recognition create quite a heady feeling. He develops friendships with some of the other Pure Men runners and gamblers, who are now wagering not whether he will win but by how much. Local chiefs offer lodging, food, and entertainment. Nathan enjoys the envy of the menfolk, the admiration of the children. Best of all, women throw themselves at him, not just desperate spinsters and widows, but young beauties. It's all too much for Nathan Provider-of-Services. His behavior mocks his "pure man" title. Though Nathan retains enough sense to eat and drink in moderation, he gives himself over entirely to carnal lust.

He becomes very conscious of his personal appearance. He trades for a metal tool for pulling hairs. Every morning he plucks his beard and body hairs like any American man—except the job takes him longer. He even plucks his eyebrows to keep the line-curve elegant. He gazes at himself in his mirror. After a race, he washes thoroughly. He combs his hair, makes sure his headband is on straight, perfumes his body with oils from Old France. Caucus-Meteor is amused by this particular Nathan, and laughs at him. "We have a saying for fellows like you," he says: "If a man could kiss his own ass, vanity would be unnecessary."

Caucus-Meteor observes yet another Nathan, Nathan the Man of God. Days go by when he doesn't pray, and god appears to be far from his mind. A great runner doesn't need a god. A great runner is a god. Then, in the middle of a night, Nathan will pop awake full of dread. He will break down, almost weeping. He will drop to his knees and pray. Caucus-Meteor wonders what he prays for. Forgiveness? Guidance? Divine grace? Caucus-Meteor doesn't think Nathan himself is even sure what it is he's praying for. The old American has witnessed these breakdowns in captives before. It's a stage they go through. When they think about returning to their past lives, they are taken by fear. They don't know why, but Caucus-Meteor knows. Part of the captive has become the savage he has been taught to despise. Usually during Nathan's bad moments, Caucus-Meteor respects his runner's privacy and leaves him alone, but one night his curiosity gets the better of him.

"I was wondering," Caucus-Meteor says, "what you are praying for."

"Light—I was asking for light," Nathan says softly.

"I have often imagined a world where one could command light, the way your god commands his heavens."

"This world cannot be commanded as long as the stain of Adam's sin is with us," says Nathan.

"I didn't say a world of easily acquired light would be heaven. I think it would be tiring."

When Nathan wakes, he's cheerful again, looking forward to the next race, the next festival, the next woman.

The last major race of the season is Chicoutimi, sixty miles up the mighty Saguenay river from the Tadousic trading center. The runners and their sponsors call it the "snow run" because on occasion it snows even in the summer. Not this year, when it might be called the wildfire run. The farther north you go, the worse the drought is. As Caucus-Meteor and Nathan canoe their way up the Saguenay they can smell smoke from forest fires many miles away. At one point they actually see half a mountain in flames.

"If it were not for your god's mercy," Caucus-Meteor teases, "the world itself would eventually be engulfed in such fires, for man, clever as he may be, is no match for a wildfire; only wind can turn a wildfire, and only rain can stop a wildfire; and only the Christian god can make wind and rain. Is that not so?"

"And surely only the savage can divine omens in such a spectacle," says Nathan, returning the gentle insult.

"Perhaps god is upset over the moral decline of his chosen people," says Caucus-Meteor.

"You joke, old American, but perhaps the joke is on all of us."

"As a practical matter, this drought has been to our benefit. We have a saying: bad weather for farmers is excellent weather for gamblers."

Nathan points out that the hardwoods and pine forests have disappeared except for a few scraggly birches. Spruce and fir trees prevail.

The old American is thinking now about the ancient gods, that he was wrong to argue with them, wrong also to reject Jesus and the priests, even if they did steal his daughter, for a man cannot consider himself entirely whole without gods. Instead of rejection, a better course might be to embrace all the gods. Let them be jealous of one another. While he's meditating over these thoughts, Nathan draws his attention. "Look, ahead."

Caucus-Meteor recognizes his village's canoe markings. He and Nathan have bumped into Haggis and his trading partners the day before the race in Chicoutimi. Surely, thinks Caucus-Meteor, this coincidence was arranged by the gods to punish or reward me for my peculiar thinking. I wonder how it will go.

Haggis brags that his crew has been all the way to Hudson Bay, where they've picked up some terrific furs in a deal for their moccasins. They'll trade the furs in Quebec for the goods demanded by their women.

"Hudson Bay region is majestic country," says Haggis. "Plenty of fish and game, no Frenchmen, no Englishmen, no Dutch-

men, no damn Scots, not even many natives. And no wars. People are too busy fighting the climate to fight each other."

Haggis is very good at concealing his emotions, but Caucus-
Meteor notes a certain strain in his jocularity. Something is not
right with Haggis. He's full of undefined sadness and anger.
Only Caucus-Meteor can smell the disturbance in the great
hunter's soul. Haggis's friends and fellow traders are fooled by
his outward behavior and their own good spirits, brought on
by the thought of heading home after a successful trading season. Now this! They're going to be treated to a footrace in which
a contestant is a member of their village, the servant Nathan
Provider-of-Services.

Nathan likes to celebrate and chase women after a race, but
never on the eve; Caucus-Meteor and Nathan stay the night in
the cabin of a local chief. They're outside by the fire eating supper when the chief informs them that one of the entries in the
race will be the great Mercuray, who has come out of retirement
solely to race Nathan. Nathan expresses excitement that Mercuray, the best of the best, has challenged him. The two Conissadawaga men are about to settle in when a figure emerges from
the darkness into the flickering light of the campfire. It's Caucus-
Meteor's old friend and Black Dirt's former lover, the voyageur
Robert de Repentigny.

The old American and the Frenchman converse excitedly in
French, which leaves Nathan out of the conversation.

"There aren't many left like you, Row-bear, a Frenchman who
dresses like an American," teases Caucus-Meteor. "These days
you have Americans dressing and behaving like Frenchmen, instead of the other way around."

"Not out west, where the Americans are proper savages," says
de Repentigny.

"Any news?" asks Caucus-Meteor. "Have they killed St. Blein
yet?"

"So you know about his crazy ideas."

"Know about them? He somehow talked me into being an informant. It was that phrase, Canada for Canadians, that impressed me." By now Caucus-Meteor has forgotten that he was the one who first voiced the rebel motto.

"He's very charming, because he's sincere, all heart, belief, and courage. And, face it, he's telling the truth," says de Repentigny. "Men in pretty rooms in Old France, not to mention some of our own merchants and noblemen, are looting this country. In the end, all that's left for the people is strife and poverty."

"I have this fear," says Caucus-Meteor, "that when they finally find him out, they'll put him on that torture contraption in Montreal—"

"The rack."

"Correct, and he'll implicate my village, all because of my vanity and stupidity."

"They may come after you, but you can rest assured that St. Blein will squirm free. He's a rich man's son with noble blood. They'll forgive his wild talk, because they know it won't lead to anything. If he doesn't get himself killed by an Englishman's musket ball, he'll marry royalty, and they'll give him a mile on the St. Lawrence complete with rent-paying peasants to work the land. He'll set aside his fine ideas and replace them with splendor and comfort."

"I hope you're right."

"Listen, Caucus-Meteor, I noticed some of your villagers camped in the woods."

"Yes, we visited them earlier. They're traders, and they'll be here for the races tomorrow."

"If they're traders, why did I see them with Bleached Bones, the gambler? Why did I hear them singing war songs or maybe death songs, I couldn't be sure? It sounded all wrong and dangerous to me."

"They seemed fine this afternoon," says Caucus-Meteor, but

he's thinking about the uneasy feeling he had seeing Haggis. And now that Bleached Bones is in the picture, he knows something is seriously amiss.

"I don't know what it means," says de Repentigny. "I just thought you ought to know."

Caucus-Meteor says nothing to Nathan about this conversation, but he's fraught with worry all night. The next morning Caucus-Meteor and Nathan leave the cabin and mingle with the traders from their village; they're sitting around a campfire, eating a breakfast of freshly caught fish. The men are talkative and jovial, but none of them touches Nathan nor looks directly at either Nathan or Caucus-Meteor. Even men who rarely smile, such as Kineo, are laughing and joking. Something is wrong. Later Bleached Bones comes on the scene. He wants to lay a huge bet on Mercuray. Caucus-Meteor feels honor bound to cover the bet. For the third time, he's gone against his fine judgment in dealing with Bleached Bones.

Haggis and the other Conissadawaga men pace in studied insouciance. They act like men looking for signs of demons, thinks Caucus-Meteor. The gods will provide plenty of such signs—from the crows in the trees, to the eyebrows on Nathan's face, cut sharply. An hour before the race, which will be run at noon, Caucus-Meteor sees the great sign that surely the traders have taken note of. The morning chill and dampness have burned off. The wildfires, which were smoldering all during the night, now flare up with the wind. Thick smoke pours down through the river valley. There's some talk of postponing the race, but it's quickly squelched. The race is too important to the bettors to halt because of a mere act of nature. The valley here is cleared, it's pasture and farmland, so no one feels in danger of losing his life. Still, the wind brings thick acrid smoke that stings the eyes and shrouds the spirit.

Nathan notices none of the intrigue swirling around him. Even the forest fire sweeping in from the west is in the far recesses of mind.

"You look ready, Nathan Provider-of-Services," says Caucus-Meteor.

"If I can beat this Cree runner, I will become a legend, the man who beat a legend. If I lose, I'll just be another good runner who lost to the great Mercuray."

In the hour before the race, Nathan paces nervously in the field with the other runners. The spectators know enough to leave them alone during this period of preparation. Nathan doesn't notice Caucus-Meteor working frantically among the gamblers, betting with more people than usual. Shortly before the race, his godfather approaches him.

"How are you feeling?" Caucus-Meteor asks, which is what he always says before a race.

"I'm fit," says Nathan, which is what he always says. In this case it's clear from his behavior that he's prepared mind and body for this race.

"Nathan," Caucus-Meteor says in the soft voice Nathan has come to understand means he's serious and not full of cow patties.

"What does my godfather want of me now?" Nathan says with just an edge of sarcasm. Since he's become an important runner, insolence, even to a king, comes naturally.

"I think it best you lose this race today."

"What do you mean—lose?" Nathan's confused.

"I mean just that. Don't beat this Cree—lose."

"On purpose? Why?"

"I'm not sure why. Call it an old man's peculiarity. The Frenchman you met yesterday, de Repentigny? I trust him. He had the same feeling. And I don't like the smell of this fire. It's too big, hostile, and malevolent."

"All right, Caucus-Meteor. I will follow your instructions," Nathan says.

Caucus-Meteor has heard that tone before, as the slave in Nathan Provider-of-Services speaks. What's in those other selves, wonders Caucus-Meteor. He supposes he'll soon find out.

Just before the race starts, the wind blows strong, bringing with it the fire. The main blaze is still miles away, but fist-sized windblown embers start small advance fires. One of these springs up in the dry grass of the field where the race is being held. The starting musket goes off, and Nathan, preoccupied by his own doubts, doesn't burst into the lead the way he usually does.

Mercuray is also slow in releasing his pent-up energy. Nathan and the Cree fight their way through flying elbows and speedy, sleek-bodied men. The course is flat, and some of it on ledge so the footing is good, but it's nasty ground to take a fall on. The course helps the fastest runners, and by the turn-around (a boulder big as a wigwam), Nathan and Mercuray have gone by the pack and are side by side. At about the same moment, the wind is carrying the grass fire to the racers. The spectators are backing away from the finish as the runners, just ahead of the fire, are coming toward the end.

Caucus-Meteor can see that Nathan is ready to expend his last reserve of energy, and then he thinks he sees a moment of doubt on his runner's face. Perhaps not, perhaps the doubt is in me, thinks Caucus-Meteor. Now, he notices Haggis standing beside him. The great hunter's hand is on his knife. Suddenly, Caucus-Meteor understands: if Nathan comes out of the smoke in first place, Haggis will plunge his knife into my heart. Oh, please, dear god in Christian heaven, oh, please, great gods of disreputed America, prays the old man, allow me this quick and glorious death, so I do not have to inaugurate the reuniting ceremony myself. He relaxes his muscles so the knife will slide through easier. And then a coil of smoke wraps around the runners and engulfs them. Mercuray emerges from the smoke three steps ahead of Nathan. The crowd shows its ecstasy at Mercuray's victory.

Haggis withdraws, his face full of shame.

Spectators and runners alike hurry to the river to watch the fire pass them by. Mercuray is happy to collect his fee and add to his legend as he goes back into retirement, undefeated. Haggis is, well, not exactly happy, but relieved that a man he adopted into the tribe was proven to be, after all, only a man and not a demon. Caucus-Meteor has collected enough winnings over the summer to pay the intendant for a couple of years, and still have money left over, so he should be happy, but he's not sure how he feels. Bleached Bones and Nathan are not happy. Nathan will not go down in the annals of this land. Bleached Bones achieved his revenge and walked away with a great deal of Caucus-Meteor's money. I know what you are thinking, old comrade, thinks Caucus-Meteor: the trouble with winning is that it removes all hope.

Haggis shakes Nathan's hand, congratulates him on his effort. "It's no disgrace to lose to the best American runner," he says.

"It was good for my character, taught me humility," Nathan grins insincerely.

"You don't look too humble to me. You look like a man who has discovered what the Englishman and the Frenchman have no conception of."

"And what is that, my friend—personal adornment? I admit to grooming myself like an American man."

"The Englishman and Frenchman are as vain as the American, their wigs and hats prove the point, but I do not speak of grooming. I doubt there is a word in your native English for what I'm thinking, but in my language it's an open sky above a herd of caribou; it's feasting after a long fast; it's forgetfulness in songs chanted over a small fire."

Nathan withdraws by turning his head away. He's in no mood for debate; he wants only to brood over his defeat.

That night Nathan and Caucus-Meteor camp on the shore of the river. The fire has moved on, leaving smoke and distant glows. Nathan tells Caucus-Meteor that something strange happened to him in the smoke when the runners were obscured. "By all accounts of mind, I left Chicoutimi, and found myself in some unknown land. I was an old man, as you today are an old man, and I was saying, 'I know it's a petty vanity, but ever since that day in Canada, I've been nettled—nettled. Did that Cree fellow beat me fair and square? I can't believe he was the better man.'"

"You were conjuring the future," says the old American king. "All men do it by accident from time to time. I am attempting to bring craft to conjuring, which is a gift from some god or other, but so far I have been unsuccessful. I envy you, and in that future time when you have this thought of your disappointment today, think of me; pray for my soul, and our shared human frailty."

Nathan recovers from the gloom of his defeat by leaving the camp and carousing. Alone, Caucus-Meteor broods. The racing season is over and they will now return to Conissadawaga. As soon as he dispenses all the money he's made, his villagers are almost certain to reelect him as king. But from that position he will be more vulnerable than in his present situation, where he is a leader except in name. As king, he'll be open to criticism from Haggis. For hours Caucus-Meteor schemes. Perhaps he should execute Haggis. But then he'll also have to execute his family. Who would do such work? Not anyone in his village. He'd have to recruit his killers from another réfugié tribe. It suddenly occurs to Caucus-Meteor that he is thinking like a European. The sickness of his ambition leaves him unhappy with his own company.

Nathan returns drunk and singing. After he falls into a dead sleep, Caucus-Meteor slips away into the darkness, following a smell, a feeling, an old intuition long buried, and a tiny light, a star on the hem of the earth. Finally, he comes to some scraggly gray birches. He hears the cocking of a weapon.

"It's only me," Caucus-Meteor says in the darkness, and walks into the light of the campfire. Bleached Bones is pointing his hand musket at him.

"Caucus-Meteor, did you come here to revenge yourself?" Bleached Bones says.

"No, I just came for a visit."

The two old interpreters sit around the tiny fire that Bleached Bones has made.

"You're an awful troublemaker, but the only man I know outside of myself who can make a proper fire," says Caucus-Meteor.

"I'd hoped that Haggis killed you today," says Bleached Bones.

"Do the work yourself. Pull your weapon and shoot me, please," says Caucus-Meteor.

Bleached Bones reaches not for his weapon, but for his belly; he hangs his head, moans.

"You are in pain," says Caucus-Meteor.

"Not enough," says Bleached Bones, rubbing where the liver bulges out. "When the pain is serious, I feel cheerful. But at the moment, the pain is merely a dull ache, like the loss of a loved one. Not that I would know anything about such matters, never having had any loved ones."

"I do not understand how you feel, Bleached Bones, since I have been cursed by many loved ones. I can only envy your solitude. I am curious. What kind of plot did you contrive against me?"

Bleached Bones laughs just a little. "First I hired Mercuray to come out of retirement with the idea of beating your man. Then when I saw Haggis and his bunch, I got an idea. I knew that Haggis was your rival in your village. I also knew that because of his old-fashion pagan ways he'd be a superstitious fool. So I convinced him and his men that Nathan was a sorcerer. How else could a white man defeat the best savages in footraces? By the time I was done, I half-believed it myself."

"So if Nathan won the race, Haggis would have killed me as the devil's agent."

"Yes, that was the plan. Either way, I was going to win. If Nathan won, I would have your life; if Mercuray won, I would have your money. No wonder I am so gloomy. My cleverness always leaves me sick."

"I knew something was wrong, so I bet against Nathan with the other bettors. I broke even on this race."

"What's more your life is your own again."

"Yes, and that is why I am as depressed as you, old criminal."

"Now that the racing season is over, what will you do?"

"I have to return to my village and take control. Control always makes me despondent, and yet I cannot stop myself from controlling."

"Do you know the birches by the black rocks a day north of Quebec by river?"

"Of course."

"Tomorrow I will hire a canoe man to take me and a cargo of brandy south. Somewhere out on the St. Lawrence river I will take the money I won from you and from the rest of the fools on the trade circuit this summer, and I will scatter it to the waters. I do it because the burden of it is too much, and because I will enjoy appalling the canoe man. I love the expression on their faces when I throw money away. The canoe man will drop me by the black rocks, and I will walk to the birches. I will sit by a fire and drink brandy until I see the devil. Only then will I be happy, and only for a few moments. But it's worth it, I tell you."

"You are more a king in your belly than I."

"I keep betraying people, hoping they'll kill me, but it never happens. I am too clever, and my enemies are too stupid. I need someone my equal to share my anguish with. Come live with me, Caucus-Meteor."

"I'm tempted."

"I will be a wife to you, Caucus-Meteor. Remember that I was a wife to you long ago."

"It was only one time. I thought of it as a test."

"Perhaps for you. For me it was love."

"I think you only wanted to get my turban, for even then you and I were bald, but I had the turban."

"Yes, I did want the turban. Your powers were in it. You told me a wild story that a king from Old India gave it to you along with your name."

"The truth is my wife made the turban, and I named myself.

When I was in Old France as a boy, my teacher studied the stars in the heavens. He used to call me Meteore, from the Old French, as one high in the air, a star that cannot stay still. And 'caucus' is the ancient Algonkian word for gathering of those who use words instead of weapons."

"Last night, I dreamed for the thousandth time that I was wearing Caucus-Meteor's turban. It's a dream that makes me feel kingly. Come, join me in my realm. We'll get on each other's nerves, and maybe one fine day we'll slaughter one another."

"I am sorry, Bleached Bones. I have too many responsibilities to fall in love. Besides I can't bear the smell of brandy."

The two old interpreters embrace, and Caucus-Meteor returns to his camp.

In the morning, as the Conissadawaga party is readying to leave, other canoe men are just arriving from the south. They must have paddled all night by the moon. From their ornamentation it's obvious that the group are Kahnawake Mohawks. One face is paler than the rest. It's young Sam Allen, who went through the gauntlet the same day as Nathan. Sam has gained weight, though he's still smaller than the rest of the Mohawks. Nathan and Sam lock eyes for a long moment. Nathan nods, Sam nods; they shake hands politely. But they have a difficult time communicating. Nathan's conversant language is Algonkian, Sam's is Iroquois. They struggle in each other's languages, give French a fling (Sam's a little better at "parlez vous" than Nathan, but not much), and finally decide to exchange pleasantries only, then with relief go their separate ways. It's not until hours later on the river in the canoe that Nathan says to his godfather, "Neither I nor Sam thought to speak English."

"So now you believe in omens, especially bad ones," says Caucus-Meteor.

"I think so, yes."

Later, Caucus-Meteor drops even the pretense of paddling, and he rests on the thwarts, shuts his eyes, and suddenly for the first time since his illness he's conjuring on the third captive who ran the gauntlet with Nathan and Sam, Captain Warren, the man whose ear he burned. He will return to his people a cripple for life. Impotent, immobile, in pain, and ugly as a clean-out stick for an English outhouse, Captain Warren will bear his suffering by displaying it, for his town will treat him as a returning hero in the wars against the French and Americans. His extravagance as the local bully will be forgiven. People will buy him drinks at the tavern. But war heroes, especially marginal ones, wear thin on the public mind until they are shunned with the coming of peace and then pushed out all together by the heroes of subsequent conflicts. Warren will pick the wrong side in the next war. He will come to be regarded as just another antique veteran. His few relatives will die off or move west. He will become a ward of the local government, an item on the town meeting agenda under Overseers of the Poor. Food will be left at the door of his crude hut. At night he will be heard screaming in pain and hatred.

"What is it? What did you say?" The voice is Nathan's, who has heard the old American mumbling to himself.

"I was conjuring over Captain Warren. He's the part of me that hides in the woods, injured, howling, alone."

Succession

aucus-Meteor and Nathan and the Conissadawaga traders are only half a day from their home village when they meet a canoe man from the south. He hails them, and paddles in their direction. It's Omer Laurent, his craft weighed down with two red-capped French trappers and their gear.

Stopped, the canoes looking like birch logs now, the men exchange greetings, then Omer shouts, "Let's visit for an hour—I have some brandy. I and my French fares have sore behinds, and need a rest."

This is strange behavior coming from Omer, thinks Caucus-Meteor.

The Conissadawaga men are full of good humor because they're almost home, so they cheer their fellow villager. The canoes pull off on a narrow beach of dark gray pebbles.

Like Caucus-Meteor, Haggis is suspicious of Omer's rare outburst of sociability, and he approaches Omer the moment they step from the canoes. "What's going on, Omer? It's not like you to slow down on the river, especially with passengers."

"Maybe Omer is happy to see his trading brothers," Caucus-Meteor says with the kind of little insincere smile that he knows infuriates Haggis.

"Omer does not lie so easily. He blushes with shame," Haggis says.

"Leave him alone, Haggis. He wants to see his king," says Caucus-Meteor. "I owe him some money. Is that not so, Omer?"

Omer bows. "Yes, for the canoe."

"I see," Haggis nods. "Apparently, Omer is now completely corrupted by money." Haggis turns, and walks off.

Caucus-Meteor starts down the beach. Omer follows, but says nothing. They walk in silence. When they're out of sight of the rest of the men, Caucus-Meteor says, "We have privacy now. What is the folly, Omer?"

"I didn't want to tell you in front of the men. I want you to know I am not afraid for myself, but for Hungry Heart and my business, which to me is like a second wife and to my wife like a second husband. If the word spreads that I helped you, it will be the end of everything that Hungry Heart and I have built."

"Your alarm concerns the intendant," says Caucus-Meteor.

"How could you know? Is it sorcery?"

"It might be. I've been incubating over a moment like this all summer."

"I don't know what you are talking about, my king, but I do know this. You are wanted for questioning at the palace. The intendant has issued a paper warrant. If you return to the village, his man will come for you."

"It's exactly as I feared. Sometimes I think I'm like a god myself in cognition. Too bad I am so unlike a god in other respects, this frail body, morbid heart. But this is not the time for a speech. Give me your purse."

Omer hesitates, then reaches for the cloth satchel which he carries in a waist band.

Caucus-Meteor transfers money from his own moose skin bag to Omer's.

"Take this money and bring it to Black Dirt. Tell her to say nothing, and to await my instructions. And, Omer, remove an amount equal to twice your fee for the canoe you loaned us and keep it with my profound and kingly gratitude."

Omer trembles. Caucus-Meteor wishes he knew what he was

feeling, probably some concoction of glee, guilt, fear, and a will to go on with his dream of a river empire no matter what, all the things that make him the man he is.

"I cannot go back to the village now to present Black Dirt with your earnings," Omer says. "I must take my fares north. It will be weeks before I can return."

"All the better. No one will suspect you then of conspiring with me. You have my blessing," says Caucus-Meteor, passing his hand across Omer's leathery head and resting it on his shoulder. Caucus-Meteor is thinking that something profound and new is about to begin. Then he bends, picks up some stones, and fills his empty money bag with the stones.

Omer no longer bothers to pretend he wants to socialize. He announces to his passengers that it's time to dig the water, and minutes later his canoe disappears into the hazy light on the river. Maybe he'll steal my money, and never come back, thinks Caucus-Meteor. We would all have nothing; we would have to depend on the hunter, Haggis. Maybe that's the way it should be. Before, when he thought he might be elected king again, when he imagined himself giving away his winnings, Caucus-Meteor had felt tense, a sickness of the spirit; his despair could only be alleviated with thoughts of the pleasures of largess. Now that he knows there will be no largess, that he is a fugitive, his life at risk, his powers next to nothing—now he is free, open, exuberant. "Let us celebrate our return to loved ones," he says. "Let us sleep here for the night, so that we can time our arrival with the high sun tomorrow."

Haggis appears suspicious again, much to the amusement of Caucus-Meteor. Later that night the men drink the brandy that Omer left them, and tell stories by a big fire. Caucus-Meteor sits by a small private fire, and waits in silence. He knows that Haggis will be the last to doze off.

The next morning as the dawn is breaking over the St. Lawrence, Caucus-Meteor is alone in a canoe for the first time in years. He stops paddling for a moment, lets the current take hold, stares into the rising sun, and shuts his eyes so that he can feel more than see the brightness through closed eyelids. He's thinking that just about at this moment Haggis opens his eyes when the birds wake him at dawn. Haggis will sense that something doesn't feel right. He will rise, walk over to Caucus-Meteor's camp. Nathan Provider-of-Services will be sleeping like stone, but the old king will be nowhere to be seen, and his fire will be cold. Haggis never panics during such moments. He'll concentrate his mental faculties, as now Caucus-Meteor concentrates his, conjuring him. I'm close, he thinks—I'm close to the conjuring trick; or perhaps what I am thinking is only speculation. It doesn't matter, since the thought is not very important. Haggis will follow disturbed twigs and bent grass. If the old king went into the woods, Haggis estimates he'll track him within the hour. But the tracks will lead to the pebbly beach. A canoe will be missing.

Out on the water, the conjuring fades and Caucus-Meteor is thinking that he doesn't like paddling, especially now when he has to do it all by himself. You can't cheat at paddling when there is only one paddler: old Algonkian saying. Well, it isn't an old saying, but it should be. In some future life and time, perhaps he will be one who creates sayings, for a people with good sayings are a good people and a people with poor sayings are poorer for their sayings. He's spent, a conniving old man; it's unlikely he can ever again give his people anything of value but the unwanted and untrustworthy commodity of advice. With his death, perhaps the intendant will leave his people alone. The idea of death comforts him for about twenty minutes, and then he thinks, but this is all so sudden. Who will take my place? It's not that a dying man should answer this question, it's that it should occur to him now that sets him to thinking, for he's always believed that when the correct moment arrives for reuniting, he will not worry about temporal matters. So, then, he thinks, I am not ready to die. With that conclusion, Caucus-Meteor is back to that comforting habit of scheming, which inevitably will lead to that terrible gnawing loneliness that has haunted him since Keeps-the-Flame died.

He estimates he's about a day away from the birches by the black rocks. Bleached Bones might not be the ideal wife, thinks Caucus-Meteor, but he'll have to do; I have no other place to go.

As Caucus-Meteor continues with the dreary work of canoe paddling, he ruminates on his destiny. He must continue to develop his conjuring gift. He's always been good at visualizing and scheming, though not at praying. He's too insincere to be good at praying. Conjuring includes all three of these tricks of mentality—visualizing, scheming, praying, plus concentration. I will try it again. I will visualize my men in their canoes. This time the conjuring trick works. Finally, he is sick enough in heart, mind, and body to visit the gods.

Led by Haggis, the Conissadawaga traders will search up and down stream for likely places that an elderly canoe man might linger. They will query Frenchmen and natives alike, but no one will admit to seeing an old savage wearing a turban. The reunion with loved ones in the village will be exciting but confusing. The men will be happy to see their families, and in great detail and with great exaggeration will tell of their adventures. The women will complain about the drought, that the crops this year are sufficient, but only because of water from the lake. Caucus-Meteor's disappearance will be a worrisome thing. The villagers will talk of spirits. They're an in-between people living in a valley between times, and they will sense that the liquid of change is about to flood their plain.

Haggis will see Nathan Provider-of-Services as a future rival. Nathan Provider-of-Services has changed a great deal over the summer. He will strut about, telling stories of his glories on the racing circuit. He will tease; he will mock. The former slave will move into the wigwam of Wytopitlock and Parmachnenee. Haggis will fear Nathan's virtues more than his vices. Nathan will impress the tribe with his nimble fingers, good at nettlesome tasks such as derhning dogsled harnesses and carving smoking pipes. There doesn't seem to be a tool he doesn't take to. The men will not only listen to him; they will respect him. The older women of the tribe obviously will want him to marry one or both of his concubines. If Nathan marries he'll become a real threat to Haggis. The people may even want to make him a chief.

For the present moment, Haggis will not be too worried about Nathan Provider-of-Services. Haggis will be convinced that without the old king around, he will be the leader of the village. For the time being the tribal chiefs are himself, Passaconway, and Black Dirt. Passaconway wasn't a chief in his prime, and he's hardly a leader in his old age. The only real threat to Haggis is Black Dirt. Eventually, Haggis figures, she'll agree to marry him, and then he will be the supreme leader of the tribe.

Black Dirt will find the uncertainty surrounding her father harder to bear than a grief. His disappearance will throw her back in time to when she was a child, and she only wanted to hide. During this summer she had thought through her plans to make Conissadawaga into strictly a farming village. The hard part would be persuading the villagers, especially her father. Without his support, the entire idea will crumble. Now he is missing. Black Dirt will deal with her anguish in the only way she knows. She will work harder; she will seclude herself.

The black rocks are easy enough to find, big as wigwams, sitting in a valley at the steep slope of a whaleback mountain, visible from the river. Where do such rocks come from, wonders Caucus-Meteor. Surely they were deposited here by gods who passed through Canada long ago, but for what purpose? Perhaps they are alive, and will one day roll on. Few things grow among the rocks, and the animals—even the birds—avoid the area; people come here only for religious reasons. Caucus-Meteor calls out Bleached Bones's name, but he hears only the mocking echo of his own voice. Bleached Bones said his wigwam was in the birches by the rocks, but Caucus-Meteor sees no birches.

Caucus-Meteor has had nothing to eat for two days. A gust of mild panic sweeps through him. He starts walking the perimeter of the rocks, resting frequently, growing weaker. After another hour of walking, Caucus-Meteor is beginning to think that Bleached Bones had been lying to him. But he knows when Bleached Bones lies. He was not lying. Maybe he was delayed, or changed his mind. Even so he should be able to find the old gambler's camp. After another hour of wandering, Caucus-Meteor is beginning to feel silly and wonderful as a bridegroom, a feeling that signals him that soon he will be delirious.

Moments later he sees the birches. They're just beyond a swamp he's been trudging through, which has taken him back toward the rocks. He'd avoided this place because of the swamp and because, looking at it from afar, there did not seem to be any birches here. But, in a ring of land above the swamp and just before where the mountain steepens, the birches appear, though every last one is fallen, split, damaged in some way, as though a giant had had a tantrum. He thinks that the original native god of this realm, Gooslup, has left his marker. Where did Gooslup go when Jesus chased him out? Maybe Gooslup moved west, to that place that Nathan talks about. Close investigation reveals the true culprit, not Gooslup but an ice storm two or three winters ago. These are not the magnificent white birches with bark for boats, or the black birches of more southerly climes that produce excellent firewood and minty aroma in the sap wood, or the yellow birches that take over a forest land through their sheer age. These are the gray birches—a short-lived tree, with weak wood, and unremarkable bark. It's the kind of forest that Bleached Bones would be attracted to, for despite his rather serious character flaws, he is a humble man.

Caucus-Meteor shouts, "Bleached Bones, give me something to eat." But there is no response to his plea. He's probably lying in wait for me, thinks Caucus-Meteor. At some moment of his choosing he'll shoot me.

Caucus-Meteor stumbles onto the camp only minutes later. First, he sees a food cache hanging from one of the disreputable birches. The cache bag dangles from a hook on a rope. It's an easy matter to pick up a stick and lift the cache off the hook. If only the animals could think as we think, we would not exist, thinks Caucus-Meteor. He eats some dried salmon and nuts. The food makes him strong and arrogant. If Bleached Bones hasn't jumped me yet, he's probably drunk and passed out, and I will jump him.

Bleached Bones's camp pleases Caucus-Meteor. It consists of a small wigwam built on a table rock, black as the intendant's heart. In front of the wigwam is a flat stone placed like a low altar on smaller stones, the site of the old gambler's campfire. Beside it is a blanket on a rotted hemlock log. Somewhere along the line Bleached Bones started sitting like a white man, preferring a rotted log for a seat because it was soft. Bleached Bones, I am disappointed in you. What makes the camp unique are the carvings, hanging from trees, whittled birch sticks of faces bearing different human emotions, all of which resemble their creator. The feeling Bleached Bones has created reminds Caucus-Meteor of the feeling in the old cathedrals in Europe—fear and awe and something else, that a man's life on this earth may have little worth in itself, but that it is part of a plan by a greater being.

Inside the wigwam is a bad smell—drink. Bottles of different kinds of brandy are neatly arranged along the perimeter of the wigwam, along with jugs of English rum. Here too are Bleached Bones's few worldly possessions. Apparently, he told the truth about throwing his winnings in the St. Lawrence, because Caucus-Meteor finds only a small amount of money in his bag. He comes across some thunderbolts, those lightning-fused chunks of earth that gamblers value as good-luck pieces; several pairs of moccasins; some snares for catching rabbits; another kind of snare for capturing migrating ducks; a set of knives for wood carving, with sharpening stone and some whale oil; and several muskets, but no powder or lead. Bleached Bones, you old bluffer, you always went about heavily armed, but with unloaded weapons. The most remarkable objects in the wigwam are costumes of sticks carefully woven together with European fibers and animal gut. What Bleached Bones did with this unique wardrobe is impossible to say, but surely, thinks Caucus-Meteor, it must have had something to do with sadness and sex.

At the center of the wigwam is a place for a fire, and a single iron pipe that projects through the smoke hole. There are plenty of French blankets to keep a man warm, but no stick frame or mats for sleeping. Like himself, Bleached Bones spends most of his hours by his fire. Caucus-Meteor sees a few pots for cooking, but they hardly seem used. Apparently, Bleached Bones's main food is drink.

Caucus-Meteor goes back outside and runs his hands through the fire. The ashes are cold. Bleached Bones hasn't been here at least for a couple of days. Caucus-Meteor returns to the wigwam until he finds some fire-making tools, flint and tinder. It takes patience and perseverance, but in a half hour he's able to start a fire. It's past midnight on a night when clouds obscure moon and stars that Caucus-Meteor, sitting on his heels by the fire, divines Bleached Bones's fate. The wind shifts as the storm rises up, and with the wind comes a smell. Caucus-Meteor goes into the wigwam to get out of the rain, taking some fire with him.

Late the next morning after the rain has stopped, Caucus-Meteor goes outside. First he eats a good breakfast, and then he walks in the direction where the wind came from last night. He finds Bleached Bones by smell. The old gambler is lying on some rocks near a ditch that he used for a privy. Apparently, he left the camp when he felt a call of nature. He did his business and started back for the camp when he must have been taken by a pain, or perhaps just a weakness. Caucus-Meteor puts his hand on Bleached Bones's belly. It's soft and distended where the liver burst.

Bleached Bones's body is more or less intact, but the face has been pecked by turkey vultures until it's unrecognizable. Birds always start with the eyes, soft and nutritious. Caucus-Meteor says a prayer aloud on Bleached Bones's behalf. "I hope, old gambler, that in the next world you can find a husband to take care of your extravagant needs. I think, too, I know a place where you can be buried and not be so lonely." Caucus-Meteor strips the clothes off the body of Bleached Bones and off his own body until he's just a naked old man wearing a turban, standing above another naked old body without a face to speak of. He kneels by the body, removes the turban, and places it on Bleached Bones's head. "You always coveted my turban—now you have it," says Caucus-Meteor.

Weeks later, in the loft of the intendant's barn, Caucus-Meteor, feeble from lack of food and rest, calls out below to Norman Feathers, who has just come in. "Norman, Norman. Bring me some water. Bring me some food." His voice is so weak that it sounds like the whisper of a ghost, and Norman runs out of the barn in fright. It's another hour before he returns. "It's really me, I'm not a ghost, not yet," Caucus-Meteor can barely speak. This time Norman drops to his knees and prays.

Prayer apparently gives Norman some courage, because he puts a ladder to the loft and climbs up. Even then, it takes Caucus-Meteor a good half an hour to convince Norman who he is. The old king is weak from hunger, he's lost some weight—indeed, he's aged in the sudden way of old people—he has a bone through his nose, but mainly he just doesn't look like himself without the turban. That bald head, pale as a white man's from lack of exposure to sun and air, takes attention away from the eyes and recognizable features.

After some water and food, Caucus-Meteor's strength returns, at least in his voice.

"Norman, have you ever wondered what your gift of memory is for?"

"For remembering, I imagine."

"No, your god has given it to you for a purpose, which I will now reveal. I am going to shut my eyes, and put my mind in a conjuring pose. You will answer my questions."

The interrogation takes several hours. Norman has no sense of what is important and what is not, so he talks on about everything. Afterward, the old American builds a tiny fire outside the barn, stares into it, conjures upon the information supplied by his kinsman.

Some French fishermen spot a canoe caught on a snag in the river. Inside is the body of an old savage. With the Frenchmen is a Montagnais fellow. "Only one man in Canada wears a turban like this, the famous king of Conissadawaga, Caucus-Meteor," he says. "We must return the body to his village."

Friends and relatives come from all over for the funeral rite, but the only close relatives the old man had were his daughters, Black Dirt and Caterina. The convent reluctantly lets Caterina loose for this pagan service, but because she's still a novice, she's required to stay in the company of an older nun, and leave right after the ceremony. Black Dirt and Caterina reconcile their differences.

"I wronged you with my anger, sister," says Black Dirt.

"And I you with my selfishness," says Caterina.

"Has Jesus been good to you?"

"Before I gave myself to Jesus, I was in a deep pit of hopelessness, dark as a well. Now I am in the light."

The sisters embrace.

Drummers make mournful music, while Caucus-Meteor's daughters stand by the fire; village women wrap the sisters in blankets, and then the mourners form a line, say a few words to the sisters, embrace them, and move on. Nathan Provider-of-Services is among the mourners. He shakes Caterina's hand, says a few words in Algonkian, then turns to Black Dirt. She doesn't extend her hand, so he refrains from touching her. Just says the obligatory words of consolation and leaves the line.

Afterward Black Dirt sees Nathan standing alone. He's looks as pained as she feels. She watches as his lips move. He's praying to his Protestant Jesus.

Hungry Heart and Omer Laurent pass through the line. Hungry Heart has gained strength and weight after her woman's illness earlier in the year. She embraces Black Dirt, then whispers into her ear. "Omer and I must return to our business, but before we go, we must see you in the wigwam when no one else is about."

The body lies under folds of tightly wrapped birch bark stitched at the ends. In the shroud the body looks like a tree trunk, except that at one end the top of the turban protrudes. All agreed that the king would want to be buried wearing his turban. After the ceremony around the fire, the mourners march in procession, through the cornfield, past the stone ruins, to the cemetery. Black Dirt and Caterina drop Caucus-Meteor's few worldly possessions into the grave. Then each of the mourners takes a handful of earth and throws it in.

Black Dirt says goodbye to her sister in French.

"Our father brought us together with his death," Caterina whispers. "After I take my final vows in a year, I can have visitors." Caterina gives Black Dirt rosary beads. "Keep these in a sacred place. Some day you may have use for them."

"I will, and when you have taken your vows I will come to you, sister."

"I will pray for you every day, sister."

The nun accompanying Caterina interrupts, explaining to Black Dirt that Caterina is forbidden to speak any further. Caterina bows her head, clasps her hands in prayer, which she offers to her sister like a kiss.

In the barn, Caucus-Meteor tells Norman Feathers that attending one's own funeral through conjuring is a pleasant if frustrating experience. "I'm happy that Black Dirt and Caterina are sisters in heart again. I knew my death would be good for something besides throwing the intendant off my trail. Now tell me as much as you can about Haggis and Nathan Provider-of-Services."

Norman tells all he can remember about the behavior of the two men.

"Listen to me carefully, Norman Feathers," says Caucus-Meteor. "You must tell no one that I am alive, because eventually the news would get back to the intendant, and I would be arrested. If I know one thing it's that there is going to be trouble in Conissadawaga revolving around succession to my throne. I've been planning a way to resolve these problems, but it will require your cooperation."

"I've been taught by my faith to be loyal to my church and my king, and you Caucus-Meteor are my king," says Norman Feathers.

"I never thought I'd be thanking Jesus Christ for what he's done to men's minds, but in this case I can only say, 'Merci.' Norman, do you know the Latin words of the Catholic mass?"

"I know them all. They are my comfort."

"I've always wondered. What do the words of the mass mean?"

"Mean? What does the meaning of words have to do with faith?"

"Why, nothing, nothing at all. Norman, I have some important work for you. If you will memorize a few words of oratory, I think that you can help me establish strong leadership for our village."

Days later, after Norman has returned with his tale, Caucus-Meteor conjures it over a fire. Before, starvation and Norman's assistance in providing him raw information helped him travel back in time. Now he can do it on a full stomach. He's already in between worlds, and eventually, with practice and more illness and hardships, Caucus-Meteor believes, he won't need Norman.

But for now he can only visualize and conjure upon what has been described to him.

Without any prior discussion, everyone in Conissadawaga senses that this evening's meeting around the campfire will be a fateful one, though no one is certain just what will transpire. Wytopitlock and Parmachnenee groom Nathan Provider-of-Services carefully—washing, plucking hairs from his face and chest, making certain his beads and pendants look right with his clothes: fresh trade shirt, leather breeches, fancy walking moccasins with frilled tops. (He's retired his plain racing shoes.) It's a pleasant evening, though on the cool side. The cold season is coming. Because he's spent more time than usual dressing, Nathan is a little late leaving the wigwam. Haggis is waiting in the circle for him.

"In the past when Caucus-Meteor returned to the village he was very generous," Haggis says. He looks at Nathan. "I know that Caucus-Meteor collected much French scrip betting on footraces."

"Not just footraces, but footraces won by Nathan Provider-of-Services." Nathan thumps his chest with his fist.

"Winning races is honor enough in American land, Nathan Provider-of-Services," says Haggis sarcastically. "For the gambler, money is the honeycomb at the top of the tree. Caucus-Meteor didn't necessarily bet on Nathan Provider-of-Services. What I want to know is before the old man mysteriously disappeared, did he give you his money, for no money was found on him. And if he did, doesn't the money belong to Caucus-Meteor's people?"

Nathan responds with haughty arrogance. "If Caucus-Meteor gave me his money, I do not owe any to Haggis."

"Haggis does not want money," Haggis says. "Haggis wants the truth. In Canada, French scrip and truth become one."

"I could have taken the old man's money any time. I don't

know where it is." It sounds like a lie, but then again a lot of truths sound like lies; the people are caught between conflicting currents of mind on this matter.

"Maybe he hid it," says Parmachnenee. "It would be like Caucus-Meteor to hide his money."

"Maybe so. He must have hidden it," says Haggis, his voice reeking with sarcasm. Parmachnenee's making excuses for Nathan has wounded Haggis in a way he wants to conceal, for he had been thinking that she might become his fifth wife, and now this from her—stupidity and betrayal.

The issue hangs there for a few minutes while the people decide what to do next. They need a firm idea to grasp onto, which presently Haggis attempts to formulate. "I believe that Nathan Provider-of-Services strangled the old king, put him in the canoe, set him adrift, and then returned to his bed with the money," Haggis says.

"Where I come from we have a thing called proof," says Nathan. He doesn't seem to be a villager anymore. His mannerisms, the catch in his Algonkian pronunciation—he's an Englishman again. Suddenly, the entire village is suspicious of their former slave.

Nathan reaches into the edges of the fire and picks up a stick burning at one end. He holds it in front of him. "Go ahead, burn me, like the old king did he when wanted to get his way out of an informant. And I will tell anything the savage wants to hear." He's trembling, not with fear, but with rage; his word has been questioned. Now he's no longer an Englishman—now he's an American again. The people are thinking he's very powerful indeed. Such a man must be killed or repositioned at a higher level in the community.

Black Dirt comes out of her wigwam, and steps into the circle.

"I heard angry voices," she says, "and I am sorry, and I confess that it is in part my fault that you are full of suspicion, for I have my father's money. It was brought to me by . . . let us say it was an angel. I have instructions from my father to pay the intendant his bribe. The angel said my father requested that I not reveal that I had the money until I heard from him, and that is why I have told no one until this moment."

"Have you heard from his ghost?" asks Katahdin.

"No, all is quiet in my head, in my wigwam. I was awaiting a sign. I think this gathering of our people is that sign."

"Is there money left over?" Katahdin addresses Black Dirt.

"Quite a bit."

Nathan Provider-of-Services throws the stick into the fire, and steps outside of its light, as one does when one has no more to offer a discussion.

Haggis is a little frustrated now. His number one wife has replaced him as interrogator. The argument now belongs to the women.

"Did Caucus-Meteor mean for you to have the extra money for yourself, or for us?" asks Katahdin.

"I am not certain what his will was, but were any of us ever certain about him even when he was here among us?" Black Dirt says. "I have been thinking about the money. I will not use the money for myself. Surely, people of Conissadawaga, you know me better than that. I will use it for the village."

Haggis thinks he had better say something important or else he'll lose this moment. "It sounds like Black Dirt wants to be chief," he says.

Black Dirt pauses for a moment, and then speaks. "Among my father's people were women chiefs, like the sachem Weeta-moo. My own mother, Keeps-the-Flame, who was Iroquois where women often serve as advisers in their later years, was elected by you to rule with Caucus-Meteor. We are not Iroquois, not Algonkian, not French, not English, not Dutch, not any tribe of the various languages my father knew so well, and yet the blood of all these peoples is in our veins, their behavior in our habits and in the construction of our ideas. Conissadawaga is a free nation where any American can be what he or she wants. If you choose me as chief, I will use Caucus-Meteor's money to preserve not only our people, but our place, this . . . this . . . holy mother land." She makes a gesture to the fields.

Haggis steps into the circle. "Black Dirt speaks with great sincerity, though she gives you no vision for a future for this tribe. Nathan, I am sorry I accused you of taking Caucus-Meteor's money. This is twice I have wronged you with wicked thoughts. The source of my poor judgment is a result of my anger over a private grief, which I will presently share with my fellow villagers. I had thought that Wolf Eyes, my oldest and dear son, would take my place as leader of my clan. But he has been lost to the French. He fights their wars, earns their money, and gives none to his people. I will lose no more of my children. If we—as a people—stay in this place we will not survive—as a people. We will be whittled down to nothing by the French or the English or the Dutch or the Spanish, whoever eventually wins out in these wars in which we are only devices. Next summer when we leave for the trade missions, I propose to take any who will follow me to the land of the Cree, my cousins to the North. I will leave this land that Black Dirt loves so much. I will take my beloved wives and children and any who wish to accompany us. If no one chooses to accompany me, I will go alone. I propose now a vote: stay in Conissadawaga with Black Dirt, or leave with Haggis."

Each person will take his or her place in the circle, then the group will vote. Some announce their predisposition with a simple grunt. Others make speeches. Nathan Provider-of-Services chooses to speak.

"My brothers and sisters," he says with outstretched and open hands. "I have prayed to my father in heaven for guidance. Even so, I am still not sure of the right thing to do. I was forcibly removed from my homeland and there are times when I want to return to it. And there are times when I wish to remain with the people of Conissadawaga and do my best for the village, to honor my master and godfather, and to promote the welfare of the people who have accepted me as a citizen. And there are times when

I find myself called to a mysterious place west of here and west of everywhere in my knowledge. West is the only direction I want in my heart to go. My two concubines have made me as happy as a man can be in exercising his manhood. In my heart, I wish both to stay and to leave, for at the moment I am a man without nation, without home, without family, uncertain where God wants him. Part of me concludes that the only way out of my dilemma is to follow Haggis to the north where perhaps I'll find word of the great river leading west to the paradise lots. I live in great confusion. My captivity was ordained by God; whether I stay in this village, return to New England, or go north with Haggis is up to God, but I do not know the course he wants me to follow. I think, though, that my fate, as it has been for these last two years, remains in the hands of the people of Conissadawaga; I think God wishes it so. By the grace of God and the guidance of my prayers, I submit myself to your judgment."

The villagers are thinking: not a bad speech for a non-native speaker. Of the men and women of Conissadawaga about thirty choose to leave with Haggis next spring, an equal number to stay with Black Dirt, and twenty announce they are undecided. Then Norman Feathers steps into the circle. Everyone is surprised. Norman Feathers is no orator, and he's never showed an interest in civic matters before. Now he stands straight and tall and addresses the crowd. "We have voted to split our little tribe of réfugiés. I have my reservations, but so be it. But we have not voted on who shall lead us."

"It must be Haggis," shouts Kineo.

"Haggis cannot be the chief of Conissadawaga, because he has elected to leave," says Norman.

Haggis is thinking that he's been tricked—and by Norman Feathers! Can this be possible? It was only Caucus-Meteor who could confound a meeting so. But he is dead. Haggis is swept with weakness, as if by an illness. Illness too was the power of the dead king. The blows he inflicted upon you were never felt like the blows of war, but like the weakness of disease.

"I will accept this argument," Haggis says with as much magnanimity as he can muster. "When I leave, those who follow me will do so with the understanding that I am chief, but as long I remain in Conissadawaga I will submit to the will of the people. But I ask you: Who will lead you now?"

It's a cunning question, for everyone knows that the leader is dead.

Crowd rumbles and mumbles follow, until Norman says, "Let Black Dirt be our chief. Like her father and mother, she is tied to this land. She is tied to this village, and she is tied to its people. You are the only family she has left. She will lead you as best she can, but she cannot do this task alone. It was not only her father who created a tribe out of a réfugié camp. It was her father and her mother. She cannot be both mother and father. Like Nathan Provider-of-Services, Black Dirt, will you submit to the judgment of the people?"

"I will," Black Dirt says.

The villagers are amazed that Norman is speaking at all, and that his words, his diction, his elocution are disturbingly familiar. It's as if their dead king were speaking through the lips of their most common citizen. Norman feels divinely inspired and divinely humbled, for he knows the words he speaks are not his own. I am, he thinks, thrice blessed: an instrument of God, of the people of Conissadawaga, and of my king. Norman, swelled by the crowd's appreciation, goes on.

"I have tried to live in two worlds, in Quebec as a Frenchman, in Conissadawaga as an American. I don't see that one side is better than the other. The French, they have two rulers, the governor-general who commands the army and the intendant who oversees all other affairs. When Caucus-Meteor was at the height of his powers as a king, he had Keeps-the-Flame to help him. When Haggis leaves for the north, he will have his wives to assist him. As a bachelor, I understand how hard it is to do the right thing alone. Black Dirt should not be the only chief of this village." Norman's voice dies without supporting his argument. He's forgotten the rest of the speech that Caucus-Meteor gave him. He steps out of the circle. Everybody laughs a little. They're not laughing at Norman, just at his sudden abandonment of his idea. But it stays with the group, and is discussed and debated by various speakers. Seekonk nominates Passaconway to be chief with Black Dirt, and the ancient runner steps into the circle.

"We are in the position of having to make this decision, because an aged king went off to die," he says. "This village does not need another old man to lead it. I have been a member of the committee of three who has commanded this village since Caucus-Meteor was ill, and I have never been comfortable with the position. I decline the nomination."

"I remember now what I wanted to say," says Norman, excited now as he steps back into the circle. "Nathan Blake came to this village as a slave, and now he is our own Nathan Provider-of-Services. Like Passaconway, he distinguished himself as a runner. Surely, we all feel both joy and envy on behalf of his success. You will recall the dream that Caucus-Meteor told us about. I understand the dream now. Nathan Provider-of-Services and Black Dirt have both agreed to submit to our judgment. You've always wondered why Caucus-Meteor, who loved Nathan so, did not adopt him as his son. It was because he thought that Nathan Provider-of-Services should marry Black Dirt, and the two of them should rule this village as chiefs."

After a moment of hesitation, a cheer rises up out the villagers. The judgment that Nathan and Black Dirt asked from their tribe, they have received.

The wedding takes place the following day. Passaconway and his slightly addled wife, Ossipee, preside over the ceremony, and it's over in fifteen minutes. Black Dirt and Nathan are polite and dutiful. Afterward there's dancing, singing, storytelling, and too much drinking, which is nothing unusual for this band. Caucus-Meteor, in the last vale of his conjuring, thinks that if he could really travel through time, really take on the powers as well as attributes of a god, he would pour all the brandy, rum, and beer into the great river.

At the conclusion of his conjuring, the old king looks away from his fire and smiles faintly. He feels like that snake that swallowed the largest rat in the rat's den, and because of his swollen belly cannot now squeeze through the rat's tunnel doorway. He's happy to be ruling Conissadawaga through Black Dirt and Nathan Provider-of-Services, and he's happy that he's successfully thwarted Haggis from being elected chief of the tribe. At the same time he didn't expect that Haggis would gather his followers for a remove to the north. The tribe will be reduced by a third to a half.

"Norman, how did you like speaking in the circle?" Caucus-Meteor asks.

"As long as I could remember your words, I felt strong. I thought: so this is what it feels like to be a king."

"The best part of being a king is largess; the second best part is speaking in the circle. All else is intrigue. I'll tell you, Norman, I was planning to die once I married off Black Dirt and Nathan, but I'm not ready yet. I have no profound feelings at the moment, and one needs profound feelings to die. In fact, if a man could prevent himself from ever feeling profound, he would probably live on as a youth until taken by war, accident, or disease, for old age cannot catch the giddy, which is why young girls appear so fresh."

"Do you want me to memorize those words for the circle?" asks Norman Feathers.

"Norman, I must teach you the difference between oratory and loose talk. What I was just giving you was loose talk. At times it might sound like oratory, but it is more entertaining, probably truer, and of no use to a ruler. The problem now is helping Black Dirt and Nathan Provider-of-Services establish a reign to allow them to hold the village together. If too many people leave to follow Haggis, Conissadawaga will blow away like fall leaves in the wind. But before I tend to village business, I have to create some stability in my personal living situation. The problem is I cannot return to the woods, for I must stay near you, for you, Norman, must be not only my eyes and ears; you must be my voice in the circle."

A House like the English Build

The Canadian summer is coming to an end. Caucus-Meteor discovers that Quebec, perhaps because it's closer to his thoughts, is easier to conjure over than Conissadawaga. All the important changes begin with names, he thinks—I will need a new name. I will pluck the few remaining hairs on my head. I will paint my face and head. I will change the way I walk. Instead of French coin earrings, I will carve tiny sticks and hang them on my ears with metal hooks. For my garb I will wear the stick costumes that Bleached Bones made. When I am finished, no one will recognize me. He stares into his fire, and sees the seasons ahead.

In late September, François Bigot, the intendant for Canada, takes a few hours from his busy schedule to solve a small but nettlesome palace problem, the hiring of a fire tender for the winter. The position itself requires no special talents but a knowledge of fires and wood. Even so, it is a difficult position to fill. The fire tender must be at the palace twenty-four hours a day, every day in the winter, for the intendant insists that the palace remain heated at an even temperature. Hence, a family man is out of the question.

The intendant interviews several men, and finally settles on an older savage, a distant relative of one of the stable men. The fellow is introduced as a Cohas Abenaki réfugié, who neither frowns, nor smiles, displaying a countenance that fulfills his name—Great Stone Face. The new fire tender speaks a northern Algonkian dialect and a smattering of English, but no French.

The intendant says in French to his assistant, "This savage reminds me of an old Jew, and he is strangely familiar to me."

The assistant bows, unsure of the proper response.

"No matter." The intendant dismisses the assistant, then turns to the savage. "Great Stone Face, you are well-named," says the intendant in Algonkian so mangled that it's all Caucus-Meteor can do not to laugh.

"It will be very rewarding to warm a palace," says Caucus-Meteor in Algonkian. He's eyeing the intendant's head, upon which is a different wig than the last time they'd met. I admire the intendant very much, he thinks.

"I'm not quite sure what you just said, Old Relic," the intendant says in French, "but I can tell from your demeanor that you are too ignorant to betray me."

Caucus-Meteor bows. He can guess what the intendant is thinking. Filling the position for fire tender presents a political problem for the intendant. The fire tender is the only man with access to all the rooms in the palace at any hour, for every room of note has a stove or a fireplace. The important intrigue of Canada is there for his ears. You need a man who is hard-working, diligent, loyal, discrete and without ambition or curiosity. Such men, like completely subservient women, exist only in our desires. Is that not so, your excellency? But we who carry the weight of command must strive, must we not? You especially do not want a Canadian as a fire tender, for then your secrets would be spread fire and wide; and a man from Old France is out of the question because no respectable Frenchman concerns himself with such matters as the burning rate of Canadian wood. So to deal with this problem you will decide to hire a savage for the task.

"I think you will do just fine, you old fool," the intendant says. He laughs heartily and clasps Caucus-Meteor's hand.

The old American takes his duties seriously as Great Stone Face, fire tender for the intendant. His natural sense of command allows him to order other native members of the staff to assist him in bringing in wood. All during the winter, the intendant will never have cause to criticize his fire tender. The palace becomes the most comfortable abode in all of Canada.

Rooms on the first floor of the palace are spacious, public, and decorated in the grand style of old France. Rooms on the second and third floors are smaller and more personal but still large, and serve as quarters for the intendant, his mistress, and scores of guests. Rooms on the fourth floor are tiny and cramped; here the servants are housed. Great Stone Face's room barely has space for a bed, a chamber pot, a chair, a wooden chest, and a stove, but he doesn't complain. He removes the door to his stove so he can eat the fire. He replaces the furniture in the room with hides and blankets on the floor. He leans sticks and bark strips against the walls of his room until it smells and looks and feels familiar. He has to admit that this is the best wigwam he's ever lived in, for it stays warm without drafts of cold air or smoke that stings the eyes. At the same time he apprehends that his comfort has come at a price. He's spoilt. He tries to explain his compromised position to Norman Feathers, who comes to visit him every day.

"Caucus-Meteor is dead if not buried," he says. "Great Stone Face shows no expression to the world; he is more a conjured figure than a man. Too bad no oratory resides within him. The house he lives in is not his house; the more comfortable and content he becomes, the less of him in me I recognize. He will take his bald head to heaven, where Jesus, having sent Bleached Bones to hell, will be wearing his turban to mock him. I am very happy, and suspicious of the feeling, Norman."

"When you talk like this I do not know what you mean, my king," says Norman Feathers.

"Forgive me. I like to test my ideas by uttering the arguments against them. How much of what I say do you understand, Norman?"

"I do not choose to understand. Understanding would corrupt my faith; I live by mysteries, not by the pronouncements of supposed solutions."

"In other words, you don't really listen to me."

"That's correct. I memorize, but I do not listen to men at all. I listen in concentration only to the lowing of my oxen in the stables. They are my true comfort. All else I do is duty to God, village, and king." He bows, a bow-legged bow.

"I suppose what's happened to you is what happens to any man who is a bachelor too long. You ought to think about getting married, Norman."

Norman goes to the village twice a week, and reports back to his king everything he sees and hears. Nathan Provider-of-Services leaves his concubines and moves in with Black Dirt; from their reported behavior Great Stone Face determines that they sleep in the same wigwam for appearances' sake, their relations cordial but unromantic. Norman's observations come without insight or color, which frustrates Great Stone Face in his search for whole understanding. He attempts to conjure the crow in his dream. Come, pick me up, carry me to my village so I can see for myself what's really going on. I'm especially concerned about my daughter. But the crow remains nested in memory. Apparently, he will have to develop the conjuring craft without divine help.

Soon Great Stone Face does see for himself, though not as he would have wished. Black Dirt arrives to pay the intendant his tribute. He sees her from an upstairs window through bars and wavy glass. She's alone, wearing a black mourning ribbon in her hair. It's a different ribbon than she wore to grieve for her destroyed family. It's for him. A moment of horror comes over him. He'd had it in the back of his mind that somewhere along the line he would inter Great Stone Face and rise from the dead as Caucus-Meteor once again, returning in triumph to his village as king of Canada. Now he realizes he can do no such a thing, for it would mean that his daughters would have to mourn him twice. For their sakes, he must remain dead. That night, for the first time since establishing himself as Great Stone Face, Caucus-Meteor cannot prevent emotion from spreading out through his skin and features. Distraught, he hides in his room, burns his arm, the physical pain relieving the torment inside his heart. By dawn the palace has grown cold, but the intendant and his mistress are out of the city, so no harm is done to the reputation of the fire tender.

Time goes by, new fires are made, flare up, die to embers, grow cold, reports come in, Great Stone Face pieces together the life lived by his daughter and her husband . . . conjures them.

For a month you and Nathan hardly say a word except in public. You are overwhelmed by a sense of responsibility for the future of your village. You pay the intendant's man the bribe, and begin to understand in the burdensome way of a chief how tentative our villagers' hold is on our plot of land. You have committed our people to a sedentary way of life, but you don't know how to establish its basis. You are nagged by the realization that you and the rest of the tribe lack experience in and knowledge of the enterprise you are about to embark on. You deal with the problem in your usual way—work work work—but eventually when the crops are in, and before the nut-gathering season, you suddenly find time heavy on your hands. You know you should act. Cannot. The villagers are waiting for you and Nathan to lead. Do not. Your husband is sullen and distracted. He obviously feels tricked into this union, and he demonstrates no love for you. He slinks off to be with his concubines.

Oh, my daughter, my godson, what a terrible thing I have

done. If you loved one another, that would be one thing; even if you hated one another, this false union I have contrived would not be so bad because then your hearts would not be so divided. Just when I think I should arrange a divorce, I see a change. In the end, it is not affection, or need, or even what you two are good at—duty—that starts you talking; it is sheer proximity.

You are in the wigwam and have just had a minor disagreement over whether to start a fire in the stove, for the nights are getting cold. Nathan: pro fire. You: pro save wood. Compromise: very small fire. The smoldering is as much in your heads as in the belly of the stove. An hour goes by in which neither of you says anything. Finally, you pose a question. You aren't sure why you ask it, but the issue has been on your mind for months and now it just spills out.

"You think we could farm this land like the English?"

"I imagine so," says Nathan, but his tone is dismissive, perhaps scornful.

"I think I will buy a cow with Caucus-Meteor's money," you say. I told you more than once that cow's milk is often offensive to the stomach of the savage, but, daughter, you never listened to me.

Nathan laughs small.

Naturally, you take offense. "A cow in an American town is a big amusement to you?"

"Let me tell you a thing or two, Black Dirt: there's more to a real farm than planting the three sisters."

"We not only plan corn, beans, and squash; we plant peas, we plant onions . . ."

He interrupts her. "True. You do well with what you have. But a cow, a cow would change everything."

"Please explain, then," you say, with a smile that mocks him.

"All right, I will. A cow must be milked twice a day, every day. It must have pasture. You must plant for the cow as well as for the people. A farm in the English manner needs more than a cow. It needs a horse, or an ox, to pull a plow to break soil. It needs a barn to house the animals."

"Breaking soil is offensive to me, and I think offensive to the corn," you say.

"There's some justification in your caution. Fact is I admire your methods of cultivation. The soil remains sweeter for a longer period. Broken soil goes bad quicker. But there is plenty of land. Endless lots for the taking. The way to deal with the problem that broken soil brings is to let the land lie fallow—that and manure. Don't break soil where the rains wash it away. In the end if you plan well, you'll have more yields with broken soil and cow dung than the three sisters in hillocks of burnt-over lands."

You ask more questions, and Nathan answers, and suddenly he is no longer haughty and you are no longer sarcastic. You are two people pleased by each other's company. Nathan's knowledge of agriculture, long buried, rises up from its grave to haunt and fascinate both speaker and listener. As Nathan Provider-of-Services talks he is rediscovering with admiration Nathan Blake. He spins off stories, descriptions, and explanations regarding the creatures of New England—cows, sheep, chickens, pigs, oxen, foxes, wolves, birds of prey; and also explanations regarding the things of New England—hay fences, manure, wells, tools, plows, surveys, rock walls. You can see that he likes just speaking the words. You respond with comments, laughter, sometimes criticism if he doesn't phrase his thoughts well in Algonkian.

So much of the building language in English is transfigured in common speech. He "hammers" out his ideas; "screws" up his face in concentration. Boring a hole with a brace and bit is a tedious activity. Hence, in Nathan's language, tedium is described as boring.

Every night thereafter, you talk as a married couple talk, mainly about farming. Eventually, the conversation branches off into . . . popped corn. Nathan raises the subject casually, and soon you are pouring rendered bear fat into a pan making popped corn over the stove. You sit on your heels like good Americans, munching the popped corn from a common wooden bowl.

"Caucus-Meteor used to demand that Keeps-the-Flame make popped corn every night," you say.

"He couldn't make his own?"

"He would always burn it. He stopped eating it when Keeps-the-Flame died."

"Back in New England in my cabin I used to eat popped corn for breakfast with cow's cream on it and maple sugar. I never thought I would have the pleasure in American land."

"We Americans invented popped corn. We were eating it before the Europeans ever heard of corn. I hope you'll give us credit."

Nathan speaks now in his native language. "Of course. We English are a fair people."

You, who know some English from your father's teachings, translate "fair" to mean a people with a white skin. You both nod in the belief that you are talking about the same thing.

Nathan returns to Algonkian and launches into a detailed explanation of how he built the first log cabin in Upper Ashuelot. "When it went up in flames, I could still see in my mind's eye my bowl of uneaten popped corn on the dining table."

I have to chuckle, for I had eaten Nathan's breakfast before I set fire to his home. You see how it is, daughter: wishing always degrades memory.

"This cabin where you ate your popped corn, it was like one of the houses in Wendake?" asked Black Dirt.

"No, it was more primitive, just logs laid square on a dirt floor, a temporary hovel."

"So not much different from a wigwam."

"That's correct. It suited me. I was a young bachelor when I built it."

"And this English wife you went and got, what were her thoughts about this English wigwam?"

"I think she was charmed by it until the children came." His voice dies to a whisper.

"Tell me her name in English."

Nathan speaks the name.

You mentally translate from the English, then say in Algonkian, "Lizard Breath. That is a good name. Usually, the English names make no sense. Like Nay Than. What does Nay Than mean? Two separate words that together as one mean nothing. American names always mean something. Tell me some more about this Lizard Breath woman."

And tell her he does. Maybe too much. Once his mouth is in motion, it cannot stop. He tells you about his courtship of Elizabeth Graves, how he'd used an old-fashioned courting tube to speak words of love to her, their remove to the cabin, Elizabeth's dreams for a timber-frame house with white-painted clapboards and glass windows and a parlor, her rages, the births of their children, the terrible distemper epidemic that took away their son, Elizabeth's sorrow and her peculiarity that followed, his own peculiar elation when he was taken from his homestead in the raid, her continual harangues that something . . . something . . . something was not right. You see, Black Dirt, daughter so dear, you and this English wife shared a common discontent.

"The glories of racing in the trade fairs removed thoughts about wife and children. I think less and less about them."

"We are teaching you how to forget."

"Aye," Nathan says in English, then switches back to Algonkian. "All that remains of my fidelity is the house she asked me to build, and which I kept putting off, partly out of laziness and self-satisfaction and partly because of outside factors, for you see the king marked my pines for his ships."

"The English king walks in your forest with a hatchet to gouge the bark?"

"That was a manner of speaking. I mean that the admiralty marked my pines for its ship masts. Such trees are called king's pines."

"But no English king has walked in an American forest—a pity. This house you would build for your wife, it is like your cabin? A big wigwam? Perhaps a long house, like the Iroquois build?"

"It's nothing. No house at all. It's a notion, a feeling, a dream, an idea."

"From idea and feeling springs the made thing, no? Like a moccasin," you say, deep into an idea and a feeling of your own. I cannot conjure exactly what it is, perhaps because it is in the mists. But the feeling is clear enough: craven want. Something you want.

Night after night Nathan rambles on to his Conissadawaga wife about the house that he promised his Upper Ashuelot wife he would build and did not, and how to keep himself whole in Canada he'd built it in a place of mind, and now as he talks through the ideas, he adds details and solves nagging problems of craft and design. You can see that the talk reawakens Nathan to his old life. Perhaps he feels pangs for his "king's" pines, his home-raised oxen, his English wife.

"You wish to go back to your New England home?" you say to him.

After a long pause, Nathan says, "I have not known what in my heart I wish for since my capture. And today I am afraid."

"You were not afraid to wrestle, you were not afraid to run, you were not afraid to hunt; even when your life was threatened you were not mastered by fear. You are the man who walked the gauntlet. What could Nathan Provider-of-Services be afraid of?"

"Forgive me. I cannot speak of it."

I know what he is afraid of and cannot speak of—contempt. Many captives who return with habits and conditions of the savage are mocked by New Englanders. He is afraid he would be first pitied, then scorned. Look how Nathan walks, pigeon-toed, like a damn savage. See how he fawns over his beard and eyebrows . . . His love of liberty does not bode well for either his soul or the peace and tranquility of this town . . . Note his pagan appreciation of those pines the king stole from him. See how he makes speeches now, instead of common talk, a pagan preacher Nathan Blake has become . . . Perhaps he'll take up residence with Mark Ferry the Hermit, and the two can comb each other's hair. Laughter . . . Pity his wife, her first-born taken from her, now this . . . You see how it is with Nathan? You see his fear? And what of the fear that even he will not acknowledge? His lust for the paradise lots?

Later that night you hear Nathan awaken, rise up from his sleeping mat, and kneel to pray to his god in English. "Oh, Lord, what do you want from me now? What work, Lord? What work?"

During one of your long talks in the wigwam, you say to Nathan, "You are troubled, husband." Something about your voice, an intimacy, touches him. You hadn't expected to speak so, and did not feel it until you heard yourself voice the words. You still haven't slept together as man and wife, and he's never given himself over to your marriage. But with your insight into his state of mind, your casual reference to him as husband, Nathan responds as one who is wed. "Dear woman, I pray to my God every day. I know he has sent me to Canada to perform certain tasks. I pray, dear woman, I pray that I can accomplish His work whatever it may be." It isn't the words that move you; it is the depth of feeling in my godson. For the first time since the plague that took your family away, you feel something inside that only a woman can feel.

Later you'll think about your mother teaching you to make moccasins. The moccasin maker cuts pieces of smoked skins into odd shapes. Laid out in front of her, the shapes suggest nothing of their fate. Your mother taught you how to join the pieces. The life of this village is in such pieces. What do these pieces make? How to stitch them? Where is the one who will teach you now?

The harvest festival brings all your people together. Americans from both bands dance around the fire, gorge themselves, drink, sing, make speeches. You will never be comfortable in this festive atmosphere, but you join them in their celebration because you must. Haggis's people talk about their plans for the fall hunt, the remove to the winter village, and of course their exodus to the north in the spring. Your village Americans have little to say; they are unsure how to talk about a life they have not yet lived. Nervous laughter is the best they can do by way of good cheer.

Haggis taunts them. "The Conissadawaga villagers grow meeker and milder. Soon they will be begging the priests for baptism to save their delicate souls."

A retort is called for, but none of the villagers can find oratory within themselves to step into the circle. If you don't do something to show strength, most of the villagers will choose to join Haggis; our own band will just drift away. Conissadawaga will be little more than the tragic Frenchman's stone foundation, a mark on the landscape, no people. You step into the circle, uncertain what you will say; you pray to the spirits of your mother and father for some of their authority and oratorical skills. Perhaps we can breathe our wisdom into you as you speak, so that your every word will be a surprise, even to you. And so you begin:

"I am sure that those of you who followed Haggis and his wives, as one caribou follows another over the edge of the cliff, I am sure you will find happiness in your northern wilderness, and I wish you well. We who have chosen to remain in the village founded by Keeps-the-Flame and Caucus-Meteor are also about to embark on a journey. My husband, Nathan Provider-of-Services, has been telling me about the life of the village farmer. This farmer, he builds a house, not just a wigwam, a house that rests on a foundation and stays there long after a man and a woman part from this earth. Nathan Provider-of-Services, I ask on behalf of our people that you build us a house like the English build."

Another long pause while the villagers contemplate Black Dirt's words. They don't know what your idea means, but they understand that it is important to their future. No one is sure what is next.

Nathan Provider-of-Services steps into the circle.

"Black Dirt is an able leader," he says "Except perhaps in a footrace, I am no leader. No place but the far place of my imaginings has ever satisfied me. I am a passable farmer. The best part of me is a builder. I built the first log cabin in an English border town; I built the first ice-fishing shack on the Conissadawaga lake; now, by the grace of God and your help, I will build the first timber-frame house on these grounds."

Nathan might have added an amen, but none is necessary. A spontaneous cheer rises up from the villagers.

Next morning bright and early Nathan calls a meeting of his Americans. For the first time they look at him, not contemptuously as a slave, nor admiringly as a trade fair runner, nor disapprovingly as a reluctant leader, but as a chief, and for the first time he presents himself as one worthy of the position.

"I have been awake most of the night laying plans, discussing them with Black Dirt," he says. "Now you—you—will put them into action. This project will take the better part of a year. You must be involved. You must pay attention. You must watch what I do and remember well, for when I am gone your teacher will be your memory." That night Nathan tells you that he repeated almost word for word a speech his father made to him when he was a boy.

And so the work ticks through time, as all work does starting with words, schemes, announcements, promises, resolutions, arrangements between individuals. Your villagers will place the structure at the site abandoned by the French family. You will re-lay and true the stones in the foundation, work that must be done before the ground freezes. Nathan picks two crews for the winter, one to fell the trees and one to make beams and boards.

"How will we move the logs?" asks Contoocook, one of the head women.

Later, in Quebec, Norman Feathers tells Great Stone Face in his quarters in the palace, "When Contoocook asked that question, I was the one who answered—I could not help but answer, my king; I said, 'We will move the logs with a team of oxen.' And Nathan Provider-of-Services said, 'Norman is correct. We will need oxen or horses to move the logs. These animals will be part of your test as townsfolk, for with farm beasts you can be nomads no more.'"

Great Stone Face feels some of the life-force drain from his vitals. He thought he'd been so clever to arrange for the marriage of Black Dirt, but as usual the God of Surprises had stepped in. His own daughter was transforming the village of nomads that he had worked so hard with her mother to construct into a village of farmers.

"What else, Norman?" he asks, concealing his anguish.

"We followed Nathan to the house site, to the pit saw site, to the forest to mark the trees. At the foundation, Nathan paced off the perimeter. He explained that the house will have a parlor, a front hall, a dining room, a kitchen, four bedrooms in the upper story, a woodshed, and a porch. His original plan called for a central chimney brick fireplace, but there is no clay in this region to make bricks. In place of brick will be a chimney made from the iron mountain near the three rivers."

"What do you mean the 'original plan?'" asks Great Stone Face.

"I do not know, except that he said he'd been thinking about this house for a long time. He said it was an omen."

Great Stone face nods. "He built the house in his imagination. Now he will build it in fact. Norman, here's what I want you to do. You will leave your employment in the stables. Tell the stable master that you have village business to attend to. You will offer to help Nathan Provider-of-Services with whatever assistance he needs. You will also inform him that you wish to return every Sunday to Quebec so you can attend Catholic mass."

"Which is the truth."

"Of course it is, and another truth is that you will visit me every Sunday and keep me informed of news in the village so I can be in a position to offer useful advice, and to conjure on these important matters."

Dear daughter, you and Nathan spend long hours in the wigwam discussing the building plans. "After my rash talk," Nathan says, "I find that we have the right piece of property for this enterprise, the materials on hand, and willing laborers. But I lack tools, Black Dirt. I cannot build this house without tools."

"I have the one indispensable tool," you say. You reach for the deerskin satchel. Inside is Caucus-Meteor's money. You show it to Nathan. "Will it buy the tools and the animals?"

"I think so, but I don't know if you'll have enough remaining for the intendant's tribute in the spring."

"Perhaps he will be merciful," you say.

"Merciful?" Nathan arches a plucked eyebrow.

"All right. Reasonable."

It's a desperate moment, for no solution seems possible.

"We have a saying in my nation," Nathan says. "Don't cross a bridge until you reach the stoop."

"Not a good saying in Conissadawaga land which has neither stoops nor bridges," you say.

"I will go to Quebec with Norman Feathers," Nathan says, "for he knows the city as well anyone in this village, and I will buy tools and beasts of burden."

Nathan and Norman Feathers canoe to Quebec, and later Norman tells his king the story.

This quest for tools turned into quite a comic situation. Here you have a white man dressed like an American who is a shrewd judge of hardware trying to haggle in Algonkian and English with another white man, who speaks only French. Then you have the ignorant savage—that is, ignorant in the ways of the housewright—but who speaks both languages of the white men. In the end, the three-way trade ceremony succeeds not because of the fluency of the speakers, but because of the money, so I supposed, dear daughter, that you were right all along about the future—it is about money.

"From my work in the palace stables," Norman says in the earnest and humorless way that so delights his king, "I was familiar with farm implements found in barns, and I'd used axes, as well as draw knives for shaping ash for canoes and buck saws for firewood, but tools for house building were strange and marvelous to me. I watched Nathan as he picked over tools with names like froe, broad axe, foot adze, pit saw, cross-cut saw, back saw, panel saw, keyhole saw, various files for sharpening same, chalk line and reel, brad awl, bow drill, auger, brace with bit, gimlet, twybil, twivel, chisel, scorp, spokeshave, plane, marking gauge, mortising gauge, cutting gauge, hammer, and nail."

Something like a musical note chimes in the memory of Great Stone Face. He's heard all these words before. Nathan spoke them in his sleep. Great Stone Face wishes now he was twenty-five again. He would like to heft those tools, not because he wants to build anything with them but because he wants to feel and smell the things behind the wonderful words if only to make the words better in contemplation.

"You can use all these devices?" he asks.

"No, but I have touched them," Norman Feathers says.

"I admire you very much, Norman. How did your trade for animals go?"

"Easier. Nathan, like myself, is an admirer of domesticated beasts."

"No wonder he is comfortable with you. Other American men know so much about their world that Nathan can never quite measure up in discussions. They make him feel petulant. But, Norman, you share in his own fascination with farm beasts, and I imagine your presence gave Nathan the opportunity to test his oratory in large-animal husbandry. I will venture that he went on and on about raising, feeding, grooming, and nurturing oxen."

"That he did."

"I'm sure he told you that the beast of burden will never turn on a master he thinks of as his mother, thus kindness and tenderness will produce more work than the prod. And you hung on every word, and he was pleased. An excellent basis for a temporary friendship."

"But you will always be my king, Caucus-Meteor," says Norman.

Even someone as thick as Norman hears the jealousy in his king's voice. The gods are laughing at him now.

"Please refer to me as Great Stone Face. Caucus-Meteor now resides in that region between dreams and waking, between this world and the unknown circle where the souls of the dead speak. Continue with your observations."

"We made the rounds of local stables, which tried to sell us sick or old animals. Nobody wanted to part with good oxen except for exorbitant prices, and they all wanted to sell the cart with the beasts. Since there is no road to Conissadawaga, there is no way to bring a cart except by expensive French bateaux. Nathan complained that a country that depends on rivers for highways can fend for itself in only a limited way. 'A country needs roads, good roads,' he said. We had to walk half a day outside the city gates, where a Frenchman with a cough that seemed on the verge of killing him agreed to sell us two young, untrained oxen. I conducted the trade, and Nathan acted merely as an advisor."

Great Stone Face thinks it must have been a painful moment for Nathan Provider-of-Services to watch a savage carry on the intricacies of trade relating to his English husbandry.

"Nathan rigged a drag for the oxen to carry our new tools to Conissadawaga," Norman Feathers says. "The village has enough pasture to keep the animals fed through the fall, but once the cold weather comes we will have to depend on cut hay. Nathan returned to Conissadawaga by canoe in less than three hours. It took me a day and a half to walk the beasts from Quebec to the village. The route was not designed by God for beasts of burden."

"The oxen were a novelty and amusement in the village, especially among the children. They'd never seen anything like this before. Some of our dogs dined on the steaming droppings of the great beasts. It did my heart good."

"And, Black Dirt—what was my daughter's response?"

"Her eyes grew large. 'Next year,' said she, 'we'll have chickens and cows and sheep and pigs. There will be no reason to depend on deer and moose for meat and hides.'"

"'I would go easy on the pigs at first,' Nathan told her. 'Pigs cause problems between neighbors. In New England, pigs have killed more children than bears and wolves put together.' And then Nathan made a speech. He named me teamster, took a drink of brandy and said in English, 'I toast thee.'... What does 'toast' mean?"

"In English usage, toast as an object means burnt bread; as an action, toast calls on the God of Burnt Bread for favors."

"English is a remarkably silly language. I can't imagine why people would want to converse or think in it."

"Then what happened?" says Great Stone Face.

"Nathan in mirth commanded that I name the great beasts we had brought to the village. Great Stone Face, I humbly thank you for inspiring me to leave the service of the intendant and return to my village. It's only by your wisdom and the grace of God that I can do the labors in my own realm that brought me so much pleasure in the intendant's stables."

Great Stone Face forces a smile. He'd freed Norman from the stables in Quebec so that he could return to the village as his own eyes and ears. Now Norman was inadvertently helping destroy his village, then reporting with glee the details. I'm receiving the punishment that Caucus-Meteor deserves, Great Stone Face thinks. "And what did you name your beasts of burden? Jesus and Joseph?"

"Right church, wrong pew—that is a French expression I learned in Quebec. I named my oxen Peter and Paul, after the saints who served Jesus."

"I believe the Catholics have a saying: may the saints preserve us."

Nathan works eighteen-hour days, training his Americans in the
work, familiarizing them with the tools. Norman reports back:
"'Some day,' Nathan said to me, 'you'll have a saw mill down
below the lake, but for now we will make do with pit saws, which
I was able to purchase in Quebec. I tell you, Norman, I enjoy this
work, and I understand now what Caucus-Meteor taught me
about being a king. A king must be a teacher.'"

Haggis' clan moves out of the summer village to the winter
village. Black Dirt's tribe remains behind. The undecideds go
back and forth. Instead of tearing down all the old wigwams as
in past years, the women in the village insulate them with more
layers of sticks, moss, corn stalks, and forest litter. The only time
the two bands assemble as one is for the fall hunt.

The leaves drop from the trees, hard frost sinks into the
ground, the snows fly. But the work goes on. Winter's a good
time for logging—no bugs to torment the wood choppers, no
leaves to obstruct their view, no heat to drain their energy. It's
easier for the oxen to skid the logs from forest to the pit saw
crews on snow than on bare ground. Rain, the friend of the
farmer, is the enemy of the logger. The work is very exciting to
everyone involved. The woodsmen hardly notice that cedars
falling on snow leave scars in the forest.

One cold night in the wigwam in early winter, Nathan has just
voiced some minor complaint about Americans and his place
among them.

"The American way of life has improved your character, Nathan Provider-of-Services," you say.

"Maybe," he says, starts to speak more, then pauses. Usually
when you and Nathan verge on personal matters, you both be-

come silent, retreat in the American way of privacy by averting your eyes and moving toward the edge of the wigwam. Not this time. He senses something within you—a warmth. But you don't feel it—not yet.

"A village should have a church, don't you think?" you say.

"I would not deny such an assertion," Nathan says cautiously.

"Would a church make the crops grow better?" you ask.

"I think so, yes, though there is no surety in such matters. We have a saying: God works his wonders in strange ways."

"Tell me how I can get Jesus to bless my crops."

Nathan responds in English, "Ye must pray."

"Then I will pray," you say in English, then return to our native language. "Tell me, and this is something I have always wondered, how is the Papist Jesus different from the English Jesus?"

Nathan bursts into laughter, a joyful, refreshing laugh, a laugh that touches a woman's heart; tears come to his eyes. You want him to reach for you, touch you. But when he does, you draw away, shy; you and Nathan retreat to your separate beds.

Two nights later you are awakened by a loud, cracking sound. It is nothing to be upset about, just the lake making ice. Still, you cannot go back to sleep.

"I'm full of energy," Nathan says. "I feel something. I think it's the power of the ice. I'm going outside onto the lake."

"Good. I will go with you."

You dress in the dark, French wool coats under deerskin wind-breakers, mink-fur mittens, mink-fur-lined moccasin boots that reached to the knee, and you go out into the winter. It is one of those windless, blister-cold Canadian nights. You both put on snowshoes, trudge through the village, to the lake. Even on a night like this with no moon, the snow cover reflects enough starlight so you can see your own figures in blue silhouettes, the glittering snow in wave-pattern drifts, the dark hills beyond, the blacker sky above, the tiny lights of the stars.

In the middle of the lake is an area swept clean of snow by

the wind. You kick off the snowshoes and prance on the ice like children.

"I wish I had . . ." Nathan searches for a word in Algonkian, cannot come up with one, and says in English, "skates."

"Skates?"

"Yes, skates—moccasins with metal blades on the soles for gliding on ice."

"Feet toboggans," you say in our language.

"That's right. You can go like the wind."

"If you can acquire the proper metal, I could make some feet toboggans."

A second later the ice vibrates. The loud, cracking noise, thunder under foot, sends a pleasant shiver of excitement through you both. You fall into an embrace. You part, embarrassed. In the sky, something happens . . . the sky speaks. Think of me now as the sky. At first I am only an exaggeration and merging of starlight, and then I am a big green silent explosion of lights bursting from the northern quadrant of the heavens. Seconds later I am a crescent of red, followed by a pulsing halo of blue. Soon I am entire as a dance of light, with shapes in red, green, blue, my silent oratory giving homage to all the gods.

You and Nathan bask in the lights for a few minutes, and then return to the wigwam. Nathan grabs his stick bed and brings it beside yours. I turn away from my conjuring, and stare at the flames in my fire.

Later, his arm around your shoulder, he talks to you. "When I was with women after racing I was all carnality and haste. With you it is different."

"You go about love-making the way you go about your work, with care and deliberation," you say to your husband.

Dear daughter, you have been without touch for so long that now the experience seems novel. You please Nathan by displaying curiosity about his hands, thick and calloused. You tell him it's the part of him you like the best. You take one of his hands into your own, and hold it against your face. You say, "It was like a conjuring. In this love I search for a future."

"Let us test it a second time," Nathan says.

And you do, and I, in deference to the sanctity of your act, leave.

Nathan's daily routine includes moving back and forth between the logging site and the pit saw mill near the house foundation, and the wigwam is conveniently placed in between for midday liaisons. Meanwhile, the work continues on schedule—despite disruptions. An ice storm halts the loggers for three days. Kokadjo breaks a leg when a tree falls on him, and several men chop their own flesh instead of wood, but we in this land accept it as a given that men will be injured or killed in work accidents, hunting expeditions, war, and sporting; and women will be swept away in childbirth; and children will die in droves from disease; and the aged will be exhausted into death by the cold; and all will starve when game cannot be found or pestilence attacks the humors or untimely weather withers the crops.

Nathan tells you that this winter is the most blissful he has ever spent, and he's sad to see it come to an end.

"The blessing and the curse of a season coincide: with a turn in weather, things are never the same as before," you say.

"Another Algonkian saying?"

"Just something my father would say."

The woods work stalls in the muddy time before true spring, and it's too early to start actual house construction, so Nathan decides to go on the salmon run this year. You join him, because lovers should not be separated, which is an idea that you received from your mother.

The salmon run is always an exciting event. Winter is over. If we've been lucky (and this has been a lucky winter), we have avoided death by starvation, freezing, and diseases, and can now look forward to months of plenty before the next hard winter, so all the people are in a playful mood upon arrival at the salmon stream. This year adds poignancy to joy because this is the last great task that this réfugié tribe embarks on in common before it will divide into two bands. The sight of cold water thrashing rocks, spray like busy fog, colorful fish slippery in the hands, sharp cuts of sunlight, stir the blood.

Does Nathan Provider-of-Services understand that the nomadic life, though more prone to disasters than the farm life, is also more ecstatic, and the salmon run is one of those ecstatic moments? This life that you are throwing away, will you miss it, Black Dirt?

Several tribes along with the Conissadawaga Americans come to this place. Each group by tradition and custom and, in another time, by force of arms, stakes a particular claim along the river to fish. Years ago I negotiated with some Montagnais for the village's fishing rights. Intruding into another tribe's space can lead to some nasty disputes, though in our epoch hostilities rarely break out because there's plenty of war to the south for those possessed by the spirit of combat.

This kind of fishing is for the nimble and the strong. It takes strength to set up the weirs in the fast water to slow the fish so they can be stabbed. It takes good balance to perch on a ledge of slippery granite while at the same time stabbing at jumping fish in frothing water. It takes agility to climb to the best spearing stations, and it takes timing and dexterity to actually spear the fish. Nathan's flaws as a fisherman are tied to his character, for as those more experienced can see he is not at heart a fisherman, and he frequently loses concentration on the river while he occupies his mind with other matters. Tell my godson that one cannot spear a fish unless one can see a fish, and one cannot see a fish unless one looks. I know, Black Dirt, I know, you are all sick of my sayings.

The men enjoy the fishing, though they don't take it as seriously as they do hunting, for they depend on their women to do the real work. By the end of the day when all have come down to the camp and drying racks, Nathan boasts that he's not only the village's best runner, he is its best fisher.

Katahdin, who is in charge of smoking the fish, says, "No. Black Dirt caught two more fish."

All the women and some of the men laugh. Nathan Provider-of-Services has been out-fished by his woman.

"Tomorrow I will catch more fish than anyone else in the village," Nathan is half-joking, half-serious.

"Want to bet?" challenges Haggis.

The good humor has spilled over into a contest. Nathan bets a comb, Haggis a walrus tusk pendant. You don't wager. Like your mother, you do not approve of wagering. But you are thinking like a bettor: I'll not let either of these men best me.

By midmorning of the following day, you, Nathan, Haggis, and the others are fishing with mad joy. Everybody wants to be the top fisher. The older women smoking the salmon have gotten into the spirit of the competition. They meet in secret and conspire to determine a method so that they, the women, shall decide the winners.

On the river, the competitors take added risks, leaning closer to the cold, roiling waters. Meanwhile, the fish, driven by lust, just keep flailing and flailing upstream for one final, exhausting, and fatal orgy. You are wet with spray, but you don't care.

At the end of the day, Nathan and Haggis are both certain they have caught more fish than any of the women, and that the only dispute will be among themselves and the other men. You know what is going to happen next, and you smile. Katahdin, who has been counting fish all day names the top fishers. All are women. It's not until the older women laugh as one that the men understand what has transpired. The men have been tricked into working harder than usual. It's all part of the mad joy of the occasion, and everyone partakes of it, even Nathan and Haggis and you, my serious-minded daughter.

The tribe is readying to leave when a group of Algonkian traders from the south happens by. Parmachnenee recognizes a cousin she has not seen since she was a child. He tells her that her clan has reassembled and returned to its ancient village on a lake of the Magalloway river in the mountains of English territory. Parmachnenee leaves with her cousin. In my conjuring I can see now that she triumphs. She will marry and lead her clan. Her name will be remembered in the waters, Lake Parmachnenee. But my people, who will be all but forgotten, the salmon fishing ends with a touch of sadness, for the tribe has lost yet another member. You, who once despised Wytopitlock for taking your man, now console her for the loss of her friend. Before, she was a woman without a man; now she is a woman without anyone.

In Conissadawaga, the two bands divide up the food stores and other community possessions. A week later, Haggis and his clan prepare to begin their long trip to the north. Even though we have had our differences on how to live, we've been together a long time as réfugiés, and parting is difficult.

Haggis, the leader who started this movement, is the most distraught. He hugs everybody, cries like a lost child, and practically has to be hauled away by his wives. He's grieving because he knows he will never see his eldest son again. Long ago when Haggis was hardly more than a boy himself, he had another wife. He married her when she was fourteen and he fifteen. They had a baby they called Wolf Eyes because his eyes were light blue. The mother died of smallpox, and the child was raised by relatives, one of whom was Katahdin. Years later Haggis returned from wandering and married Katahdin mainly to be with his son. But Wolf Eyes never returned his father's love, and insisted that he be treated and referred to as an adopted son. Haggis will never see his son again: that is the source of his pain. For Haggis, love is not in the behavior, but the blood. I gave Wolf Eyes Nathan's gun, knowing it would increase the rift between him and his father; I brought Wolf Eyes together with the French soldiers. Without my influence, he never would have given himself over to the army. Daughter, we used to burn prisoners for religious reasons—now we do it to gather information. The king used to wield powers through oratory and largess; now it is done through killing-prowess and cunning. Oh, daughter, I have a need for Christian penance for my sins; thus I burn myself.

Haggis and his followers leave with three of the undecideds. The rest, including my old friends Passaconway and his wife, Ossipee, stay in Conissadawaga. Three others also leave that day: Omer and Hungry Heart Laurent go off to tend to their summer business in canoe transport. With them is a new apprentice, Freeway. There is no celebration on the night of departure. No drums, no conversation—a great silence. Next day our people remain grim and quiet, immersed in private thoughts. It's struck them all that the world that Keeps-the-Flame and I set into motion has begun its descent into the oblivion of time. The following day the mood is a little less somber. A passing stranger might hear a laugh, a bit of easy talk. After a week, the villagers have regained their good cheer. Haggis and his band have fallen deeper into memory.

All through the winter and into the spring, Norman has watched his king replace his facial paint with tattoos and piercings. All the native peoples have heard stories of the great stone face in the mountains to the south. Great Stone Face drew the profile with the ashes of his fire, memorized it, and described it to a tattooist in Quebec. With various colors—blue, red, and white— and by dislocating the nose and adding scarrings to the bare skull, the tattooist was able to transform the bald head and face of Caucus-Meteor into a good likeness of that profile in the mountains. Great Stone Face has become the great stone face, the Old Man in the Mountain. If his face represents stone, his stick body garb represents the palisade protection of an ancient American village. Did Bleached Bones have this idea in mind when he created strange clothing? Norman thinks that even he, who sees his king every week, cannot recognize him as Caucus-Meteor.

"Only your voice betrays you," Norman says.

"The Great Stone Face of the mountains does not speak, except perhaps to command the weather of the notches in the language of gods to which we are not privy, so if I am to speak it must be with the voice of Caucus-Meteor. Now, Norman, tell me what's going on in the village."

"It is as you predicted. I have become Nathan's apprentice."

"He likes to have you around to hear himself speak, and because he knows you are agreeable. Tell me now about the house-building sorcery."

"It is not sorcery at all; it is a matter of tools, tricks, and application."

"So, then, it is like anything else that is hard and of value. Your king believes houses are unnecessary, also unwholesome."

"Yes, I relayed that information, as instructed."

"What did Nathan Provider-of-Services say?"

"He said, 'Your king is dead.'"

"These English are short-sighted. Tell me some more of this work you are doing."

"Though it will take all summer and into the fall to complete construction of the house, the frame is raised in one day by the entire village. That event is traditionally known as a 'house-raising' and it is accompanied by a festival."

"That is some rite from New England?" asks Great Stone Face.

"Correct. With rum, dance, and good fellowship. Black Dirt says she will roast a deer and pretend it's a pig."

Great Stone Face does not change his facial expression, but a moan of anguish escapes from his throat. Norman is not listening, for he's occupied with what he's going to say next.

"The house building actually began with Nathan building an English wigwam, just poles covered with bark. 'This is our tool shed,' Nathan said to me. 'Our instruction begins here. Then he picked up an axe. 'This is the axe you're familiar with, the European trade axe?' he asked, and I nodded. 'Most Americans and French and many English still use a European trade axe to split firewood,' he said. 'Note how it's made. An iron strap was heated white hot, the ends spread, the piece bent over a rod to make an eye. A small steel bar welded between the ends to make the blade. But this axe'—he held the axe straight out like a soldier presenting his arms, paused, repeated—'this axe has poor balance compared with this axe.' He picked up another axe. 'This is called an American axe. It has a weight over the eye, which balances the swing. It's a little harder to forge than the trade axe, but it cuts deeper and with less effort in the chopping of large trees. As in everything else, balance and weight make the difference.'

"I said to him, 'Nathan Provider-of-Services, why would an Englishman call his axe 'American'?"

"'In the English colonies,' he said, 'many people are using the word *American* to mean more than native peoples.'"

"Norman, if an Englishman is an American, then what does *American* mean?" asks Great Stone Face.

Norman does not know how to answer, and after a long pause says, "Your majesty, I am stupid, forgive me."

"It's all right, Norman. You're not stupid—well, you are stupid. But your god will forgive you. As for me, I too am stupid, for even in my best conjuring I see only partially into the future. One day all the English may be French-American. Or, more likely, since they are a stronger people, all Americans will be English. Still, it's not necessarily the strong that prevail. When the wind blows hard, the strongest trees are often the first to topple. It's doubtful, though, that all English will be French or all French will be English. You see how it goes, Norman? The future, even for a conjuring man, is all informed guesswork. It's our partial understanding of matters that makes us stupid, laugh material for the gods who require us for entertainment."

"It makes me happy, great king, that we are stupid together. In fact, Nathan Provider-of-Services said something like that to me; he said, 'Norman, you remind me of your king kin, Caucus-Meteor, a thinker, a dreamer, who dwelled in the hollow of his notions. I'm more practical-minded—solid clean through—

and what we are about on this day is for the practical nature.'
And then Nathan hefted the axe.

"We spent all day chopping, sawing, hewing, planing. 'You
will learn joinery later,' Nathan said. 'You will learn the ruse of
sharpening rip saws, crosscut saws, and the blades of plane irons.
You will learn the artful secrets of wood-working: sharp tools,
good measurements, balance of body, repose of mind. You will
make boards of differing sizes to fit over beams, to frame window shutters; you will make and hang a door.'"

Great Stone Face suddenly feels a decade older. From these
days forward, his people will no longer look at a tree as their ancestors did, a living thing with a spirit; they will look at a tree and
see boards. They will become competent carpenters and marvels
at putting a file to a saw. But will they remain as Americans?
"What other changes in the village have you noticed of late?"
Great Stone Face asks.

"Now that Haggis is not around to set the standard for American manly behavior, the men are less appalled by the idea of
doing women's work, such as house construction . . ."

Great Stone Face interrupts, alarmed, "Our men are not
making moccasins, are they?"

"Not yet, but in addition to house building they are planting
like women—even hoeing, and weeding in the fields."

"It's as if they're treating all crops as tobacco."

"I imagine so."

This is the problem with living too long, thinks Great Stone
Face. You live not only beyond your years, but beyond your con-
victions.

The day of the frame-raising, Nathan and his crew are busy and
very excited. Nathan had explained to you that a house- or barn-
raising back in New England is always an excuse to carouse with
a barrel of rum, a pig roasting over a spit on hot coals, entertainment by fiddle players, and dancing all around. You tell him that

we Americans can sympathize with this particular English ceremony. Substitute brandy for rum, venison for pork, drums for violins, and Canada and New England achieve congruence.

Two posts with a cross beam and top plate are pegged to form frames, called bents, to be raised by people power. It's tricky work, requiring an organizer to position a crew to raise the frame, a couple of men to hold the safety rope to keep the frame from falling over the other way once it's raised, as many bodies as possible to heave the beams upright, and pikemen to push against the top plate once the frame is above shoulder level. If Nathan has planned or measured wrong, the bents might not line up properly with the girts. It's almost as if Nathan were back on the foot-racing circuit—invigorated by thoughts of victory or defeat. After the bents are in place, the rafters are raised; collar ties and purlins are pinned in place. Following the tradition of Nathan Blake, Nathan Provider-of-Services nails a tiny fir tree to the peak. I am looking at your face. You are radiant. Is it love that has made it so? Is it this house? Something I cannot fathom? I think I do not know everything about you, dear daughter. This much I do know. All agree that it's a great day that a house frame has been raised in an American réfugié camp. The rest of the summer will be devoted to enclosing the frame. For me, however, the house building is more punishment for my many sins.

One Sunday Great Stone Face's reliable informant doesn't show up. The next Sunday, he arrives late, stays a short time, and leaves nervous. Something is wrong. Great Stone Face conjures over the matter. Perhaps his spy in the village has been turned against him through sorcery or bribery. He decides to spy on the spy. The next Sunday Great Stone Face waits in the shadow of a doorway across from the church that Norman attends regularly with the faithful. When Norman arrives at the church accompanied by a woman, Great Stone Face understands the source of his unusual behavior. Great Stone Face listens to the church singing for a while. It's less the music than the words—incomprehensible Latin—that he finds relaxing. Wailing Catholic singing brings him back to his slave days in Europe. He misses the old priests who taught him the various ways one can pronounce words in French, English, and Dutch, all the useful languages but the sacred Latin. When the music stops, Great Stone Face returns to his room in the palace. The weather is warm, but he makes a fire anyway.

Two hours later Norman Feathers comes for his weekly audience with his king. "Norman, where is she? What have you done with her?"

Norman's mouth yaws open, but no sound issues forth.

"Norman, you cannot speak because you cannot lie, so let the truth pour out."

"She is in the stables waiting for me. She knows only that I have private business in the palace. How could you know about her?"

"Norman, I am a king, or have you forgotten?"

"I have not forgotten."

"And a king always knows more than his subjects. Norman, I will not punish you—I am merely curious. How is it that you, a confirmed bachelor, are keeping company with a licentious woman like Wytopitlock?"

"Because she is an angel." Norman drops to his knees, folds his hands, and bows his head all the way to the floor. Great Stone Face puts his hand on his subject's brow and whispers some nonsense Latin words mixed in with some archaic Algonkian. Through this invented incantation, Norman understands that he has been forgiven by his king, and, relaxed now, he relates a tale.

"I was walking with my oxen in the woods to fetch some logs when I could see a figure by the lake. Something about the way she moved troubled me, so I left Peter and Paul to forage and went down by the water. Wytopitlock had tied a stone about her neck. By the time I arrived she was about to drown herself; I went in after her and pulled her out. I made a fire, and gave her my blanket, for she was shaking. She told me she wanted to die; I told her that Jesus wanted her to live. I know that I compromised your safety, but I had to bring her to church. We attend mass every Sunday. All I think about during the week is Wytopitlock and myself in church. I do not dare broach this subject with my confessor. My king, am I in sin?"

"Norman, don't you understand anything? You are not in sin, you are in love."

With the arrival of warm weather, Great Stone Face is prepared to leave the palace and move into the woods for the summer. He plans to establish a camp at Bleached Bones's place, spend the summer eating a fire; maybe his conjuring skills will improve sufficiently to allow him to save his village. He'll raise a few vegetables, and gain his meat by fishing and running a trap line, for Bleached Bones left some excellent snares. Great Stone Face has already given his wages to other servants in the employ of the intendant; this is not the kingly largess of old but it is enough to make him feel clean and expansive. But his plans undergo a change when he is summoned to the personal quarters of the intendant himself. Great Stone Face thinks maybe the intendant has found him out, and is going to execute him personally. This is possible good news! But of course he knows that ideal prospects true better in the thought than in the deed.

They meet in the petit salon. The intendant stands by a velvet couch to greet him. Sitting on the couch is a middle-aged woman in wigs, her skin giving off a strong scent of perfume that tells Great Stone Face that she has recently arrived from Old France. In the background are library shelves, the true source of the Frenchman's power over the native. But it's the sight of yet another wig that excites Great Stone Face. He envies the French folk only for their wonderful wigs.

"Is this the one you saw outside that you asked for?" the intendant addresses the woman in French.

"Can there be another? I didn't know the savages lived to such an age. Do I offend him with my frank talk?"

"He speaks no French, my dear countess."

"Could I offend him in his own language? Does the savage have sensitivities as we do?"

"He neither gives nor takes offense, for he lives by his name—Great Stone Face," says the intendant. "As for the sensitivities of the red race, they are of no less nor greater concern to you and me than the sensitivities of the peasants of old France. Any cur off the street has sensitivities if only we sacrifice our own sensitivities to apprehend the cur's, and what's the profit in such an act? God cares not for our sensitivities to one another, but for our faith in Him, so it is between man and his dog, squire and his servant, nobleman and his vassal, merchant and his creditor. I will tell you that Great Stone Face is my fire tender, tender most extraordinary to hot and cold, which is more than I can say for some of his savage kinsmen who often ignore a shirt on frigid days."

"So much for sensitivities. I would like to hear the old savage speak," says the woman.

Great Stone Face feels like a boy again in Europe when his master would display him before royalty. In those days young Caucus-Meteor used to imagine that one of the women would adopt him; now he has the same feeling, an ache to see his mother so profound he would accept a pretend mother.

The intendant says a few words in his crude Algonkian, and Great Stone Face launches into a long speech concerning ancient religious practices revolving around the great turtle and its twin daughters that he knows the intendant with his limited vocabulary will not understand. However, as Great Stone Face knew he would, the intendant translates his speech to suit his own purposes.

"The old savage praises the countess's beauty and poise. He says all Canada is at her feet."

"What else—he spoke at length?" asks the countess.

"Modesty prevents me, but if you must know he praised our

benevolence here at the palace. He says without us he would freeze and die in the Canadian wilderness."

The encounter gives the intendant an idea, and the day after the countess has left, the intendant summons Great Stone Face once again to his quarters. He says in crude Algonkian, "You go with me . . . come there . . . gods across the great waters." Even Caucus-Meteor, that linguist who resides in the ink of the tattoos of Great Stone Face, can make no meaning from these words. It takes a while, but the intendant finally makes himself understood. He wants Great Stone Face to accompany him when he entertains dignitaries from Europe. Great Stone Face nods in compliance.

Throughout the summer Great Stone Face is put forth in front of visitors for their entertainment. His aged tattooed face, his stick garb, his stoic unchanging expression are admired and commented upon. Often he's likened to a Greek. Great Stone Face becomes an emblem of the New World savage, so much the better that he is old and therefore no threat. The intendant comes to enjoy having him around and when they are alone he often talks to Great Stone Face in French.

"My grief is that I have no confidant here in Canada, except for my mistress, and regarding matters of state and commerce one can only go so far in intimacy with a woman," he says, "but you, Great Stone Face, because you don't understand a word I say, you make the perfect confidant. In your presence I can pour out my thoughts and feelings without fear of reprisal, scorn, or whispers behind my back.

"My tragedy, dear savage, is gambling. It's not just the money I win or lose in games, it's that gambling is in my soul. I truly believe that at my death, Jesus and I will wager where I will spend eternity. I gamble on everything. I gambled on you, for I was advised not to hire a savage fire tender; I was told by the Canadians that you would be indolent, indifferent, rash, that you would fly away like the crow for no good reason. I won that bet, for you have been exemplary in your service to me, especially when one considers the piddling that I pay you. I have your stupidity to thank—I thank you ..."

At "merci," Great Stone Faces bows, as if in recognition of this lone word, and the intendant laughs aloud, then breaks into a small flood of joyful tears.

"You don't know, Great Stone Face, what a relief it is to have you with me. It is secret satisfaction, like breaking wind in a crowded room." He laughs again; more tears come to his eyes. "My biggest gamble is against my king and his ministers. I'm stealing from the royal treasury not to enrich myself, but for the pleasures of the test, the unbearable tension, the knowledge that in the end I must lose. It's as if at a table a gamesman continually doubles his bet. No matter how much he makes with each throw, eventually he must by the odds lose everything. I wonder who will catch me first, the king or Canada. It might be neither, for the king is under the sway of Madame Pompadour. You met one of her ladies, that dreadful countess. Perhaps I will cut off my French wife's head, as the English king did, divorce the pope, and marry Madame Pompadour herself. Now there's a gamble.

"At the moment I'm being protected by the English. They know that without a French Canada necessitating British troops, their colonies would rebel. But it's a delicate balance. If we French become too strong, connecting Quebec with Louisiana through the west, we will surround the English colonies. Thus it's in the interest of the English to allow just enough Canadian strength to threaten the colonies, but not to conquer. As for France, well, only Protestants could be persuaded to settle in this cold climate, and, by the grace of holy mother church, Protestants are not allowed; thus France can never match England man for man in the new world. Praise the Lord for small favors. In this endeavor, which serves both Old England and Old France, I am the perfect agent."

Great Stone Face wants to tell the intendant that there is nothing like hearing oneself talk to know what one is thinking, but he remains, as he must, impassive in expression.

Through the summer the intendant entertains lavishly, while his savage is admired by visitors from across the seas. During these times Great Stone Face eavesdrops on scores of conversations. It becomes clear to him that St. Blein was right in his assessment. The intendant is robbing Canada blind (blind is something he knows something about). What St. Blein doesn't know is that the intendant is also stealing from his own king in France. He buys stores under the king's auspices at low prices from French cronies, and then he informs the colonial minister that it would be to the crown's advantage to buy stores from Canadians. He then sells the stores he has already bought with the king's money back to the king for high prices paid for, again by the king, and shares the profits with Quebec merchants, among them St. Blein's father. Then instead of distributing the stores to the natives and the army, he sells them again to merchants, who ship them back to France for more profits. This is only one of his schemes. Such a man, if he were selfish and haughty, would be despised, but the intendant is generous, without malice, and evenhanded in his treatment of all. Quebec society is small, with nearly everyone related by blood or enterprise, and if Quebec society understands one thing it is that they are better off with the intendant than without him, so they overlook his corruption; indeed they share in it. Great Stone Face recognizes in the intendant's generosity a figment of his own largess as Caucus-Meteor. He admires the intendant very much, but thinks that his criminality must weigh heavily upon him, for he drinks huge amounts of brandy and wine; he gorges himself with food; he gives himself over to sexual excess, and yet cannot find satisfaction.

As the weeks go by Great Stone Face's interest in the intrigues of Conissadawaga gradually dissipates, for his role in the intendant's household has changed him, and therefore he loses kingly ambitions. The intendant has inadvertently stripped Great Stone Face of his pretensions to royalty. Great Stone Face realizes that he has become a slave again in action if not in fact. Like any slave, Great Stone Face grows anxious when his master is upset or out of control. He calms when his master fawns over him. This happiness in submission cannot last, thinks Great Stone Face; I'd best enjoy it while I can. He tells Norman, "The intendant has reduced my worth—I am grateful. Norman, I release you from your obligations as informant. Live your life as you wish. Visit me as a distant relative and friend, not as a subject."

It's almost the end of the summer when Great Stone Face learns enough from various sources to divine one of the intendant's more exotic schemes. Bigot is a civil magistrate, his misdeeds revolving around paper and profit. He is no soldier, and violence upsets him. Still, he must do what he must do. The intendant has heard the echoes of St. Blein's seditious talk. The young ensign is his only real threat in Canada. The intendant worries less about a rebellion in New France than he does about word of his crimes reaching Old France, for some well-placed information in the hands of his enemies in Paris and Versailles could lead to his demise. St. Blein has been assigned to lead another raid along the New England frontier. The intendant's man will be among the soldiers. During the heat of battle, the intendant's man will shoot St. Blein.

Great Stone Face knows it's imprudent for a savage to involve himself in the intrigues of white people, but he feels duty-bound to aid his former commander. He cannot tell him who the assassin is, but at least he can warn him that one exists. One Sunday he borrows Norman's canoe and paddles two hours to the campsite of the raiders. He'd forgotten how much he hates canoe paddling. He thinks: I wish I were with two or three strong paddlers, so I could cheat.

At the campground are the usual collection of mercenaries recruited by the French—the Algonkians from Odanak, who fight to avenge the loss of their lands; the Iroquois from Kahnawake, who fight for profit and out of habit; the Huron from Wendake, who fight out of loyalty to the French; and a few unaffiliated réfugiés who have been brought into the regular French army and who fight because they can do nothing else.

Great Stone Face stops a Huron fellow, and says, "I am looking for your commander, Ensign St. Blein."

"He has gone to Quebec. He will be back just before the sun goes down."

"I will wait for him," says Great Stone Face, and he builds a private fire out of sight and earshot of the men. He will spend these next few hours eating this fire. He's been in Quebec a long time, and it's good to be in the woods again with trees, rocks, birds, and grand design.

Great Stone Face has been by the fire an hour when he hears a familiar voice behind him, calling softly, almost sweetly, "Caucus-Meteor." The sound of his true name sends a shiver down his spine. How to thank the man.

Great Stone Face turns slowly, and finds himself looking at a handsome, powerfully built native wearing a French soldier's uniform.

"In my father's time to speak the name of the dead was to risk execution," says Great Stone Face. "My father himself killed a man who spoke the name of his deceased father."

"But Caucus-Meteor is not dead, and anyway these ancient beliefs mean nothing to me."

"Wolf Eyes, you left your village barely a boy, now you are a man. How did you recognize me?" says Great Stone Face.

The former réfugié child of Conissadawaga pauses before he speaks. He's gained perhaps fifty pounds of muscle, and grown another two or three inches in height. Great Stone Face guesses that he would easily defeat his father in a wrestling match today. He wears his hair short and without feathers or headband, like a soldier; no paint or adornment of any kind marks him as a native. Except for his darker complexion, he looks more French than the Frenchmen from Old France, and like those he emulates his manner is superior and aloof. Though his family band has left the village Wolf Eyes will ask not a word about them.

Great Stone Face marvels that a man could be so without curiosity. I admire Wolf Eyes very much, he thinks.

"Just as you recognized me—by your voice," Wolf Eyes says. "A man can change his apparel, as I myself have done; he can change his face, as you apparently have; he can change, even, the appearance of his gender, if he but have the will; but only sickness will change his voice. Are you sick, Caucus-Meteor?"

"Sick at heart on occasion, but apparently such illness does not disguise the voice."

"And a false face is only a mask, as a Mohawk might make."

"How did you find me?"

"It's all around the camp that an old native with tattoos is waiting for Ensign St. Blein. I knew it could only be Caucus-Meteor, and then it was an easy matter to smell the air for a small fire."

At that moment Great Stone Face hears in his mind the screech of an owl as the mouse hears it. "Wolf Eyes, how could you recognize my voice when you did not hear me speak?"

"You did not have to speak . . . here."

"You've been to the palace. That was where you overheard me, but you did not reveal yourself to me, nor did you betray me."

"That's correct, old king. I heard you ordering one of the cooks to release a helper to gather wood for you. The intendant told me about his fire tender, how he was handsome in an ancient way, but very stupid for he could not speak French. I know that Caucus-Meteor speaks better French than most Frenchmen. As the palace fire tender you must hear about every intrigue in Canada."

Suddenly, Great Stone Face understands everything. "I see you still carry Nathan's musket," he says.

"It was meant to kill Frenchmen, was it not?" Wolf Eyes laughs.

"I will leave now; I have decided I do not wish to visit with my former commander. I will not warn him against you." Great Stone Face makes the old sign of trust.

"So, then, you will not reveal me, and I will not reveal you.

You see, Caucus-Meteor, we are both at heart the devil's children, for we've made a devil's bargain."

"Not exactly, Wolf Eyes. It would be a great relief to me if you did reveal me. But I will not reveal you, for my loyalty to a citizen of Conissadawaga is greater than my loyalty to my former French commander. If you have a chance, tell him I am sorry before you kill him."

"If the opportunity presents itself, I will honor your request, for as sure as you are in no part my father you remain in part my king."

The romance between Norman Feathers and Wytopitlock builds slowly over the summer and along the same time-track as the construction of the house. The coincidence does not go unnoticed by you. Wytopitlock and Norman confide in you. She tells you that she and Norman have long discussions. He tells you how a great calmness of spirit came over him after his conversion to Christianity, but how no amount of prayer could overtake his loneliness until he met Wytopitlock. She tells you how her husband clipped her nose and cast her out of their village after he discovered her unfaithfulness; she tells you about her rage, her fears, her passion, her wanderings, her wish to die, and, finally, of the calmness that came over her when Norman brought her to church. You advise Wytopitlock to press Norman on the issue of marriage, not to entrap him—he is already entrapped—but to guide him. Norman is the kind of man who must constantly be led. In this respect, as it turns out, you are partly right. Wytopitlock guides Norman, as any woman of need does at entry, and Norman proposes marriage. But he goes a step further. He visits you and Nathan Provider-of-Services and tells them that he and Wytopitlock insist that a priest wed them in the sacrament.

"Your love, its peculiar need for sanctification, is an omen," you say. "It is time that the priests return to this village."

I am shocked. I had begun to think that with the conjuring

gift came some control over events, or at least some blessing from outside powers. Now I understand that conjuring is a mere window pane of wavy glass that admits only the eyes. You, Nathan, and the lovers canoe to Quebec to visit with Norman's confessor, Father "Spike" Morrissette. The priest lives with others of his kind in a huge stone house full of echoes.

"My kinsman and his betrothed wish to marry with the blessing of Jesus Christ," you say to the priest. "Will you come to our village to perform the ceremony?"

"I am elated at the opportunity to return to Conissadawaga," says Father Spike. "I hope you will allow me to spread the gospel."

"Will you tell us about heaven?" you ask.

"I will bring you the word of Christ. Heaven will follow."

A few days later, Father Spike shows up in the village in response to your invitation. He stays a week, saying mass, reading the gospels, preaching on faith and morals. Everyone turns out for his talks. At first the priest is viewed as a curiosity, but soon his message of salvation through submission to the son of God takes hold. The villagers' thoughts can be summarized by the idea that now that they are no longer nomads but a settled people, they require a settlers' god. Father Spike makes no promises, but he does bless the crops in the name of Christ, and the villagers are impressed by the ceremony. I wonder about you, Black Dirt? Is it a need for faith that led you to call the priests? Or are you like your father, full of ambition and schemes? I think your decision encompasses both, or even something else I cannot conjure. Subsequent events only add adornment to my perplexity in this matter.

You ask Father Spike to arrange a meeting with the chief of the church. That would be the new bishop, says Father Spike, and he speaks the name of my old adversary, the reverend Esubee Goulet. You go alone to visit the bishop. Nathan would be no help since he does not speak the bishop's language, and anyway you wants the bishop to understand that you, not your man, are the village chief. Since you last saw him when he took Caterina away, Bishop Goulet has grown fatter, softer, redder in the face. You are impressed.

He welcomes you to his rectory, bows slightly, leads you to a chair. It's awkward to sit on, but you could get used to the position.

"What is your name, my child?" he says.

It's obvious that Bishop Goulet has forgotten that you've met before. You are aware that your name, Black Dirt, cannot be pronounced in French, and that in translation it is a bit of a puzzle. "I wish to be called Marie," you say.

"Very good, Marie. And do you have a last name?"

"Meteor," you say. Your pronunciation in the bishop's tongue doesn't quite take in the bishop's ear, but he adjusts. "Metivier, is that what you said?"

"Oui."

"I'm pleased to make your acquaintance, Marie Metivier," the bishop says. "Now what can I do for you?"

"My village has undergone many changes in the last year," you say, your first utterance as Marie Metivier. "I believe we are ready for a priest. Our people wish to be baptized so they can receive Christ."

"It's not so simple," says the bishop. "Children, those holy innocents, may be baptized, but adults must be instructed before they are allowed to take the Eucharist."

"We are not stupid, Bishop Goulet. We will learn the instruction."

"I am sure you will." The bishop pauses. "Something about your voice now seems familiar to me."

"I am the daughter of . . ." You pause. Among our people, it was forbidden to speak the name of the dead. But I did not follow the custom, and you yourself spoke the names of your dead mother, husband, and children. But with the name of your father you find yourself under the sway of ancient gods. You bow.

"Yes, of course, I remember now," says the priest. "You are Caucus-Meteor's daughter."

"He was my father and king."

"Your sister is in the convent."

"What covenant?" you say, misunderstanding.

"What convenience, yes," he says, equally puzzled. When it's clear to both that you've lost yourselves in words, you drop the subject. "I heard that your father passed away," says the priest. "I am only sorry that he could not take the sacraments, but I am sure that God has a plan for him."

"I am sure."

"Marie Metivier, I must tell you that my last meeting with Caucus-Meteor was quite disappointing."

"Yes, he too was disappointed."

It occurs to me now, daughter, that through the sorcery of religion, nation, language, luck, and malice, Father Goulet has managed to name both of my children. I admire him very much.

"Enough of these old wars," says the old priest. "I've been to your village of Conissadawaga. If we are to send a priest, it must have a church with a stove. If I remember correctly, your village is abandoned in the winter; your people live the old northern Algonkian life of the nomad; you are hunters and fishers."

"I am here to tell you that today we are farmers. We live in our village year-round. We have farm animals. We have built a house, not a wigwam, a true house. It is almost complete." You are no longer thinking of yourself as Black Dirt, but as Marie Metivier; you pause, then add, "We can use the house for worship until we build a proper church, bishop, for we know now what it takes to build."

"All right then. I will assign Father Morrissette to visit your people to instruct and serve them."

"It costs much to build a house, a church, a village. We cannot afford to pay tribute to Jesus and to the intendant."

Up until now, Bishop Goulet thought Marie Metivier was an ignorant savage to whom he was ministering for the purposes of his church, his nation, and of course her salvation. Now he realizes she's been ministering to him. There's a long pause while the bishop mulls over this matter, prays silently, and finally says, "How much in tribute does the intendant extort from you?"

Marie Metivier tells him. They strike a bargain, souls in exchange for church influence in the palace. At the conclusion of the meeting, you ask the bishop for his blessing.

I'm thinking that God's wonders in expanding the meaning of that word "blessing" are quite extraordinary.

"Kneel, daughter of Christ," Father Goulet says, rising. You kneel before him and bow your head. And so now I have lost my second daughter to Jesus. I admire the Son of God very much.

Minutes later, agreement ratified by the blessing, intendant taken care of, Conissadawaga committed to Catholicism, leaders parting in mutual respect and suspicion, Marie Metivier on her way out asks, "I've always wondered, Bishop, what's the difference between the French Jesus and the English Jesus?"

The bishop is startled. That moment of doubt within him is my only satisfaction. He's thinking that even here in Canada the savages are somehow exposed to dangerous ideas, or perhaps— and this strikes him as an unexpected blow—the savages are the source of the dangerous ideas. "The difference," he says, "is antiquity."

When Great Stone Face learns that his conjuring was correct— the priests have returned to Conissadawaga at his daughter's request—he senses another of those great turns in the scheming roll of the imperfect circle of things. He used to think the world's muddled landscape was made of the footprints of animals, but now he understands that it consists of wheel ruts; the gods of old or the three-persons-in-one god of the Catholics, or the Protestant god whose entertainment is to listen to prayers of individuals, whichever of the gods is in control these days, wish for us to live by the wheel. Conissadawaga, as conceived by Keeps-the-Flame and himself, is falling into the abyss of memory. When he believed that Haggis would take over his village, he was jealous, as a man is jealous to keep his woman or his best beads or his weapon, but he did not feel pained by his rival, for he and Haggis agreed over the important matters. They both looked back in time for inspiration; they both believed that to be a savage was to be a nomad, for it is only the man who wanders as part of his way of life who is forever at home. Haggis, like himself, was merely ambitious for power and preservation. If only they could have worked together! Now this: his precious daughter was destroying everything that her parents had wrought. This understanding, this vision of impending destruction, thinks Great Stone Face, is the true nature of my pain. I am very grateful. Surely this feeling is what the priests call penance for sins. Maybe in spite of myself I am bound for Christian heaven. I hope not, for it is all clouds and worshipping, hardly an environment for a curious king.

You and the other villagers are so busy with building and farming and, of late, praying that you hardly have time to notice how quickly and profoundly you are changing. No more nightly celebrations around a fire. Our people spend more time with loved ones inside the wigwam, where they discuss such matters as the cramped and dark quarters they live in and how nice it would be to have their own house, one with glass windows. Festivities are reduced to one or two nights a week, Friday and Saturday. Nubanusit and Pisgah leave the village in search of more gatherings for drinking. I look for them in Quebec, but I think they have gone south to Montreal, and will never be heard from again. Sundays everybody goes to church, the service held by Father Spike outside if the weather is good and in the house if it is poor.

The house now has a roof and floor, though no doors or windows. Only two windows will have glass panes. The others will be shuttered so they can be thrown open to let in light or closed to keep out cold, wind, rain. Trade missions this year are strictly local, for the tribe can obtain just about everything it needs in nearby Quebec. The women confirm what they had always suspected, that the trade missions were mainly an excuse for the men to travel and have adventures. The men miss the trade missions, which exposed them to goods and ideas far and wide and gave them a sense of importance. As a group, the men are thinking that though they work these days with their women in the fields, though they have given up summer trade and travel, though they confess their sins, no woman, priest, or God almighty is going to stop them from going hunting in the fall. Men are funnier than women in their vices.

The women also see a disadvantage to their new social cycle. They have more control over their immediate families, a safer environment for their children, but less control over the tribe as a whole. Men are taking over the farming and building operations of the tribe. In the old days, women set up the wigwams; now men are building the house that will replace the campfire circle. Some of the men are talking about more construction projects—houses, a church, a shed to store moccasins.

You see, my darling daughter, how it is with a ruler. All is excitable refinement refuted by loneliness.

It isn't until the first snow that Norman Feathers canoes to Quebec. The ice will lock the river in a few weeks, but now it's navigable. It's only when he speaks of his own bliss that Norman's powers of observation grow foggy, but by close questioning Great Stone Face is confident he has the entire story by the time Norman Feathers leaves.

Wytopitlock is baptized and takes the name of Anne. The wedding of Norman Feathers and Anne of Conissadawaga is the first public event held in the new house. A celebration follows, both for the house and for the married couple, what Nathan Provider-of-Services calls a house-warning or warming, hard to tell from Norman's description. Norman says that something, something better than oratory, told him he was in the presence of a greater power. Something better than oratory! How easily people throw around language today; Bleached Bones, you did right to die when you did. But Great Stone Face conceals his bitterness. Nothing is left of the old ways of Caucus-Meteor. He should have died with Bleached Bones.

Then Norman says he has been talking to his confessor about a sin. Now that he has a wife this secret he carries, that his king is still alive, has become a sin of omission. He must renounce his king, for there is not sufficient fidelity for God, family, king, and secret. Trembling, Norman asks his king for release. He kneels in front of him, and Great Stone Face puts his hand on his shoulder and mumbles ancient Algonkian incantations well mixed with as much pretend Latin as he can muster, and then Norman leaves him forever to be with his wife, his oxen, his own life.

The old king no longer can wield power or even influence. With Norman lost to him, he calls upon other sources—the reports of visiting natives, voyageurs, priests, soldiers, and his own conjuring gift, which grows more powerful as his worldly faculties decline.

A Far Place

By speaking with my mind's voice in oratorical tones directly to you, I speak to all the women in my life—to you, Black Dirt, to my adopted daughter, Caterina, to my wife, Keeps-the-Flame, and to my dear mother, whose name I will not voice out of respect for the old superstitions. These words within my conjuring, these are my embraces—words have always been my embraces. I am beginning to see how it should be between you and Nathan. An old Algonkian saying tells us a heart mended after heartbreak makes for the strongest heart.

For two months, Father Spike instructs the villagers in the requirements of the faith until one day, speaking in the three main languages of the villages—Algonkian, French, and Iroquois—he says, "Now you are ready to receive Jesus." The priest baptizes everybody in the village and gives communion to all except one. The demands of the priest remind Nathan that while he might in good conscience love a pagan woman, he's hard put to love a papist one. He says to you, "I'm too much an Englishman to offer my soul to a priest." While I fear that his intransigence will be the ruin of you both, I cannot help but admire him very much. Dear daughter, you are not sure what to think, what to feel. You gave yourself over to this man for reasons mysterious and perhaps (you are thinking now) temporary. These Frenchmen and

Englishmen, they presume to court Jesus, but they quarrel over how to love Him, and in the end the quarrel supplants the love. How can a poor savage woman determine a correct course weaving between these and those?

The house that Nathan built serves variously as a meeting hall, a Catholic church, and a residence for the builder and his wife. But, Black Dirt, a house like the English built is not a wigwam! It is not like the den of the wolf or the nest of the bird or the burrow of the mouse, abodes in the village of the earth. A house is apart from the earth; it separates you from the very dirt that you love. Nor is a house heaven. Don't you understand what I am saying? A house is a place to grow lonely, and the lonely grow ambitious for comforts. What is happening in Conissadawaga supports my proposition. The villagers treat the house as if it belongs to them, and after a fashion it certainly does, for they have put their labor into it and their king paid for its necessities. But Nathan behaves as if it belongs to him and you alone. He snaps at the villagers, as a squire snaps at his servants. You draw back in sullen criticism of his actions, but you do little to dissuade him because secretly you, too, want the house for your own. The house has made the villagers envious, you and Nathan jealous. The ancient idea of sharing fades into the yaw of want.

Religion, too, is making the people lonely. When they were pagans they always had good company, for a pagan can feel like a brother to a stone or a tree; a pagan can laugh with the foolish voices in a brook. Now that the people have been baptized, they feel, as the priests told them, removed from the garden; they start to leave Conissadawaga. A great orator might yet hold them together, but neither you nor your husband are orators; you are only hard-working and good people. Over the course of the months where summer flows into fall and abruptly drops off into winter, the tribe grows smaller and smaller.

Omer and Hungry Heart and Freeway move permanently to Montreal. After Wytopitlock changes her name to Anne and marries Norman Feathers, they set out in search of great teams of oxen which require great teamsters, who have great wives to make them happy so they can impart happiness to their beasts. Others leave for Quebec to live as Frenchmen. Most have either left or are planning to go to réfugié villages where relatives reside, for now that they are in the faith they will be accepted. A few go North searching for Haggis. Ossipee wanders off and falls from the river bluffs on the rocks below. Passaconway stops eating, and he too dies.

Haggis was right. Once the village turned to the papist Jesus, the tribe broke apart. You see how it is? Do you? No you don't. You still hope to remain a member of a people in this place. What is it that holds you? The land? The past? The folk? The future? I think it is the dirt. I know how it is with these réfugiés, for I am one myself. As a boy I was a true savage, but I lost myself in slavery. Because of that experience I cannot just be. I must become. I am a conscious act, I am a decision, I am a labor. With all my effort, I can never be entirely the savage that Haggis is. Part of me will always be a slave with a European way of thinking and feeling.

You bring up the subject of loss and dissolution with the priest. Father Spike tells you that Jesus takes away our dream for a life on this earth in return for eternal life with Him. I admit his is an unbeatable answer to the question.

You draw closer and closer to the church, and by the tenets of that proximity a distance between you and Nathan lengthens. You have been searching for something that neither family nor village can provide; now you have found it in the papist Jesus and the difficult order he brings. Perhaps it is the very difficulty that makes submission possible. Or perhaps it all a ruse with you, and you are more conniving than myself or your mother. I cannot tell. Oh, this feeling of wonder and suspicion makes me happy to be alive.

As one by one the people depart, Nathan attempts to console you. "I know how difficult is for you when even one of the villagers leaves."

"And now they are all going or gone. The few who remain

have voted to divide up our fields and hunting grounds into . . . I forget the word in English?"

"Lots."

"Yes—lots. My people are becoming like the French and English: paradise is in their own lots, their own houses, their own farms. I plead with them but my oratory fails, and the votes go against me. I cannot blame them." You say no more. You are thinking that the English house that Nathan Provider-of-Services built is a lonely place; even so, something in you wants to remain there.

Full of conflict, you visit your sister in the convent. She tells you to look for a sign from Jesus. You think maybe that sign comes later in the month.

You meet with your confessor, Father Spike. His tiny hands, hands soft as a girl's, embrace your own. You wonder if Jesus had hands like his priest. Jesus, like Nathan, was a builder, so perhaps he had big rough hands. But Jesus is never seen building; he builds with the heart, and uses his hands only for blessings. So perhaps the hands of the Son of Man were tiny and soft like the ones belonging to Father Spike.

"I have something troubling to tell you," you say.

"I know what the trouble is in your heart, and I've been meaning to talk to you about it," the priest says. "Your marriage is not sanctified by the church. In the eyes of God, you are not man and wife." Sorry, priest, wrong trouble, but you don't correct him.

"My husband wishes to worship his Protestant Jesus," you say.

"Marie, I cannot marry you to a Protestant. You are risking the pains of hell for this illicit love."

"I will test it," you tell the priest.

A week goes by, and you do not test it. You have something very important to tell Nathan, but you cannot because of the pronouncement of the priest. You are afraid. You feel events moving toward something you can't quite fathom. On Sunday Father Spike returns to the village with the omen. He asks to meet privately with you and Nathan.

"Three Englishman have arrived in Quebec under a white flag of truce," he says. "With them is their prisoner, a French military officer, one Ensign Pierre Raimbault St. Blein. He was captured on the English frontier after being wounded in a raid last fall. Shot accidentally by one of his own men. The Englishmen are negotiating with the governor-general to exchange the ensign for their countryman, known in New England as Nathan Blake. What is your wish, Nathan?" says the priest.

"I wish to remain with my wife," he says haltingly. Even a fool can see that he's not sure what wife he means to be loyal to.

"Your face is full of doubt," says Father Spike.

"I am surprised by this news, yea, stunned. Let me think on it some," Nathan says.

"To guide your thinking I have instructions from Bishop Goulet," says the priest. "If you choose to return to New England, so be it. If you elect to stay in Canada and convert to the Catholic faith, the church will give you sanctuary. If you keep your Protestant faith, the church will step aside."

"What does this mean?" you ask.

"It means the determination for Nathan will be made between the governor-general and the English," the priest says. "It's likely soldiers will take him back to the land of his birth."

You see how it is, daughter? When the priests say they want your soul for Jesus, they mean they want your soul for Jesus.

Nathan is silent, betwixt and between words as well as worlds.

In your secret heart you've thought about this moment since you married Nathan Provider-of-Services. Now that it is here, you are oddly calm. No amount of work or worry can save you now. The ancients say it is better to keep the wind to your back. The priest tells you that Jesus constantly tests one's faith. You know only that it is your wish for your fate to be determined in Conissadawaga, on your grounds, in your house; this is your land, your home, your dirt.

"I must tell you," says Father Spike, "that the Englishmen have been informed of your whereabouts. I expect they will arrive here on the morrow. You will have to render them a decision."

"Time is what I have been passing in Canada," Nathan says. "Give me some time."

You send the priest away, and tell your husband that you wish to build a fire outside the house, as in olden times, and you wish also that he join you. And so you build a fire. Once it is going well, you say to your husband with a shy smile, "My mother and father both made small fires like this when they did not know how to conduct their lives, and from the fire they gained comfort and guidance, as well as warmth." You pause, and both of you stare for a moment at the fire. You continue, "I lost a husband. I lost two daughters. I lost a mother. All I had remaining was a sister and a father, and the sister left me and the father went to heaven. The village was my family. It wasn't until you became a father to my village, teaching them the house-building sorcery, teaching me the farm-life sorcery, that I felt like a woman again. I will always admire you, Nathan Provider-of-Services. But now there is something else. I was able to become a woman because I had a mother and a father. A child needs a mother and a father."

"Who would deny such an obvious assertion?" Nathan says. He's annoyed. Your way, indirect, is not his way. Already, he is parting from you.

"Nathan Provider-of-Services, I am carrying your baby."

You can tell by the look on his face that he didn't expect this. Perhaps he had it in the back of his mind that while creatures of different kind can copulate, they cannot produce offspring. "I do not know what to think," he says. "Nor what to feel or do." You can tell that he wants to hold you by the way he retreats from you, for he is one of those men who often draw away when they feel great things.

"Perhaps we should pray," you say. "Stay here. I will return." You go into the house and come back with rosary beads. "They were a gift from my sister, Caterina. Will you pray with me?"

He points at the rosary beads. "I cannot pray with those

things." They are made of the same trade beads that decorate the moccasins he is wearing. Perhaps he notices that the cross is carved wood, cherry, if the burnished red color is evidence.

"I half hoped," you say, "that you would come to the Catholic faith."

"We must pray in our own fashion," he says cautiously, for they are in the familiar territory of marital discord.

You and Nathan kneel in the snow, hold hands, and pray all the way through the completion of the rosary. Meanwhile, the fire dies to smoky ashes. Nathan listens while you repeat the papist Hail Marys and Our Fathers in French. His jaw drops open during prayers, but his lips do not move. Probably I am unkind, but seeing two such people so desperate and wedded in the snow amuses me. Forget all you know and follow your hearts, lovers, and pretend you are the same in kind; your child will be one, not two.

Upon conclusion of the prayers, Nathan rises, holds out a hand to you, and says, "The music of your voice reminds me of my first trip to Conissadawaga when I was on the river and the wind brought the singing of a farmwife working in the fields."

"And what of your own prayer, husband?" she asks, as you walk hand in hand back to the house, the wood-burning stove, the hard comfort.

"My prayers are worn from too much use brought on by captivity. I ask only for guidance."

After an uncomfortable pause, you whisper, "Nathan." And at that modest promontory before house entry that Nathan calls the stoop you fall into his arms. Perhaps he can feel your child pressing against him. Surely, the message from heaven is: Nathan, your place is with this American woman and her—your—child.

Both you and Nathan are uncertain what course he will take, but I know. I cannot write parchment script, but I understand what is written in a man's behavior. Nathan Provider-of-Services in the time he was my slave, especially during that winter we spent on the ice, talked often of his regret for rash acts. In 1736, as a very young man, Nathan was among those who pioneered a village on the New England borders. With the coming of winter, the other proprietors retreated to the established towns to wait out the severe weather, but Nathan on a whim remained in his bark shelter. Eventually, he ran out of food and had to flee, leaving his oxen behind. Two winters later he risked crossing a pond, and his horse fell through thin ice and was drowned. This is the man who abandoned his family in the stockade merely to let his animals out of the barn during an attack. This is the man who walked the gauntlet, who defied a people in renouncing his slave status. How a man behaves during moments of crisis is of great interest to me in this my last epoch. In Nathan's day-to-day life, he is pious, reliable, predictable, controlled, uninteresting. But during moments of inner turmoil he is rash, a subject worthy of inquiry.

He protects himself against fear and tedium with the thought of a "far place." It was this thought that made a pioneer of him, that killed his horse, that starved his oxen, that drove him out of the stockade that April day in 1746, that created behavior within him that helped push his wife over the edge into madness. It's the thought of the far place that grips him now, and he tells you about it, his language often lapsing into English, for his grasp of Algonkian is insufficient to reproduce in words the emotions of his childhood.

"When I was a boy," he tells you, "I was often restless. No activity or encounter seemed agreeable enough to me. And then I heard the stories of the west where, it was said, there were paradise lots for the taking. This story has stayed with me as a feeling, as a directive. Times are I think it's the devil that's in every man who gives me this feeling, but when it is upon me as it is now, I do not care if the source is out of Providence or below. I wish only to follow the feeling. Black Dirt, I'm a man no longer English, who can never be a proper savage and who will forever despise the Frenchman. You see how it is with me? I have to break paths to the far place. You must come with me to the great west. With our child we will people the paradise lots; we will build the barns, the houses, the towns—not for France, not for England, not for any native tribe, but for our own nation."

And so you pack food and stores, and leave by dog team. Conissadawaga lies before you with the helplessness of a deer with a broken leg. Smoke twists up from the chimney of the house Nathan had built, and from perhaps a half dozen wigwams surrounding it; it is a village reduced and it is the saddest day of your life since your children were taken by the distemper. Nathan does not notice. He's in the middle of something. I remember sailors in Quebec telling me about a peculiar feeling. A man will climb the mast to do some chore. High up he will look down. The sway of the ship will make it appear as if the mast is still and the ship moves out from under him. Men under the influence of this effect often fall. The sailors call the feeling "rapture in the rigging." It's this rapture in the rigging of mind that steers Nathan west. You travel until the dogs need to rest, and then you travel some more. You spend that night in a shelter made by the sled and skins.

The next morning is thick with a cold, malevolent fog. Nathan hadn't reckoned on this. He'd said the north star would guide you in the long night, and the sun would guide you in the day. But this—fog—means you have to work just to stay on the path. By noon the fog has cleared, only to be replaced by dark clouds. A storm is coming.

In an hour you reach the gorge, the place where Haggis and his hunters slaughtered the deer herd, where I told Nathan, teasing him, that the opening to the western lands lay ahead. The fog is lifting.

"There, there, through the gorge is our beginning," Nathan says, though he's not looking at land but at heaven.

You turn your thoughts to the baby in your belly, and you think that Nathan's mad love for the far place will kill the three of you. And yet a woman's place is no further than with the father of her children.

"We always traveled by rivers and known paths," you say. "All I've heard of the land beyond the gorge is stories of swamp, and great rock ledges, little sustenance even for beasts," Black Dirt says.

"Don't you see? It's the wastelands that discouraged your people. You must persevere."

You look at the sky.

Nathan says, "If the weather holds . . ."

"It is winter, it is Canada—how can the weather hold?" you say.

For a moment Nathan doubts his rapture, but the rapture is too strong. It orders his thinking. "Remember the lights we saw the first time we made love . . ."

"They were in the north . . ."

"They started from the north, they spread to the west. Don't you understand?" he says. "We start one place, and we spread to another. Our dreams, our hopes, our faith—these give us vigor and purpose. We have provisions for a month. We will find the paradise lots."

"I've prayed to the Son of Man, and I hope, as so many women do, that the Son of Man is not as crazy as a man. I would go with you, Nathan. But this child in my belly wants to stay where it is safe."

"At least come through the gorge with me. If it's a wasteland beyond . . ." He stops, he can't bear to promise her he'll turn back.

Who can say if he would have turned back or if you would have gone on? The old trickster intervenes. You are almost through and in some thick spruces, when five men step from the shadows. One is Nathan's New England friend John Hawks, a stalwart soldier. With him are two dough-faced, well-fed, jolly fellows. These three men have come all this way under a white flag of truce with a fourth man, their prisoner, Pierre Raimbault St. Blein. As Nathan will soon learn, they also carry ransom money that Elizabeth, his English wife, has raised. You take note of the fifth man, the guide who brought the men to this point, a native you've never seen before, an old buzzard with tattoos covering face and head. Since I started this conjuring business, I'm only half myself, hence half my hopes, so I half hope you'll recognize me, but you don't.

You stand aside as the reunion progresses. It is very awkward. The Englishmen rejoice when they see Nathan. Something like love crosses Nathan's face, but it quickly fades into confusion. He looks at you, at his fellow New Englanders, at his own skin, and then buries his face in his hands, and weeps. The bottled emotion of three years or perhaps even a lifetime, pours out of him.

At first the New Englanders think he is happy to see them, and surely he is. But there is something else in him that he is weeping for, a loss behind all the other losses, an ache that seems like gladness in the knowledge that he'll never know in this life whether a wasteland lies before his dreams or paradise. Whereas before, with you, daughter, he had to reach into English to express himself, now that language of his birth deserts him. Finally, he says in Algonkian to John Hawks, "I can never return as the man I was. Nor can I remain as the man I am."

Hawks doesn't know what he's saying, and perhaps neither does Nathan, for sometimes the lips speak the truth hidden from the mind; the moment slides past him, until he finds some English on his tongue. "My wife, my girls—are they well?"

"Your family is sound. They are staying with your people in Wrentham. Come, let me bring you to them."

"John, I cannot."

"Cannot?" Hawks draws back.

"I have a wife here in Canada. I have, I think, a destiny in Canada, an account payable to God."

Hawks snaps at his countryman, "This being in buckskins is not you speaking, Nathan Blake. It is the demon who lurks in the anguish of your captivity. Come, we will make you whole again in New England."

How certain in their opinions these English are. They are easy to admire, if difficult to love.

Nathan answers simply, "I will not go." I think his voice lacks conviction.

Hawks is a soldier, and of course a soldier knows only one way. He points his musket. "Nathan, I'll return your body to your English widow, before I let you remain in Canada with a savage wife."

In the middle of the argument, you creep away. You have decided that your fate is not with this man. Nathan doesn't notice you until he hears your sharp command to the dogs, and they bolt forward. "Black Dirt—Marie!" he calls out. But you never give Nathan a backward glance; he stands watching you until he can just make out the sled's shape on the horizon. You are thinking that the far place is too far. And with your departure, dear daughter, I feel the conjuring powers leaving me. Once again, I am nothing more than an old man. I know only that my place now is with Nathan.

He starts south as he had gone north three years earlier, a captive again. He isn't bound, but he's closely watched. The old American thinks that one day Nathan will understand that Black Dirt taught him about woman's grief, about his New England wife's grief, and about his own grief, how all along he had been fleeing from it, but for now he is merely in the stupor of the first stage of captivity, as he was the day Caucus-Meteor captured him.

Great Stone Face stays clear of Nathan, makes his wishes known through Hawks in grunts, sign language, and the corrupted phrases of traders and soldiers. As the men start back for Quebec on snowshoes, Nathan walks with head bowed between the two New England underlings. Nathan will be in this state all day, thinks Great Stone Face. He'll not eat, for the stomach rebels against insult as well as injury. Hawks and St. Blein walk with their guide at the front. It's an effort for Great Stone Face to pretend that all this walking is not tiring him out. He muses that though he has taken on a different appearance, his body is as frail as Caucus-Meteor's. His predicament reminds him of an old Algonkian saying: a disguise is full of nerves but has no muscle.

Hawks talks with St. Blein in English, believing that this old savage cannot understand him.

"How could our guide know that Nathan would flee and that he would go west to this forlorn gorge?" Hawks asks.

"Some of the savages enjoy strange powers," says St. Blein. "I'm surprised that he even exists. I thought I knew every wise tracker, guide, and interpreter in these northern lands, but this fellow is as much a mystery to me as he is to you."

"He says he's from the south, if I understand him. He speaks in such a crude way." Hawks looks back at Nathan, head down, in a daze. "I fear for my countryman, that he's lost himself in Canada."

"That may be," says St. Blein. "I will take you to my father's house in Quebec. We will celebrate this prisoner exchange with drink, food, and carousing. Then you can start south. Perhaps your man will have his wits about him then."

Two days later when the men reach Quebec, Nathan's torpor gives way to sullen unappreciation of his predicament. Nathan, thinks Great Stone Face, you are a man between worlds—see them both, be grateful. But, no, he's the kind of man to do a duty without asking for thanks, or offering thanks for a duty received. Great Stone Face is thinking that Nathan, as he did upon his capture in New England, is scheming to escape. It's a thought that has struck the New Englanders too. They are suspicious of all Canada. They've grown to respect St. Blein, but they don't trust him any more than they trust any Frenchman or savage. After the formal prisoner exchange, the party will be vulnerable in Canada. The Englishmen fear that Nathan's savage friends or maybe even French soldiers will pursue them.

The guide takes the men's fears as an omen that suits his own purposes. He assures them he knows a route that will be safe. It's a route he has been thinking about for months. It's the wrong route, he knows, but he must take it, for it's his last chance to plead to the old gods for a father's succor. In this matter, he knows he is destined for failure. Good! The old feeling of the gambler, all anticipation, is in him again. Bleached Bones, I miss you, he thinks.

At the celebration at the St. Blein house the New Englanders get roaring drunk. That is their phrase—"roaring" drunk. One roars when one is the grips of the liquor. Great Stone Face is offered wine, but he refuses with a phrase that disconcerts his hosts. "Where I come from we have a saying. 'Under the influence, the savage does not roar like the bear—he howls like the wolf.'" The New Englanders know this is their last safe night in Canada. The rich merchant's family, ecstatic to see the soldier son back home, offers them hospitality and sanctuary, but after they leave they will be enemies once more.

Great Stone Face mingles with the crowd, where he's admired for his strangeness. Soon, he's recognized as a member of the intendant's household. That leads to the big joke of the evening among the Canadians. It seems as if the intendant's palace has grown cold, and the intendant is furious. It's only the Canadian cold that can bring heat to the Frenchman, thinks Great Stone Face.

The drink clouds over Nathan's anger and confusion. Hawks recounts the circumstances of Nathan's redemption. A new governor from France has taken the place of Galissoniere, and he did not recognize St. Blein. The governor informed St. Blein that a field officer has no authority to negotiate prisoner exchanges. Hawks pleaded on Nathan's behalf, told how Nathan had left a distraught wife and family behind; in the end, the governor threw up his hands and said, "Take your man back to New England, and keep your ransom money." It's a story that Hawks will tell over and over again for years to come.

Nathan is surprised to learn that he's been exchanged for St. Blein. Surprised also to learn that the war is over, and has been over since October when a peace was signed in Europe, though word did not arrive in Quebec for more than a month, and many in both New England and Canada are pretending that the war is still on.

"A fine house it is, I've seen nothing like it in New England, not even in Boston," says Hawks.

"A bit fussy for my tastes," Nathan says. He seems about to speak again as a New Englander, but holds back. Perhaps he was going to tell of the house he built for the savages, but the tale is too strange or disturbing to relate.

Toward the end of the evening, St. Blein and Nathan talk. The Frenchman's English is much improved after his months in captivity. He'd been shot by a man from Conissadawaga, name of Wolf Eyes. Perhaps Nathan experiences some satisfaction in the knowledge that St. Blein's discomfort had come as a result of Nathan's musket. Nathan is no marksman, but he understands the gun as a tool, and he could have told Wolf Eyes that because of scours in the barrel, the compression in that weapon flagged at times. The ball hit its mark, right in the middle of St. Blein's chest, and it knocked him down senseless and slightly fractured the breast plate, but it hardly broke the skin. He came to hours later, alone and abandoned, and made his way to a farmhouse where he surrendered. He was brought to Boston, where, taking advantage of his birth as a nobleman, he managed to conspire with Governor Shirley over matters of state and craft, for though he was a prisoner he moved about as a free man in Boston.

"I met thy wife," St. Blein says in the formal English popular in the generation before Nathan's.

"Aye, and you drove her away."

"I was speaking of your English wife."

Nathan stops breathing for a moment. "Is she well?" he asks with great caution.

"You're a lucky man, Nathan Blake." St. Blein's voice is full and colorful, but he averts his eyes from Nathan's. It's the last time Nathan sees the Frenchman, who drifts away, out of house and festivities.

The Englishmen spend another day in sleep and lounging to

get over the effects of the celebration, and start on their trek bright and early the following morning, proceeding on foot over trudged paths, led by their scarred and tattooed guide. If there is a storm, they will don snowshoes, which they carry tied to French roll packs. At the Richelieu river, the guide, telling Hawks he knows a route safe from pursuit, takes the men east away from the river and normal routes into New England.

In a strategy to bring Nathan back into the English hearth, Hawks makes frequent attempts to engage Nathan in conversation. The soldier's task, as Great Stone Face divines it, is to make Nathan realize that his love of Canada and savages was the result of despondency and savage cunning; Hawks uses the European trick of turning love to hate. I admire John Hawks very much, thinks Great Stone Face.

"You know," Hawks says, "our guide reminds me of Mark Ferry."

"I knew another native who reminded me of Mark Ferry," Nathan says. "How is the hermit of our New Hampshire village?"

"I cannot say, for I have heard nothing about the man during these three years."

Nathan takes Hawks's arm. "John, my village of Upper Ashuelot, what has happened to it?"

"It's been abandoned, Nathan. But now that the war is over, I imagine folks will be going back."

Hawks continues to speak, but Nathan's attention wanders. He's a man between home and a far place. Using the old English of his grandfather, Nathan says, "I can see that my aloof behavior distresses thee, but you took me against my will."

"You have no will—the savages burned it, as they burn flesh. But the burn that does not kill, heals over if in a scar; we will be friends again."

Nathan cannot look at Hawks. Great Stone Face knows why. Nathan can't bear seeing the reflection of his history in those eyes, distorted now by Canada.

Great Stone Face turns the party south, and three days later the men enter the country of the highest New England mountains. A snowstorm holds them back a day. Now that their tracks are covered the men aren't sure they can stay on the path, which comes and goes according to whims of snow. They're dependent on their guide.

Hawks calls a halt on some level ground to bed down for the night, but the old guide motions for the men to continue. Hawks barks at him that he is in command, but the guide simply goes on walking.

"We can find our own way home now," Hawks says. "We don't need this sullen savage." But his voice lacks conviction, and they follow the old man.

Great Stone Face has the desire to make a Caucus-Meteor speech, or maybe he just wants an excuse to stop walking. He's not sure. Suddenly, his reuniting ceremony is in doubt. He's too exhausted. Or perhaps it's just the effort of pretending not to be exhausted that is exhausting him. Such contradictions have dominated his entire life. I am very grateful, he thinks. And then all too early he sees them—the stars in the heavens, the eruption of light from the great north. Then total darkness. For a minute or two he walks blindly, though pretends to see. And, then, does see as well as ever. They've entered one of the notches between mountains.

"Look!" says Hawks, pointing to the mountain top.

Silhouetted against the setting sun is a rock formation in the shape of the head of their guide—the great stone face.

Great Stone Face does not notice the presence of the Englishmen. He is looking up at the rock formation; he calls out to it, "Speak!" After a pause, he says again, "Speak!" And finally a third utterance, "Speak my name!"

Nathan Provider-of-Service looks down at him still kneeling in the snow. It is as if the strength of Nathan's sight has material weight, for the old guide falls over. He holds out a hand, and Nathan takes it. Great Stone Face can feel eyes upon him, can hear his own mouth still sucking and blowing air, can feel the

cheek muscles on one side twitch. He is between the old man in
the mountain and the far place. The sight of the stone face, the
silence that followed his plea has stripped him of his disguise—
he's Caucus-Meteor again. He understands that while his father
may not be able to speak without a jaw, he can inspire a son to
speak. Now, he thinks, now I will again be able to speak. "Thank
you, father," he says to the mountain.

"What's going on?" Hawks asks.

"This old fellow has had a shock," Nathan says.

They build a fire and make the old invalid as comfortable as
possible. "Bring him closer to the fire," Nathan says.

"Nathan Provider-of-Services," the old guide says in English.

Nathan's breath catches. He whispers, "Caucus-Meteor—are
you a ghost?"

"I soon will be."

"You know this ancient?" said Hawks.

"Shut up, John, and feed the damn fire."

Nathan gives Caucus-Meteor some pemmican and water, and
as he has done so many times, the old king finds strength to go on.

"You had a shock," Nathan says in Algonkian.

"I'm grateful for the attack from the gods to my faculties, for
finally I understand everything now," says Caucus-Meteor, and
now the need to make a speech charges him with energy. "My
reign in Canada has come to an end. What will happen to my
people is best left to the two sisters of time and fate, their brother,
Jesus, the unborn, and the mysteries. Or something like that.
I have always been a little confused about religion. Did we all
arrive on the back of a turtle? Were Adam and Eve carried on
the wings of carrier pigeons? Crows? Huge black-purple crows?
Pigeons or crows? Eagles perhaps? I prefer crows. I half believe
everything and half believe nothing; together everything and
nothing make men and mud. You are equally complicit in understanding and confusion with me—you are, thus, this: my
son. You have passed all the tests in Canada. You are ready for
other tests in another place. Which is why I conspired to take

you back to New England with these fine, if stupid, English soldiers."

"What is he saying?" Hawks asks.

"He said, 'God bless the English,'" Nathan says.

Caucus-Meteor chuckles, pleased by Nathan's ability, after three years, to deceive, if crudely. "Ever since that day you let an old man live who wanted to die, I have always wondered what force directed your actions," Caucus-Meteor says in English.

"My behavior was nothing strange. I was only acting out of my manhood as I knew it."

"What in hell are they talking about?" says Hawks to his men. They shrug.

"You prayed, and your god said do not kill this savage; that much I have determined," says Caucus-Meteor.

"My God said, look at this man you are about to kill. So I looked, and as you drank, old king, it seemed to me you were kissing the water like a lover. I thought, why should God let me have such a thought if not to prevent me from killing you? So there you have it, for your life you may thank the God you have so often mocked." With that utterance, Nathan's face changes; he's less confused, less angry, suddenly brimming with affection. Some obstructing tumor has passed out of him. He turns to Hawks, and says, "You came all this way, risked your life, and I, I treated you like a stranger."

Like Caucus-Meteor, Hawks too is reading a change in the face of his countryman. "It's all right, Nathan," Hawks says. "This land is marvelous strange, and one can expect nothing else but strangeness."

Caucus-Meteor takes Nathan's hand.

The men loiter for a day while Nathan works. The other New Englanders watch Nathan with axe and crooked knife and make-shift birch-bark steam box bust a sled out of a young ash tree. Caucus-Meteor, the man who never slept when he was healthy, dozes, his eyes shut, his breath fast and labored.

"This old fellow, he was your savage mentor?" says Hawks.

"He was my king," Nathan says.

"Where are we taking him? Back to Canada?" Hawks asks. "And, if I may be so bold, why? And why are you the agent of his removal?"

"We're taking him home."

"Canada?" Hawks repeats.

"No, New England. As to your question of why I am the designated agent, I cannot say. I am only a farmer, a builder, and a believer in the Divine. In this endeavor, I feel ruled by the Divine. I think for a while the devil was in me, pulling me west, and that was why I could not see into my fate. Now I know it; now I follow the whim of the Divine as it is felt in me."

Over the next three days, the New Englanders drag the sled over trails that twist through mountain notches. Luckily, they have good weather. When they come out of the mountains into the lower hills, the snow suddenly gives way, and they have to abandon the sled. But by now, as he has done so often before, Caucus-Meteor has rallied. He is able to walk, with head bowed, back bent, and a shuffle, as one in a funeral dirge.

Two days go by and the party comes upon some New Hampshire men. The ice has cleared on the Merrimack, they say, and though the water is still fast, the river is navigable. They lead the party to some river men, who guide them to the next series of cataracts.

And so they make their way south in various crafts on the big river, crafts not recommended to one accustomed to swift travel by birch-bark canoe, and then over hill and dale by horse cart, and on foot, until they are only half a day from the Blake family farm in Wrentham.

"Go to Wrentham, and tell Elizabeth that her husband will join her soon," Nathan says to Hawks. "From here, the old king and I go on alone."

By now Hawks and the other men have come under Caucus-Meteor's spell, for he's delivered long oratories in English that would shame a minister at the pulpit. There is no need to swear these men to secrecy. They know they are in the presence of some profound if indiscernible moment; they leave Nathan and Caucus-Meteor in full knowledge that the captive and his captor are part of a ceremony in which discretion, intimacy, and mystery are one.

That night it rains. Caucus-Meteor and Nathan stay under a bark shelter and keep warm with a fire.

"You've gained some pluck," Nathan says.

"Just enough," says Caucus-Meteor.

"I feel at peace," Nathan says.

"It's because your service is almost complete, and thus you are relieved of whatever confusion was inside you. You only needed a bit of rescue from the devil that draws men west. Otherwise, on your own, you behaved well; you submitted yourself to the judgment of the village. And now the village is no more. Never mind that you were in part the agent of its demise. All that remains is your God, and I think your God was telling you that you had an errand. You were so long in Canada, because you were waiting for the circumstance to reveal itself. Now it is manifest."

"Yes, I understand now that my place is here in New England. My only regret is Black Dirt. What will become of her, Caucus-Meteor?"

"Like you she is practical-minded, and her love for you was practical, just as your love for her was practical. I tricked the two of you into marrying, and you both made the best of it. She never really loved you, Nathan. She never really loved her first husband, Adiwando, either, else she wouldn't have grieved for him so long. I never should have arranged that marriage. Women who lose husbands they love get over their grief quickly, and remarry. It's only women who are never sure of their love who grieve long. I know the man Black Dirt really loves. I love him myself, but I prevented her from marrying him because he belonged to a different race. She still loves him, he still loves her— I know it from their behavior, though they won't admit it themselves. My last act before coming to you was to go to him, and explain to him the feelings he has been denying for years. He will seek her out, and he will marry her, and they will raise your child. Of this I am sure. You've provided your last service to me, Nathan. Now you are wholeheartedly my son." And the old king gives Nathan his blessing.

By the dawn's light, the fire has gone out, the rain has stopped, and Caucus-Meteor can feel warm moist air pouring in from the south. As Nathan sleeps, Caucus-Meteor blesses him again, and whispers, "Go home, reclaim thy family."

Caucus-Meteor, walking alone south, stops frequently to drink water, but he takes no food. He thinks: I'll never again have need for food, which is one of the conveniences of dying. I am very grateful. He walks all day, following childhood memories. It's only toward the end of his journey, when he sees the ocean bay through the trees, that he falters. He breaks from the path and walks through the woods to the shore. From the rocks he can see little hills across the water, small English sailing vessels, and circling sea birds. He cannot remember what the birds are called. This sudden failure of memory troubles him. He returns to the path, feeling old and weak and sick. Soon a man on horseback appears on the trail headed toward him. He hails the man, and asks, "Is this Mount Hope Bay?" His pronunciation, like that of the men of Old England, throws the rider off his mental course if not off his horse. "What in helldom are you, an antique statue cast from the rum barrel?" he says.

Caucus-Meteor repeats his own question.

"Aye, this is Mount Hope Bay," says the man. "Would you be a savage old whaler from Nantucket?"

"Nay, I am the king's son," says Caucus-Meteor.

Puzzled, the horseman rides away.

It's the smell of the sea that finally relaxes Caucus-Meteor. He breathes it in and goes on. The air temperature has warmed, and he sheds his clothes until he is naked.

Caucus-Meteor comes to a fork in the path. The low road leads into a swamp where his people hid from the English. He slogs through it for the experience, then climbs a gentle bank to the pasture of an English farmer. He walks the edge of the pasture to a stand of oaks with no path, no obvious signposts, but he knows where he's going. He's finding his way by reading rock shapes. A field, a swamp, a river will change with the seasons, and over a human lifetime might vanish all together, but a rock takes a century or two to change even its color. He walks maybe a mile on gradually rising land when he comes to a place that floods him with the sweet longing of home. At a spring where his mother often took him as a child he drinks deeply.

The path narrows, winding through oaks and maples, their leafless branches in multiplying embraces.

It's afternoon when Caucus-Meteor reaches his destination, the rock formation that local people call King Philip's Seat, a half-crown-shaped ledge surrounded by oaks and maples. With the ledge at his back, his father would step into the circle and deliver long and eloquent speeches.

Close by is a downed maple. Caucus-Meteor pauses at the maple for a minute, then returns to the rock face. He climbs along a split in the ledge, puts his hand in a crack, and feels around until he finds what he's looking for: a human skull.

Caucus-Meteor is at the end of the reuniting ceremony he contrived many years ago in the despair of his slavery. He's thinking back to his boyhood in Europe now. He's in a great hall of art, but instead of images of Jesus and the saints, he sees himself in the statues and picture frames: Caucus-Meteor as a young slave, unctuous and articulate; Caucus-Meteor running in the woods, fleeing dogs and men with guns; Caucus-Meteor exhausted, about to die of exposure, found by a Seneca war party that surprises his pursuers with a hail of arrows. His thoughts return to the hall of art in Europe. The sun sets through the arched windows of the great stone castle, and soon it is dark, and now he is remembering in words only—Algonkian, Iroquois, English, French. He calls out, "My name, please—my name."

The Seneca took him prisoner, put him through tests, and

decided he'd make a good American. Caucus-Meteor never belonged to any particular tribe, never excelled as a hunter or warrior, but because of his skills as an interpreter and orator he
gained respect and prestige. Even after his escape from slavery,
he was subject to unaccountable sorrows and terrible loneliness.
All that kept his mind sound was the personal mission he had
envisioned to tolerate his slavery.

Under the moon one night he went to the gates of Plymouth,
Massachusetts. Here his grandfather, the sachem Massasoit, not
only befriended the English, he saved them with gifts of food
when they were starving. Here too was what remained of Massasoit's son, Metacomet, derisively called King Philip. After Philip
was betrayed and assassinated, his body was drawn and quartered, the limbs and torso strewn in the forest for the animals to
eat, the head impaled on a stake at the entry of Plymouth for
all to see. Cotton Mather, only a boy of twelve himself at the
time, defiled the body further by ripping the jaw from the skull
to silence Philip forever. Caucus-Meteor's mission was to rescue his father's remains. The head had been on that stake for
twenty years when Philip's son climbed the pole, removed what
was left, just a skull without a jaw. He had held the skull up to
the moonlight, and he had said, "I will be your jaw; I will speak
for you."

Caucus-Meteor returned the skull to Mount Hope, wedging
it into a crack in the ledges. Now the skull begins to crumble in
his hands. This is good, he thinks, this is as it should be.

He takes a place in front of the ledge, imagines himself in the
circle where the Wampanoags gathered. "You've heard all my
speeches," he says. "I hope they have entertained you. I am too
tired to deliver my own eulogy, and anyway such vanity is beyond
even my scope. I am happy to be here. I will not say, 'Goodbye,'
but 'Hello.' I search the gathering for my mother, Woostone-
kanuske. I see her now. I will come to you mother." He's forgotten now what else he wanted to say. It's better when you don't

finish the speech, because filling the omissions gives the audience something to do.

He walks slowly down the path holding the skull in one hand by his side, carrying it the way the priests in Europe carried their holy books. Still in sight of King Philip's seat, he comes to the large, mossy, downed maple tree. He remembers the day it fell, struck by lightning during a violent storm. It was during the war, and his father said to him. "If the English soldiers should come, run away from me and hide in the hollow of this maple." The soldiers did come, but the young son of Philip never had a chance to escape. Now he kneels beside the tree; now he will hide himself, as any child does, to await rescue. He crawls into the hollow of the tree and lies on his back, the skull resting on his chest in his hands. At any other time in his life, the soggy rot would feel cold and clammy, but now it feels warm, the wet like the velvet on the Intendant's couch.

Caucus-Meteor breaks the skull into little pieces, scoops them up and sprinkles them on his head, the only crown this king will ever wear. Muscles in his body twitch involuntarily. His face and body contort into a knot. The hours go by. Gradually, his muscles loosen and he arrives at a state of partial consciousness. For a moment he thinks he will recover from this illness and rule over Mount Hope Bay. And then a bright flash of light, and he is blind, his left arm suddenly useless. Only his voice remains strong. He says aloud, "Speak, speak . . . speak my name." The great silence of a lifetime continues.

A minute later the old man's body shudders briefly, a gargling sound comes from his throat, then he's still. One more miracle —he can see again. He can see as well as any man has ever seen. A crow flies by, circles, alights on a branch, watches. Caucus-Meteor finds himself greatly entertained by the crow, its black-purple sheen, its ironic eye. "Keeps-the-Flame?" he says. Now his understanding of the dream three years ago is complete. Now he can die as he must. "I will take you to the place where the names are spoken," the crow says. She unfolds her wings, and the ghost grabs hold and they fly away.

Elizabeth Blake has shut her eyes. Her husband puts his hand on her forehead. It is cool to his touch, her breathing rapid and faint. "If you can hear me, Elizabeth, give me a sign." There is no change in his wife.

Nathan Blake stands from his chair by the bed. His back is still straight and his mind sound, but he moves slowly; after all, he is ninety-one years old.

He looks out the second-story window of what everyone in town calls Blake House. Not the biggest or the best house in Keene, New Hampshire, but a fine timber-frame structure that he'd built with his sons and for that reason house enough for a Blake. From the bedroom window he can see the wide Main Street and the road to Marlborough, other fine houses, barns, stores, the streets full of carriages. A town measures its pride by its traffic, he believes. It's a fine town in a fine, if brand new, nation. He wonders what that old pagan, Caucus-Meteor, would think today of the village, then called Upper Ashuelot, that he burned to the ground so long ago.

Earlier in the day his wife, who was eighty-three years old and had been ill for several weeks, called him to her bed and told him that she meant to put her affairs in order and die. She asked him to remember back into the middle of the last century, and to tell her what really happened to him while he was with the savages. She guessed that his mysterious yearly visits south were somehow connected with his experiences in the north. And, too, she carried her own burden from those years, and he should know her story. He turns to look at her now. Her eyes, those blue blue eyes that he has marveled over for a lifetime, open.

"You're awake," he says.

"I was resting."

"Ready to go dancing?" he teases, with the same words he often used to suggest they make love.

"I might dance in heaven with you one day, but for now sit with me and go on with your tale."

Nathan returns to the straight-back chair by the bed. It's a chair that young Nathan made, cutting the red oak tree, splitting out the rungs and slats with a froe, smoothing them with a draw-knife, doing the boring work with brace and bit.

"Wife, what do you want to know all this for?"

"I think, husband, you are wiser in an understanding of an answer to your question than you let on." She'd grown plump in her middle years, providing his hands with entirely different sensations than in their earlier years. During odd moments, often when working alone with his oxen, it would pass through his mind that in Elizabeth he'd had by touch what it had taken two women in Canada, Wytopitlock and Parmachnenee, to provide.

"Why bring it to the fore in these your final hours?" he asks.

"I think perhaps in tales told truthfully heaven remembers to forgive."

"I daresay heaven is absentminded."

"You were always rueful, Nathan."

"It's my way. Started being rueful upon my return from captivity to find that my wife had been restored in spirit and sensibility during my absence and without any help from myself."

"You made the most of your adventure, and I made the most of mine."

"Aye." He's thinking about St. Blein, that damn Frenchman.

"I think I lack the conclusion to your story," Elizabeth says. "I wish to learn here on earth, not in heaven, why my husband visits Mount Hope Bay every year."

"All right, then. Twenty-five years after my return, a young stranger passed through Keene. He found me in the barn. I recognized him immediately, for he greatly resembled me, enough to be able to pass for white. It was my son by Black Dirt. His

mother had taught him English. He told me that as Marie Metivier she had married Robert de Repentigny. They operated a
saw mill at the falls by the lake, and lived their lives as French
Canadians in the house I built. This boy of mine went by the
name of Philip Provide. He informed me that he planned to
leave Canada for good and establish his residence in Mount
Hope Bay, Rhode Island."

"And that is why you go there every year."

"Yes, he has a family, and he works the housewright trade. But
I think you wanted less to hear my story than to tell me your own."

"That's true, for my tale is equal to yours in amazement.
Listen . . ."

After Elizabeth Blake finishes her story, she says, "Go now,
gather our children and grandchildren, and bring them to my
bedside, for I am ready to pass on." Nathan takes her pale, white
hand in both of his. He kisses her brow, and leaves the house to
perform this last errand for her. First he will fetch her son. He'd
known all along about the boy's paternity, born only six months
after his return. Nathan the younger had been a good son and
Nathan the elder had been as good a father as he was capable of.

He walks with a cane through the streets of Keene; he needs
the cane not for navigation, but for balance. Despite his age, the
old man dresses carefully every morning, always makes sure his
thin hair is combed, his boots shined. Local people hail him,
bow before him, treat him like royalty. He has a number of nick-
names about town: Old Nathan, the Old Pine King (because he
is known to have defied the crown by cutting the king's pines in
colonial days), the Old Speech Maker (from his sometimes long-
winded oratories at town meeting), the Old Selectman (because
he served for many years on the town's board of selectmen), the
Old Pioneer (because he built the first log cabin in the town that
would become Keene); but because he was a strong supporter of
the revolution in 1776 and reflects the values of the new nation,
they also call him the Old American.

Author's Note

The Old American is fiction, but I've stayed close to the facts of the Nathan Blake captivity as I've been able to divine it from the history books. I used very few original sources; most of my information comes from the work of others, scholars and writers to whom I owe a debt of gratitude.

For purposes that should be apparent to the reader, I took liberties in my novel with the words *American* and *Algonkian*. The New England colonists referred to the natives as Americans during the Puritan era, but by 1746 when the Blake drama began, most colonists were already calling themselves Americans, and the natives were being called Indians. I combined Algonquian (referring to languages) with Algonquin (referring to peoples) to create "Algonkian." Some Indian characters in my novel are named to honor place names in New England and historical personages without regard to the actual meaning of the names in the native languages.

François Bigot, the Canadian civil magistrate known as the intendant, was eventually arrested by French authorities, convicted, and jailed for his misdeeds. Ensign Pierre Raimbault St. Blein was killed in a raid the year following Blake's release. My characterization of Blake, St. Blein, and Bigot is a fiction, as is my characterization of all who appear in this novel, for while the histories tell us much of what people did they tell us little of who in their hearts they were. Samuel Allen, like Nathan Blake, was redeemed and lived to a great age as a New England farmer, but he insisted to the end that his time with the Indians had been the happiest period of his life. A man named Warren ran the Gauntlet with Nathan, turned on his tormenters, and in retaliation

285

was crippled for life. The historical Nathan Blake may not have walked the gauntlet, but he did get through with superficial wounds by being passive. He claimed also that he had a moment when he could have killed his captor when he bent to drink, but Nathan prayed and the message he received from God was not to kill. Nathan the great runner and Nathan the house builder also existed in fact. It struck me as remarkable that the pioneer who built the first log house for an English border town also built the first timber-frame house for a tribe of Canadian nomads. Nathan comes through as gutsy and athletic, but also nonviolent and pious, though he did leave a record of occasional rash and risky behavior—attempting unsuccessfully to winter over in a hut on the frontier, losing a horse on thin ice, and leaving the safety of the fort during an Indian attack.

Nathan Blake neither criticized nor praised his captors; he told his story in spare and descriptive language, but said nothing about his feelings; unlike some captives, he never attempted to set down on paper his experiences for memory or profit. Elizabeth Blake did indeed die at age eighty-three when Nathan was ninety-one. Three years later Nathan remarried an "interesting widow," as he wrote in a letter to his children, the only document I could find in his own hand. He died in 1811, his hundredth year.

Of the Indian who captured Nathan Blake, little is known. Blake reported that his captor had two "pretty daughters," that he died from disease in the second year of Nathan's captivity, and that the tribe elected Blake to take his place as leader of the family. What set the fiction of this book into motion was a line spoken by this unnamed captor. Blake related that he left the stockade to free his animals from the barn. He accomplished that task, then fled through a back door, but an armed Indian was waiting for him. Blake told the Indian it was mighty early in the morning and he'd had nothing to eat. He never expected to be understood. But the Indian surprised him by saying in English, "It's a poor Englishman that cannot go to Canada without his breakfast." I built the character of Caucus-Meteor out of those few words, out of my own loony imagination, and out of the inspiration provided by two dear men to whom this book is dedicated, the old Americans in my own life, my father, Elphege Hebert, and my father-in-law, Leo Lavoie.

I was born in Keene, New Hampshire, and grew up there in a family where Canadian French was the primary language in the house, and I did not speak English until I started kindergarten. As a young man, I believed I was 100 percent culturally French-Canadian. After a few visits to French Canada, the Quebecois made me realize that I was a lot more American and New England Yankee than Canadian and French. As a young man I believed my bloodlines were purely French. Then I learned that my great-grandfather on my mother's side was an Italian who immigrated to Canada. When my distant cousin Connie Hamel Hebert presented me with a genealogy of the Heberts, I discovered that a Cormac McDonald had worked his way into our gene pool. My mother, shortly before she died four years ago, confessed that her Italian grandfather's thirteen-year-old child bride, Flora Galarneau, may have been an Indian who, like many natives, took a French name. So the Blake captivity means a lot to me personally not only because Nathan Blake was from my hometown, but because his story touches on my heritage, in this land where surprises of culture, blood, and history lie in wait to abduct our cozy notions.

On the corner of Main and Winchester streets in Keene is a small stone monument. When I was a student at St. Joseph's parochial school next door, I was curious about the monument just barely visible through a hedge. One day I crept through the hedge and read the plaque.

Site of first log house built by
Nathan Blake
1736
He was captured by Indians and taken to Canada
1746
Ransomed by his wife
Elizabeth Graves
1749
Six generations of Blakes lived on this spot